THE RED LION

THE ELIXIR OF ETERNAL LIFE

Alchemy brings to mind an obscure laboratory in the Middle Ages where a sinister figure clandestinely conducts experiments to produce gold. What is less known is that the true alchemist's primary aim was not so much to get rich as to find the Philosopher's Stone and thus the tool to attain immortality.

The "Elixir of Life" is the secret of immortality, a magic serum that grants eternal life and "supernatural" abilities to those who are sufficiently developed and will not misuse its power. As written in the ancient texts, alchemy is the process of transmuting base metals into gold or the ultimate transformation of the alchemist's mind. However, if acquired through greed or malice the consumer of this terrifying potion is swept into a vortex of horror: The psychic mind opens, one sees all that is hidden, and the body is condemned to supernormal life. Consciousness is not lost in death or in reincarnation as one is carried deeper into agony and inescapable torment on the soul's journey to again find the path to enlightenment.

In 1553, Hans Burgner, an impatient young man determined to acquire the secret of eternal life, becomes the servant and pupil of Eduard Anselmus Rochard, an alchemist who possesses the potion. Rochard refuses to give him the Elixir and in his obsession Hans murders the Magister. As a consequence of this crime, the reader of this novel is conducted through the bloodstained labyrinth of alchemist rites and mysteries spanning four centuries as "Hans" searches through lifetimes for the only possible key to escape his torment – the *Prima Materia* and secret of the *Philosopher's Stone.*

Reborn in 1760 in Cassel, the home of the secret brotherhoods and the occult sciences, he is gradually initiated into the nine degrees of the Order. He becomes the student of Count St. Germain, the famous magician, travels with him, and is finally invested with the ranks of Magister when fate decrees a fitting resolution to his original crime.

His last return to earth is in this century, to offer hope and unveil occult secrets which hereto have been under many seals.

"Very few entities in all the centuries have made their voice louder than politics, personal religion, or the worship of a multitude of Gods. Very few have ever made their voice sound through the ages to the present time, but those who did were the great alchemists, the great scientists from Arabia and Persia all the way to Israel and into Europa and China.

You may not have any room for alchemy in your life because you have no history of what a student went through to true mastership. Those hidden schools, those hidden academies, left no reading material behind but only oral tradition, and those were scraps of information.

The ancient schools — where great students had learned to overcome age and death — sent their greatest students into the world to save or to change or to augment world history. And we see great students such as Comte de Saint Germaine in testimony and diaries about his great life. Then there are the alchemists, those illustrious beings that we go to museums and see their confiscated gold that actually brought the fortunes to England. It is the alchemists who made England wealthy. Historians like to bury their achievements and science likes to debate it. Nonetheless, the remnants of that great art survive today and historically made the great powers what they were.

In the end the greatest alchemists ended up being the greatest teachers of destiny because ultimately they knew they could make all the gold to buy anything they wanted. When you have the power of securing anything you want, the need to want diminishes greatly.

A true alchemist never got bored with burning the fire because they knew that in the end it was their observation guiding molecular structures. The faith and knowingness that they were going to change an incredulous idea of heavy iron into heavier gold drove them to sell everything to burn that fire, to come to that ideal. Their guardian angel, their guiding light, was the faith of turning a piece of iron into several weights of gold. They held that foremost because the art — when dissolving a relationship, when dissolving a metal — the art of holding the perfect idea is very important for the reconstruction of what you have destroyed to re-form it under the new idea."

Ramtha

The Red Lion
The Elixir of Eternal Life

An Alchemist Novel

by

Mária Szepes

HORUS PUBLISHING, INC.

THE RED LION
THE ELIXIR OF ETERNAL LIFE

Original title: *A Vörös Oroszlán*
First published in Hungary in 1946
Copyright © 1946, 1984, 1989, 1994 Mária Szepes
Published in Hungary by Sweetwater Publisher Establishment, 1994, 1997

Translated by
Laszló Vermes and Gizella Józsa
Revised by
Catherine Hill
Edited by
Ardi Lawrence
Cover photography by
Marc Hazewinkel

Acknowledgments

I wish to thank the people who helped in the English-language publication of this book: first, my friends, László Vermes and Gizellajózsa, who translated The Red Lion and gave it its initial life in English; Catherine Hill whose work in revising the book was essential; Ardi Lawrence for the excellent editing; and Francis Hollo, who helped it reach the people for whom its message was intended. - *Mária Szepes*

ISBN: 0-9652621-7-0

Introduction

In my introduction I would like to recount for the reader the events that led me to write this book, and how, like a magnet attracts iron filings, the subject drew me into its power.

I most prefer to speak about *The Red Lion* in the third person, because it has taken on a completely independent and wondrous life. It has a fate of its own now. I will not claim that the fact that I am a born writer was not a prerequisite for its genesis; I have worked with almost every literary genre since I was eight years of age. I let my mind, my imagination wander, and needed only to have historical and scientific sources of inspiration to come my way. Still, I felt that I was only a tool, a medium for a force greater than myself. Call it inspiration, although I do not know if that is the fitting term. But I know that it does have a name.

If I had guessed what a sea of flames was about catch fire just as I began writing in 1939, I would have not have had the courage to go through with it. In 1939 my little boy died. I was born into a wonderful family, actors, film makers, musicians and writers whose "Bohemian" liberties never meant libertinism but an open mind and curiosity for art, philosophy and science. We were not petty bourgeois, nor gentries, but we got to know all kinds of people and trends and followed the events taking place in our country and the world. We were aware of the dangers, but we never became attached to any ultra-political movement or party.

My husband, Bela Szepes, an Olympic athlete, graphic artist, caricaturist and journalist had worked for both Hungarian and major international papers. He made it possible for me to do all the things I am interested in, and to obtain German and English back-ground literature; I have reading proficiency in both languages. At that point I was into alchemy. I decided to write a short story about one of those fascinating alchemists. I was touched by the tragic fate of these experimenters who had been forced to function in hiding. They were misunderstood by the power-hungry lords just as were all great minds in our bloody history. The real initiates into mental alchemy were never out to "make gold" but to transmute their own being from "human dreams to human gold".

They worked to generate the "philosopher's Stone", or "portable gold" in their very souls and spirits, which was the true Elixir of Eternal Life. When they fell into the hands of omnipotent lords and were unable to fulfill their masters' lust for wealth they were tortured and executed. In the meantime, however, they made countless interesting discoveries as they searched the secrets of nature. Modern science continues to prove that like elements can be changed into other elements through energy by the invention of plastics. We also know that gold and gems, vitamins to unclog our arteries and extend our life spans, medicines, antibiotics and serums to conquer epidemics and infections can be produced.

Chemistry is alchemy's offspring, only it produces "Arcanums", deemed useful but often just as damaging, at a much higher financial cost and failure rate than nature's ingenious bio-magic which it is trying to imitate.

The Red Lion's fascinating plot spans four centuries, really the history of alchemy, and holds the secret key to eastern philosophy for those who in several readings will realize how many and always new psycho-archeological layers they come upon.

I remember how I was shaken by the fire that ignited within me when I was writing the book. I came to realize that what was engulfing me this time was not a short story but an expanse I was catapulted into by some cosmic vehicle and which made me dizzy. I was unable to end this interstellar journey, it extended ever further the more I proceeded. It raised me over the waves of a sea of flames. While I did know the outline of the plot, my pen produced surprising phrases such as I had not conceived of just seconds before.

It was a sort of schizophrenia. One part of me filled my imagination with pictures, colors, passions, strangely credible characters which my "sound mind" considered alarming and shirked away from. "My God what is this? What are people going to say?" My internal struggle I always countered with my conviction that it would never be published anyway. Writing took five years. In Leanyfalu, the recluse I called 'Noah's Arc', a neighbor who was an experienced typist noticed the manuscript piling up on my desk in our little room. Until then I had no idea I was actually a writer. I was simply interested in the subject. The lady suggested I should go to her place and dictate to her, she could type thirty pages a day. We were living the final horrors of war. Budapest was surrounded. The capital, twenty-five kilometers away, was being razed to rubble.

In the evenings salvos of red tracer shells pierced the sky, and during the day thick black smoke hovered over the horizon. Huge blasts shook also our little house. A nearby hit shattered our windows. Explosions pounded our closed doors. We had no idea which of our friends and relatives trapped in the city cellars were still alive or who was killed. Amidst the commotion of air raids, cannon and machinegun fire, in the apocalyptic blare I dictated and dictated this strange book, thirty pages each day. No one knew it, no one read it, until typing was completed.

Not my husband, nor my brother, parents or friends. And what I had not thought of, much less hoped for, came true: in the three years of freedom that followed *The Red Lion's* first edition was published by Hungaria, in 1946. It became a bestseller. In 1947 the publishing houses were nationalized, and like all other books in the shops and libraries whose content digressed from the only official "ideology" *The Red Lion* was shredded. Which did it a lot of good. *The Red Lion* is about immortality, and it could not be killed. It rose from the ashes like a Phoenix.

Raising eternal human questions and offering a solution to them *The Red Lion* thus continues on its own designated course to pass on a never outdated message to the contemplative reader in search of spiritual support in a most disquieting era.

- Mária Szepes

Table of Contents

THE RED LION

Prelude

Adam Cadmon's letter reached me in the summer of 1940.

At that time I was living in a small house, the existence of which no one except a few intimates was aware. It was a low peasant house with wild vines shading the verandah and kelly green shutters that set off the whitewashed walls. The house was on a gentle, sloping hillside, hidden under a tent of sweet smelling linden trees. There was no access by either car or train; the road to the nearest railway station wound through the hills for a good hour. Even the mail reached the place only once a week. I had named my hideaway "Noah's Ark."

The inside of the house had been made into a comfortable dwelling, but I still had to pump water into the reservoir with a hand pump and depend on oil lamps and candles at night. But then in 1940 everyone of a sensitive nature longed to go back to the "primitive" past, away from the berserk blessings of "culture." From my verandah I could look down on vineyards sprawling over the hills whose feet brushed the waters of the Danube.

I had intentionally chosen this inaccessible home after much searching for a suitable one, for I felt if I did not get away from the pestering city atmosphere I would never finish my research. Yet my occupation tied me to the city. I was head of a large mental hospital, and it seemed impossible to get away from my numerous obligations. Perhaps a doctor is more a slave to his profession than any other man. In my territory, nothing can be set aside; each and every event has a terrifying unexpectedness and will not brook delay.

The field I was pioneering presented a grave dilemma. Both my profession and my book required my full attention. I had been collecting data for the book for years, but I still had a great deal of reading to do to clarify a number of details. At first I tried to use a portion of the night for this purpose, but my health suffered and my work suffered with it. The areas I was working in demanded a concentrated effort to keep my theses from being

1

weakened and open to attack. I could not use mediocre arguments to set forth an extremely important idea.

So after many delays and compromises, I finally asked for four months' leave of absence and threw myself into the matter like someone jumping off a precipice. My disturbed conscience was suppressed by the overwhelming clamor of an inner urge. After all, I had put my best assistant in charge of the hospital before I walked out of that world.

At first I could not accept the magic peace of solitude and work. During the first week my unfinished cases swarmed around me like disquieting caricatures, but I firmly quashed them. If people were indispensable, surely death would not exchange them continually like governments taking printed money out of circulation. Making known the method I had discovered and successfully tested was far more important in the long run than the treating of a few isolated cases.

My role in this book is not an important one; I merely dwell on the nature of my work because it makes Adam Cadmon's appearance more understandable and has a part in his compelling story.

I had been treating mental disorders for twenty-five years. Approximately ten years before, I had turned to an entirely different theory from the cul-de-sacs of the prevailing authorities, but I had not made my experiments public. I well respect the caution of science and her sometimes exaggerated defenses against pioneers, so I was prepared for my own work to be drowned in ridicule, viciously attacked, or simply passed over in silence. These considerations did not bother me. Some of my students were of such talent that they could not be banned from the field; they had already been "contaminated" by my theory and were using it in their practices. We were getting remarkable results and, more important, our patients became human beings again.

I called my system metapsychoanalysis. By my definition, the psyche is the immortal intelligence which in this world is most highly developed in the consciousness of man. The peak of man's awareness unfortunately compares to the limitless Spirit as does a speck of dust to the Cosmos. A disease of the soul means there is some kind of damage to the bridge, the organs that transmit between the individual and the spirit. He who would doctor the soul must diagnose and correct this malfunction with all the efficiency and thoroughness of clinical research. If he only treats the symptoms, he may well fill mental institutions — and the world — with raging living dead. Of course, I am not speaking of organic diseases of the brain which can have such a baleful influence on a man's entire life. I am talking about diseases of the soul which seem to be invisible and defy analysis.

Now is the time for a general revolution of the spirit and with it the art of healing. I believe in Hermes Trismegistus, who revealed the law of analogies in an ancient tradition whose roots go back to the prehistoric past. His truths have constantly reappeared but people with small, wicked minds, have failed to recognize them. There is the example of Paracelsus, whose envious colleagues crushed the skull for which they would have given thousands of their own.

But as for Adam Cadmon's letter, which precipitated all these reflections, it contained only a few lines.

Very Honorable Professor:
I hope the results of my forthcoming visit will justify the interruption of your work. I will only be with you for two days. I do not yet know exactly when I will arrive, for I have other matters to settle first, but I believe I will be able to start this week.
Until we see each other, heartfelt greetings from

Your friend,
Adam Cadmon

Yes, he actually signed it Adam Cadmon. The letter had been mailed from Budapest.

At first I thought some of my friends were playing a practical joke. Only three people knew my current address: my assistant, my housekeeper in Budapest, and the bachelor colleague with whom I played endless chess games. This last was in the hospital recovering from gallstone surgery and nevertheless I did not believe that any of them would give out my address. But how had "Adam Cadmon" gotten it? And why did he call himself by the Kabbalistic name that means "Cosmos"? And what did he want with me?

Every morning my first thought was will he come today. The third day I strolled out to the railroad station, pretending I only wanted to go to the village for some matches, candles, and food. When I got back, he was there.

★

He was sitting on the verandah when I came up. He stood and offered me his hand and I studied him curiously. It was impossible to determine his age. He was not old but he was not young either, despite the lack of wrinkles on the narrow, fine-drawn face. For some reason the concept of age didn't seem to fit him at all; he seemed to be timeless, a part of the eternal present. Though his features were slightly Mongolian, his complexion was that of a southern

European, and I could hardly look away from those brilliant, almond-shaped eyes. His head, with its noble forehead and concave temples, would have been a delight to the phrenologist. He wore an ordinary white summer suit, and his straight black hair came to the nape of his neck. However, I cannot describe the essence of his being, that penetrating glance that seemed to pierce through forgotten memories. The man was not a stranger to me, but I did not know the origin or nature of our bond.

He inquired about my work, displaying a soft, even voice. We became absorbed in conversation, and I was somehow not surprised to find him well-informed. Even when he mentioned details of my as yet unwritten book, I thought he must have read them in some of my magazine articles. Then I remembered I had never mentioned these things in print. I stopped and stared, and he smiled.

"It isn't witchcraft! I'm just a step ahead in the territory you're exploring, that's all. The whole book is in your thoughts, and I have read it. Every man has this latent ability; it only needs to be developed." This statement expanded my world by a few dimensions.

Then we started talking about the war. He had come from Lublin, he said, to visit me, and he would return there day after tomorrow. I was quite surprised at this. Why had he been in Lublin, where the war was then at its worst? Was he Polish? But he spoke perfect Hungarian, with only the slightest accent. And he had spent only one day in Budapest before coming to see me. Who mailed the letter in Budapest four days before? How did he know about me? And how could a private individual travel through the war zone?

"I'm not Polish," he responded to my unspoken question. "I moved to Lublin in July of '39."

"You're a German!" I said with choking suspicion. "Are you . . . ?"

"I came from Tibet," he replied simply. "I decided to visit you before I ever left. If you will clear your soul of the distractions of your ephemeral consciousness, you will realize that you were waiting for me. Naturally the man destined to such a revelation awaits it with his emotions and subconscious feelings as well as his intellect. You feel that an inexpressible essence not susceptible to the laws of science will reveal itself. The only difference between us is that you *guess* what I remember. But that is not important. What is important is that you know the facts, do the work you were meant to do, and preserve your personal entity."

"But what is this work I was meant to do? And what is all this about my personal entity?" The questions were torn from me.

"The biggest problem with using words," he replied, "is that they mean something a little different to everybody. When I said I remember what you only guess, I mean I remember previous lives. You believe in reincarnation yourself, you have had experiences, and you have feelings about it. For instance, I know you feel this is not the first time we have met. And you followed an inner command when you came to this Noah's Ark to finish your work. The future needs that work. And I know that this inner command of yours is really a mission from that place where spiritual revolutionaries are preparing the New Age with the help of conspirators who have renewed souls. You are one of them," Cadmon continued, "though you don't remember it in this life. I assure you that at a time in the past you consciously pledged yourself. The thing is clear now, isn't it?"

I nodded involuntarily though this explanation dazzled rather than enlightened me. Throughout Adam Cadmon's visit I was filled with a strange, elated feeling. In his presence I could not bring myself to dispute or analyze any of his statements. Sometimes I thought I must be a victim of the power of suggestion; his every word, even when it was directly contradictory to all logic, hit me with a force that exterminated every germ of doubt . . . Yet I had experienced enough of that type of suggestion to know that this was something different. Adam Cadmon was not trying to influence me; I could feel no aggression emanating from him. He was just being himself, in possession of tremendous illuminative power and controlled spiritual forces and abilities. His utterances had an air of certainty.

That evening we lounged in the garden after supper, sitting under a star-studded sky. The constellations shone all around us, and the Milky Way flowed through the heavens like a pale, mysterious river. Near the full moon shone two clear, brilliant stars: Saturn and Jupiter in close conjunction.

I began to watch the two planets and to think about their powers that both oppose and complement each other. Jupiter is the great benefactor, a fiery and constructive being; Saturn is the obstacle, a source of the chilling suffering which yet teaches. Jupiter is the friend of the sun, Saturn a celestial loner. The danger from the one is fire, from the other is freezing. How does the struggle between these two giants affect the world?

"The Constellation of the Messiahs," Adam Cadmon said softly. His voice seemed to be the distillation of the incomparable night round about me. Again he answered my unspoken thought. "The birth of Christ was also preceded by this conjunction. At that time it was in the sign of Taurus, and it brought us Christianity. Now it will bring a philosophical and social revolution, a redemption of the spirit from its prison of matter. The Messiah being born now will open the gate of the New Epoch."

"The Messiah being born now — Where? When?" I could not comprehend him.

"In Lublin in April of '41. In the ghetto of Lublin, to be exact, where there is the greatest suffering and darkness. The signs of his coming are here already; the Man of Sin, the Great Lawbreaker, has appeared in the power of his deceit. And the Messiah will follow his signs, contrasting reality with illusions; he will come as a Liberator from the Antichrist. To fulfill the scripture and make the eternal rhythm of the surf of time audible, he will come as the illegitimate child of a Jewish girl, a girl burdened with the sorrow of her people, their frightening cleverness in their sufferings, and the terrified tenderness they show one another in their persecutions. She is the counterpart of that other mother who gave birth to her son in a stable nineteen hundred and forty years ago."

His voice was soft and his story was simple, but they kindled a fire within me. I was certain, with an unbounded, unreasoning certainty, that what he said was true and was more real than the visible world around me. "And you — Why did you go to Lublin?" This was the first question I had dared to ask about him.

"When Wisdom is to be born in the stable of human hate, those who are invited to the Baptism will reach him by following the star. I have already been invited. That is why I came back from Namelessness to prepare for Him and announce Him. I am here to make the True Ones aware that these are the times of which the prophecies spoke. The days are coming when the fast-grinding mills will crush every human support. Fires will burn the last refuge of matter. There will not be a single foothold on earth or shelter for fleeing humanity. The golden calf will tumble off its pedestal forever. Floods of tears will not soften the merciless demons who are coming. Oceans of blood will flood nations, cities, houses, and fields; blood always washes the world clean before it is covered by the cool ocean of Aquarius."

These dispassionate, apocalyptic words did not penetrate my mind immediately. I looked at the dark, soft landscape that murmured all around. I could hear the crickets and smell acacia and elder. Dogs were barking somewhere on a distant farm. From the river I could hear the soft, hoarse voices of the frogs begging for rain. The whole idea of blood and death seemed far away from this clean, peaceful night.

Then suddenly I felt a premonition of the horrors of the coming years. I was overwhelmed at the thought of unsurpassed destruction, the mouthings of rabid hatred and their corresponding oppression of defenseless masses — the whole was an uninterrupted, suicidal St. Vitus's dance. Suddenly the landscape about me was filled with ominous life, a murmuring of fearful voices, pulsating in a heart-rending anticipation of horror. The feeling was so real that my heart began thumping violently.

"No!" I cried. "Human beings cannot descend that low! No one could endure such a time!"

"The human soul is both divine and demonic," Cadmon replied. "Which side predominates depends on which of the two forces reaches the control levers first. The elemental influences that pour into the soul attack it irresistibly at every weak point. That is the way hate works, and anyone who has the slightest inclination toward it must fight against it with all his might or else he will be drafted into the demonic army of hate and be lost. Hate is the most frightening and magical force that has ever appeared on the earth. It can conquer every other human weakness: selfishness, hedonism, and even the fear of death. It whips a man's fanaticism into a white hot glow and melts him into its own mass. It will even risk its own destruction to destroy."

"But why must these things happen?" My shout echoed among the sleeping trees. "If there is a Planner with a plan for visible things, how can he give way to the forces of destruction?"

"Precisely because there *is* a plan behind visible things," was Cadmon's sober answer. "This is to be the time of a great transmutation of the earth. Her entire essence is to be altered. She will cast out the contaminated and refine the remaining few into precious metal. The coming cataclysm is by way of a provocative injection; it will bring the latent disease to the surface in those who are tainted with it."

"But the people are weak and ignorant and they act without responsibility," I pleaded. "It is their leaders who are educated and unscrupulous. It is they who misuse the black magic of propaganda, not the ordinary man. The transgression is theirs. It is their poisonous editorials and broadcasted word bombs that beleaguer the bewildered skulls of the people. How can they defend themselves? They don't have any independent ideas or lines of moral defense, only their wants. They're just children, flocking to their doom after the Pied Piper of Hamelin. Why should they be punished?"

"You are quite right. Most people are children — children who play very cruel games, harming themselves and all other living creatures. The earth can no longer be their playground," Cadmon explained. "It is to become the home of reasoning adults."

We were silent for a time. I couldn't argue with the man. His words were similar to the visions of Enoch, Baruch, Ezra, and John; you had to accept them or reject them.

Presently I spoke again. "Why did you come to me, a single individual, all the way from Tibet through Lublin to Noah's Ark?" As I spoke I suddenly saw the grave implications of my whimsical name. Noah's Ark! Cadmon's next words reinforced my feeling.

"I've brought something that must survive this new flood of blood. I had to come now to bring it; otherwise it would have been too late." A mad joy raced through me; I thought he referred to the whole of Hungary. "I'm only talking about this little house," he answered my thought, "Noah's Ark. And even it will be shaken when the tempest begins to blow."

"So you think this nation won't be spared from . . ."

"No, it will not escape."

"Oh, well — I'll help you in any way I can."

"I know," he replied simply. "I came to bring a manuscript I want you to keep until I can send you instructions on what to do with it. It wouldn't be safe with me where I am going to be for the next few years. You can read it if you'd like."

The next afternoon he left.

★

That's how I came to have Adam Cadmon's manuscript. I am now executing his written instructions to make it public for those who have survived the bloody flood and are trying to find their way back to life.

I never saw Adam Cadmon again.

ADAM CADMON'S MANUSCRIPT

THE PRIMA MATERIA

No one should start thoughtlessly down the path of the arcane sciences, for once be starts he must persevere to the goal. Otherwise, he will be lost. Once on the path, a single doubt will produce madness, a single stop will cause a fall, a single attempt to shrink back will plunge the luckless soul into a bottomless abyss.

You who are now beginning to read this book will be either a king or a madman once you have finished. You can do what you want to with it; you will never hate or forget it. If your heart is pure, it will be a shining torch; if your heart is strong, it will be a weapon in your hand. If your heart is wise, it will become still wiser. But if your heart is base, this book will be hellfire to you; it will brand your soul and weigh your conscience with eternal sorrow and restlessness.

Eliphas Levi — *Rituel de la Haute Magie*

Sebastian, Who Never Succeeded

Hans Burgner is as alien to me now as his body that died and was replaced, but a few centuries ago I was he, a creature of excited joys, anxieties, and ambivalent feelings. He was a miserable, greedy, and confused creature, but the spiritual ferment that lifted my life out of the cycle of ceaseless repetitions began with him. And so he must start my story.

Come with me. Like a priest of the Orphic Mysteries, I will lead you into the darkness of night through deep, moonless forests, down the paths of the nether world leading to the gates of Hades. Do not be afraid; I have a torch and I know my way. You will not get lost. And at dawn we will come to the temple of the rising sun.

★

I was born in Swandorf in 1535. I suspect my father had little to do with the matter; it was more likely the work of his robust, arrogant young workman. My father was a miller, fat, pale, short of breath, and meek; my mother cared about as much for him as she did for a flour sack.

My mother was the most emotionally unstable woman I have ever known. The entire house was saturated with her shifting, unbearable personality. You never could be sure who you would meet there: the romantic, gentle noblewoman, the self-flagellating Puritan ascetic, the drunken, wet-lipped courtesan, or the screaming fishwife who cursed everybody in the vilest possible terms. She would change her opinions from minute to minute and, since it was her nature to enforce her will, not even a flea could rest peacefully in her presence. People were always running around trying to obey her contradictory orders. When everything was total confusion and even the animals were nearly insane, she looked very happy.

"I am surrounded by sheer idiots!" she would screech suddenly, then burst into the tears brought about by her enjoyable excitement. She often cried publicly over her fate. While my father sweated in terror, she would sob out all the sacrifices she had made for him, how she had buried her youth and hidden her beauty in his dusty mill . . . At this point she invariably brought in the traveling nobleman who had sworn eternal love to her. "I could be wearing silk and velvet," she would sob pathetically, "and here I am rotting in a stinking hole where everybody uses me. None of you have ever said a good word to me in my whole life! I work my fingers to the bone for you and nobody even says, 'Thank you, Theresa.'"

My mother always talked about her beauty as if it were one of the Seven Wonders of the World. If any man so much as looked at her, she thought he was already her "slave," whether he was a skinny apprentice or a decrepit sack carrier. When the awkward peasant women were waiting to get their flour ground, she would wink and wave behind the back of some unsuspecting workman and show them how he gobbled her up with his eyes or tried to touch her.

She was a tall, large-boned woman with legs like pillars. Her large, pear-shaped hips made her shoulders look narrow. But her face had a certain beauty, with a clear, blooming complexion and regular features. Only her sharp nose and the cold glare of her eyes betrayed her. Her laugh was like tin pans rattling together. My first conscious feeling toward her was utter repulsion. Because she allowed no one any privacy, I became reticent and introverted.

Our employees changed like clouds in the sky. The lad whose bitter, jealous affair with her resulted in my birth took off shortly thereafter. But my father and I had no escape. He was obese and sickly; I was but a helpless child. I had to endure my mother's possessive bursts of love, punctuated with thick, sloppy kisses, as well as her frequent slaps in the face. If I had to pass her room, I knew I would get one or the other. I tried to avoid the place.

In addition to all these things, my mother was a miser who begrudged every bite of food anyone ate. She would eat delicacies in secret and then preach to my father and me about the sin of overeating and how the scriptures forbade it. I was growing rapidly and always hungry, so I stole from the pantry continually, eating everything I could lay my hands on. My father also suffered from hunger; it was both pitiful and amusing to find him in his own pantry, stuffing like a thief. Whenever I caught him, he would hand me a sausage or a piece of beef, blushing at the thought of being my partner in crime.

"Here, Hans, I'm already on dessert but your mother mustn't find out about it," he would whisper. "It would hurt her deeply to know we were eating like this. It's useless to explain to her that God gave me a disgust for fish cooked in water. She is so — dogmatic about religious matters."

"Father, do you really believe she fasts herself?" I asked through a full mouth. "Why, I saw her in the outhouse eating a duck stuffed with chestnuts!"

"You were spying on your mother in the outhouse?" He looked reprovingly at me, but he couldn't sustain the pose for long. Finally he waved his hand. "You don't understand her, Hans. Our salvation is really important to her. Here, I have left a little jam for you. Throw the jar in the creek when you get through."

But my father escaped from her sooner than I. One evening during dinner the spoon stopped halfway to his mouth. His face turned red, then purple, and he fell from his chair and died.

My mother mourned in a wide variety of characters. At first she became the dramatic widow of "my poor, sweet darling." She invented sentimental fantasies about his last hours and what he had said to her when he felt death approaching. "You were the most magnificent woman in the world, Theresa. If I had a hundred lives, I could not repay what you have done for me. What would I have been without you?" The truth, of course, was that she had cursed the dear departed most terribly just a few hours before he died because his linen trousers had split when he bent over. Later I heard her tell someone acrimoniously, "I knew he would end up this way! He just gorged himself to death."

But otherwise life at the mill was varied and interesting. Peasants from the neighboring villages brought news along with their wheat to be ground. And not far away was a broad highway that bore distinguished coaches as well as peasant wagons. I did not spend much time at home, for I heard the songs of the traveling journeymen, free spirits marching toward the great magnet of Nuremberg. Frequently I would accompany them until I was forced home by fatigue and hunger. I drank in their tales and inhaled the atmosphere of joyous restlessness and the search for the wondrous unknown. Then I would dream of the highway stretching to infinity under my feet, and in my dreams I never went back.

★

My mother had an uncle named Sebastian who came to see us occasionally. She was greatly ashamed of him, but for some reason she was also afraid of him and gave him everything he wanted instead of throwing him out. He was a tall, lean man with a dark complexion and a nose like a vulture. His eyes were always bloodshot and he had yellow teeth. He had lost an ear somehow or other and he was always dirty. But even though he drank heavily he could read and write, and when he talked everyone listened. My mother said he was an incorrigible liar, but even she listened. He would tell about foreign countries, islands peopled by dark-skinned natives, giants and dwarfs, one-eyed monsters, and flying people, and he made them all as real as the people around us. In addition he could prepare amulets and love potions, tell the future, and cast spells. To put it plainly, the man was a sorcerer. He impressed me tremendously; I thought he was the most wonderful person I had ever known.

Gradually I realized why my mother was afraid of Sebastian. She thought he would cast a spell on her, and his mere presence would curb her horrible temper. This made me idolize him all the more, and I began following him everywhere. I would watch with a mixture of wonder and horror as he talked and gesticulated to himself.

"No!" he would say. "No one stands a chance unless he was born under the sign of Saturn." Then he would stop and bleat scornfully, "*Quide virgis fecit aurum, Gemma de lapidibus . . .*" Then he laughed piteously and would run so fast that my short legs could hardly follow him. "Fatheads! Blockheads!" he would yell periodically.

At first he didn't notice me but gradually he began to take note of my constant presence. "What do you want, hey?" he snarled.

I was so frightened I broke out in a sweat. How could I explain feelings I hardly understood myself. I stammered, "I — I want to be — just like you."

He looked taken aback. "So — why?"

"Because you're different and everyone is afraid of you — even my mother."

He stared at me, and for the first time since I had known him the mocking, bitter expression left his face. Suddenly he seemed a different man, old, tired, and defeated. "Run along and play, my son," he said colorlessly. "Don't try to follow my example. Make the sign of the cross and banish me; I am accursed. Someday you'll have this mill. Grind flour there and prosper and don't even think about anything else. Don't pay any attention to me. I'm just a crazy old duffer who talks nonsense. I have no real learning, and I've never made anything out of myself. I've frittered away my life chasing the will-o'-the-wisp of gold. I wanted to rule three worlds but I'm going to die in the gutter." Tears filled his eyes and my heart was filled with infinite pity.

"Don't say things like that!" I begged and began to cry myself.

"Why are you crying?" He demanded roughly. "Cry over something that's worth it. You do see it's no good being like me, don't you?"

"No, I do not," I insisted. "I want to learn spells and practice magic so people will be afraid of me and do what I want them to."

Sebastian broke into loud laughter. "You're stubborn, boy, just like I was." He grasped me by the shoulders. "Well, if I don't take you in hand, someone else will deceive you. At least I can see to it that you don't lose your head completely. It wouldn't do you any harm to learn to read and write." He was wrong even about that, poor soul.

★

And so Sebastian began to teach me. He became very attached to me, so much so that he could not leave. Before that he had never stayed more than a few months until his restless spirit would drive him on; now he stayed to be with me, to the intense irritation of my mother. He told me all his secrets and sorrows, and I came to love him like a father. I learned to read, write, and count easily, because he made it so interesting and I even managed to learn some Latin because he would translate for me the quotations with which he always prepared his speech.

He had a few books on alchemy. I threw myself into them and read them all until I knew them by heart. Once I understood all the words, the books intoxicated me. The one that made the greatest impression was the story of Nicholas Flammel, the famous French alchemist. Flammel had gained possession of the Philosophorum Lapide, the Philosopher's Stone.

Flammel had been born in Pontois in 1330. He was just one of the teeming poor of Paris until suddenly, in 1382, he became a very wealthy man, so wealthy his funds seemed inexhaustible. He founded fourteen hospitals and built three churches. Even the King began to notice him, and the Estates General made an investigation. All they could learn though was that Flammel had the Philosopher's Stone and had acquired his wealth by turning nonprecious metals into precious ones. His own story was that he had bought a cheap manuscript on a piece of bark and, after twenty-one years of trying to decipher it, had taken it to Spain as a last resort. Here he had found a learned doctor at Santiago de Compostella who was able to decipher the document and translate it. It turned out to be a letter by a Jew named Abraham in which he told his brethren how to make the Philosopher's Stone. Flammel also stated that the miraculous substance could not only transmute metals but could also prolong life . . .

Prolong life. I wasn't much interested in gold. It was the possibility of escaping death that filled me with fever, stirring my soul to its depths. Sebastian realized how much the tale had moved me, and he was frightened.

"Listen, Hans! For God's sake! It would be better if you didn't believe a word of this. I was dazzled by alchemy, too — did everything I could to find the Philosopher's Stone. Once I worked for a charlatan who spread the rumor that he had the *Aurum Potabille.* It was just a cheap confidence game. He tried it out on a baron, got found out, and paid for it with his life. His Elixir didn't save him. And the adventure cost me one ear."

"Still that doesn't prove every alchemist is a fraud," I declared stubbornly. "Can you prove to me that the Philosopher's Stone does *not* exist?"

He was silent for a moment, turning his eyes away. "No, Hans, I can't say it doesn't exist because it does. But people like you and I can never get it. The passion for it simply ruins our lives; we fly into its flame like insects. Alchemy is an amusement for princes. The beggar on whom the yellow flame shines winds up in the torture chamber. If it is even whispered that some wandering mountebank has the 'Red Lion,' some king, prince, or priest will capture him. Then the poor fool will gorge himself on the food they offer and begin to drink because he knows he doesn't have it. Then he will hem and haw until his patron tires of him and takes his head from his body. Of course not everyone caught like that is a quack; the lunatic gets caught too. He's the fellow who believes that just one more experiment will bring him success. He walks into the web of his own will just to get a well-equipped laboratory."

"And the real ones," I asked eagerly, "where do you find the real ones?"

"Nowhere, my son. You don't see them. They submerge in the crowd and dissemble, taking on the color and form of their environment because they know the truth. You can follow them from village to village or from city to city, and you'll always find they've left just before you got there. An Adept will perform, or get someone else to perform, a transmutation so that the fire of knowledge will not stop burning and the tormenting desire will remain in people's hearts. Then he will leave without a trace."

"But why do they disappear like that? They could be more powerful than kings."

"That's it in a nutshell. They want to avoid the torture rack. A king will tolerate no one but servants, but a true Adept is a ruler. He has conquered the worst tyrant of all, death, and he doesn't have to stay alive by filling the coffers of debauched princes and insatiable conquerors. You see, making gold is just the surface of alchemy. The mystery of alchemy is like a deep sea, Hans, that gives its true contents only to the chosen. That doesn't include you and me; I know that now for certain. The Adepts who can make gold, you see, won't make it for themselves. They don't have any desires, and the life they have gained means nothing to them. As for me," Sebastian added, "I tremble when I think of gold, and I would like to live for centuries to wallow in every mud puddle on earth. That's why I've never succeeded in alchemy, Hans, and you won't either. You're just like me; we were born under the same sign. So forget about alchemy or you will become an unwanted vagabond and lose the life you have, instead of becoming immortal."

He might have spared his breath, for I was contaminated to the roots of my soul. The only part of Sebastian's words I had really heard were his assurance that the Elixir really existed. And if it existed, I would get it. Just because Sebastian had failed didn't mean that I would fail. I didn't mean to die; I had to live a long time — forever. I didn't want to turn into a stinking, puffy corpse as my poor father had; he had started to rot in a few hours in the summer heat. I could not bear the thought of that; it was hateful and degrading.

Meanwhile Sebastian began to drink more and more. "I'm drinking partly because of you now, Hans," he would tell me when I reproached him. "I see you're irrevocably committed. I only wish the example of my own fate could save you."

I tried to keep him from drinking. I would beg him not to ruin himself, for without him I couldn't bear to live with my mother. He cried at that; he had begun crying more and more lately. Finally he gave me his word he would not drink any more. The next morning I had to bring him home from the tavern in a wheelbarrow while everyone jeered and laughed. But I was obstinate. "Even dead drunk," I thought, "his little fingernail is worth more than all your hollow heads put together, you imbeciles."

Death found him in a drunken coma. He lay motionless, with his fallen jaws colorless and wizened; I could no longer hope that he would crawl out of bed coughing and complaining of a beastly headache. Suddenly he lifted his bloodshot, tear-stained eyes to mine and spoke.

"Don't say anything, Hans. Please don't say anything! Why should you believe my promises? I'm just a rotten animal fit for the rubbish heap. But this is the last time! Spit in my eyes if you find me getting drunk again. You'll find out!" And then I knew what it meant to be all alone in the world.

I ran behind the granaries and cried, angrily stamping my feet. Why had Sebastian left me here? I needed him like meat and drink. He held the key that could lead me to my goal.

This was the second time I had seen death at close range and I knew I would never get used to it. A few minutes before, he had been alive with thoughts and feelings, telling about islands in the warm blue sea where treasure palaces rise, wondering aloud what types of beings lived on other planets, watching the moon, and talking about Cyclops and other monsters — and now he was dead. His nails were violet and his body rigid, and there was an alien smile on his mute face . . . No! It was wicked and meaningless! Sebastian should have lived so much longer. And as for me — I would not die at all!

★

My mother became more intolerable as she got older. As a widow she no longer had any inhibitions about her passions, and our workers made fun of the maneuvers she used to crawl into their beds. They openly called her a whore. Anyone who had an affair with her immediately considered himself master of the house and started ordering me around.

Finally she fell in love with one of the hairy-chested gorillas and decided to marry him, even though she was twenty years his senior. I of course didn't agree with her decision at all. I knew he was only stringing her along to get control of the mill, but it was no good talking to her. Her sensual desires controlled her completely, and during our violent arguments she always sided with her lover. She called me a big, malicious lout jealous of his mother's happiness. She had never had any real happiness in her life, she told me. First she had been a slave to my father, then she had "nurtured me with her heart's blood," and now, when she could find true happiness, I was causing trouble.

That was enough. Not even the pleasant old house and familiar landscape could keep me there any longer. They were alien now anyway; Sebastian seemed to have taken all their warmth and light with him when he died. Beyond our home was the golden highway where wagons and coaches rolled into the sunrise. I was filled with feverish impatience. What was I doing here? Every day I lingered I was missing something out there in that wide, unknown world. Even at the mill we could feel the pulsation of Nuremberg's fiery heart; the wandering journeymen brought it to us in all its richness. I could not wait.

I didn't bother to say goodbye to my mother. I just filled my knapsack with food and one book — the story of Nicholas Flammel. So at the age of eighteen I set out for Nuremberg, the free city.

2

Eduard Anselmus Rochard

It took me fully half a year to reach Nuremberg.

First I had to make the necessary money. To do this, I tried manual labor: chopping wood, carrying water, digging, and hoeing, but the pay was miserable. In the evenings I would drop like a log onto my cot. No, I decided, such work was for animals, not for men, especially a man like me, who was striving toward something entirely different.

So I joined up with a carnival magician. He was an Italian, a jabbering little man who was as swift and pliant as a lizard. His name was Vincenzo Giacomini. He knew only one science but he knew that one thoroughly — the science of profiting from ignorance and gullibility. He could tell fortunes from palms, make diverse miracle medicines for aging men and barren women, compose love letters and poems for various occasions, and, if he had to, extract teeth and draw blood. He was also a first-class expert at opening latches and locks and conjuring small objects out of strangers' pockets — or back in again, if it seemed necessary. His expertise was such that the Italian authorities had requested him to keep his operations outside their borders.

His pride in himself and his "art" knew no bounds. "This is a very serious business, Hans," he would say with a comic mixture of cynicism and self-importance.

"The very fact that you met me proves you were born with a silver spoon in your mouth," he would continue. "Watch and learn. You can make gold with this science. If someone stretches out his palm, pretend to be studying it deeply but really watch the man in front of you. It won't be difficult to determine what type he belongs to. Learn the twelve schemes; one of them will fit him."

"The important thing," the magician's lecture would conclude, "is to talk constantly. Mix, weave, and cast spells with your words. Your victim will

21

find seeds in them that he will swallow gratefully and afterward he will crow about what great things have happened to him."

"Now the basic material of all miracle medicines is water, and don't you forget it. The magic power is on the label. That's an exact analogy of man himself — water on the inside and name and title on the outside. And the more disagreeable the medicine is, the more they'll believe in it. So salt it, pepper it, and put vinegar in it so that sheer horror shakes the person who tastes it; make it burn through his guts like hellfire. I've coaxed the Bengal light from many an extinct volcano that way; I have a whole legion of godchildren. My patients all believe they begat those sons in their happy agony. Luckily women aren't inclined to talk much about the source of the fruit of their wombs. That's how the legend of the immaculate conception has lasted so long."

But Messer Vincenzo had one incurable problem: He did not want to pay his help. Though he acknowledged the justice of income, he passionately denied that of outlay.

"Now don't be an ingrate, Hans," he would say, looking deeply offended that I had asked him for my pay. "I don't pay you with money. Your pay is the secrets into which I have initiated you. After all, I'm getting old, and when I retire you can have this territory. Just be patient."

It was just because he had initiated me into the "secrets of his arts" that I refused to tolerate his deception. Here I was, his beast of burden, miracle medicine peddler, barker, collector, laundress, cook, and famulus all rolled into one, and he would not pay me a cent.

But when I left the old impostor, I had exactly the amount of money we had originally agreed upon in my pocket. Presumably he lamented over the loss of such a skillful student; I took it out from under his pillow while he slept.

★

Ever since I had first heard of Nuremberg, it had lived in my imagination as a fable with limitless possibilities. Whatever I had expected of that city, then boiling up to the dramatic culmination of its fate, I was not disappointed. Its beauty captivated me — an enchanted, sparkling jewel box embedded in the hilly, emerald forests. The Gothic spires of its churches and chapels were awe-inspiring, melodious psalms.

Here the many types of people I had met during my wanderings were present in crowds, jamming the sloping, cobblestoned streets among warm gingerbread houses. I would hear scraps of conversation in Czech, French, and Italian, as well as the various German dialects. I drifted through the city with wide eyes and an open soul, taking in the narrow funnels of the streets where the guilds were, the wide bays of church and market squares, and the whole din of humanity upon them. There were boisterous groups of students, stout market women, wandering journeymen in velvet jackets, flat-chested virgins, sleepy looking nuns, jolly monks with ruddy faces and pot bellies, ascetic priests, beggars with horrible-looking sores, peasants who smelled of manure and led red-spotted cows, men on horseback loudly demanding the right of way, and apprentices shouting obscenities as they hustled baggage.

For a few weeks I roamed through the city, happily aloof from the clattering of humanity. Then when I ran out of money I got a job at a small inn near Sebaldus church. I chopped wood and carried water and luggage to the rooms, careful to conceal the fact that I could read. If I had let it become known, I would have been set to crouch all day in the dark office by the kitchen, well away from the mainstream of events that I so vitally needed to observe. I had to be in a position to watch, in case fate threw before me the one man out of all those people, or even the one possibility, that would lead me to my goal — the Philosopher's Stone.

This water and luggage carrying provided me with some very interesting insights. I discovered, for instance, that titled ladies and respectable burgher's wives, once they had gotten rid of their servants or chaperones, behaved very much like smitten kitchen maids. I was a muscular, handsome lad in those days and I liked to keep myself clean. This combined with the quiet, closed rooms and the transitory nature of the situation was an irresistible attraction for these women. I marveled at how much alike they all were in their barely disguised lust — the same faces, the same small, foolish sounds, movements, and coquetry.

Whenever I happened to get a fleeting appetite, I tasted this particular fruit of the tree of knowledge but it didn't mean much to me. I was too burdened with a feverish, transcendent restlessness to see life through the eyes of a Boccacio. One idea, grown to an obsession, filled my every thought — the stench of death ruins life. Life is beautiful, yes, but it is also pointless if man is to live only a few years, if he is to be a burnt-out wreck after only a few pleasures. Yet the muscles become flabby, the teeth fall out, and life flickers out like a candle.

I could not understand how people could have the heart to jostle about, show off their importance, marry, pursue a vocation, or engage in any other activity when at any moment their lives might come to an end. At best they could only live a few more decades. Why didn't they run away when they went to funerals and saw their own death sentences in the faces of the dead? Why didn't they run from the cemetery, away from their homes and family and profession and look for the Elixir of Eternal Life — infinite pleasure and youth? This Elixir does exist, though it is more difficult to acquire than the greatest treasures on the earth. Yet what good are earth's treasures if we must die?

I would think about these things as I watched the surging crowds on the streets, chattering, laughing, and enjoying the sunshine. The thought would strike me with shock as I watched the face of the woman in my arms contort with pleasure. Didn't they know it? Didn't they think about it? Did they believe death would pass them by? Couldn't they see their own death masks looking back at them from the mirror when they smiled into it? Why did they bother with anything else? Didn't they realize that every instant was precious, that the next might be too late?

★

One cool October day a modest guest arrived at the inn. I didn't notice him immediately, for his figure did not catch the eye. In his dark clothing he blended in with the crowd and became lost. He had carried his own luggage too, a blue iron-handled wooden chest. He rented one of the cheap rooms that opened into the yard. When I overheard him talking with the innkeeper, I noticed casually that while he spoke German well, he spoke with an accent. His pronunciation was like that of the Frenchmen I had had dealings with, and his name also sounded French — Eduard Anselmus Rochard.

The first night he was there I brought warm water to his room. He was sitting at a table drawing strange figures, a compass beside him, an open book by his elbow, and Chinese ink and paper before him. He was drawing unintelligible signs in an ink circle that had been divided into segments by several diameters. This strange occupation aroused my interest. Quickly I stole a glance around. There were books on the night table; I hurriedly read the title of the book on top — *De Alchymia*. My throat felt parched and my heart beat wildly. In my excitement I forgot myself completely and stood rooted to the spot. When I looked up, Rochard was watching me with a cool, inquisitive gaze.

"Are you waiting for something?" he asked quietly.

Painful embarrassment washed over me. All my hard-won cunning and poise dissolved in the cold light of those bluish-green, penetrating eyes. "No . . ." I stammered. "Forgive me, my lord." I left quickly.

What was the matter with me, I asked myself when I was alone in my cubbyhole. Why had the sight of that book upset me so much? I had seen other guests with alchemy books; the spirit of the thing permeated that age. People were still ignorant and greedy enough for it to be a fad, and they were shallow enough to want only the yellow scum off the deep sea of alchemy — the method of making gold.

No, it wasn't the book that had upset me. It was the aura of Eduard Anselmus Rochard himself — his eyes — yes, those eyes, and his face, that flashing revelation of personality that confused me so deeply. When we had looked into each other's eyes, it was as though a magician had conjured up a magnificent castle with a wave of his wand. That quiet, somber figure, so modest and aloof — suddenly something had burst forth from him. What? Power, yes. That was it, power. I had met many kinds of people, idiots and scholars, braggarts and beggars, lords and peasants, eccentrics and rogues, but none of them had had this power. What if — my pulses pounded as I thought of it — what if this were the person for whom I had been waiting?

I spent a sleepless night. If I fell into a troubled doze for a few minutes, I would start awake with a stab of fear that he might be gone in the morning. This fear tortured me so much that I finally crawled out of my cubbyhole and ran silently through the sleeping inn to Rochard's door. There I flattened myself and listened to his breathing.

In the morning I could hardly wait to get to his room. He was not there and his books were gone from the night table, but his padlocked blue chest was under the bed.

Later that morning I had to go to the bar for some reason, and I saw Rochard there with a group of drunken students and idlers, spinning a yarn for them with great gusto. It must have been an amusing and somewhat disreputable tale, for his listeners frequently burst into lusty guffaws of laughter. I hid under the stairway and watched this many-faceted, incomprehensible stranger. Yesterday I had seen him as an extraordinary Adept, but today he was acting like a drunken bum — like Sebastian. This similarity struck me forcibly.

How often had I seen Sebastian sitting with flushed face at a tavern table surrounded by an audience that drank in the magic of his words with shining faces and stupid, open mouths. He was always bitter after one of these "orgies," as he called them. I could hear his words echoing from the past.

"Did you see my performance today?" he would laugh with bitter self-scorn. "I was a big success, wasn't I? I could have had the same success with a bunch of sheep. They wondered, laughed, and were horrified by turns, but then they just went right on grazing. How I envy and hate people like that! They're a dim-witted herd of animals, but at least they are never lonely. They all snuggle up to each other's warm, smelly bodies and have the same foggy thoughts about food, drink, and love-making in their dull brains. I am terribly alone among them, Hans. My soul has already died of loneliness. I'm really dead. The only reason I shout and agitate so much is that I am afraid of the corpse that is my soul. If I didn't have you, Hans, I would have hanged myself long ago . . ."

Then perhaps this thin, pale man with the greenish-blue eyes was also trying to run away from something by diving into this "herd" and covering himself with laughter. Maybe it was a disguise, as it had been with Sebastian. The way he had looked last night and the way he looked now — there was too great a difference. There was some secret here.

Now Rochard interested and attracted me more strongly than before. I watched him and did not let him out of my sight. That night I brought hot water to his room again. He was sitting at the table reading. For a moment he looked up, absorbed in thought, and then he turned to his book again. This Rochard was still different from the two previous ones. Now his face was intent but infinitely gentle, like the quiet surface of the water with the sun reflected on it. I puttered quietly about the room, pausing to wipe up a few drops of water on the floor so I could read the title of his book from underneath. When I was just about to leave, because I couldn't make myself inconspicuous any longer, his quiet voice stopped me.

"What do you want from me?"

The question was so unexpected that I could only stammer, "I . . . I don't . . ."

"You have been spying on me. Today when I was in the bar you watched me for over an hour from under the stairway. Now you are spying on my books. Can you read?"

"Yes." I felt naked and paralyzed under his penetrating gaze.

"Who taught you? Who are you?"

A tremendous impulse, such as I had never felt before, drove me on. I fell on my knees in front of him and heated, jumbled words rushed from my mouth. "I want to serve you, my lord. I wouldn't ask for pay, just to be allowed to learn. That was the reason I left home. I am Hans Burgner, my lord. The only friend I ever had, an old relative, reared me. His name was Sebastian Dorner, and he was an alchemist. He died before he had succeeded. But I — I still want to go ahead," I implored.

"You want to make gold, don't you?" There was more sadness than scorn in his voice.

"No, I don't care about making gold!" I exclaimed vehemently.

"Then what do you want?"

"The Elixir . . ." My voice trembled, and I choked in my excitement.

"Why do you want to live longer than other people?" he asked quietly, studying me intently as he spoke.

"Can *you* accept the fact that you are going to die? Have you never seen a corpse, sir? Have you never seen those you loved, whose words gave you pleasure and comforted you in sorrow, dissolve into rotten flesh? Isn't death really our only enemy, the thing that snaps at our heels and whispers terrible words?"

He looked away. "You are a strange fellow," he said tonelessly. "Please get up. I am not accustomed to being mistaken for an altar." I picked myself up shamefacedly, and he stood also, his face stiff. "I really don't see why you have come to me with your request. I'm just a poor physician on a study tour. I travel on foot and I don't need any servants."

I stared at him. Suddenly he seemed to be a worn-out old man. What could I want of him? He was so convincing that it seemed everything I had thought of him had been the creation of my own exuberant imagination. I grew more ashamed of my foolish behavior every second, and I could hardly wait to stammer out my apologies and leave the room.

"I must be going crazy!" I growled to myself in confusion. "I'm seeing every fool who turns up as an Adept with the Philosopher's Stone under his cloak!"

But for some strange reason the further I got from Rochard, the more this last image wore off, and I saw the many-sided stranger who could read Albertus Magnus, sham in a bar, and was now hiding from me behind a mask. I suddenly realized that this also was a mask. But why was he pretending so much? Had he committed a crime and been forced to flee the consequences? No, Rochard could not have committed a crime. A criminal was scared, and there was no sign of fear in Rochard. Then why did he hide as one of the drunken, debauched rabble, make himself gray and insignificant? Again I heard Sebastian's words. I had asked him where true Adepts could be found. He said, "Nowhere, my son. You don't see them. They submerge in the crowd and dissemble . . ."

So why did Rochard travel alone and on foot? "I am a poor physician; I don't need any servants!"

Then I became certain that Eduard Anselmus Rochard could be nothing but an Adept.

★

Next morning, when he wasn't in his room, I used the skill acquired from
Messer Vincenzo Giacomini to open Rochard's chest. There were books in
it, astronomical instruments, writing materials, and a large supply of French
gold coins.

Now I do not deny that I burglarized his room. Hans Burgner was not
choosy about his methods in those days. He was still primitive, filled with
dangerous passions and untouched by ethical considerations.

Inside the chest there were two books by Albertus Magnus, the book
written by Arnoldus Villanovarus, *Testamentum Duobis Libris Universam
Artem Chymicam Complectens,* three textbooks on astronomy, and, under all
these, a locked notebook with a red cordovan binding. Naturally the lock was
no obstacle. I felt this book contained the key to Rochard's secret.

The first page was entitled "Secretorum Tractatus"; I had not been
mistaken. But the text was mostly in Latin with inserts in French and short
passages in German, and I could read only the German and a little bit of the
Latin. My hands trembled as I thumbed through the notebook, my ears alert
for the slightest noise outside.

Rochard apparently dated his notes like a diary. Suddenly one German
text caught my eye:

> Spying on my secrets is useless. I could shout them from the rooftops and they
> would still be secrets.

This scared me, as though I had received a personal rebuke. I began to sweat
as I read on, and my heart pounded wildly.

> I could proclaim this secret as the sun, moon, and stars proclaim the sky, as
> the earth proclaims itself under human feet, as water, fire, wind, plants, and
> animals proclaim themselves, and they still would not understand it. How can
> they understand the large Universe when the small one — their own bodies and
> souls — is a mystery to them, sealed with seven seals?

Then there was a French text, and then a sentence that began in German and
finished in Latin.

> Gold and Elixir. If they could get hold of them, they would adorn corpses with
> the first and stuff the other into the mouths of the putrefying worms to fatten
> them . . . Raris haec ut hominibus est ars, ita raro in lucem prodit. Laudetur
> Deus in aeternem qui partem suam infinitae potentiae nobis suis objectis-
> simis creaturis communicat.

Further on, again in German:

> He who lives too long should change his name. The name Flammel, for example, is known to too many . . .

I didn't have any more doubts. Excitedly I thumbed to the end of the notes and found what I was looking for.

> October 12, 1555 — His name is Hans Burgner. He is wild, unpolished, dangerous, and touching. Perhaps he interests me because he reminds me of a face I have seen in the mirror somewhere during the time of Chaos. This chest is heavy, and I am getting a little bit lazy. I must be on guard to keep the weaknesses of my body from defeating me — pity, for example. He knelt down and spoke of the Elixir. He is intelligent, as a young animal is, and terrifying reflexes slumber within him, reflexes of which he himself is unaware. His eyes follow me everywhere. Unfortunately, dogs have always moved me . . .

Now I possessed the spark that could melt the icy wall of his reserve. He felt sorry for me, and he was interested in me.

It would have been unwise to stay in his room any longer. I relocked the notebook, put everything in the chest back into place, padlocked it, and shoved it back under the bed.

★

Even now I find it difficult to trace the interweaving currents that boiled inside Hans Burgner that day when he left Rochard's room. There were so many powerful contradictions — dark and light, fire and water mingled. Thus the chaos whirls in the incandescent, seething spiral nebulae of nascent solar systems. The youth was exalted by finding the "Magister," admired him to the point of worship, and wanted to serve him humbly and unconditionally. Yet at the same time he was treacherously scheming to force this Master to take him into his service.

Nor did his burglary and lying trouble him. Naturally he had to know for sure, and naturally Rochard must never learn about it — otherwise he would never even speak to the boy again. Fortunately, Rochard did not know about it. And the deed that is not known — might never have been done.

★

That evening I knocked at Rochard's door, excited but determined. His expression was not unfriendly. His notebook lay closed in front of him, but he must have closed it when I knocked, for the tip of his long reed pen was still wet. I came and stood quietly in front of him. The humble respectful entreaty in my eyes was an honest emotion, but it was only a fragment of those that seethed inside me.

"Well, what do you want, Hans?" Rochard asked. It was an encouraging sign that he called me by my first name.

"I would like to ask the — Magister to permit me to become his pupil. I make good money here at the inn, and I would pay. I could take lessons in the evening if . . . ?"

"But what do you want me to teach you?"

"Well, I know a little Latin, but I would like to learn some more. And I have always been interested in the physician's art. I don't want to haul luggage all my life. Perhaps I could become a gentleman or even a scientist. I learn quickly, so I wouldn't give you much trouble . . ."

Rochard looked at me thoughtfully, his lips tightly closed. Then his gaze glided past me and I felt him receding, disappearing once more into the unfathomable.

"Please don't reject me, sir. I beg you!" My voice trembled with emotion. "I want to learn so much. I want knowledge the way most men want a woman. I'm poor, and there's no one in the world who will help me. Sebastian, my friend, the only person who ever cared about me, died. Don't you turn away from me too. I cannot bear to keep living as I am. Please help me!"

Suddenly his eyes turned back to me. He stared at me quietly for a long time, and I felt his gaze burning through to the innermost depths of my soul, reading my deepest secrets. Presently he spoke.

"I know that you're telling me some of the truth and making some of this up. I know the real reason you cling to me. You are still an unripe fruit, in spite of your sharp mind. Knowledge in your hands could become either a key or a weapon. I ought to send you away, but I cannot. I feel some kind of obligation to you, something I don't understand. It worries me. Yet perhaps it is better for me to keep you with me; otherwise you would be sneaking around behind my back. I'll take you into my service and teach you — but only the science of this world. You needn't expect me to do anything more. If you are industrious, I will see that you get to take the necessary examinations and get a diploma. Then you can be a respected citizen, raise a family, and acquire as much money and fame as your ambition desires. But I repeat,

I will only teach you knowledge that pertains to this world and the ordinary human life span. Do you understand, Hans?"

"Yes, sir."

"Do you still want to join me? Wait. I will not pay you. In a few weeks we will be leaving for Padua, and you will have to carry my chest, make my purchases, and make all the arrangements for our travel and lodging. I will pay your room and board, and I will furnish you shoes or clothing if yours should wear out while you are working for me."

"Thank you, sir. That is more than I had ever hoped for. You have made me so happy! You will see; I will show my gratitude. I will be worthy of your trust, so help me God!"

At that time I meant every word I said.

★

And that was how I became the servant and student of Eduard Anselmus Rochard, the alchemist. At the time I thought I owed my success to my own cunning. And although Rochard was very shrewd and saw through me, he could not yet see his own fate in me. He only sensed it, but this had been the reason he could not turn me down. My craving for knowledge was genuine, of course, and so was my Elixir monomania. He was fully aware of my immaturity, but this was canceled out by his deep, humane kindness and his empathy for me.

Thus the Great Planner's design was woven into the vast fabric of destiny according to its predetermined plan. The two of us had searched and waited for each other and had finally met in sixteenth century Nuremberg: I to start a new cycle on a strange arc and he to end his earthly cycle.

★

I soon learned that though Rochard had many passing acquaintances with whom he would converse in the Sebaldus bar, he had only one friend. This was Amadeus Bahr, the librarian of the Count of Zellern. Almost every day he would visit Bahr in the adobe house inside the castle park where the weak-chested little man had been sent to live when guests overflowed Zellern Castle.

This isolation was no particular burden to Bahr. He enjoyed living among the heaps of books, manuscripts, and dust that surrounded him. It was almost as though he slept on, ate, and breathed books. He used to lend great, heavy volumes to Rochard and I would have to carry them to our quarters. For this reason I was sometimes allowed to go with him on his visits to Bahr.

On one such occasion I managed to listen to an exciting debate on alchemy, even though Rochard had sent me home. I had carried back the heavy book Bahr had lent and, when Rochard had selected another one, he sent me home to study. But I had other ideas.

I went around the house and sneaked through the thick trees to the open back window. There I lay flat on my stomach in the dense weeds under a prickly gooseberry bush. Amadeus Bahr, I had learned, was a genius at debating and loved the art, while Rochard merely discoursed. Yet his gentle, smiling tranquility would slowly wear down the tiny Lucifer with his flaming sword. I had instinctively sensed that Rochard had the more powerful personality, and Bahr, who was a perceptive scholar, recognized this.

Bahr had a clear, analytical mind, and until he met Rochard he had been an outspoken opponent of alchemy. He had rejected it only after intense study, and his arguments against it were excellent and amusing. Now he began the battle by making some categorical statements.

"All this fable of universal medicine simply deceives the masses," he declared, "and the 'transmutations' that are proclaimed from the housetops have always turned out to be merely worthless metal coloring that did not change the specific gravity of the substance."

Rochard quietly asked if anything like this had been proved in the case of Nicholas Flammel. The name Flammel made my heart jump and roused my senses to fever pitch.

"No!" There was mocking laughter in Bahr's voice. "Of course it wasn't proved; human stupidity clouded the evidence. Flammel was a more skillful scoundrel than most, that's all."

"Perhaps," Rochard replied. "You will probably think I am stupid also, but I make bold to confess that when I talked to him not long ago he gave the impression of being an honest and modest man."

"You talked to *whom*?" Bahr asked incredulously.

"To Nicholas Flammel."

"When?"

"Two years ago when I was in Egypt. I had gone with a commercial caravan to get a certain plant that can be processed to relieve festering eye diseases; one of my rich patients had been happy enough to pay my fare. One day we saw a small group of five people crossing the desert ahead of us and we caught up with them in the noon heat, when we joined them in the cool shade of an ancient tomb. The group turned out to be a French couple with three servants. Since they were my fellow countrymen, I greeted them. It was a very interesting meeting."

"Excuse me," interrupted Bahr. "I don't quite follow — your fellow countryman told you he was Nicholas Flammel?"

"Nothing of the sort. I found out for myself that the couple was Nicholas Flammel and his wife."

"But how did you find out?"

"By very convincing signs."

"You are joking, making fun of me," Bahr exclaimed angrily. "If I remember rightly, Nicholas Flammel was born in 1330. This is 1555. Do you mean to tell me you've met a 225-year-old man? You don't really expect me to believe that, do you? I'm not a credulous fool. I myself have seen a one-hundred-year-old graybeard; he sucked his thumb and somebody had to wipe his nose. No man could live 225 years unless he filled himself to the brim with the mythical Elixir."

"Yes, only then."

"But there's no such thing!"

"Are you sure?"

"I am sure that Flammel was devoured by worms, just as you and I will be!"

"Who watched him die?" Rochard asked gently. "He was rich, respected, and famous, surrounded by numerous followers and friends. But which one of them attended his funeral? Who knows where his tomb is?"

"No one. But that's not proof!"

"No, but it is interesting. A number of travelers claim to have seen him in various parts of the world, and the old records also record such instances."

"That's not even worth debating," protested Bahr. "Flammel simply disappeared from Paris and changed his name. He wanted to appear immortal, so he died somewhere else under an assumed name and thus became a legend. That's not unusual in our pitiful age. Just look around you! Alchemy is a greater reality than the plague. Even you are contaminated with it. Just because nobody knows the true story of Nicholas Flammel's death, somebody sees him in every French confidence man who comes along."

I had seldom heard Rochard laugh, but he laughed wholeheartedly now.

"Why are you laughing?" Bahr asked suspiciously.

"Don't be angry." Rochard tried to stop laughing as he spoke. "It's the situation that's funny, not you. It reminds me of an amusing story. Let me tell it to you."

"By all means." Bahr's voice still sounded suspicious.

"Once upon a time there was a clever and learned Chinese named Hui-Shen who lived in the province of Shan-shi on the Huang-Ho, or Yellow River. He was so clever that people came from all over the country to gather around his bullrush mat and listen to his endless debates with a gentle old village priest. For years they had been debating the existence of spirits. The priest insisted that spirits existed, but his only proof was that he regularly saw and talked to them.

"But Hui-shen had exactly seven hundred and seventy-seven arguments to prove that spirits did not exist. Anyone who claimed to see them was either sick or drunk; anyone who talked with them was only mumbling a senseless dialogue to himself. The air and the sky were really empty, and only the graves were full — full of rotting bodies. Man was the spirit, and when he died everything ended.

"Hui-shen would crush the old priest's arguments like eggshells and, if others spoke up in support of the priest, he crushed their arguments too. He would not allow the slightest possibility for even the tiniest spirit to squeeze into the Universe. His arguments were invincible. Finally the old priest got tired of these fruitless debates. He told Hui-shen that his health was no longer good enough for him to continue with them and he would send someone better prepared to argue. This left Hui-shen alone with a whole storehouse of unused arguments. No one would debate him; if he so much as opened his mouth, people backed away out of fear.

"One evening Hui-shen was preparing for bed. He was restless and dissatisfied because he had had no one to argue with for days. Then he noticed a skinny, dark man sitting on the other rush mat. Hui-shen was amazed, for he had not seen or heard him come in. He was about to reprove him for bad manners when the stranger spoke.

" 'I am the one for whom you have been waiting. A friend of mine sent me to convince you of the truth; he says you don't believe in spirits.'

" 'But of course not!' Hui-shen burst out in his relief. He forgot all about his plans for going to bed; already he loved this white-robed stranger, and he would not have let him go for anything in the world. He began to present his arguments in a sarcastic, mocking voice. He stated and refuted, argued and proved without ever giving his opponent a chance to open his mouth. Every time the stranger took a breath to say something, Hui-shen would raise a hand to forestall him. 'Wait! I know what you're going to say. You needn't tire yourself.' Then he would raise his voice and enumerate the other's every possible argument, then dissect and kill it. The stranger grew increasingly gloomy and restless and kept trying to speak, but Hui-shen would stop him before he could utter a single word.

"This went on until the silver rays of dawn lightened the window and a rooster started crowing in the yard. Then the stranger lost patience, jumped up, and interrupted Hui-shen's steady flow of words.

" 'Silence, you wretched fool!' His angry voice shook Hui-shen's tiny house. 'I cannot refute your damned reasoning; what you say sounds like the truth, except that it is not. In spite of all you say, there *are* spirits, damn it, because *I myself am one!*' With that, he disgustedly evaporated before the eyes of the deflated Hui-shen."

Bahr could not help laughing at this story but, when he realized what it meant, he stared soberly at Rochard. At this point I peeked through the window to look at the two still figures in the circle of candlelight.

"Why do you use every possible means to confuse me, Anselmus?" Bahr demanded. "There's something irritating and unfathomable about you. Damn your innuendoes! You'll get me sent to the exorcists yet!"

"I don't see why," Rochard replied innocently. "I only told you a Chinese tale, and you are not easily taken in, Amadeus . . ."

"No, I'm not," Bahr growled. "But no matter how I fight them, your words affect me. For the first time in my life I can refute something and still not be able to dismiss it altogether. It worries me. You were joking just now when you said Nicholas Flammel was still alive two years ago, weren't you?"

"No, I wasn't joking. He's still alive now."

"The Elixir keeps him alive?"

"Yes."

"I simply can't understand it. I know your mental ability, erudition, and your intellectual honesty. How can you believe this — this madness?"

"You're wrong, Amadeus, I don't believe; I'm not so gullible either. I *know.*"

Bahr turned red. He jumped up from his chair and then sat down again, fuming. "Well, that's that, I suppose. What am I going to do about you? And what am I going to do about myself when you leave me alone with all these questions? I can't even sleep anymore."

"Why not?"

"Why not? Because something in me is drawn to you by some illogical, invincible magic. I don't know how to explain it; I've brooded about it a good deal. Your most nonsensical statements radiate an irresistible force. Yet I'm no worshipper of authority; in fact I'm a passionate iconoclast. All these abstracts and transcendental fogs just annoy me. I put up with them in you and I can't understand why. I had given up faith in everything and resigned myself — complete nihilism brings peace, you know. Now you come in and disturb my personal religion and urge me to become a heretic. You have made me doubt my own doubt. And the most astonishing thing is that you haven't done it by arguments — it's your very personality. It's not what you say; it's what you are. You radiate certainty without direct communication. It's like — well, it wouldn't occur to me to doubt the existence of an oak tree when I'm standing in front of one."

"I must confess that I'm not a bit sorry to disturb your religion, Amadeus. In fact I am going to try to bring about your total damnation."

"But why did you choose *me*?" Bahr asked. "The world is full of pious jackasses who would offer you their faith on a platter. I'm a hard nut to crack, a rebellious, cantankerous, backsliding old sinner."

"Well, I would tell you the parable of the prodigal son, but you'd throw something at me. I won't even mention the Saul who became Paul. We'll stick to the facts. The blind faith of jackasses is like a puddle in the summer heat; it will take the form of any basin offered it. Your icon-smashing, Scorpio individuality is much more attractive. You might say I have a weakness for that sort of personality. You and I are walking the same path, you know — the path of intelligence. I've struggled through the same labyrinth myself. Why shouldn't I shorten the path for a friend, especially an old friend to whom I owe so much?"

"Answer one question for me, Anselmus."

"More than one, if need be."

"Will you sit down with me and explain this conviction of yours clearly without any hazy hints or occult references? Will you tell me what experiences brought you to it and what your proofs are?"

"Yes."

"Then let's make an engagement. When will you do it?"

"Soon. Before I go to Padua."

Now was time for me to leave. I ran back to the inn as fast as I could, panting and sweating, spread my books and papers in front of me in my cubbyhole, and stared at the blank sheets. One thought overwhelmed me, filling my whole being. "He who lives too long should change his name. The name Flammel, for example, is known to too many . . ." Rochard's conversation with Amadeus Bahr had revealed the meaning of these words. "Who saw him die?" "You were joking just now when you said Nicholas Flammel was still alive two years ago, weren't you?" "No, I wasn't joking. He's still alive now." Still alive! Flammel was a Frenchman and so was Rochard. "He who lives too long should change his name . . ." Nicholas Flammel — Eduard Anselmus Rochard.

But what about his wife? They had discovered the Philosopher's Stone together, and she also drank the miraculous Elixir. Well, why shouldn't they have separated for a little while? They had a staggering vista of centuries before and behind them; they didn't need to dog each other's tracks. There was no hurry; they had time for everything.

Rochard had not hidden anything from Bahr. In fact he had practically stunned the little bookworm with his openness. Why did he reveal so much to *him*? Why did he lavish the treasures of his wisdom on a skeptic and refuse them to me, who longed for occult knowledge with my whole soul? I studied like a fanatic and got my homework done ahead of schedule and all I got was "Very good, Hans. Well done, Hans," — just like he would talk to a well-trained dog. Any time I cautiously turned the conversation to alchemy, he would become uncommunicative immediately and, if I persevered, he would stop me.

"This isn't the road for you, Hans," he would say. "Stop thinking about it. You would only learn enough to get you in trouble. Your passion for the Elixir is a dangerous one; it springs from a greedy, dark desire. I will never lead you to your destruction."

That evening I was so obsessed with my idea that Rochard was really Flammel that I had to say something or burst. So when Rochard came to hear my lessons, I didn't hesitate to tell him I hadn't done them. I had been completely engrossed, I told him, in some words I had accidentally overheard while I was leaving Bahr's. It had been something about the Elixir and Nicholas Flammel.

"Oh, so you were eavesdropping. Well, I'm not surprised. I should have known . . ." To my surprise, his face did not show its usual rigid rejection. He seemed to be musing, and there was pity in his eyes. He sat down at the table with me.

"I feel sorry for you," he said quietly. "I am sorry because I have grown to like you, Hans. You are a talented and intelligent child — but you're still a child. You still have a childlike mixture of tenderness, unpredictable passions, and dangerous curiosity. Don't think I'm belittling you. You do very well indeed on your own level, but nature can't be hurried. Life cannot be conceived in a child's womb. I am keeping these things from you simply to protect you. Please try to believe me and understand that there is no Elixir for a person in your stage of development. Adult Elixir would poison both soul and body."

I had heard only two points in this lecture. One, he had mentioned the

Elixir as a reality to me for the first time; two, he considered the doubter Bahr an equal and me just a child. I erupted in bitterness. Why, I asked, did he trust the sour librarian of the Zellern Court more than he trusted me, when I was a diligent disciple on the mystic path?

"He is mature, Hans." Rochard spoke to me tenderly. "He is mature mentally as well as physically. Many evil passions have burned out in him. Now he only needs his eyes opened."

"But what *could* happen to me if I tried the Elixir?" I asked heatedly. "I'm not afraid of anything!"

"You are wrong. There are still things you need to be afraid of. When a certain level of development has been reached, fear can indeed be cast aside so the soul can soar. But until then it's a necessary ballast. He who is weightless inside is swept away by every gust of wind. You asked what could happen to you if you attempted to seize the occult forces of the Elixir," Rochard continued quietly. "I will tell you. You could get into a state worse than death. You see, the books don't mention the secret effects of the Elixir. Let me warn you about it now, Hans. It might even kill a person whose soul is full of the lower impulses. Even if his body should overcome the terrible shock, he would still become a mental leper trapped for eternity in a torment of painful, festering sores.

"Here is what I mean. There is a beneficial veil over the eyes of mortal man that keeps him from being aware of the demonic beings who fill the ether. The Elixir breaks through this protective barrier, even in the case of Adepts. But Adepts are prepared for it; they had already rid their souls of demonic characteristics and they are able to overcome these astral beings. But when all the bonfires of passion still rage in a man, the demons rush in and capture him. They use his own fear and weaknesses to weave a noose around his neck."

Rochard paused, then continued gravely. "When the Elixir is acquired by force, it infects the disobedient disciple with a horrible disease that drives him from disaster to disaster. He can never again become a part of the normal, slow process of evolution. His life is one long agony of insatiable desires, unquenchable thirsts, and incredible loneliness. Nor can he hope to escape through the universal exit of suicide; that route is closed to him. He can die only at the violent hands of another; otherwise no hatchet, dagger, sword, rope, fire, or any other agent can smother his burning consciousness or his memory. That is all I can tell you now, Hans. Don't ask any more; otherwise you will have to leave my service. Do you understand?"

I understood that he had refuted me. I would not believe in his dark threats nor would I accept his refusal. After all, he hadn't wanted to take me as his servant either; yet I was his servant. More than that, I had become his pupil. Now I only had to wait — wait and observe with unbreakable tenacity. Eduard Anselmus Rochard had in his possession the only thing that meant anything in life — the Divine Substance. I had to stay with him. I would have to keep on with limitless patience and equally limitless pretense, taking every affront, and sacrifice everything to reach my goal.

★

One afternoon we sat in the Sebaldus bar. Though it was still comparatively early, the rain-bearing autumn clouds made it dark as evening. Rochard was surrounded by a large crowd of noisy students who bore all the marks of their strenuous night life. I withdrew from them and went to the fire, where I began to study a book my master had borrowed from Amadeus Bahr. The only light was a floating wick hung from a sooty beam, and I had to stop reading, for my eyes began to hurt.

I began to watch Rochard again, stealthily. As always he was the focal point of all my thoughts. There he was calm and sober, sitting in the middle of that drunken crowd whose hot breath smelled of sour wine. But I was the only person who perceived him this way; to the students, he was a companionable tale teller whose every word brought laughter. Now he was telling them a story about a well-known "woman of the city" who would give herself to any man who could cover every part of her body with gold coins. Once she lured in a tattered old alchemist; she could sense the smell of gold about him. She fed him sumptuously and then led him into the bedroom, disrobed in front of him, and stretched out on the bed, placing large chunks of lead on her soft, white body. Then she challenged the old man to turn them into gold if he would have her. The poor old fellow did the best he could, but he was so inflamed with desire that the precious red powder slipped through his fingers at the wrong time. Instead of turning the lead to gold, he had made gold of those parts of the woman's body which were valuable only as flesh and blood.

This story aroused the students greatly, though they tried to conceal their feelings by laughing. One of them started to sing, but his hoarse voice faltered and choked frequently from drunkenness.

The many contradictions in Rochard's personality did not bother me anymore for I understood that a sage can hide only behind a shield of foolishness. This was why he acted the charlatan.

Suddenly the water in the iron cauldron over the fire began to boil and hiss over the sides. An old woman came up with a bowlful of big dumplings, which she began to roll in her clawed hands before throwing them into the steaming water. As if this were a signal, Rochard got up and came to where I was sitting.

"Let's go," he said curtly. I rose and followed him.

★

Heavy, cold rain was beating down on the narrow streets, so we hurried. We moved with long strides across the market square, along the city wall, and into the dressmaker's street where we found the tailor's house in which Amadeus Bahr was now living. Even his modest adobe house had been needed for the swarm of servants who had accompanied the Count's guests. We were both soaked to the skin by the time we knocked at the door.

The little man cleared his throat and called, "Come in!"

We entered the windowless little room Bahr had rented. There was a rancid smell from the tallow candle that burned almost constantly, and the whole room stank of onions. Bahr turned toward us. He was emaciated, and his clever black eyes shone from slack, wrinkled lids, but he smiled at us cheerfully.

"You've come just at the right time, Anselmus! I'm engaged in struggling with your famous Tabula Smaragdina."

"A divine pastime," Rochard replied, shaking water from his cloak. He cautiously pushed aside a large pile of books and papers and sat down on the squeaky bed. "What wretched weather! Are you soaked, Hans?"

"To the bone," I replied, shivering. I moved closer to the small iron stove, feeling elated. Rochard couldn't send me home in this heavy downpour. I found a seat on a wooden chest by the stove, well out of range of the candle-light. Here I sat patiently, like a wild beast awaiting his prey.

"His Grace wants me to give him the exact meaning of the Emerald Tablet. He wants to serve it to his guests as a dessert after the larded bear shank." Bahr was really a secret rebel. His weak body, menial position, and great mental ability had combined to make him miserable, awkward, and haughty all at once. Thus he took note of all the ridiculous, cruel, and stupid things at his master's court with the black daggers of those sharp eyes. He frequently wrote scathing pamphlets with irresistibly humorous — and recognizable — characterizations. These works were carefully hidden in his wooden chest; he knew that even one of them could send him to the torture rack in the Pagan

Tower if it got into the wrong hands. But he could not give up writing them; they were the only satisfaction in his miserable life.

"This isn't a difficult assignment, Amadeus," Rochard said with a smile. "There are already a number of confusing interpretations of the Emerald Tablet in circulation; the worst you can do is add one more. The important thing is to make it exciting enough to help the digestions of the nobility."

"I suppose I'll have to shove in a lot of sex for that and then soothe them with a bunch of lies about how they'll still go to heaven after their no-good, stupid lives!" The two of them laughed, but Bahr's laughter turned to a choking, barking cough that shook his whole body and brought tears to his eyes. Rochard looked at him with concern. When the attack had subsided, he spoke.

"And have you found anything to amuse the guests suitably?"

"No," Bahr replied grumpily. "What really irritates me though is that I can't find a single sentence in it that makes sense. I suspect it is one of the greatest frauds in human history — a fraud of genius, of course, since both the intelligent and the stupid have been fascinated by it for centuries."

Rochard nodded wisely. "That is certainly one explanation of the Emerald Tablet," he replied, his lips twitching with that curious smile that even seemed to provoke Bahr. "I am surprised though to find you among the spiritually feeble, Amadeus. Are you trying to save your sense of superiority by refuting something just because you don't understand it?"

"Of course not! You are wrong." Bahr jumped nevertheless, his face livid. "But for Christ's sake, are you telling me *you* understand this Dodonaen hocus-pocus?"

"Understand it? No, I wouldn't say that. I have not yet fully grasped its meaning on all three levels. But I do know that it contains every solution to the problems of the body, soul, and afterlife of man."

For a few moments Bahr stared at him silently. Then he spoke almost with humility. "The seeker who does not want to hoard the blessings of learning for himself cannot afford to have prejudices. Knowledge is more important to me than this sick body, or the drudgery of having to serve those fools up there, or even my pride. Please tell me about the Tablet."

"I'll be glad to," Rochard replied. "What do you already know about it? I don't want to be repetitious."

"I don't know very much," Bahr admitted. "I know it was written by Hermes Trismegistus, whose tomb Alexander the Great found during one of his campaigns. His Greek name was first mentioned about the fourth century after Christ, but his figure was undoubtedly surrounded by religious legends long before that. During the Roman Empire, the Egyptians erected obelisks in his memory, and they always covered these obelisks with engraved alchemical formulae.

"Some people think that Hermes Trismegistus is simply the Greek name for the Egyptian Pharaoh Thoth or Theut who is mentioned several times by Plato," he continued. "According to Plato, Thoth lived several millennia before Christ and founded and encouraged numerous sciences and arts. He is credited, among other things, with inventing arithmetic, astronomy, and the game of dice. The Egyptians even believe it was he who made the distinction between vowels and consonants. Of course some people believe that the name Thoth refers to the embodiment of a concept rather than a person. The ancient Egyptians had had a god named Thoth who represented wisdom, skill, and swiftness, and they pictured him with a caduceus, just like the Greek Hermes. That's as far as I've gotten in finding out about Hermes Thoth."

"Getting that much was a nice accomplishment, Amadeus," Rochard said approvingly. "The most charitable thing that can be said about the documents concerning Hermes Trismegistus is that they are ciphers understood only by initiates. And don't think I'm being arrogant when I use the word 'initiate.' Every initiate has had to go through hard physical exertions, equally difficult tests of will, and unceasing spiritual effort. The use of esoteric terms is not just a greedy device to conceal material pleasures that anyone might enjoy. Anyone who wants to enjoy these treasures must laboriously work his way to the summit where the Temple of Knowledge stands open."

I dared not stir for fear they would notice me. I simply sat on the chest, numb in my steaming clothes. I understood the words Rochard was using, but I only became aware of their true meaning after much time and suffering.

"Hermes-Thoth was unquestionably an Egyptian priest, physician, and astronomer," Rochard was continuing. "His actual dates have not been established, but they are probably earlier than Plato's estimate. It is also possible that he was the Pharaoh as well as a priest; the ancient world didn't separate these two functions. At one time the Pharaoh was the man of highest intellect in the nation, quite a different figure from the bloodthirsty tyrants of later times. He had to be an initiate because, according to the ancients, only he who ruled himself and his own spirit was fit to rule others.

"Hermes is a title, like Mann or Buddha, but it has a threefold meaning. It can mean a man, a caste, or a god. The man Hermes was the first great initiate, but his name also refers to the entire priestly caste. Referring to a god, the name means the planet Mercury, the spiritual sphere where divine initiates live. In fact Mercury is the leader of divine initiation in the regions beyond earth. The Greeks, who studied the Egyptian religion, called the person who largely originated it Hermes Trismegistus, the threefold master of all natural sciences. Many thousands of works are ascribed to him; most of them were written by his disciples and adherents. The most profound and the most authentic is the Emerald Tablet. If you have it by you, Amadeus, please read it aloud."

Bahr leaned over the large open book, and his knotty finger traced the beginning of the Emerald Tablet.

Verum sine mendacio, certum et verissimum
quod est inferius est sicut quod est superius,
et quod est superius est sicut quod est inferius,
ad perpetranda miracula Rei Unius.

Et sicut omnes res fuerunt ab Uno
meditatione Unius, sic omnes res natae fuerant
ab hac Una Ra, adapatione.

Pater eius est Sol, mater eius Luna,
portavit illud ventus in ventre suo;
nutrix eius Terra est.

Pater omnis telesmi totius mundi est hic.
Vis eius integra est,
si versa fuerit in terram.

Separabis terram ab igne,
subtile a spisso,
suaviter, cum magno ingenio.

Ascendit a terram in coelum
iterumque descendit in terram,
et recipit vim superiorum et inferiorum
sic habebis gloriam totius mundi.

Ideo fugiet a te omnia obscuritas

Hic est totius foritudinis cortitude fortis
quia vincet omnem rem subtilem,
omnemque solidam penetrabit.

Sic Mundus creatus est.
Hunc erunt adaptationes mirabiles,
quarum modus est hic.

Itaque vocatus sum Hermes Trismegistus
habens tres partes philosophiae totius mundi.
Completum est quod dixi de Operations Solis.

English Translation of the Emerald Tablet:

The truth without lying, certain and truest;
Inferior things are like superior things,
And superior things are like inferior things,
To perpetuate the miracles of the One Thing.

And just as all things came about through the
meditation of the One, so all things were born
from this One, by adaptation.

Its father was the Sun and its mother the Moon;
It was carried in the womb of the wind
And nursed by the earth.

It is the father of all good things on earth.
Its power would remain whole,
even though it were directed against the whole earth.

Thou shalt separate earth from fire,
the subtle from the simple,
gently and ingeniously.

It ascends from earth to heaven,
And descends to earth again,
And receives the vital force of both planes.
Thus thou shalt have the glory of the whole creation.

Therefore all darkness will flee from thee.

This is the strength of all strengths,
that conquers all subtle things
and sees through that which is solid.

And thus the world was created.

From this there were marvelous adaptations,
and this is the method of them.

And so I am called Hermes Trismegistus,
for I have the three parts of the philosophy of the whole world.
I have told everything about the work of the Sun.

Bahr sat looking expectantly at Rochard, his aquiline profile outlined on the wall by the flickering candles.

"There are three levels of meaning to the Tabula Smaragdina, just as there are usually three meanings to each Egyptian hieroglyph," Rochard told him. "There is a physical, an astral, and a mental meaning. The revelation of Hermes Trismegistus contains the most profound secrets of creation and the forces which created this world and the astral regions.

"But the Tabula is also alchemy in the strictest sense of the word, the very essence of it. It contains the spiritual recipe for the great Elixir of Life, the Aurum Potabile, that can heal sickness, rejuvenate, cleanse the blood, and revitalize the body fluids. I ought to mention that this so-called 'potable gold' doesn't make people immortal, as ignorant fanatics believe. It simply lengthens the life span by eliminating aging.

"The Tabula Smaragdina also deals with the other, more esoteric goal of alchemy," Rochard continued, "the transmutation of metals. Now you can understand why Trismegistus hid his meaning in a complicated labyrinth. The young priest who sought the deep mysteries of the Egyptian religion had to undergo difficult tests before each new concept was unveiled to him. The more he learned, the more severe the tests became, and he had to suffer physical death before he received the full illumination of the ultimate secret. Trismegistus constructed the Tabula Smaragdina so that it not only reveals but conceals its essence from the spiritually inferior. Truth gives strength to the strong, you know, but it wounds the weak, just like a carelessly handled sword. That makes the Emerald Tablet fascinating not only for its content but for its structure. It in itself is the test that polishes the spirit that overcomes it to maturity and makes it capable of understanding the conclusion. Another basic tenet of Trismegistus' philosophy is that only he who can transmute himself on the physical, astral, and mental planes can bring about the Great Magisterium," Rochard concluded.

"Tell me what the thing means!" Bahr broke out. "You have led me to the mountaintop and now you cover my eyes."

"Next visit, Amadeus. It is getting late and you need some rest."

I knew that he wouldn't discuss the meaning of the Tablet because I was there, and the knowledge filled me with bitterness. Bahr, alert as a little owl, was also dissatisfied.

"You can't go now! You mustn't leave me now!" he protested vehemently. His words ended in a coughing fit that shook the fragile little body frighteningly.

Rochard stood up, uneasiness reflected in his face. "Spare yourself, my friend."

Bahr shook his head, still gasping, and waved an impatient hand. "It's too late for all that now. There's no reserve left in me to call up. The only time I feel good is when I forget this physical coffin."

"That coffin is precious when it houses a spirit," Rochard replied. "It deserves your care."

"*You* say that? You've been talking about being liberated from matter. Or was that just an abstraction?"

"You misunderstood me, Amadeus. To follow the teachings of Hermes Trismegistus, the cornerstone of spiritual life in the millennia, one must have strength and good health. A sick body produces unhealthy imaginings and blocks the organs that transmit spiritual light with a clog of emotions and strangulating anxiety. He who has a message must keep the vessel for that message pure."

"But do I have a message?" Bahr asked scornfully. "And, anyway, who wants a message these days?" He paused, then continued thoughtfully. "But maybe we really do. You and I, anyway, are persuaded of the value of these letters. Since we can't have real meat, we make do with imaginary food. We satisfy our appetites for power by studying theories that justify our lives and make us phantom monarchs of dream kingdoms. Our weapons are carved from worthless feathers. We dip them in poison and take shots at those who have this world's power and pleasures." He stopped, sighing.

"There's alchemy going on right now in your soul, Amadeus. That acid which is called doubt in human beings is separating your gold from your dross — a very useful acid indeed. There's a great difference, you see, between the two kingdoms you just mentioned. One is the kingdom of death and the other is the kingdom of life. The flesh, after all, however gorgeously desirable, inevitably decays. It's just a toy of the spirit or, if you prefer, an exciting experiment in the self-expression of the spirit, just like a picture drawn in sand. The fleshly world is a wonderful and profound expressive device, just like music, sculpture, painting, books, and cathedrals. The creative joy of the spirit is in all these things but they are transient." Rochard wrapped his cloak around him. "Keep on fighting, Amadeus. The chosen one must serve with all his capacity, including bitterness and doubts."

"I have never felt so worthwhile," Bahr said. "You have given me transcendent feelings and ideas that might well make me conceited, something no worm of a man has a right to feel. I'm going and look in the mirror."

"Look inside yourself," Rochard replied. "The mirror image is just reality's shadow."

★

I plodded along beside Rochard, silent as the sleeping houses we were passing. The rain had stopped and a raging wind was ripping apart the clouds. Already the pale sky was beginning to show through, though Rochard was not heading for our lodging.

"I'm going to take a walk, Hans," he said. "Go on home."

But curiosity drove me after him, and I trailed him from a distance. He went outside the city wall and headed for the thickly forested mountains. The wind kept inflating his loose cloak, then lifting it and flapping it about him like bat wings. Suddenly I was inexplicably afraid. I felt I had to run away; formless premonitions gripped my throat. I turned and tottered back to the inn, threw myself on the bed and sank into a troubled sleep.

The next evening Bahr's landlady burst in on us just as we were finishing our lessons in Rochard's room. She was gasping and panting and managed to choke out that Bahr was vomiting blood and the Count's doctor thought he was dying. Bahr had sent her to bring Rochard at all costs.

We started immediately. Rochard didn't seem to care whether I came or not. We all went out into the bitter cold night pierced by brilliant stars.

There was a candle fluttering on a table beside the bed, revealing the shadowed, yellow face sunk into the pillow. When I first saw him, I thought we were too late. His landlady, the tailor's wife, stood in one corner and cried.

Suddenly Rochard turned to her. "I saw a butcher in the next street. Go get me a pail of ice from his pit. Hurry!" She just stared at him, not seeming to understand. The coin he threw at her spoke her language though and she scurried out.

When she was gone, Rochard laid his palm on the sunken forehead. The flickering candle revealed his grave, intent face. I could almost feel the life force radiating from his palm into the immobile body; living light glowed in his eyes. Suddenly Bahr looked up and saw his friend, and the ghost of a smile played on his lips.

"I'm sorry." His voice was barely audible. "I would have liked so much — the Tabula Smaragdina . . ."

"Don't try to talk." Rochard's voice was soft but firm. "I know what you're thinking. But now I'm here; I made it in time, and you will live." The soft voice was charged with conviction. He pulled a chair over to the bed and sat down very close to Bahr's head. Then he stretched out both hands over him and, as far as I could tell, made strange stroking motions over the sick man's body from his head to the pit of his stomach. The painful gasps from the bed subsided.

The tailor's wife clattered in with the pail of ice. She burst on the scene like a blast of coarse reality and brought in the terror of death. Bahr opened his eyes very wide.

"If I could just believe! But even you can't grow me a new lung!" he moaned.

"Keep still," Rochard ordered. He wrapped the ice in a towel, uncovered the suffering body, and placed the ice pack, all the while speaking gently to the sick man. "If the lizard can replace a torn-off tail between sunrise and sunset, why cannot we learn this secret also? God gave us the intelligence to try. He didn't just say have faith; we are also permitted to turn our faith into knowledge and conviction if we will make the effort . . ." Abruptly he turned to the tailor's wife and me. "I want to be left alone with him. If I need help, I will call."

I waited for Rochard in the stuffy tailor shop. Three people worked in that tiny place where cabbage brewing on the hearth gave off a foul odor. The smell of the place turned my stomach, but I stayed, listening nervously for every sound behind the door. Once in a while I met the eyes of the tailor's wife and became conscious of her hungry, treacherous curiosity. She too was watching that door and was probably cursing me as a hindrance to her eavesdropping.

From the sickroom came only the soft murmur of Rochard's voice. Once he came to the door and sent one of the workers for red wine. He opened the door a crack to take it in, and then all was silence once more.

Presently the pale, consumptive looking little tailor quietly asked me my master's profession. Was he a physician?

"He is," I replied.

"That's not what they say in the city," the woman told me.

"What do they say?" I asked apprehensively.

"That he is a warlock. He and his shadow have been seen to walk separately. He has sold his soul for the gift of making gold. God help us!" She crossed her fat bosom hurriedly.

My heart sank when I heard this dangerous news, but I forced a smile.

"If I weren't in the presence of death, I would laugh at that. Surely I'm in a position to know just how much we could use some gold ourselves. They're always after us to pay on our account at the inn. What kind of gold maker and warlock would stay up to his ears in debt?"

"Oh, that's just his cleverness, to lead people by the nose," the woman replied. "He couldn't stay here if his true skills were known. He would find himself in the pentagonal tower, and that would be a fine cage for a gold-laying goose!"

I shuddered. I remembered what Sebastian had said and the horrible stories that circulated among the tavern tables about people who were tortured to death or killed trying to escape.

"Rochard is just a wandering physician." I spoke out of a dry throat. "He goes to church every Sunday, and he wouldn't even kill a fly. What can they possibly want from him?"

"Gold." The woman giggled. "Like this, see? By the basketful." She opened her hand and a French gold piece flashed in the light.

I stared at it, mesmerized as though by a viper. Rochard had thrown that at her when he sent her for ice. I had forgotten all about it. Now it was obvious I was lying about our poverty and debt. The gleam of that gold piece would illuminate the whole city long before the sun did. Now all we needed was for Bahr to recover after the Count's doctor had given up on him. It was not affection for Rochard that made me frantic with anxiety; it was the fear that violence might take this repository of the Great Magisterium away from me before I could learn his secret.

But I was not alone in realizing the danger. Rochard also knew he must leave before sunrise. As soon as he was able to leave Bahr, we rushed to the inn and packed our bags. I managed to get some food too, thanks to a smitten kitchen maid. The grimly beautiful gray and blood-red dawn found us already on the road. A damp coolness arose from the valley, and little rags of clouds hung among the trees.

We didn't go very far. There was a weed-covered, deserted farm just outside the city with a rickety old barn where we could find shelter. There were gaping holes in the roof and stinking puddles on the dirt floor, but we were hidden.

Rochard had been very quiet and grave all this time. There was something unapproachable in his manner. Silently I found a dry corner for the chest and Rochard sat down on it. Then I managed to make myself a dry seat from a few bricks and some straw. I began to grow increasingly anxious as the minutes crawled by. Why were we here? We were still too close to the city to be safe, and the place was dust laden and full of filthy bugs. A fat spider descending from his thread bumped into my face, and I shuddered. I began to feel bleak and hopeless as the minutes passed.

"Eat!" Rochard handed me the leather bag of food. He didn't eat himself but got out his astronomical instruments, book, and writing materials and became absorbed in some kind of calculations. First he drew a circle, divided it into twelve parts, filled in the signs of the zodiac, and wrote a date. He must be calculating our journey by the position of the planets, I thought, for he wrote them also in his circle.

It was cool in the barn, and a drizzle drummed softly on the roof and into the puddles. A dank draft swept through the building. Rochard looked grim and worried in the dim light, and I could feel his apprehension like a physical force. Finally I felt I could not stand this waking nightmare any longer; I would jump up and yell, somehow break the tension. Then I felt Rochard's eyes on me. He might have been looking at me for some time before I noticed, but he did not speak until I returned his gaze.

"Are you afraid?" he asked in a peculiar voice.

"Afraid of what?" I asked; my voice broke in terror.

He didn't answer immediately; he just kept looking at me. I wanted to run away from that stare but I couldn't evade it. I began shivering and I could feel the sweat start out on my forehead. "I feel sorry for you," Rochard said finally. There was real compassion in his voice. "I can't help you."

Suddenly my fears took shape. "You saw my destiny in the stars, Magister?" I choked out.

"Yours as well as mine."

"Am I going to die?"

"Sometime . . ."

"When? Now? Don't spare me. Will it be violent?"

"No, it won't be now or for a while yet. First you will be afraid. You will be afraid for a long time and you will finally curse your life. You will try to die, and life will cling to you like the death grip of a monster. You will try to run away from yourself, choke out your life, dull your perceptions, shake yourself loose from your body. But life will cling tenaciously, burning and rising to an infinite pain. My poor son, I can't help you with this. You will live . . ." His soft voice sounded dull.

I was flooded with happiness, completely oblivious to the dark prophecies of his words. All I understood was the promise of life — indestructible life. Finally he had quit being contemptuous of me and told me I would live. This could only mean he was going to give me the essence of Trismegistus' secret, the Aurum Potabile. I fell on my knees and bowed my head on the insect-ridden straw at his feet.

"My lord, my lord!" My heart overflowed and my eyes filled with tears. "I am not worthy, I know, of the treasure you give me but I shall become worthy, so help me God! I'll be your servant forever and smooth the road for your feet. I will see that you are never troubled with the cares of this world. My own body will be your shield. You are my father, my brother, my ideal next to Christ. I will destroy every evil desire in my soul. I won't lie and steal anymore because of your favor."

"Stop, you miserable wretch!"

My heart turned to ice. I studied his face, trying to find some reason for the change, but it was like looking at a blank wall. In the gloomy shadows he looked frighteningly old. Why did he keep turning me away, I asked myself in despair. I heard his voice through the gloom speaking tonelessly.

"Nothing but emotions," he said. "Just a dark turmoil with no spiritual sunrise in sight. All-consuming longing and exuberant devotion today, blind passion and destructive hate tomorrow — death . . ."

"I don't understand!" I was trembling all over and I realized I had shouted.

"There's no reason why you should. You are just a hurled stone, matter to destroy matter. Adonai uses you to take this transitory house — I am grateful. Amen." Suddenly he stood up and looked through the narrow window. "It will be dark soon and luckily the sky is overcast. Would you obey me one last time, my son?"

"Of course. Anything you ask!"

"Go back to Bahr's lodgings. You needn't be afraid; no one will hurt you. The tailor and his wife will be gossiping six doors down if the Count hasn't already called them to the castle. And of course the workers won't be there either, with no one to make them work. You won't see anyone. You can get into the sickroom without being seen."

"But what if Amadeus Bahr is already . . ."

"He is alive," Rochard replied simply, "and I want you to take a letter to him."

I wondered how he could be so sure of what was going on in the city. He took out a piece of parchment and wrote thoughtfully. Presently he dried it and rolled it into a scroll. Then he pulled off his heavy silver ring and pushed it over the scroll to keep it from unrolling. A large ruby winked from the middle of the silver phoenix that formed the ring's crest.

I was frightened as I set out, but I was curious too. If I were caught, of course, I knew I would not escape without leading the pursuers to Rochard. I knew well enough there were ways to unlock any lips.

The scroll under my broadcloth jacket practically burned my chest. When Rochard had handed it to me, we had both known I would read it as soon as possible. Yet he had trusted me. Obviously he didn't care whether I read it or not. When I got to a place in the forest where I could be sure of privacy, I took out my tinderbox, piled up some twigs and leaves, and built a small fire to read by.

Rochard had written the letter so that it covered his meaning like a shell, and my mind was too soft and weak to break it open. I read it word for word, struggling through the text till I knew it by heart, and it still seemed utterly foreign. Occasionally I would grasp one word, but I lost the meaning when I tried to relate it to the rest of the sentence. It was such a peculiar letter in those dim woods that I trembled as I read it again and again.

> He who is leaving greets the one who was sent back, one who was his friend and companion on the road. This was a bond that came into being long ago and is now being dissolved. He who leaves has paid all debts save one, and that will soon be collected. Humbly submitting to the law, he will not speak again in a human tongue until the resurrection of the Only Truth, but he pauses to say a few words to his old friend.
>
> The House of Life has three keys, and he who is dying has sent them back to you from the grave. The hands with which he sought them are Scorpio and Aquarius. He himself must get into that house so that he may set a light in the window for those who seek. The Apocalypsis Chemicae has taken place. From the seed sown in the coffin, the triple fruit of Life will come forth — the all-remembering, the all-knowing, and the all-dissolving medicine. These three together are the only great Arcanum. This is the formula, the way, and the explanation. E. A. R.

Things at the tailor's house were exactly as Rochard had said. I didn't even have to knock; they hadn't bothered to shut the door. The workshop was dark and empty. My heart pounded as I scurried to Bahr's door. What if he was dead after all?

Bahr sat at his rickety table. He was bent and yellow and had wrapped himself in his cloak — but he was alive. When he saw me, his face lit with joy and then worry sprang up in his eyes. He jumped up and came to me with firm steps that showed nothing of illness. His breath came naturally, with no sign of the wheezes and gasps of consumption, and his alert bearing shook me to the bottom of my soul. The miracle was tangible, in giddy proximity to me.

Carefully Bahr locked the door; then he turned, and I felt the firm grasp of fingers that yesterday had barely been able to scrabble at the blanket. "Where is he?" he whispered excitedly.

"In a safe place," I replied softly.

His hands dropped from my shoulders. "I have been terribly worried about him." Relief sounded in his voice. "This city is like an anthill that's had honey poured into it. The Count himself has been here twice. He used to ignore my existence, even when I was half dead. But now he has gone so far as to touch me." A shrewd, sardonic smile appeared on his lips. "I've pretended to be an idiot. I told him I had vomited blood because a blood vessel burst in my throat. You know it was my lung, Hans — thick, black chunks of it amid the blood. I felt it." His voice grew softer still. "Tell Rochard the Count has learned nothing from me. He wanted to question me about what medicine I had had, but I denied being given any. The rumors will settle down, but he had better keep under cover until they do.

"Hans, tell him how much I miss seeing him." Emotions tumbled out as he continued. "I don't dare try to see him yet. I would rather lose my own new life than endanger his. But some day . . . Tell him I'm looking forward to the things he promised. Not only has he brought me back to life, he has made me a new person. Tell him that, Hans. My soul that fluttered like a blind bat has died and risen like a bird rising to the light. Tell him I will make an eternal building on the foundation he has laid for me. His words used to sound like improbable theories, but now they have become real inside me. Tell Rochard that I believe, and some day I shall know!" His small, lean face was wet with tears, and the fire of his joy lighted up my own volatile soul. I wept and trembled and rejoiced with him in his miracle.

Then I gave Bahr the parchment, and he took it eagerly. The ring struck awe in him; he leaned closer to the candle and put it on his finger. For a moment the candle blazed brightly, then it died as an overcast dawn crept into the room. This meant I must hurry. Bahr simply raked another candle out from under the bed; he was so absorbed in the letter he hardly heard me say goodbye.

It was late morning when I got back to the barn and I was completely exhausted. Just when I had almost reached the city limits, some of the drunken students from Sebaldus recognized me and came after me. I tried to flee by sprinting wildly but they kept after me, and one of them nearly caught me. I hid in a hole in the forest until they had clattered by and lost the scent.

Rochard was waiting patiently for me. I was flooded with happiness and gratitude at seeing that thin, extraordinary figure again. This morning he looked old and tired, but it was the silvery peacefulness of a serene old age — the old age of a learned sage. It may have been my knowledge that colored my vision, but there in that filthy barn he seemed to be the Magus, the master of the Divine Science and the Great Magisterium.

I told him what Amadeus Bahr had told me, and the telling brought back my emotional tears. Rochard's face showed no emotion throughout.

"Tears, fervent emotion — the scale tips up and tumbles down to balance death," he said softly.

I stared at him, trying to understand. "Amadeus Bahr understood you only after you had healed him, Magister," I said cunningly.

"Amadeus Bahr healed himself. I only made him aware of his ability."

"If you would make me aware too," I whispered, "as you promised . . ." I was trembling.

"I promised you nothing."

"But you said I would live!" I was utterly taken aback. "What else could you have meant?"

"I meant something entirely different," he said firmly.

"No, don't talk like that," I begged. "You have the power; I know you do. I have seen the dead come back to life. My lord! In Christ's name! I don't want to die; I have too much to live for. I have had so little experience, just a few short years. I want to go all over the world, to learn and experience and find out what will become of man. But at the same time I want conscious awareness that I am the man Hans Burgner, your servant. Why is that a sin? God and Christ, the saints, prophets, Magi, and sorcerers all have this everlasting life."

"You have everlasting life too."

"That's not the same thing. That's just an elusive mental fog. Why there are trees out there in the forest older than the first man, and you yourself have seen the course of many generations. I want to see things as the trees and the stars see them — as you see them, Magister. The only desire or prayer I have ever made is just to live. Please have pity on me." I crawled to his feet and embraced his knees. My yearning desire would have overwhelmed the average man but not Rochard. His cool eyes stared at my emotional storm like blue-green ice crystals.

"You are like a child demanding a star from the sky. How can I extinguish your insane fire?"

"Give me life!"

"You yourself are the only one who can achieve that. The most I could do would be to make you one of the living dead who wakes to find himself alive in a walled-in crypt. Pray you never learn what I mean by that."

"You're just saying that, Magister." I lost my self-control and shouted. "You didn't say things like that to Amadeus Bahr. What did he do to deserve the sacred potion that brought him back from the dead in a single night?"

Rochard made a hopeless gesture. "I'm arguing colors with a blind man. What can I do with you? You talk about life but what you really mean is death. You want eternity when your every thought is tied to earth. Listen, Hans. Everyone in this transitory carnival of life is really wearing a costume, and often you cannot recognize your own brother behind the mask. But he who knows that it is his best friend, his dear and long-missed companion inside that costume of a human body doesn't care about the externals. He is concerned only with the essence and timeless personality of the other."

"Then Amadeus Bahr was such — a friend of yours?"

"That's right."

"And that's why you healed him?"

"I couldn't have done it if his spirit had not been ready. The medicine I gave him would have been pure poison to someone else."

"But if I asked for it, I would take the responsibility."

"The responsibility remains with me, Hans."

"You just don't want to understand. Surely you can't be that cruel! I can't stand to live as I am any longer! I am literally under a death sentence and the executioners may come any time. I need time, infinite time to learn about life and resign myself to its passing. How would *you* know — you who have enjoyed centuries? What a terrifying, humiliating crime it is to send intelligent, sensitive people to be eaten by the worms of the grave! It's easy for you to refuse and say it's not good for me, but I'm not going to budge. I *must* make my desires and demands break through that selfish deafness! Or else kill me right now. Kill me because I won't back down. I'm not going to sit here any longer waiting to be slaughtered like an ox. I want all or nothing — now!" I was trembling with emotion. My very helplessness filled me with rage against the barricade of Rochard's body — the obstacle between me and my maniacal goal.

"It would only cost you a gesture, a single compassionate moment, Magister," I whispered, pressing closer to him. My hand glided from his knee to his shoulder in a convulsive move. "You have it right on your person, I know. You must give me some, only a little bit . . ."

He quietly removed my hand from his shoulder. "I have nothing to give you." His voice was firm.

This calmness infuriated me and I spoke in a hoarse screech. "Oh, well, I understand now. I know what kind of man I've been unfortunate enough to get mixed up with. I could move a stone before I could move that soulless shell of yours. A stone would weep with pity for me, but you —" Suddenly I stopped. Two tears had rolled down his cheeks. "Why are *you* crying?" I yelled. "*I'm* the one who ought to cry."

"I'm crying over you," he said softly.

Then I got to my knees and looked him in the eye as though I could drag what I wanted from him merely by my glance. "Are you going to give it to me?" I asked, whimpering.

"Never." He spoke with absolutely no emotion. "You'll never get it while I'm alive." It was like a final judgment.

I collapsed as though I had been struck unconscious. There was no strength or will left in me as I lay on that straw, my brain parched and my limbs incapable of moving. I had been exhausted by the unequal fight. All my arguments were used up and lost; my toy weapons lay broken at his feet, and he stood there — a tranquil, immovable fortress.

Imperceptibly my stupor became a deep sleep. I had been up two nights in a row, made long treks, and been emotionally consumed by excitement.

When I woke up, the sky was already gray with twilight. My bleary eyes searched the desolate place and suddenly saw a dark, motionless mass in the corner. Then I realized Rochard was asleep, wrapped in his dark cloak; presumably he was waiting for nightfall to continue our journey. I stared at his motionless body — nothing but a breathing, fragile vessel in the rotting straw. Yet it was able to set itself invulnerably against me. It was ridiculous — the taboo was vulnerable and in my power. Only the invisible forces protected him — or was it my own superstition? Because — what could keep me from just taking what I wanted? It was on his person, I knew, because he did not part with it for a minute. He had had it right at hand to give Bahr . . . It was just an arm's length from me, and I sat there helplessly, gnashing my teeth. It would just take one quick moment. Rochard was only a bundle of rags in the corner, his life force gone from him in sleep. He had no particular physical strength. His lips were closed; the magic of his words was gone, and nothing remained but a frail, cruel old man . . . I crept closer.

Perhaps the thing was in his belt or on his chest; my trembling hand was groping over his body. He did not move, so I cautiously leaned over to open his shirt . . . Suddenly terror stabbed through me. Rochard's eyes stared unwinkingly into mine. He had been awake all the time! I broke out in a sweat as I drew back. My hand clutched for support, and I found a wet half brick. Without conscious volition I grabbed the brick and smashed it between his eyes as hard as I could. A thick, warm wetness splashed in my face . . . I had not known I was going to do that.

When it was over, I still couldn't realize what I had done. I had only meant to extinguish that motionless gaze that guarded the treasure like a demon, to eliminate that last resistance and tear my own life from Rochard's obstinate body.

The box was under his shirt, sewn up in a leather bag. I took it. By simply blotting out what I had done, I made my brain function with precision and cunning. I gathered my own baggage, being careful to leave Rochard's. I didn't even take his gold.

By now it was completely dark and overcast, aiding my escape. I knew I would have to change clothes and wash myself before I could afford to be seen. I managed that at the well in a sleeping village, and I buried my bloody clothing under a tree.

3

The Walled-in Crypt

Only one thought occupied my mind for the next few weeks — escape. I moved at a frenzied pace, stopping only to eat and drink at some remote farm and sleeping in haystacks and forests. I always moved on as soon as I could stand again, driven by blind fear. My clothing became tattered, and my horrifying experience that I dared not even face carved lines on my features.

Since I looked like a beggar, I started begging on the highways and in villages. Every time I came to a fair or a wedding I wrote congratulatory verses and told fortunes to lovesick young people. Slowly I began accumulating money in the bag next to the box under my shirt — that box for which I had done murder and damned my soul. I felt it touch me every time I moved, and it never failed to fill me with joy and horror. At night its pressure against my chest caused confused dreams. But I was not yet secure enough to try it out. To do that, I wanted the shelter of four walls and a locked door.

I got my opportunity at Regensburg. The city was ideal for my metamorphosis; no one knew me and I could change my rags for decent clothing without fear of discovery. I even had enough money to rent a private room at an inn. At last I was alone — alone with It. The room was quiet and had a wrought-iron decorated door. I turned the rusty key in the ornamental lock and carefully covered the window with my cloak.

Then I put two thick, expensive candles on the white damask table cloth. I might have been drunk, for I was filled with a wild gaiety that almost masked my lurking uneasiness. Tremors took over, and my cold yet sweaty fingers beat a tattoo on the table.

I opened the leather bag and took out a gold box about the size of a man's fist. It was decorated with crowns of iron, silver, and gold, and there was a Latin inscription under them, "Curso Completo." I raised the lid carefully

59

and saw a lion's head set with jaspers that sparkled in the light. It was strange that the goldsmith had hidden this perfect work on the underside of a lid. The box contained a powder that was deep red as the jaspers and sparkled like gold. The color and brilliance of it so filled my emotions that I had to cry.

I filled a silver goblet with some red wine I had bought, then sprinkled a few pinches of the box's ample content into it. The thin, light wine turned blood red and then took on a blinding brilliance. I was careful to wait until the powder had dissolved completely, stirring it gingerly with a spillikin. Then I lifted the goblet to my lips. The divine potion felt cool and light on my throat and its sweet balsam fragrance woke an unquenchable thirst. I refilled the goblet, sprinkled in more powder and drank greedily, filled with euphoria.

Suddenly I fell into a stupor, and the goblet fell from my nerveless fingers. I heard it clang but it sounded far away, drowned by the wild rumbling in my brain. The cool, light liquid had become molten fire within me. It burned and distended my organs, and the inarticulate sounds wrenched from my throat relieved me not at all. I was paralyzed and helpless, watching with horror the unbearable pressure that should have shattered a frail human body.

I heard voices now, multitudes of them, and colors and forms joined in a bursting crescendo, just as though I was thrown into the midst of a witches' Sabbath. Screams of agony and desire, the racket of grinding metal, sobbing, and obscene whispers filled my being. Shapes swam before me, wet, black, and writhing. While I stared at these ominous sights, two glowing points of light appeared and rushed toward me, spinning and forming themselves into a fireball as they came. It burst in my face with a deafening shriek.

I thought I had seen the whole carnival of hell, but now colored vortices swirled toward me, vortices with monstrous faces that changed before I could even become fully aware of them. The faces were part animal and part human, the distorted products of a twisted mind. I saw an egg-shaped tree trunk covered with elephant skin where open mouths drooled and writhed. Another jellylike mass had gaping eye sockets from which sleek snakes swung, their heads blazing eyes. There was an obscene black hare with giant tusks and bloody eyes. I saw dogs with curved beaks, birds with elephant trunks and bat ears, an ape whose cheeks hung down like a woman's breasts. Then there were human faces — dreamy-eyed women with erect phalluses for noses, obese men with genitalia for eyes, and an octopus with baby's hands and an evil human face. And all these faces laughed at me. How mean and destructive laughter can be!

Suddenly a hurricane rose in the deafening chaos and whirled it all away, the screaming mouths, clinging limbs, twining tentacles, and fragments of color and sound. Now the hot wind clutched at me too, filling me with pain and terror and perverse desire. I felt the suicidal pleasure of self-destruction as the emotional tornado forced me through the basest of desires. But I kept pulling out; my body was a heavy stake that jerked me back to earth. I was alive — "one of the living dead who wakes to find himself alive in a walled-in crypt." Now Rochard's warning seemed terribly real to me. For had I not just awakened to eternal life in a tomb?

My enlightened vision saw the inferno that was my spiritual home — a place of obscene decay and the lowest passions. I was helpless against the forces I had unleashed, for I had jumped into the deep sea of transcendental laws without knowing my way or the meaning of the warning signs. And I was terrified beyond the capacity of human emotion. I did not know how to conquer the fear.

"Be afraid," Rochard had said. "You still have things to fear." Now I understood him. I was one of the weak mortals who had been blinded by grace because my soul was not sufficiently developed to bear the truth. Now I had rejected the natural evolution that would have developed me properly for the great transmutation. I had stepped out of the stream of mortal necessity that guides, polishes, tempers with suffering, and protects its hapless subjects throughout time. I had broken unprepared into another plane of existence. My body was now unnaturally resilient, in truth a glass coffin in which my soul raged in terror, unable to die or find release. Now I was truly a leprous beggar in both worlds, at home in neither, persecuted in both. In the mortal world I was a demon-possessed sinner; in the other I was an ignorant weakling.

★

From then on my life was a dazed nightmare. The events in the physical world appeared only as pale shadows of the supernatural world. Sleep did not bring me rest. Solitude, crowds, and change of scene could not serve to drive away the phantoms. Oddly this spiritual stress that seemed to be beyond mortal endurance did not produce any abnormalities recognizable to others. My brain could still function even in the deepest hell of fear; it could force me to be cautious and maintain my self-control when I was around other people. Outwardly I was still the muscular lad who had embraced voluptuous women at the Sebaldus Inn, but my face was drawn with inner tension and I avoided other people's gaze so assiduously that they realized

I was in the pit of hell. Old women made the sign to ward off the evil eye when I passed, and children ran away in terror.

I could not remain anywhere long. I wandered from village to village and from city to city, living on charity because no one would trust me to work for him. People would give me alms just to get rid of me. Soon I began to take a grim delight in the terror I aroused; that was the only power I seemed to have gained. Even though I myself was afraid, I could still frighten others. I didn't notice that I was becoming just like the monsters that swarmed around me and just as miserable as they. So I begged and starved, got soaked in rain showers, and shivered through many nights with that box on my chest. That box could have brought me the greatest riches and most voluptuous pleasures of earth, but I didn't want them. My world was a gray, hazy blur in which only two things stood out — my fear and my guilty conscience.

4

The Transmutation

*Why does man live within the rigid walls of time until
his evil stupidity is burned out of him? It is because
each of his weaknesses may become his assassin.
Benevolent blindness protects man from his only real
enemy — himself. Stealing the Great Arcanum is vain,
for his own imperfect character is his trap and he will
perish with his loot.*

I came into Straubing during the mayor's birthday celebration.
Since the day was also the fifteenth anniversary of his election, he had opened
his garden to the public. Spitted whole calves and lambs were being roasted
over open fires for public consumption, and beer was being brought from the
cellar by the barrel. An intoxicated, happy crowd was an excellent hunting
ground for a man of my talents. Soon I was surrounded by a dense ring of
humanity, looking at palms and predicting love, marriage, children, and good
harvests. While I worked, I listened to the gossip about the mayor, gossip
touched more with envious curiosity than with active malice. It seemed his
name was Anton Bruggendorf and he was newly married. Although he had
grown sons, he had married a poor and beautiful young widow.

Meanwhile I had accumulated a great many coins, and I was about to
leave when a fat, white palm slid into mine — quite a change from the cal-
loused, black-lined hands I had been handling. I looked up. It was the mayor
himself, for whom the people had respectfully made way. His fleshy face
was wreathed in smiles.

At that moment something strange happened. As if by magic, I ceased to
see and hear the forms of the underworld. I was once again a man fortunately
blinded to the other existence. I was only a man, a normal man. Suddenly

the warm, golden sunlight, the odor of human bodies, the delicious smell of the meat, trees, flowers, sky, and children all became real again. I bowed to the mayor and, feeling generous because I had regained my normalcy, I pretended a great interest in his hand.

"How interesting!" I pretended to be surprised. Then I told him his name and as much of his personal circumstances as I had learned from my other customers. I rounded off my reading with a few favorable predictions — more wealth, recognition from higher authorities, and a son by his young wife. "But these are not the things that surprise me."

"Then what is it?" His smile was anxious. "Speak up, my good man. But wait! I don't want any bad news today, though I'll pay for a good fortune."

I looked steadily into his eyes, my face impassive. Finally my penetrating gaze made him fidget, and he stopped even pretending to smile. Then I knew what kind of man he was — superstitious, weak, and vain. He was like the clapper of a huge bell, swinging to and fro as fear and ambition jerked him. Here was my man, my raw material. Now I had someone to open the gates for me.

"This is something completely different, Your Honor," I said emphatically. Then I hesitated as though I could not continue on such an important subject.

"Oh, something dangerous and ominous. I see it in your face." He tried to hide his apprehension with a jocular wink.

"Well, it is of utmost consequence," I said quietly. "Here," gesturing to the crowd, "I would hesitate to mention the matter."

"We could go inside the house." He was pale and serious.

"I must talk with you alone," I said firmly. "The presence of guests would be disrupting. I'll come back tomorrow."

He grabbed my arm. "There's no need; they won't disturb us. Won't you come?" Now his condescending, familiar manner began to switch imperceptibly to awed politeness.

So I had achieved my first goal. I had him in awe of me and he was curious. I had no idea how I was going to continue to trick him, but I felt exhilarated and trusted my ingenuity and cunning. We went around the big house, which was made of pink hewn rock and trimmed with a wooden balcony. Anton Bruggendorf led me to the door of the cellar in the backyard. Here he carefully and with great importance took a rusty key off his belt and opened the reinforced door. At first I thought he considered his wine cellar a suitable place to bathe his portly person in the mystical pleasures, but I was wrong.

We were going down a dark stone corridor. Very little of the light from the summer garden filtered through the narrow windows with their iron bars. There was a blackened pine torch in an iron ring on the wall, and soot stripes running to the ceiling above it showed it had been well used. My instincts began to signal danger. I stopped and my host looked at me questioningly.

"As it happens," I said out of a dry throat, "I don't have the proper instruments to make a thorough computation, but your palm evokes signs of a most beautiful science — and you and I know that palm-reading is just the antechamber of the truth. Astrology is the inner room for the initiates, a regal hall of the past and future under a vast tent of stars . . ."

He became more excited than ever. "I understand. Don't worry about instruments. I have everything you need." Misunderstanding my hesitation, he leaned close and whispered, "Don't worry. My family and guests won't know who you are. I know you have secrets you do not wish disclosed. It would make me very happy if you accepted my invitation. My whole house is at your disposal, Magister."

That name — Magister — made me quake, but I was also elated with a vain joy. In that weak moment I felt entitled to the name. The nightmare world retreated even farther; now it seemed like a dream from which I had wakened just in time to avoid stepping over a precipice. The homage of the fat mayor went to my head like wine and silenced my doubts. I would live well for a few weeks, frighten and dazzle this simple soul, and then disappear. He would not dare make a complaint. And, after all, I could not give a new direction to my life while being a beggar in a ditch. Accepting the offer of Anton Bruggendorf would cost nothing and might gain much.

"The stars truly do not lie," I declared majestically. "Your invitation was fated; the Great Cosmic Forces are directing us. I accept your offer."

Now my host led me into a well-equipped alchemist's workshop. Bruggendorf was one of those fascinated fools who sank a fortune in searching for the yellow goblin without getting one step closer to the goal. He had neither the brains nor the perseverance — the eternal dilettante. The expensive leather folios might as well have been in Sanskrit, for he could not begin to understand their symbolic language. Mere possession of them made this dolt conceited. I could tell from his bursting self-satisfaction that he had put the whole room together as a child puts together a building set. Once he had it, he had no idea what to do with it.

Bruggendorf went to great trouble to open the lead-ringed window panels so I could better appreciate the dusty stuffed animals, reptiles, and owls that hung from the ceiling. There was a melting furnace of imposing dimensions in the middle of the workshop and he forced me to investigate it in great detail. Proudly throwing out the proper Latin phrases, he opened the "latera" or side wall of the furnace, practically pushed my head into the "camera" where the fire is kindled, and pushed his fat fingers into the "os" opening as delicately as any midwife. When I asked what kind of success he had had, he looked embarrassed.

"Well — heh, heh — the metal yellows rightly enough, but the essence — there's a lot missing." He grabbed my arm and I saw naked desire in his red, sweaty face. "You don't know how I've longed for a visit like this!" He winked slyly. "I always knew my man would come in a crowd. A crowd is like a thick forest at night — a perfect shelter for the royal game so many are after."

I became cold all over and stepped back involuntarily. For a second I saw again the witches' Sabbath of the other world — then the silence returned. The yellow grains in the giant sandglass on the table continued to tumble in their glass time coffin. "I must get my luggage," I mumbled.

"I'll send for it." He embraced my shoulders, blocking the outside world with his huge bulk. Then he led me into a corner to look at a skeleton; he was as proud as though he had made it himself. "Disgusting, isn't it?" he said cheerfully.

Then I had to admire the distilling pot, barrels, crucibles, grates, bellows, mixing spoons, containers of cinnabar, iron-powder and saffron — plus the big pieces of lead he hoped to change to gold. I was becoming progressively uneasier.

"I have never seen such perfect equipment," I said with pretended elation, "but I don't see the instruments for my own science — the astrolabium and sextant to prepare horoscopes."

He didn't show the slightest disappointment; in fact he grinned like a cunning accomplice. "Horoscopes, of course. Those instruments are in the tower room. I'll give you the room right next to it, but I hope you won't neglect my humble little shop, Magister. I myself spend all my free time here, and I would be honored to have your valuable advice . . ."

"I would be happy to help you," I replied eagerly, "but actually I've concentrated so much on astrology I've had little time to practice this divine art. At best I would be an unskilled and ignorant pupil to you. But now I understand the mystic triangle in your palm. I am anxious to learn from the stars what their forces have designed for you."

At last I had diverted his attention and his greed. But how long could I keep it up? Obviously I had not convinced him I was ignorant of alchemy.

He treated my denial as a natural defense he could dissolve in time. I had badly underrated this greedy fat man. He had guessed that I was the golden goose and decided to cage me for himself. Now I would have to be alert and slip out of the trap at the first opportunity.

★

Anton Bruggendorf introduced me to his family and guests as the son of a dear school friend, hired as a secretary at the father's request. And my host saw to it that I was dressed very nicely indeed. His lanky adolescent son glared at the white linen shirt and plum velvet jacket I wore; until lately they had been his own.

My belief that I could soon escape calmed my anxiety. After all, why shouldn't I enjoy this marvelous evening amid the colors, smells, and luxuries of riches? Even my torturers were silent. But I dared not even think of them lest they should come back. Now I could enjoy gourmet dishes, spicy wines, fragrant and beautifully dressed women, glittering candles, everything I had missed out on until now. The heavy golden wine resolved my inner dissonance into a dazed, peaceful harmony. I began to feel confident; what had looked so threatening before now seemed childishly innocuous.

I even allowed my thoughts to stray down to the grave in my soul where I had buried my memory of Rochard's corpse. Maybe he hadn't really died; surely he had just fainted. After all, he couldn't die any more than I could. And if he wasn't dead, I wasn't a . . . But if he wasn't dead, he could be anywhere; he could confront me on any street corner. I ran away from the thought in terror; even being drunk couldn't make *that* endurable.

But the wine was cool inside me; it filled me with a fierce joy. Now I felt no remorse whatever over what I had done. After all, I had been made alive by the Aurum Potabile and I had withstood the side effects. Since I had gone through hell, heaven must be in the offing.

Across the table from me was a woman with copper hair and emerald eyes who wore a garment of shimmering violet cloth. This was Charlotte Bruggendorf, the mayor's young wife. Her eyes sparkled brighter than the innumerable candles, and she seemed the most desirable woman in the world to my wine-fogged eyes. She looked at me frequently, silently asking, "Who are you and where have you come from? What can you mean to me?" My own eyes replied with boldness. "I am Somebody, not like these people around you. I want you, and I will take you. The only law I respect is the law of nature — a beautiful woman for a strong man!"

Charlotte couldn't bear my gaze for long at a time. She would turn aside, and I would see with a stab of desire that her bare shoulders shuddered sensuously above the silk gown. But presently she ignored me altogether and listened to an oily dandy who pretended to have traveled in foreign parts. He was prattling about alchemy, playing the witty and enlightened agnostic. His spicy, humorous stories of how he had discomfited various quacks had everyone rolling with laughter.

The mayor laughed till his belly shook, and Charlotte was giggling excitedly. She was leaning on her elbows, and the white hills of her breasts swelled out of the low cut gown. I found I could not tolerate seeing her stretch her body toward another man and flashing those eyes at one I knew to be an empty-headed idiot. Drunk with wine and lust, I decided to interfere.

"You state, young man," I said pontifically during a pause in the general laughter, "that alchemy is just a delusion and the Great Arcanum a fool's dream?"

This remark produced dead silence. Everyone turned to look at me, but I saw only Charlotte's wet lips and snub nose.

"Yes, that's what I said," snapped the dandy. "So far, the only thing our Adepts have transmuted has been words. If any gold has ever appeared in a crucible, I can guarantee you it has already *disappeared* from somebody's pocket."

"I see. You have investigated, of course, and read all the literature on the subject. You must have experimented for years to come to such firm conclusions," I said guilelessly.

The guests all laughed and one, who knew the fellow well, positively yelped with laughter. "Heinz experiment? Where? At the Golden Cock or at the fencing hall?"

Heinz, his pride at stake, stiffened. "Just a minute, ladies and gentlemen. Let's see if this respectable gentleman is a sufficiently learned scientist to get on his high horse. I personally have never known anyone who could disprove what I've just said. Not even my Uncle Toni, and he's been experimenting for years. All he's managed to do is transmute gold to lead! I take it you yourself believe this nonsense about alchemy."

"I do," I replied. In the deep silence I heard Charlotte give a quick gasp.

"Do you believe there's such a thing as the Great Arcanum?"

"I do."

We faced each other in the suddenly tense atmosphere. "I take it *you* have experimented and got results?" my opponent sneered. I allowed a haughty and provocative stare to serve as my answer. Heinz stood, leaned across the table, and articulated his words straight in my face. "Your opinion is obvious. But if you've really gotten results, show us! Then we'll believe and repent of our mockery. We're willing to follow you but warn you we don't forget failure either!"

Suddenly I saw Anton Bruggendorf's huge head behind Heinz's challenging figure and a warning bell rang in my fogged head. Was this a conspiracy? Just then I felt a light touch on my arm. There was Charlotte standing beside me. I could feel her warm breath and smell her lavender fragrance.

"Don't pay any attention. They're just teasing you. They'll laugh at anything you do."

"Oh, will they?!" I looked up into those emerald lakes with golden flames in their irises. "Not while I have something to say about it," I added hoarsely. Grasping her hand, I deliberately spread her resisting fingers and laid them on my palm. "I accept your challenge, sir." I stared around contemptuously. "This very hand will shame you, my young friend, simply because your ignorant laughter irritates me. I'm sure our kind host will put his workshop at our disposal."

At that Anton Bruggendorf went off to make preparations as fast as his short legs would carry him.

But now Charlotte's hand had turned cold on my palm. I looked up and found her staring at me with a strange, frightening gaze. The emerald lakes were now a cold, deep green.

"Are you afraid of me?" I asked softly.

She withdrew her hand abruptly. "No," she replied quietly. "It's just that all of a sudden you seem different."

"Different?"

"Different, yes. And more than that!" She stopped suddenly as though unwilling to say what was on her mind.

Meanwhile a bewigged old woman, Charlotte's aunt, leaned closer to me. "I'm afraid I didn't quite catch your name."

"My name is like the label of an unfamiliar bottle, Madame. It reveals nothing of the bottle's contents."

The woman's toothless mouth opened in a screech of laughter. "How witty! Isn't he darling?"

"In any case," Charlotte threw back her head, "we'll soon find out what's in his unfamiliar bottle — down in the workshop." Her provocative laugh snapped the last thread of my self-control.

"Come with me," I choked. "I've got to show you how to help me with this experiment."

She followed me into the backyard, then led me into a screening bower. I pulled her to me, and she pressed herself against me. Her kiss was like the bite of a hungry animal; it surged the lust pounding in me. Abruptly she jerked away and sat down a little way off. I stared at her wicked eyes and closed lips, my senses greatly disturbed.

"Charlotte, don't go away now," I panted. "Oh, Charlotte!" I grabbed her again. She allowed the embrace, then whipped me into ecstasy with an experienced variety of kisses, then slid away again, as strong and cunning as a snake. Time and again she brought me to the threshold of fulfillment — and then emerged cool and reserved from my passionate caresses. I began to tremble in helpless rage. "Witch!" I pushed her away from me.

The tip of her tongue glistened. "Yes, I am a witch," she murmured, "I prefer the unfulfilled desire; that is all that attracts me."

"You're a monster!" I pressed my throbbing head between my hands, dizzy and nauseated.

"So are you." Her hot breath tickled my neck as she spoke. "That's why I'm attracted to you. That's why I wanted to share sweet pain with you . . ."

Anton Bruggendorf could be heard calling our names from the direction of the house.

"Let's go." Charlotte straightened abruptly.

"I won't!" I bounded out of the bower — straight into the mayor.

★

The oil lamp hanging from the workshop ceiling made curious lights and shadows on the faces of the crowd that stood around. They being ordinary folk were suppressed by the strange atmosphere; they all spoke in whispers and glanced about anxiously. Ignorant people are only certain of their prejudices when they are in familiar surroundings. Here in the alchemist workshop, they shivered at being in such close proximity to stuffed animals and the time-ambered skeleton.

Anton Bruggendorf bustled around the fire like an obese volcano, his panting breath even louder than the huge bellows he used to stir up the embers. It became almost unbearably hot in the low, closed room where nervous red shadows danced on the walls.

The workshop was very full indeed. The others only sensed it, but I saw. *They* were back again; the avid astral entities were leaning over the furnace. Their cold, sinuous extremities clung to the ceiling beams like spiders' legs.

They also were watching. Long, swamp-green faces watched me with a tense, gloating malevolence.

I stood in the inky shadow of the furnace to make my wax pellet. Charlotte was right beside me, watching over my shoulder as I fumbled underneath my shirt. A million demon faces stared behind hers; now I hated her.

The lid of the crucible rattled as Anton Bruggendorf lifted it. The fire had melted the gray chunks of lead into one silvery mass. "It's ready now, Magister!" he called.

"All right." I moved forward, hoping to get away from Charlotte. Her body had become one of the demon bodies as soon as the elementals had reappeared. I saw them swarming around her, controlling her like a live puppet pulled by the strings of her emotions. Fear kills lust, and now all I felt was fear.

Charlotte hurried after me into the red circle of light and held out her hand. Now it seemed loathsome to me, and I drew back as I handed her the pellet. She walked over to the crucible and threw it in. Then Bruggendorf replaced the lid and added more fuel to the furnace. The coals crackled in its greedy maw.

Charlotte's aunt was beginning to feel faint with the heat. "I've got to get out!" she gurgled. "I've *got* to! It's my heart!"

"Nobody can leave now!" The others did not even glance toward her as they spoke; the possibility of making gold had completely removed their thin veneer of politeness. They didn't care about this miserable flushed old woman whose wig had fallen off in the jostle. I got some water from the cooling tub and sprinkled it on her face, then used the bellows to blow some cool air onto her. Maybe I prolonged her wretched, empty life. But why? Was it kindness? Brotherly love?

No, impossible. I wasn't a good person. But I wasn't a bad person either, even though I had committed an insane and beastly murder. Except for that one incident, my feelings were not too different from those of the ordinary human being. I had pity, compassion, desire, ecstasy — even though I had robbed and murdered a defenseless, innocent old man.

In the meantime Bruggendorf turned the hour glass. The time was up now. The crucible, which hung on an iron rod, was submerged in the tub, and the water hissed and sputtered. Heinz's hand trembled as he held the oil lamp over the crucible. A dense crowd gathered around the tub, pushing, tearing, and shoving each other without noticing it.

Charlotte's aunt was gasping in a corner, her balding head hung down. But even she, bad as she felt, tried to push her wig out of the way under her skirt. At that instant I saw that these people with their gold lust differed from my swarming demons only in that they had denser bodies. I was disgusted.

Suddenly there was a small opening in the human circle and I could see the open crucible. Something in it glittered yellow in the lamplight. The impossible had happened.

Charlotte broke into meaningless laughter, and the others made repulsive sounds between sobs and laughs.

"Look! It's yellow! . . . Let's test it . . . There's so much. If it's real . . ."

Anton Bruggendorf sweated as he worked tenaciously. Physical pain did not seem to exist in the presence of this powerful idol. Finally he finished his test and straightened up. Even now I can see how he looked when he made his awed announcement. "It's gold, all right. Real, pure gold."

"And it's still hot!" The cry burst from Charlotte's lips as though it would fulfill all her lust.

They forgot all about me as they pried their precious gold out of the crucible. Everybody wanted to hold it or pet it or touch it. I moved quietly to the door and went out.

But the dark powers didn't want me to escape. It was the fact that I could *see* them that tied me into knots. The corridor was pitch black because no one had remembered to light the torch in all the excitement. This provided a thick darkness that made an excellent backdrop for the demons whose appearances are enhanced by dim light. They glistened and changed colors all around me as they screamed. I could smell their stench, feel their reptilian touch, and hear their screeching voices poisoning the air. My abject terror mounted with my need for fresh air. I forgot the number of turns in the corridor. Malicious demons steered me into a wall, then, while I was still dizzy, headed me back in the wrong direction. Finally I plunged headlong down a long flight of stairs that led to the lower cellars.

It was a terrible fall and Hans Burgner's mortal body would have been crushed but, thanks to the gross elasticity given by the Elixir, I merely sprained my ankle. Unfortunately I did not have the reptilian regenerative powers Rochard had talked about. I was a helpless captive for just a few decisive days. And that's how my own vanity and weakness tripped me.

★

No sick man ever got better care than I did at the mayor's house. Charlotte herself changed my bandages; her stepson read me poetry. Anton Bruggendorf brought up all my meals himself, and the old aunt brought me the chamber pot. I always had visitors in my room. But I knew it was all a demon mockery, a carnival masquerade at my expense. I knew they were really weaving a rope around me. There was never any doubt about my fate; I could hear it coming for me. Its shadow already hung over me and the shadow seemed to raise its fist.

5

The Magic Name

The Marquis of Brandenburg-Ausbach's coach came for me the third evening of my convalescence — came complete with the "guard of honor" of a whole cavalry troop. There was even a physician who bled me in spite of my strenuous protests. Anton Bruggendorf pretended great distress, but he must have sold me to the Marquis for a fancy price. His smug satisfaction kept showing through his hypocritical anxiety. After all, he had gotten a good deal out of me — gold, recognition, and almost a child.

The Marquis had been on his way to his summer residence in Dreisesselberg; Bruggendorf had probably sent him a messenger at the border. And so they came to an agreement and I was sold like an object. At the time I was defenseless; my leg still hurt too badly for me to think of escape.

As we were saying goodbye, Charlotte slipped a tiny red heart on a chain into my palm. Vengefully I put it into the mayor's hand as he paid his massive homage. The only satisfaction I had out of that whole wretched affair was seeing Charlotte's fright and Bruggendorf's bafflement. Probably the ugly old aunt whose life I had saved in the cellar was the only one really sorry to see me go.

I was carried to the coach like a sacred relic. A heavy brocade blanket was spread over my knees and my back was propped up with an armorial silk pillow. The Marquis and his group had already gone on; my companion was the fox-faced doctor. He gave me plenty to eat and drink and was very solicitous of my comfort. He was gravely worried about my welfare, for I was a tremendous responsibility. Like all other court parasites, his own welfare and security hung by a slender thread. All courtiers, I had realized, revolved around a moody sun that was far less trustworthy than the industrious one that centers our Cosmos. Kings, Princes, and Counts indulged themselves at will throughout the boundaries of their power, held back only by the leash of their own impulses. Their insectlike subjects, terror stricken, either avoided or imitated the St. Vitus's dance of their rulers' passions until they got too close to their fire and were annihilated.

★

I was brought to a castle that was designed to be impenetrable. The barred windows looked like deep wells in walls that were five-feet thick and cleverly designed and tended promenades spanned a gaping dark chasm. It took us a week, even using relay horses, to get to it by the winding mountain roads; twice we had to spend the night in the open. This grim castle in the middle of a forbidding forest was the Marquis' summer residence.

I was put to bed in the highest room of the rectangular tower. From my bed I could look through a broad window into the valley below where there was a toy village of red roofed houses, colorful fields, and a silvery little river. In the mornings it would rise out of a milky fog and in the evenings it would fade slowly from my sight, as though a magician had made it disappear peacefully. This prison of mine was beautiful and terrifying at the same time, for the castle itself perched over this sunlit valley like an evil vulture.

For a while no one disturbed me. I saw no one but the servants and the doctor, as I was supposed to be ill.

From the very beginning I was aware of the aura of malevolence around this castle. It was the home of dark emotions, fears, and unnatural passions. The wraiths of spilled blood and unconsoled sorrows wailed unheard in the rooms at night. The atmosphere was so pervasive that even those who did not have tense nerves and cursed eyes were aware of it. I noticed that the servants who cleaned the room and even the doctor were afraid.

An old man with sunken eyes brought me my meals. He had a low, receding forehead, and his tangled hair stuck out around his ears. He would be a dangerous man if angered, I thought; those thick, red fingers and clubby thumbs revealed a blind, murderous temper. But he could be handled, just as one handles a ferocious animal. He liked to drink, and drink loosens the tightest lips. This violent monster would become a whining child under the influence of wine. He would tell about walled-in countesses, skeletons that embraced you, and worm-eaten cabinets in the corridors from which cold, misty ghosts glided every night.

The old man dreaded the coming of night. His room was right under the attic, and every full moon the demons had a hellish ball over his head.

"There's a slimy, many-armed monster living in one of my old chests," he told me. "He's my enemy, the one who is buried under the seventh barrel in the cellar. When he was alive — he was in the Marquis' service not long ago — he managed that wine cellar. He was a handsome, loudmouthed fellow, and he loved to tease me. He was always asking how many mistresses I had, when I had last looked in a mirror, and how I could stand to sleep with myself.

"One time we went down together to get some wine, and I choked him to death in the middle of a laugh — the laugh changed to a death rattle in his throat. I enjoyed that. Of course I've repented since because from then on I've heard that laugh from the chest — that and the slithery noise of a reptile's body."

"Didn't anybody find out you had murdered him?" I asked, astonished.

The old man gave a grotesque, frightening laugh. "Oh, yes, he knows. He wanted me to."

"Who did?"

"Our most gracious lord."

"The Marquis? Why?" I shuddered.

"The cellarman — heh, heh — he mentioned the Name in the Marquis' presence . . ."

"What Name?"

His repulsive face showed a flash of cunning. "I'll tell you if you'll stop the laugh in the box. I know you're a warlock."

I had to get this information to save my own skin. "All right," I said, "I will stop the laugh in your chest. Here's what you do. Take the chest into the cellar, put the remains of the corpse in it and roll it into the chasm under the promenade. The swamp goblins that live there will cling to it and keep it from surfacing. Then you must send a binding spell after it to paralyze it. Lean over the chasm every evening and shout slowly and distinctly, 'I have killed the laugh. I won't hear it anymore.' "

" 'I have killed the laugh. I won't hear it anymore!' I've got it. How long do I have to repeat the ceremony?"

"That depends on when you first heard the laugh after the murder."

"The first time? Last year, about this time of year."

"Then you must do it for a full year. Now what is the Name for which the Marquis wanted the cellarman killed?"

The old man leaned very close. "Solomon Trismosin." He said the words softly and fearfully.

At the sound of that Name I felt a surge of power around us. A wave of horror swirled through the castle's tepid silence as he finished speaking. But this insane horror did not come from the famous and immortal alchemist Trismosin; it came from the Marquis' fears which were nourishing a legion of demons.

"Did you know Trismosin?" I asked in a whisper.

The old man nodded. "He was here," he stared around fearfully, "in this very room for a long time. Our most gracious lord had him here under guard. He wanted him to make gold and poison that works from long distance. The Marquis has many enemies. But Trismosin refused. He disappeared suddenly from the torture chamber — disappeared without a trace. But before he left, he wrote on the wall in his own blood that his very Name would hinder our lord in committing his sins. Why, if the Marquis even *thinks* of the name Trismosin — God help the man who utters it in his presence. His days are numbered. We finally managed to scrape the traces of blood off the wall, but the spoken Name acts just as effectively. That's why the mouth that utters it must be shut forever."

"But what's the use of shutting mouths if the Marquis has only to *think* of the Name?"

The servant winked. "You'll see how the Marquis takes care of that. He has a whole company around him all the time — clowns, musicians, whores, quack doctors. He even buys cripples to amuse him and he employs two thieves to invent diversions. Diversions can make him deaf to the Name. And at night he takes a stupefying drug so he won't dream. He drinks too. . . . My God, *how* he drinks! . . . I'm sure what he wants from you is a potion that will make him forget what he doesn't want to remember."

"But what does this Name do to him anyhow?" I asked. "Does it really keep him from doing what he likes?"

"Oh, no, he has done many evil things since then, but somehow the deeds seem to cling to him. You know how it is with a powerful lord. He gets rid of anyone who is in his way or has insulted or threatened him. It's a God-given right; he's not accountable to any man. But Trismosin did put some kind of hex on our lord. Now all the people he has killed throng around him all the time. They appear to be more alive and outrageous in death than they ever were in life, and they can accuse and torture him with impunity — but only when he thinks of that Name. You'll often hear him moan as he tries to push them away. He raises barricade after barricade but they always get back in through the door of the Name. Nobody has ever been able to close that door; the key is missing. If you are lucky enough to find that key for him, you'll be set up for the rest of your life."

Thus I learned my function at the castle of Dreisesselberg. I also learned that there lived another miserable soul like myself who was sizzling alive in the boiling oil of his own fear and was defenseless against his fate.

6

The Centaur

The most striking thing about the Marquis von Brandenburg-Ausbach was the flatness of his skull that was covered by thinning blond hair. No eyelashes protected the protuberant watery blue eyes, and his nose was as dainty as a woman's. Though his upper lip was narrow and curved pleasantly, his lower lip was full and hung loose, giving him a petulant expression. His fair skin was splotched with freckles. As a whole, he appeared to be a sickly, stunted man, full of capricious desires but lacking the strength to carry them through.

His power was a grave misfortune to him, for his servants complied with even his most whimsical request as soon as it was made. He was a man too weak to be good and yet also too weak to do effective evil. He was afraid of his victims, horrified of his actions, and paralyzed by remorse. For every evil plot he conceived, he had to find a scapegoat — someone to punish. The result was that he committed irrevocable deeds like a debtor makes loans to ward off the evil day.

This wax centaur image was really a helpless pawn in the great eternal battle between the forces of light and darkness. He was even now sizzling in purgatory, and both sides were waiting for the roast. Solomon Trismosin had indeed known where to write his name. That one bloody name lived perpetually in the Marquis and fought off a vast army of demons. I knew the truth of the matter before I even met him. The name of Solomon Trismosin was more powerful than the darkest demon.

The Marquis was graciously pleased to receive me in his dressing room, where an animal trainer was entertaining him with a mock wedding enacted by dogs. A grimacing monkey was driving a small gold coach pulled by four black dogs.

The Marquis laughed like a child.

"Come in, Magister, and watch this!" he said motioning to me. "Aren't they cute?"

Just then the veiled bride dog uncovered a basket in the coach to reveal a tiny white puppy. Then she put her paw bashfully over her face. The bridegroom, shaken, ran away whimpering, and the Marquis picked up the puppy and kissed it as the parade moved on. Then he sent everyone away.

Now we were alone, the Marquis with the puppy snuggling in his lap. The man's insecurity was immediately apparent; he who had unlimited powers in his own domain seemed awkward and flustered as he addressed me. He spoke with obvious embarrassment, skirting the one subject that really interested him. First he asked after my health and if all my needs had been tended.

After briefly expressing my gratitude, I decided to get to the root of the matter. "There is an ominous atmosphere in your castle, my most gracious lord," I began without preamble. "Hostile forces work here against someone."

He winced, and the skin around one eye twitched convulsively. "What have you noticed? And what kind — whom are they working against?" He stammered, flushing. I did not answer immediately. "Speak!" he screeched, his eyes burning like blue pits in his gray face.

"Against your own most noble life, salvation, and peace," I replied quietly.

He leaned forward eagerly. "Who is it that you're talking about? Where is he?"

"He is not a tangible entity to have a specific location. He has not body or visible form and yet is always present. His name means death, and he is deathless."

Now the Marquis' face was a mask of horror with apparently dead eyes. He collapsed in the chair and I thought he had fainted, but his trembling fingers still convulsively kneaded the puppy's fur. Suddenly he burst into tears and before I knew what was happening, he was kneeling in front of me, clinging to me as though he were drowning. He garbled all kinds of pleas and promises. Deeply shocked by such pitiful behavior, I made to raise him.

"No, let me stay here!" he panted. "This is my proper place — on the ground like a worm." He twitched away from my outstretched hands. "You don't know what I really am. They ought to shake a rattle when I approach, like they do with lepers. Leave me alone — or else give me some deadly nostrum so I can die forever and become peaceful dust and ashes. Merciful Father! Miseracordia!" He beat his breast. Suddenly he looked at me with the whites of his eyes showing, and I knelt beside him to hear the secret he whispered in a choked voice. "I'm afraid! I'm afraid to live *or* die; do you understand? Dying is the more terrifying. I know it will all end sometime — the carnival diversions and spells and drugs and liquor. They're already getting a place ready for me in hell; I saw it. It was under the reversed cross during the Black Mass. They were all there, right in front of me, the ones I — I — they were *alive*. I ordered them tortured, their flesh torn off in shreds, their bones crushed to pulp . . ." He leaned toward me and I smelled his sour breath. "They are here now — always, always around me. They mock my gestures and threaten me. It is their faces I see in the mirror instead of my own, and during Holy Mass . . ." his lips worked soundlessly as he struggled to continue.

I silently lifted him and set him back in his chair. His condition frightened me and oppressed my jangled nervous system. What could I tell him — I who myself had no defense against fear? How could I help him when I couldn't even help myself?

Abruptly he raised bloodshot eyes. "I order you to conjure him up," he said weakly. "You must summon him here by any means that are possible. The more I try to forget his name, the louder I hear it. He has won; I surrender unconditionally. He's the only one who can bring me peace — so I can pray undisturbed and be forgiven. He's the only one. Go. Prepare the act. That's what I brought you here for. I will do whatever is necessary . . ."

"Whom shall I conjure up?" My voice was anxious, not because I didn't know the answer but because I fondly hoped I had misunderstood what he asked of me.

"Him . . ." The Marquis tried to say more but his voice refused to function. He covered his face with his hands. "I will write it . . . have it written for you. When you have prepared, let me know!"

★

Summon someone who wasn't dead? Someone who was an initiate in the powers that ruled the three worlds? Would he summon a powerful Magus by the lips of a sinful, ignorant slave? Must I shout silly commands from hell to heaven? What kind of success could I possibly hope for? Yet the Marquis had ordered me to make the attempt, and I had to do it for my own sake. I knew well enough what would happen if I refused to try. In the torture chamber my cursed life would cling to me as a bloodhound clings to its victim. I would not faint to relieve the agony and — I suddenly realized — I couldn't even die . . .

★

The Marquis had given me free access to his extensive library. Here in this dusty, cold chamber the astral beings had reigned for centuries like bats in an otherwise uninhabited tower. It contained a rare collection of the occult — manuscripts so ancient they crumbled to the touch, forbidden works on black magic, treatises on alchemy, the Kabala, religious works, and the profane works of excommunicated priests. They filled the shelves and overflowed onto cabinets and tables.

The wet logs that crackled in the poorly vented fireplace managed to generate more smoke than heat. The smoke rasped in my lungs and made my eyes water, while the noisome fire provided no protection whatever against the icy mountain winds that blew through a large open window. My only light was the wavering torches in the wrought-iron rings on the wall; I could barely make out the faded lines written in indifferent longhand.

I was sick and miserable, and the vultures from the other world that had been bound here by the books' dark formulae hovered over me.

Here was a manuscript copy of the famous *Clavicula Solomonis* written on heavy parchment. Initials and diagrams studded the illuminated Latin text. There was Dr. Carter's *Book of Raziel*, along with Abraham von Worms' *Book of Ancient Practices*. Somehow these two had managed to live peacefully under an Old Testament with an ivory cover. The monsters immediately drew my attention to the infamous *Sorcerybook of Honorius* of Grimoir. It was surrounded by clusters of reptile bodies with writhing tentacles and curved talons; when I picked it up, they screamed in rage and fear.

But by now I knew these creatures could not kill me. They could only terrorize me, keep me in perpetual tension, and confuse me. I decided to pretend not to see them and sometimes I succeeded. We managed to establish brief armistices this way, and thus I was lulled into making a dangerous mistake — I began to underrate their power.

I took the books I needed to my room to make the necessary notes to prepare for the conjuring the Marquis ordered. I won't relate in detail those nightmarish days and nights in which I was thrust into the vortices of both hells and locked into place there by a fiery circle of formulae, words that summoned demons, and horrible, living spells. This period of intense terror changed my appearance so drastically that even the Marquis was frightened when he saw me again. I had wasted to skin and bones, and my eyes had sunk in their sockets.

Respect and hope conquered the Marquis' fear, and he grabbed my arm. "I can see, Magister, that you have been spending your time on pursuits that burn through the body and liberate the spirit. Tell me what you've accomplished."

I told him that we both had to make a twenty-one-day preparation for our conjuring and that I needed certain articles made by craftsmen and weavers.

He impatiently gave a series of frenzied commands and his servants promptly flew into motion. He himself performed his magical exercises with fanatical diligence and fasted faithfully at my instructions.

This exact following of a manifold ritual was an escape for me as well. I didn't want to think about the object of our preparation — that experiment that loomed in front of me like a tunnel leading into the unknown. And that ominous day that was the end of our anxieties rushed at us as though drawn by wild horses.

7

The Conjuring

Soon the day I had set to perform the conjuring arrived. All the preparations were complete. It was new moon; the sharp arc sparkled in the autumn sky among the impossibly close stars.

I had selected a tower chamber with eastern windows for the experiment. At my instructions four greenish concave mirrors without frames had been hung to face each other on the walls. There was a large white marble altar against the northern wall. It had been hung with a magnetized iron chain, and the pentagram was set into it in gold. I ceremoniously stretched a fresh sheepskin in front of the altar; it too had the pentagram embroidered in various colors. There was a copper incense burner of charcoal and bayleaves on a tripod on the altar, and I put another on a small three-legged table.

Then the Marquis and I changed into long, loose robes of purest white specially woven for the occasion. We crowned ourselves with wreaths of vervain strung on gold chains. When this was done, I drew the magnetic lines on the Marquis' body to put him into the state of wakeful sleep in which the mind can take in astral light. It was in this state that the great Sabbath orgies confessed by various sorcerers to the Inquisition occurred.

I could feel the Marquis tremble as I drew the lines. I kept hoping he would tell me to stop, finding at the last minute he couldn't endure the great trial. But he said nothing — his desire to be free of his curse had conquered his weakness.

I unrolled the parchment on which I had written the incantation. I stirred up the fire in both burners, then began reading. At first I spoke softly but gradually my voice grew louder.

The fire began to glow in the burners and a thick, spicy smoke rose over the room. Nervous flames leapt from the embers, throwing wild, evil patterns on the wall. Then suddenly the flaming tongues collapsed — as though an invisible hand had smothered them. The glowing coals dimmed slowly, straining our expectation to the breaking point. White clouds rose from the altar, and I was horrified to feel the floor shudder underneath me as though I were in an earthquake. I heard the deep tolling of a bell and my heart thumped wildly. I was able to continue only because I had memorized the procedure thoroughly.

I threw more charcoal on the burners and stepped into the chalk circle I had drawn between the altar and the table. Closing my eyes and pronouncing each syllable distinctly, I shouted the name of Solomon Trismosin three times.

My eyes opened of their own volition. Suddenly I became extraordinarily cold. Now the embers were blazing again, illuminating the room with the light of oppressive dreams.

The apocalyptic light revealed the figure of a powerful old man, his hazy shape multiplied by the four mirrors. Every other sound and motion in the room froze abruptly. Even the tongues of flame stood still and the astral hordes that surrounded us shrank from the being. I felt a numb tranquility, the peace that comes to the wretched outlaw when he is finally caught by the forces of justice. I knew that my presence in this magic circle had been predetermined; the circumstances were merely the bloodhounds of fate.

I forgot about the Marquis. I was staring spellbound into the eyes of the apparition. I knew the look, of course; I had never forgotten it. It was something I had feared because I couldn't understand it, and its peaceful coolness had lived on behind all my desperate barricades. The face that belonged to the eyes took form as I watched. It wasn't quite Rochard's face but it was so similar. I could hear the Marquis moaning near me. As I began to relive my memories of Rochard, the face changed to the one I remembered after I had crushed it to a bloody pulp in that single moment of frenzy.

The room was filled with the silence of surrender and defeat. One thought only pounded through my head — how could I have killed somebody who was immortal? I had just shattered the form, broken the mirror that reflected the one indestructible being. I don't know if he really spoke or if I just heard his voice in my head coming up from my subconscious mind where knowledge is not yet formulated into words. But now I understood. It was just one person who stood before us — Nicholas Flammel, Solomon Trismosin, or Eduard Anselmus Rochard. All were one after the Great Transmutation had condensed the divine essence from the disintegrating satanic element.

So the contact had been made with the other world, the sphere of the divine initiation. It was not the word of a sinner dragged to hell by the weight of his deeds that had penetrated the sphere of Mercury; it was the call of the divine EGO that lives in every being, the essence that cannot murder and cannot die.

For an instant the spirit mirror played over my past and future lives as though over some ravaged battlefield. My spiritual landscape had not changed; it still smoldered with crime and mad destruction. The road of my future faded into an infinity of frightful desolation. I had built an empire of clotted blood. The victims I had killed, hated, and feared had become my eternal companions, nourished by my energy. I was bound body and soul to the morgue of this world by handcuffs of desire and selfishness.

And now the Law was here in front of me. No, not in front. *In* me. The greenish-blue eyes into which I stared seemed to speak within me.

"I have forgiven you. It is not I who punish you. You yourself are both murderer and victim. The sin and salvation from it lie in yourself alone. The earth is just a dark reflection of the astral ocean, a reflection that shows everything upside down. What seems bad is good and what seems good is bad. What seems to be destruction is really construction. Birth and death are really interchangeable terms. Suffering is atonement and pleasure is downfall. What is hoarded is really borrowed. Redemption comes from martyrdom.

"You can begin to move toward the highest goal from the lowest point of the deepest depth. There is yet a nucleus of divine light in the womb of deepest darkness. When a change of direction occurs, the result is not necessarily visible immediately. Still the necessary step has been taken.

"Remember, you must repay to the last penny, and suffering is the payment. The point of greatest pain is the turning point toward the highest goal."

I heard moaning in the distance and only later did I realize it was I myself who had moaned. I was too deep within myself, listening to that voice. It took some time for the Marquis' feverish and disjointed words to register in my consciousness.

"Take your Name off that wall! Get it out of my head, out of my soul! I can't bear it anymore! Leave me in peace! Ahh!"

Now the flames danced madly, and the voice resounded through the whole room.

"Only blood can wash away blood.
My name is written here in blood!"

A mighty wind swept the room and the figure disappeared. Darkness closed in on us, and the censers smoked like gigantic chimneys. There was a moan beside me, followed by a prolonged crashing. The Marquis had fallen unconscious on the floor and had dragged the table holding one of the censers with him.

Still dazed I tried to pull out my tinderbox, but suddenly I was too weak to move. My knees shook and I broke out in a sweat under the long robe. I had to sit down again. I couldn't seem to get in touch with my body. Time and again my consciousness submerged into the spiritual ocean. The Marquis was an island of reality somewhere near me, dead or fainted in a room full of smoke and smells. Someone else hunched beside him in a backless chair, fingering a withered wreath of vervain. All this had no connection with me.

Now even the spiritual sea grew dark. I don't know how much time I spent in the twilight world of the formless subconscious. It was almost as *if* I had died and not yet been reborn.

A cold, overcast dawn breathed through the narrow window onto the white altar, the overturned table, and the body in white linen. The wreath had slipped off, I noticed, and his fingers seemed to be trying to grasp the floor.

Someone was knocking on the door and there was a babble of voices outside. I couldn't move my sluggish, newly returned body, and my mind was yet too hazy to fear or escape what must come. Gradually more voices had assembled in front of the door and the knocking was now a frantic pounding on the door. I couldn't move even when they broke it down.

Shocked servants lifted the Marquis to a chair, and the frightened looking doctor drew his blood and administered vinegar and anise. The Marquis' grim priest, Frater Bertholdus, sprinkled holy water on his face. Under these ministrations the Marquis opened his eyes and looked around blankly. When he saw me, his eyes lit with horror and he clutched Frater Bertholdus convulsively and whispered in his ear.

The priest turned to look at me. I could read my fate in his malicious satisfaction.

8

The Lowest Point of the Deepest Depth

I did not try to resist the violent hands; I was helpless and only half conscious. They dragged me bodily down the corridors that ran under the castle. Here the stones sweated green slime. I thought they would lock me in one of these windowless cellars, but I was wrong. An iron ring was set into the middle of the floor in one cell. They attached a chain to it, ran the other end over a hook in the ceiling, and began pulling on it with all their might. The fat round stone came up with a dull plop, and an odor of rottenness welled up around us.

Then they tied a rope to my waist and pushed me into the hole. As the ground disappeared from under my feet, my terrified life instinct reawakened. I realized I was being lowered into a narrow well shaft cut in solid rock. Many things were atoned for during that descent, as I banged into the sharp rocks that opened bleeding cuts. A howl of mad fright burst from me as this descent into hell continued, apparently into eternity. But then I found my feet in icy water which swiftly moved up past my knees to my waist. I had reached the bottom and the rope was thrown after me. It crashed onto my head with a painful wetness even as I heard the heavy stone close over me.

My hands groped on the slippery stones as I tried to find the dimensions of my prison. The Marquis wanted to make sure I could not escape, like Solomon Trismosin.

Certainly no one could escape from this. I felt under my garments. The box was still there. The box containing the Elixir. . . . of eternal life. I jerked the leather bag from around my neck and threw it into the water.

"No!" My voice rang in the confined space. "Almighty God, my God! No! Help me! Forgive me!" Then I fell silent, horrified. Mechanically I began to notice the darkness and the stench and the dripping of water from the stones.

Time had no meaning. I counted the drips to measure it but I finally had to give up. My body felt like lead, pulling me into the depths.

If I could just sleep, I would perish. Die. Oh, my God, not die! But I would be free from fear. I lowered myself into the water until finally it was over my head. Stagnant water rushed into my mouth and nose, and my blood pounded in my ears. I waited — and then terror forced me to surface. My lungs couldn't take the strain. I should have suffocated with the fluid rattling in my lungs, but I was alive. I hadn't been able to endure the agony.

Thus I could not commit suicide; my body had been damned to life by the Elixir. Life clung to me indeed "like the death-grip of a monster." I would have to live in this walled-in crypt without light or food, rest or hope, forgotten by everyone, as long as my damned body would last.

This was surely "the lowest point of the deepest depth."

Wracked with hunger I cried, shouted, and cursed — cursing myself, Rochard, God, and my own life. Then I started begging for mercy.

Meanwhile the water dripped on — a hundred, a thousand, ten thousand, one hundred thousand drops . . . I began praying to demons, to the powers of darkness. I pounded on the walls until my fists were a bloody mass. I gnawed my arm in a desperate attempt to relieve my hunger — and the water kept dripping. I counted the drips.

What time was it? Was it day or night? How many days had I been here — or maybe it was years? It was a hundred thousand drops of water — a million.

I went through periods of rage, followed by apathy. As I became weaker, the periods of apathy grew longer. At last I fell into a troubled sleep and my feet refused to hold me up. My muscles and flesh had slowly degenerated, and the struggling life flame flickered within the wasted form. And as I lay motionless in mute surrender, death finally came.

9

The Valley of the Shadow

For a long time I didn't realize I was no longer attached to my body. I thought I was still slumped in that prison of uncrushable bones. Then suddenly I saw the skeleton under me, crumbling in the phosphorescent light of decay. I was both attracted and repelled by the sight. Now I was formless, a bewildering, tormenting sensation.

Abruptly I was swept away by a howling astral current. The well disappeared but my phosphorescent corpse stayed in my mind's eye for a long time before it faded. Then I saw my demons again. They were being swept away with me, and they bumped and jerked me about in the merciless elemental flood. We were united now — horrible embryos on long, mysterious umbilical cords. I was swimming in a nightmarish twilight among other shades like myself, each chained to its attendant cluster of demons.

I yearned desperately for an escape, for light, rest, and freedom from these demons. I clawed to a level where I could dimly see ahead of me a clear and open tranquility where I could surely find it. But it was like trying to swim against a tidal wave; I continued to drift with the gyrating forces, plunging and struggling.

Suddenly the forces concerted in a tightening spiral. I was caught in the vortex and propelled through the astral matter by writhing human bodies. A cry of lust was distinguishable in the chaos around me. Then the core of the vortex opened and sucked me in.

Now I was captured — impaled on a new stake. It was a thin thread that tied me, but it was tough. And the thread kept growing shorter with the passage of months. I was revolving in a mother-body whose womb was provided by astral beings with the necessary substances of life. This was my new refuge.

10

The Professor of Marburg

I was born again December 2, 1560, the sixth child of a poor Lutheran potter. My name was Heinz Knotek.

My father belonged to one of the drunken and fanatic fringe groups. He constantly poured out accusations and descanted on divine grace, but his family and fellow men might have starved in front of him for all he cared.

My mother was a soul worn out by labor, poverty, and continual child bearing. She was a silent, self-sacrificing woman, so busy tending the bodily needs of her family she had no chance to get to know them. Her sixth child must have been a distressing event to her. That which had been mildly pleasant the first time was an almost intolerable excess in a house where there was never enough food and absolutely no peace.

The child of this worn womb had a withered, timeless face. No one noticed him in his fifth-generation hand-me-downs when he became aware of his past life and its horrors. My awareness did not merge with this new body until it had developed past the point of simply performing bodily functions. Thus Heinz Knotek learned his past when he was five years old. His large family was indifferent to his sudden introverted silence and the big eyes that looked on the terrors of the other world. They weren't even curious when he began to scream in the night. An angry older brother would nudge him "awake" — he who had gone astray in the past and lived again in the castle depths at Dreisesselberg.

★

After I had become fully united with Heinz Knotek, I found my new family utterly unbearable, perpetually bogged down in mud and quarrels. We lived our whole life in a big, dirt-floored kitchen, at close quarters with each other's bodily necessities, noise, and smell. There was always a pervasive odor of food from the huge fireplace, and there were always dirty clothes soaking in a bucket in the corner.

We all scattered as far as possible during the day. The older boys were already learning a trade. My oldest brother was a barber's apprentice and ridiculously proud of the fact. He always spoke to the rest of us condescendingly and used as many complex words as possible. Apparently standing in front of a long mirror all day had gone to his head. The mirror image had somehow become a suave, independent personality to be aped faithfully by its original. My older sister worked for the apothecary, and the younger one tended cattle for Hlavanak, the rich miller.

But in the evening everyone crowded into the kitchen, even the chickens, who blundered among us in their stupid, panic-stricken way.

My father always sat under the lamp, which cruelly illuminated the long, hollow face, drooping mustache, drink-sodden eyes, and narrow, disputatious mouth. He had the complexion of a sick man and indeed he was frequently ill, with pains in his heart, left arm, and fingers that incapacitated him for work. I had inherited his weak constitution to a far greater extent than the other children, for I was the last child and had been conceived during a drunken stupor.

As for my mother, I never saw her sit down anywhere. She even ate standing up. She was always working, the heavy, large-boned body slaving silently. Sometimes she groaned, but that was only when she had the pain in her legs. I was the only one who knew about it. Once I had asked her if something was hurting her. She looked at me and smiled, a smile that transformed her into a beautiful and intelligent gentlewoman.

"I have shooting pains in my legs sometimes; don't worry about it, Heinz."

"But you ought to lie down when you get them."

"Lie down? When would I find time for that? A nice thing that would be! Whatever would your father say! Someday, my son, I'll catch up on my rest — in the grave."

That was the only private conversation we ever had. But from then on she would smile at me occasionally, a communication fuller than any words. It was only for me that she smiled this secret smile; for the others she kept on scrubbing, washing, and cooking with her usual silent, dull face. She suffered her drunken husband's beatings stoically, with compressed lips.

My father made up for her silence by talking continually. Everything that happened to him became the subject of a bombastic, trivial sermon. He flushed with violent anger if anyone contradicted him and quickly descended to personal abuse. He was always picking quarrels, and anything that deviated in the slightest from his preconceived ideas was twisted to fit his distorted pattern. Abnormally sensitive to even imaginary opposition, he had no sensitivity at all in the areas where he really needed it; he trampled down that which was most delicate in his own household. Woe to him who disturbed Knotek's sleep, but if he himself woke up in the night he shouted the house down. During his frequent drunks, his verbosity was both overpowering and abusive. He would seek a victim for an endless, insulting sermon, shouting questions he never gave anybody a chance to answer and damning the unfortunate to hell for all seven cardinal sins.

I'll never forget how angry I was one Sunday when I saw my mother pause in her scrubbing of the slate entry, a cloth still in her swollen hand, to stare at my father as he stood sternly before her. He began to instruct her in the rules of religion; mother lacked the time to follow these petty regulations.

"You mustn't risk your soul, you wretched woman!" he intoned in a repressed voice, raising two rough fingers. "Do you think that in our religion you can buy God's mercy with a little piece of paper? This is a religion of action! The devil is always on the lookout for slothful souls," he ranted. "Missing even one meditation opens a gap to hell. And I won't be there to take care of you on Judgment Day. Cast out this abomination of indolence from your soul, or you'll call to the Lord in Judgment and He will say, 'I don't know you!' "

Of course the night before two of his cronies had had to carry him home from the inn; they had managed to drag him through every mudhole on the way. My mother had calmly induced vomiting, cleaned him up, and put him to bed. By the time he woke up from his drunken stupor, the house was immaculate and breakfast prepared. But now all the other children were out, and I was lying hidden on top of a large cabinet and there was no one else on whom to vent his temper. So he towered over the weary figure and dared to preach to her about duty.

★

I got away from home as often as possible, following the grassy shore of the river Lahm as it wound its way through the city. Our ramshackle house was in a rank alley some distance to the left of it. On the other side of the river, a castle sat on top of a gently sloping mountain. I dreaded seeing its silhouette against the sky; it reminded me too much of Dreisesselberg, where the disintegrating skeleton in the icy well still seemed to belong to me.

One day when I was almost nine years old I happened to see Amadeus Bahr, the Count of Zollern's librarian. He was walking along with a loaf of bread under one arm and I recognized him immediately as the friend of Eduard Anselmus Rochard, whose miraculous recovery had triggered my tragedy.

I was so surprised I forgot myself. It didn't occur to me that I was a completely different person since the last time he had seen me. Now I was a fugitive in the body of a nine-year-old street urchin. But I was too happy to see him to think. I ran up to him.

"Magister! How did you get here?"

He stopped and looked at me in his absent-minded way. "How — What do you mean? What do you want, little boy? Who are you?"

My voice froze in my throat. Suddenly I looked down at myself, then ran away in confusion. I heard him shout hoarsely after me.

"Wait! Don't run away! I'm not going to eat you!"

But I kept running as fast as my legs would carry me, over the wooden bridge that crossed the Lahm and along the muddy streets. I didn't dare stop until I was in the tool shed behind our house with the door shut.

Amadeus Bahr's question echoed in my mind. "Who are you?" What kind of answer could I, should I, have given him? I am Hans Burgner, who murdered a gentle, wise, old man, a Magus who knew what I was going to do and made no resistance. He even felt sorry for me, the victim crying over the executioner. Of course now I know why. I know because he told me much later in the magic half circle. "The earth is just a dark reflection of the astral ocean, a reflection that shows everything upside down. What seems bad is good and what seems good is bad."

I could not rest knowing that Amadeus Bahr was in the city; I was too full of curiosity. How had the awesome Arcanum affected him? Did he have horrible visions too? If not, why not? Why was I poisoned by what had cured him? If I could only approach him without rousing suspicion, he would tell me about Rochard, how they found him, and what happened after my flight.

I stopped being afraid of his recognizing me and turning me over to the authorities. In the body of Heinz Knotek I was completely safe from earthly justice. I did not realize then that earthly law merely executes spiritual justice, even when it seems to punish the innocent. No innocent man is ever punished; he is always caught by his own actions. You cannot escape the past by putting on a new body.

★

It was easy enough to find out where Bahr worked. There were only two places he could follow his profession: the university and the Count of Hessen's castle. I learned to my surprise that he had a chair as a professor of German literature at the university. I wasn't at all surprised to find he had a different name; naturally he would shed his own name as a precaution.

Bahr was now greatly respected. His invincible sharp wit in debate had brought him great recognition here in Marburg, which was still in the throes of the Luther-Zwingli debate of 1529. That debate had made the city a center of the spiritual struggle and kept it in ferment for forty years. Even the most impoverished tradesman demanded clarification of the most abstract articles of faith, and he was always willing to spill blood to support his viewpoint.

It was only in this kind of atmosphere that Bahr could really blossom. He had a wealth and quickness of wit and an intensity of personality that no one could match. The Count himself felt honored to have him at his table and condoned the stinging sparks of humor that flashed from him continually for the sake of his great intellect. For Bahr's satire spared no rank, authority, custom, or dogma. The Inquisition would have killed him years before, but in this city of nascent faith he found a home. The age had arrived when man felt free to doubt, not God, but the rulings of his fellow men.

The genius of Rochard's friend had been discovered. Now the musty bookworm was a professor of great authority whose witty remarks achieved instant fame. People in high society decorated their conversation with his aphorisms. They might amuse or anger, but they were always admired.

Outwardly Bahr hadn't changed at all. His cloak looked like the same one he had worn in the tailor's shop in Nuremberg, and his graying hair still hung down his neck. He was even still missing a clasp on one shoe. All this was overlooked because of his great intellect.

I hung around the house where he lived, waiting for an opportunity to be of service to him. He rented the upper room over a gingerbread maker's shop. In good weather I would go to the top of the house across the street so I could see him bending over his books. Sometimes he would stand up and wander aimlessly about the room, stopping abruptly to make an impatient gesture or talk to himself. At first I thought that he also was molested by the astral rabble. I watched them throng around him continually in a wide circle, but to my surprise they didn't approach him. There was a pure, shining clearing around him, like a fire in the jungle that animals must circle at a respectful distance.

Later when I got to know Bahr better, I realized that he was battling something much more abstract during those spells of pacing. He was having inner debates in which he was both advocate and opposition. Sometimes he would stop by the window and stare unseeingly into the street for a long time. I would try to attract his attention on these occasions by jumping up and down, but he never noticed.

It was weeks before he finally noticed me, and even then it was his own hunger that roused him from his absorption. He had been writing at his desk for hours and it was getting dark. He hadn't eaten a thing all day, but he still could not seem to break away from his subject. Finally he leaned out the window and his eyes met mine. Perhaps my obvious readiness to help influenced his decision; he threw down some money and shouted for me to bring him some bread and milk. Then I understood that every desire can be fulfilled by applying willpower and patience.

My heart pounded with excitement as I walked up the broad wooden staircase. I had a fresh loaf of bread under one arm and a warm, foamy pitcher of milk in the other hand. I knew I needed to establish a relationship with the little scholar, and I had a plan to go about it.

I had to knock, for Bahr was again in the Milky Way of his own thoughts. First he asked me who was there, because he had forgotten he had sent me on an errand. Then when he realized who I was, he couldn't find the key to the door. Finally I was admitted to a wildly disordered room, where household utensils were scattered in the most unlikely way among folios, scrolls, and ragged manuscripts. He began scraping a candle out from under the bed, alternately grumbling and speaking kindly to me.

"Where has that stupid candle got to? Just a minute, young fellow. I'll have some light soon." My God, he had done that very same thing the morning I brought him Rochard's letter! "I'll give you something for your trouble," he muttered, continuing his search. As my eyes adjusted to the dim light, I saw him staring with nearsighted surprise at a beret he had fished out. He threw it away impatiently and tried again. This time he produced a candle. "Last time it was behind the bed," he explained. "I have no time for these things. Do you want money or candy? I should have both, if I were you."

Now was my opportunity. I spoke out of a dry throat. "I don't want either, Magister. If you want me to, I'll be glad to bring you bread and milk every day. I could also clean your room and perform other services — chop the wood, make the fire, carry water . . ."

Now candlelight illuminated the scene, and the professor was able to stare at me in his surprise. His sharp little eyes looked me over thoroughly. He leaned closer. "I've seen you before, haven't I?"

"Yes," I replied. "On the street near the university one day and recently near this house."

"Of course! Now I remember. Now tell me what you want, and don't run away this time. Who's your father?"

"My father is a potter. He's always drunk, except when he preaches, and I like him better drunk. His name is Stephan Knotek, and I am Heinz Knotek. I'm already nine years old. I have five older brothers and sisters at home, and that would still be too many even if I never came back. I realize it sounds ridiculous under my circumstances, but I would like to become a student. I'd like to be *your* student, Magister; that's why I've been haunting your home ever since I heard you were here." I was intentionally speaking precociously.

The little man was speechless with amazement; he just stared at me. I leaned closer, beseechingly. I could tell he was moved and intrigued, but he was also reluctant. "Please, Magister, don't turn me away. I can already read and write."

"Where did you learn that?"

"From an old book I found."

"All by yourself?"

"Yes. I can see you don't believe me."

"No, but you can prove it." He turned reluctantly, went to the table, set down the candle, and pulled out a book. "Come here." He opened the book at random. "Sit down and read."

I took the book from him and pulled the candle closer. We were both as solemn as if we were performing a ceremony. It was an improbable and strangely tense situation. I was amazed in this setting to see my own finger that of a dirty child with the greenish-white complexion of malnutrition. Putting this finger between the pages, I turned back to the title page; it was the second volume of the Old Testament Apocrypha and Pseudepigrapha in a rare, hand-copied edition. The designated page was part of the first vision of Ezra. I began reading the ornamented words slowly, syllable by syllable.

> "The day will come when a mighty terror will shake the inhabitants of the Earth.
>
> "The region of Truth shall remain hidden on that day, and the land of faith will bear no fruit.

> "Injustice will grow and multiply, more than thou seest now or hast ever heard. And the land which thou seest rule today will become a trackless desolation. If the Most High permits thee to live, thou wilt see chaos after the threefold times.

"The sun will suddenly brighten the night;
the moon will appear by day.
    "Blood will drip from trees,
and the very stone will shout.
    "The nations will all rebel,
and no help shall be found on any hand.

    "And he whom the inhabitants of the Earth do not expect will gain power. (This is the Antichrist.)"

My thin, childish voice trembled over the weight of the words. Silently the professor took away the book and placed paper, quill, and ink in front of me. Then he began to dictate, leaning over to watch me.

    "The fishes will migrate. The sea of Sodom will cast them out utterly, and the night will howl with a loud voice which few will comprehend.
    "Chasms will open in the earth,
and fires will burn without ceasing.

    "The wild beasts will leave their dens, and women shall bring forth monsters. Sea water will mingle with that which is fresh, and the friends of a man's bosom will suddenly become his enemies.
    "Knowledge will hide.
    "Wisdom will go down to the grave.
    "Many will seek her and find her not."

At first the weak and inexperienced hand of Heinz Knotek made a clumsy job of transferring Hans Burgner's literacy to paper, but gradually the letters attained a better form and the speed increased. I wrote with regular spaces between the lines and without an error.

Suddenly the professor spoke. "Enough!" I looked up to see the wondering disbelief in his face. "God be merciful to you, my son! I only pray that this ability came from the Lord and not from the Evil One; dark knowledge is worse than the worst ignorance. But whatever the reason, fate has sent you to me for some purpose and I will not frustrate it. Tomorrow I will talk to your father."

Thus I entered the service of Rochard's friend as his pupil and servant. I — who had murdered his mentor. He shared his food with me and I slept in the room next to his. Sometimes he showed his dislike of my inappropriately mature behavior, but he also pitied me and came to grow fond of me, giving me the emotional surplus of his lonely life.

The only really peculiar thing about the situation, of course, was that I knew who I was and remembered what I'd done. People who tortured, persecuted, and killed each other often meet in new bodies. Mothers give birth to the souls of their greatest enemies and put them to bed with brothers who may have been their executioners. And I was really less dangerous than those miscreant souls whose thirst for vengeance merely hibernated. I literally could not kill again, for my terrible experience had wrought a living truth within me. Murder would rob me of the gentle gifts of a normal evolution. All I wanted was to be free and find the formula that would save me from hell.

11

The Magister and His Enemy

My father made no difficulties; in fact he was proud that his son was accepted as a pupil by the famous professor. And anyway my constitution was so frail that I couldn't have learned a trade. As for my mother, she performed the miracle of the loaves and fishes, given by Our Lord to all mothers who have bent backs and swollen feet. To these women it is given to make bread multiply, to make clothing appear from the bottoms of drawers, and to produce pennies from nowhere. Thus when I took my place in my new quarters there were two sets of underwear in my little wooden box, and a little money was hidden between the hand-knit socks.

My new room had heart-shaped holes in the window panels that were supposed to let in light; since they let in cold air instead, I covered them with thick paper. It was a dark, unfriendly little room, with sooty beams curving over my bed. Fat spiders were spinning webs that seemed to cling to my face whenever I moved. Still it was a place of refuge, a foothold on the way to my goal.

★

There was really an unshakable order behind the professor's absent-minded, disordered life. The only things that were real to him were his studies, notes, and contemplations. Rank, authority, success, wealth, pleasure — all the things that occupy the average man were peripheral to him. Soon I began to realize that he was plagued with an inner conflict; his sharp, dry humor and his compassion fought in him continually. He had a devastating perception of the distorted and the stupid, and his observation was promptly relayed in fiery flashes to his brain, whose creative wit formed it into some irresistible phrase. So he would launch a verbal missile and annihilate the misshapen oddling.

But the success and applause he gained did not please him nor did the malicious gloating his sharp missiles afforded the average man. He became troubled and unhappy, for he could actually understand and feel for his opponent. The moment of victory nauseated him. He knew that stupidity is really an illness that should be pitied and that evil is only a symptom of that stupidity. He knew that there was Divine Essence waiting only to be liberated within even the man who seems totally lost. The world is densely populated with such unfortunates, stumbling through their lives in a heavy stupor.

"I fought shadows again just now," he told me one night when he returned home from one of his "orgies." He had been at a meeting with his colleagues and had verbally vivisected a bigoted and hateful professor of theology, much to the delight of everyone else. The great man had been knocked sprawling, gasping and speechless, among the carcasses of his slaughtered arguments. Not a single person had felt sorry for him, for they had all suffered under the lash of his tyrannical, sensitive ego. But Bahr himself had been moved with sudden empathy, which attacked him almost like a physical pain. His colleague's red-rimmed, darting eyes and trembling hands had reminded him of a cornered rat he had seen stoned to death during his childhood. "He was just like that — just like that, believe me, Heinz!" he told me. "And it doesn't really matter that he is a stupid dunderhead and that his ideas and teachings are like obnoxious insects; he doesn't know any better! He can't do anything else. In effect I've mocked a blind man for stumbling and further frightened a man who was already crazy with fear. I pilloried him simply for being deformed! If I didn't know that flagellation was an evil, I'd gladly scourge myself. Oh, Christ, why can't I stop doing things like that?"

★

Bahr was good to me in a kindly, awkward manner. Whenever he gave me some heavy work, like carrying in the wood or copying a rare book from the university library, he would feel bad and want to compensate.

"Do you get enough to eat, son?" he would ask frequently. "Be sure to tell me if you need anything. You know my head's always full of my work. But you look pale and your eyes are sunken. I'll have a stove put in your room. Go buy some honey cake from the landlord; here's some money. It will put some meat on your bones. Or wouldn't you like to play with the other boys? I'd be glad for you to."

"No, Magister. Thank you for your kindness but I want to stay here with you. The boys are wild and stupid and they bore me. Books are more interesting; they are quiet and friendly."

"You talk like you were a hundred instead of ten," he remarked.

"Maybe I'm older than that, Magister."

He looked at me with new astonishment. "Of course you are, but how can you know that with your child's mind?" he burst out. "At your age I was chasing butterflies and determined to be an armorer because I envied their muscles and their deep voices. In the ordinary course of nature, the soul is only a dim mirror during the years when the body is maturing; it reflects only the shadows of the past."

"In the ordinary course of nature," I repeated slowly. I looked up at him from my small chair, where I had a heavy volume of manuscript on my knees. "You are right, Magister. But who is to say there are not creatures among us who have stepped out of this order, some up to the heights above, and some down to the depths? Are not some blessed with the pure light of vision and others cursed with dark knowledge?"

He stared at me seriously, and I could see a strange aversion in his face. "Heinz, Heinz, I cannot understand you! I can only fear for you. You know better than I do why you came to me. Won't you tell me? Who are you and what do you know about your real self? What can you remember?"

I didn't give him the answer I had intended to. Already I had said more than was really safe, but I was flooded with a painful desire for absolution. Yet I could not confess to him. He was the first person who had really cared for me since I had become an outcast, the first to put out a selfless hand and support me. Aloud I said, "I remember a lot of things I'd rather forget — images, secrets I daren't share with anyone. If I could, I'd tell you, Magister, but I just can't, even though it would relieve me."

The professor leaned forward. A warm, all-understanding compassion seemed to flow from him. "Unburden yourself. No matter what you did, I'm not going to judge you. There is no abyss that has no way out."

"There's no way out of *my* hell, Herr Bahr!"

His eyes narrowed and I felt a surge of fright. "You were born here in Marburg, weren't you?" he asked.

"Yes," I replied in a low voice.

"Have you ever been out of the city, perhaps as far as Nuremberg?" I was silent, not knowing what to say. "Answer, son!"

"No, I've never been to Nuremberg but, after all, you're a famous man, Magister. Everybody was talking about you when you first came," I jabbered confusedly.

"Did anyone tell you I was Amadeus Bahr of Nuremberg?"

"Yes!" I spoke in a rush, then became numb with terror. Suddenly I knew what he was going to say.

"Amadeus Bahr drowned himself in the river because he was afraid the Holy Inquisition had issued a warrant for his arrest. The fact was established beyond doubt; his clothes and papers were on the riverbank, and his body was washed up near a neighboring village. Several people, including the Count of Zollern's doctor, made the identification, and a certain tailor's wife even swore it was the wicked old heretic's corpse. He was declared legally dead about ten years ago."

"But you're Amadeus Bahr nevertheless!"

"Undoubtedly." He leaned back. "No one knows that, however, but myself and the old friend who gave me my new name and papers; he's since passed on. And yet you called me by the name of the Nuremberg librarian, Heinz. Let's see — someone I knew in Nuremberg must have come here and seen me, then mentioned my name in your presence — is that how it was?"

"Precisely!" I agreed eagerly. "My father is acquainted with the owner of the Sebaldus Inn; he came through Marburg on his way to settle an inheritance matter and saw you on the street — from a distance."

"You mean Wilhelm Drumann?"

"That's right."

"He's been dead for twelve years." His eyes were two penetrating, almost tangible rays of thought that seemed to scan my very brain, deep into the seat of my odious secret. I was seized with an instinctive desire to run. Getting up, I stepped back a little. "Stand still, son!" he said firmly. "You needn't be afraid of me. I am sure you joined me for some definite purpose, for I know I cannot measure you as though you were an ordinary person. You want something from me and I may be the only one who can give it. Why won't you be honest with me? I can't help you unless I know your problem. How did you know who I am? Who were you in Nuremberg and where did we meet?"

I just stood and stared at him. I was being torn apart by the desire to confess to him and ask his forgiveness, but I remained silent. Fear, mistrust, and self-loathing shut my mouth as effectively as any prison gate.

"Are you burdened with some great sin?"

I bowed my head and suddenly gave way to convulsive sobs that shook Heinz Knotek's puny body to its depths. I no longer had the force of the Elixir to hold my body together, and the emotional shock generated by my conflicting desire and fear was too much for my delicate child's nervous system. Amadeus Bahr pattered around to me awkwardly, patting my shoulders and soothing me.

"Now, now. For goodness sake, stop crying. I won't ask you anything more if it upsets you so much."

I wanted to stop crying but I couldn't. I was shaking all over and there was a sharp pain in my chest. It was as though all the repentance and hopeless suffering of wicked, tragic Hans Burgner flowed out through Heinz Knotek's tears. I was helpless, wracked by a fever of nervous collapse, and the Magister undressed me and put me to bed with cold packs over my heart.

In the stupor of my fever, time's hobgoblin lured me into the past. Again I was with Rochard in the rickety barn, kneeling and begging, demanding the Elixir in Heinz Knotek's thin, trembling voice. Then, swimming in perspiration, I relived the murder. It was as though the demons were grinding an old-time roll through some devilish barrel organ, and I had to repeat it over and over just as it had happened.

My own screams jerked me back into the present, and I saw Amadeus Bahr's troubled face close to my own. He was using all his strength to pin my arms to keep me from jumping out of bed. Then the fiery waves of fever rolled me back to the rotten, damp barn and left me beside the dark mass that was Rochard's body. His open eyes stared at me in his gentle, old face, and I brought down the brick between them. I had to hit and hammer with the merciless automatism of relived past action, and I felt the warm, bloody pulp smash into my face.

Now the whole thing started again and my horrified, raving spirit protested wildly. The childish throat of Heinz Knotek screamed madly in that Marburgian attic. Through the red haze of fever, I could hear the voice like something cast up from a deep canyon of the past.

"No! I don't want to! Please — help me! Help me stop it! It's my hand; you must stop my hand! Thou shalt not kill . . . hit *me*, kill *me*! Kill me just like you would a rabid dog! Don't you understand? Please close your eyes, Rochard; please close them! Don't look at me like that. You are Flammel, and Flammel cannot die — but me — I have to kill again and again. My God, please help me! Don't let it happen, God! I don't want to kill. Oh, God, I don't *want* the Elixir — not if I have to get it this way. Thy will be done — *Thy* will — Help me!"

When the attack was over, Heinz Knotek's life force was spent, burned out by the fever of the terrible upheaval. There was barely a flicker of life in the feeble body, but rationality returned and clutched at the last frail thread of life so that I could hear the Magister's last words. For the wise old man had kept the vigil beside my bed, and he had heard and understood the secret Hans Burgner, the murderer of Eduard Anselmus Rochard, had shouted through Heinz Knotek's mouth.

12

The Cosmic Inoculation

When I regained consciousness, I realized that the Magister knew everything. "Forgive me," I whispered, gasping.

He waved me to silence. "You don't need to say anything, poor boy. I know what you mean. And there's nothing for me to forgive. What is alive cannot be destroyed. Rochard still lives, even though he is no longer reflected in time's mirror. But you are enmeshed in a horrible trap. Desiring life, you've gotten lost in the swamps of death. Now I know why you came to me. I know the whole story, and I want to help you — as much as one human being can help another. I will show you the beginning of the road, but you will have to set your own feet on it. I'm going to tell you everything it is safe for you to know." He saw my grateful joy and forestalled my efforts to speak by placing his bony hand on my head. "Be quiet! You must to conserve your strength. Every moment is precious; that's why I haven't sent for your parents. Do you want them?" I shook my head violently. "All right. Now you understand I can only speak in allusions, and that isn't going to make things any easier for you. The Elixir you acquired by murder has made you a prisoner at the lowest point in the world of emotions. It has literally poisoned you. The only remedy is transmutation, and you'll have to do it on all three levels at once. Transmutation will be your salvation.

"You'll have to work hard, studying and experimenting until you find the secret of the three keys that open simultaneously. Nobody else can do it for you. Listen carefully! You've got to find the *Prima Materia,* the matter that contains death, decay, and resurrection all within itself. You must find the great, dark womb from which life is poured out. This is the lowest point in the matter of the world and only there can your bond be dissolved.

"You see, you cannot succeed by using only the two higher planes, the astral and the mental. If you did, the matter would still be bound. The material plane is not present in the other two, but they are both present in it. I know you can't understand all this as yet; I'm just inoculating you with it. Search for the meaning. Your whole existence and your every experience are guarantees that there is a meaning.

"There is simultaneity only in the nightmarish world of matter. People pray in one room, curse in another, kill in one, and beget in yet another. Two will be harvesting in the evangelistic meadow, and one will be taken and the other left. It's only in that meadow, on the material plane, that the two can stand side by side, subject to the laws of material existence. There's the potential for everything on this earth — damnation as well as resurrection. *Man is the spiritual equinox of the Cosmos. The boundaries of everything meet in him.*

"That's why the transmutation has to occur simultaneously on all three levels," Bahr continued. "The process is a motion directly opposite to the drive for physical existence; this makes it a motion tending away from desire, begetting, and birth. Birth is merely a motion toward matter; death is its antipode. Sages and philosophers all knock on the door of death because they can sense that the solution of every mystery, freedom, and resurrection are all found behind it.

"By the laws of alchemy, something has to die and decay before it can rise. To sum up, transmutation on the physical plane is a converse motion to begetting and birth. It is analogous but in reverse order. It too needs male and female principles; the process is called the *chemical wedding.*

"During this chemical wedding, which takes place in the ancient womb of the Prima Materia, the irresistible Word is spoken; the Summons is sent out to call together all the physical and astral forces of the Magus, all the created material and emotional forces. Even those that have wandered in separate directions like Golem and those that are latent are summoned.

"The Prima Materia may be defined as that bottle into which the Magus, if the transmutation has been successful, deposits the whole power of his spirit, his creative complex that has previously moved without direction. Now the spirit serves him and fulfills all his wishes. He becomes vested with his full forces and controls them; there is no limit to his power. But the prerequisite for a successful experiment is the elimination of the desire for power. Only he who will really use it wisely, who can see in it the key to the three gates of liberation, can produce the Philosopher's Stone."

Then the waves of the great ocean broke over me and tore me from Heinz Knotek's puny body. The attic and the haggard face of the blessed old man who bent over the bed stayed in the three-dimensional world. I myself was again tossing about in the dirty green-black astral densities, again trailing my terrible entourage.

But this time I knew that the train of apocalyptic monsters was really myself. They were part of me, my own creations, and would control me until I could control them. We were all tossing helplessly in the raging hurricane of emotion, all chained together.

If people could only understand and see the true origin and essence of these bizarre, depraved forms, they would never give in to one single lustful or evil thought. They would stamp out their impulses as they stamp out cobra's eggs.

But the state between life and death was different this time. I was impregnated with an idea. I clung desperately to the little seed of idea about transmutation all through the stupefying cacophony of the violent, sucking vortices. I clung to it as though it were a buoy and surfaced again and again from the dirty foam.

A few of the whirling lust vortices pulled me toward them and carried me toward the dark narrow gate, but the idea on which I concentrated with all my strength proved to be a barrier that would not let me through that gate. Because of the magic idea of transmutation, I was special.

It was not easy to go through any vortex with this strange soul-pregnancy of mine. If I found a mother womb whose sensitive vibrations made contact, she could never carry me full term. Either she miscarried or produced so little life force I couldn't live longer than a few months. I went through many ordeals of conception, development, birth, exhaustion, and death before I finally succeeded in getting on firm ground. This was in Milan on December 25, 1616.

13

The Sun and the Moon

My new name was Giuseppe Francesco Borri, after my father, who was advanced in years when I was born.

The name Borri, translated as Burrhus, was to play an infamous role in the history of alchemy. And yet most of the epithets commonly hurled at it were founded on shortsighted and irritable incomprehension. Burrhus was not by any means "an unscrupulous con man who used every possible means to secure his end — a comfortable life." I was already far from desiring "a comfortable life." The portion of my life observed by others was just the outline of a puzzle whose solution lay elsewhere. What could I have told my contemporaries about my goal? Whom could I have permitted to guess at my cataclysmic, haunted personal Cosmos? And to what mortal could I have told the truth about my bizarre and tragic alliance with Homonculus?

★

My father was a physician and amateur alchemist. He was a gentle being who shied away from the passionate arguments that were then raging about alchemy; thus he allowed himself to be satisfied with partial results. Nowadays he would be an obscure professor in a small college.

My mother was a fragile, oversensitive creature who was much younger than her husband. She was a poor distant relation of his who had come to town to act as his housekeeper, and she had brought gentle cheer into his house. He came to love the charming, delicate girl dearly, but it would never have occurred to him to marry her. It was her idea from the beginning and everyone thought it was merely a whim. They all tried to talk her out of tying herself to a man twenty-five years her senior. But my mother held out stubbornly, and she advanced arguments that embarrassed, touched, and astonished her intended.

At first he shrank back from raising so violent a storm so late in his life. He had already discounted the possibility of marriage and did not even want it. He liked tranquility and solitary contemplations.

"Why we could search the whole world," my mother declared, without finding anyone else with whom we could converse in such peace and friendship! And you know I am too weak to endure the passion of a young, virile man, and you are not young enough to find an understanding partner easily, someone who would provide you with everything and not disturb your peace. Neither of us really likes being alone; we feel happiest when we're together. So why shouldn't you take me as your wife? Just because the world disapproves? Because it is unusual? Well, I thank God we are not usual people. It is only a matter of whether we dare to get on the right path in spite of everyone — whether we dare to be happy in our own way."

It was my mother's fascinating originality, not the magic of her young body, that won the day. My parents frequently joked about the circumstances of their marriage, even in my presence, laughing at how the passive and submissive young woman had gotten her own way.

The results of the marriage justified my mother's efforts. The two of them were true friends, infinitely tender without the need for passion. Each needed what the other had. My father admired my mother's mystic dreams and visions, which she related softly; he respected her as the possessor of these holy things. He drew her into his work, asked and accepted her advice, accommodated himself to her sensitive moods, and truly suffered with her during migraines and menstrual problems. As for her, all she asked was to play a leading role in his life and deserve his faith and admiration. Their personalities fit together like the two pieces of a broken dish. Alone, each was strange and difficult to understand. Together, they formed a whole.

This setting was particularly appropriate for me. At last I was in an environment as unusual as my own personal makeup. I felt like an animal hiding behind a successful camouflage. I didn't have to conceal my anguish and constant awareness of the other world. My father believed wholeheartedly in the presence of the other world, and my mother not only sensed but sometimes saw it. Her underdeveloped body and oversensitive nervous system that responded to the slightest influence placed only the thinnest of veils over her third eye, which was open and observant of the spiritual kingdom.

Even now I am overcome with emotion when I think of those two. How much they loved me! It was a tireless, unbounded love. How often they kept vigil by my bed when I was an infant, silently holding hands and watching me while my soul wandered in the astral labyrinth. Whenever I awoke from these wanderings, I always saw their gentle eyes.

My mother sensed what my problem was and always knew what to do. She was the first woman who showed me the most profound mystery of that other sex. In her I saw through the petty, superficial existence of the human female the image of the mighty and tender mother. When I was with her, I sensed for the first time that the solution for all ills may be found in the protecting and healing feminine being.

My mother was the only person who could drive away my tormentors. She would pass her narrow, long-fingered hands over me three or four times. I can still see her tense, introspective expression as she worked, with her curved eyelids draping those sparkling, caressing eyes. Slowly she would repeat the motions over my convulsed body, never quite touching it. I could see a space between her hand and my flesh, but still I felt her balmy touch. Then the convulsions would cease and the astral world leave me. I could breathe clean air again without the putrid scent of decay. Then I would relax and sleep.

I had a recurring vision that would slide me into a gentle, dreamless sleep. It seemed I was lying on my back in a boat, eyes half closed, looking out at the quiet, translucent water on which I was floating. Someone wearing a long, cowled cloak stood in the prow with his back toward me, rowing slowly and soundlessly. We were in a world of calm water, translucent air, and clear sky, traveling together through endless space to an unknown destination, gradually to become absorbed in peaceful light . . .

My mother had boundless spiritual ingenuity where I was concerned. She besieged her inner world with a persistent clamor until she broke through the gate of secrets. Without ever having heard of them in her current life, she uncovered profound mysteries unaided and learned procedures that were sealed in occult tradition. She managed to find real solutions by this inward listening. When she saw how I was being persecuted and realized that her magic lines only helped me for a short time, she searched with the delicate instrument that was her soul and brought from the Akasha the secret of the "protective cloak." Every night she would wrap me in this invisible, protective cloak of concentration.

"Now I am going to cover you," she would say gently as she stood by the bed. Then a wonderful and incomprehensible drama would be played out. I would feel something like a soft, fine linen winding around my body, twelve times longways and twelve times sideways. It was a restful feeling, and I knew I was in an impenetrable cover through which the angry astral claws could not pass. This covering poured from my mother's soul and eyes. It was stronger than any sin or passion because it was woven of the will of unconquerable love.

My mother always wore blue. Her long velvet dresses had high collars and high waists, and there were often light blue stripes among the dark blue pleats. She usually had her tiny blonde curls caught up in a blue silk net. She always wore an old-fashioned silver brooch and matching ring. They were worked with the figure of a triangle standing on its apex in which a slim, flat-chested female figure trod on a serpent's head. These pieces had been left to her by an aunt who had been a nun. I was fascinated by the Gothic silver virgin in the blue enamel dress and the serpent she trampled, but my mother wouldn't tell me what they meant. She got upset when I asked; it was some time later that I learned why.

★

I did not try to hide most things about myself from my parents, but I could not bring myself to tell them that I remembered my previous lives and names. I didn't conceal the fact that I was mentally mature beyond my chronological age or the dark connection I had with the other world. But I was terrified that they would reject me in horror if they learned my crime. For the paralyzing awareness of my true identity didn't leave me for a second. I knew the body was only a disguise and I in it was Hans Burgner, the murderer, fleeing the consequences of his crime.

The average human being who slowly drifts between the barriers of time and space cannot understand the mercy of that lack of memory, *tabula rasa,* that is the gift of every new birth. No one could bear the full truth all at once. Even today doctors have to work long and carefully to bring to the surface and deal with the subconscious hurts and petty crimes of a single lifetime. Even these emotional pebbles prove to be great obstacles, causing considerable trouble to the nervous system. So how could one vulnerable human being balancing on the high wire of a single life bear the burdens of a long series of lives?

Once when I was about eleven I overheard my parents talking about me. They were sitting in their little backyard, which was singularly peaceful with its black and white flagstones. My mother was sitting in her straight-backed chair under a cypress tree, embroidering flowers on a piece of silk. My father was resting his aching feet on a small footstool — I am sure he must have had rheumatism — and sorting colors for her. He was a tall, strong man with childlike blue eyes who radiated the gentleness of the big man and his characteristic awkward willingness to help others.

I had been suffering from a slight fever that day, so I went to sleep after lunch. My mother, with her usual excellent instinct, had made me a slightly sour drink to arrest the fever — lemon juice with honey and water. When I woke from my subsequent rest, I was alone in my room. I got up and went toward the backyard where my parents always sat that time of day. I was just in the act of pulling back the door curtain when I heard my father's voice.

"Francesco?" He sounded perturbed.

"Yes," my mother replied, "he is burdened by some great sin."

"If only I knew where you get these ideas, Marietta!"

"I can feel them."

"But this time you are mistaken, my little one. Francesco wouldn't hurt a fly. You know how he begged old Lena not to kill that chicken."

"That just proves my point. Most children are cruel and bloodthirsty because they have drunk the water of forgetfulness at birth and don't know what the blood and screams really mean. But Francesco knows. He remembers but he doesn't dare talk about it. If you could just see his invisible surroundings and his fears! They're far more serious than any childish scares."

"But what is it he's afraid of? What does he remember?"

"The day he realizes nothing in the world could ever make us reject him, he will tell us," my mother answered calmly.

"But if you really think he is burdened with a torment like that, why don't you encourage him to tell us about it?"

"For the same reason I don't stand in front of a tree in the spring and urge its buds to ripen promptly. Francesco's trust is not yet ripe because he is too lonely, introverted, and frightened. It's usually that way with persecuted people."

"Oh, Marietta! You confuse and disturb me so greatly!" my father burst out.

"I'm sorry, Giuseppe, but what else could I do? I can't keep carrying this burden of concern all by myself."

"You are an alarmist, Marietta, dear. Who would ever persecute our timid little Francesco? Why he hardly ever even leaves the garden; he's growing up right in front of us."

"Francesco's crime is old; he didn't commit it in this body."

"Oh, so that's what you mean!"

"Yes."

"But, Lord God, if we accept that idea, we would have to look for a murderer behind the innocent face of every child!"

I watched through the curtain as my mother leaned forward and covered my father's hand with her own, her brow wrinkled with earnestness. "Listen and try to understand. Francesco has suffered more than anyone else I've ever heard of because he has carried over his memory into his new body. He is like a man with his eyelids cut off, forced to stare forever. He is not blessed by the restful blindness of death's dream or the unawareness normal to birth and childhood. If only you knew how he is perpetually tormented to the bounds of human endurance. And I can't help him. Sometimes I feel so helpless I'd like to die and forget the whole thing!" Her voice broke and she put her face in her hands and sobbed.

My father reached out and lifted her into his lap as though she were a child. Their features grew indistinct as the silvery twilight settled on the garden. I heard my father's consoling murmur in the dusk. "Calm down, dear; don't torture yourself so. You know you could never try to escape sinfully from suffering and responsibility. We are all being burned through and through by the pure fire of love. Don't we have more faith in Francesco than we have in ourselves? Who would understand him and protect and encourage him if we evaded our responsibility? We shall live as long as God allows and stand by him. If he is guilty, we will beleaguer heaven for his forgiveness; if he is weary, we will make him a bed of our tenderness; if he is frightened, our bodies and souls will be the barriers to protect him."

"My darling Giuseppe!" I heard my mother's tearful voice through the dark garden. "I'm so weak, weak and feeble as the moon up there. What would I do without your life-giving sun?"

"That is the way it should be, Marietta. The Sun and the Moon are indeed a mystic couple, and no two beings can come into true union unless one soul has the attributes of the one and the other soul those of the other. Then they radiate toward each other and provide love and light."

My mother stood up in the shimmering light of the half moon and wiped her eyes. "Francesco's sleeping a long time today."

"It's because of the fever."

When she came in with her candle to check on me, I was lying on my back with my eyes closed. I could hear her dress rustle as she leaned over me, and her fingers caressed my face. "He's been crying," she whispered over her shoulder.

"It was in his sleep, my dear."

★

Why did I pretend I was asleep? Why hadn't I run into the garden and knelt before them, beating my breast? Did I not trust them? More than I trusted myself. Did I fear to lose their love? No, I knew it to be boundless and unconditional. Why did I pretend to be asleep and reject such living, healing love? My whole inner being was in burning upheaval to rush out and confess to them. All my horrible memories expanded within me in my desire to pour them out, but I knew I had to remain silent. I was paralyzed by a feeling completely new to me — compassion.

If I had been selfish, I would have been eager to seek relief by transferring my heavy burden. But for the first time in my memory I was restrained by a tender desire — the desire to be considerate of someone else. It had been fear and shame that had kept me from confessing to Amadeus Bahr, but now I wanted to remain silent so the burden would be mine and mine alone. No matter how much my parents were worried about me, the situation would be easier for them to bear if they didn't know my past and its terrible consequences.

The desire to tell them fought inside me for days and weeks. My mother, who seemed to feel my conflict and realize that her own time was short, broke down and tearfully urged me to unburden myself. When I was away from her, the memory of her pleas would break my resistance, and I would run to tell her everything. But as soon as I would see her, her physical condition would restrain me.

For she was pregnant again and she got terribly thin. She couldn't keep down any food and her back hurt. As the pregnancy progressed, she grew so weak she could hardly walk, and finally she had to take to her bed. My father was nearly prostrate with worry.

Then one night the event we had dreaded happened. She began to deliver prematurely with massive hemorrhaging. She must have been in excruciating pain for she kept breaking into inarticulate screams, intensifying and diminishing like a blood-curdling aria by a mad composer. The heart-rending cries filled the whole house with alarm and despair.

I can still remember my emotional chaos as I stumbled through the darkened rooms where scared women whispered softly together amid an odor of sickness. Suddenly I was a homeless stranger, panic-stricken in my sense of total loss. I ran to distant rooms to get away from those horrible screams. My teeth chattered as I moaned, shouted, prayed, and cursed.

But the screaming didn't stop. It lacerated our bodies and souls for two whole days and nights. I remember watching Maddalena, the midwife, help my father out of the sickroom on that second day; she had to lead him like a child. He was crying.

"You won't let her die, will you, Maddalena? For God's sake, don't let my little girl bleed to death!" There was blood on his shirt and he tottered like a drunken man. Maddalena helped him to a chair.

"Just leave it to us, Signor Borri. We're doing everything that can be done for her. You can't do anything else; you'll collapse from fatigue."

"No, I must go back. I must help . . ." the poor man said mechanically. Then his eyelids drooped and he slept the sleep of exhaustion for a few minutes. He came to with a start, jumped up, and went back into the sickroom. My own physical suffering, all the fear, shame, and guilt I had ever felt paled into insignificance in my compassion for my parents.

There was a deathly quiet the third day. My mother's strength was spent; her voice began to break and fade. Then suddenly there was total silence, more horrible than those ravaging screams. Life itself froze in the disheveled rooms caught between sunset and death. The women were working in grim silence, muted by their awareness they had lost the struggle.

Then I heard a soft, shuffling motion, and my father came and took my hand. He seemed suddenly old and stooped, and his hand was icy cold as he led me into their bedroom. My mother lay stretched out on the ravaged bed. All around it were overturned chairs, blood-stained bandages, tubs of horrible contents, and pools of blood. The room was filled with a nauseating odor. Yet the waxen, bloodless figure on the bed was majestic and commanded respect. We came closer.

I was surprised to see a joyous expression on the wasted face. It was as though behind her closed eyes she listened to some hopeful sound from the ethereal distance. The silver ring with the Gothic virgin treading on the serpent's head shone dully on her smooth hand. As I stared at it, I seemed to hear her voice.

"Do you understand it now? The message of Sister Beatrice, the nun, was that the initiate must crush the head of the serpent. I should never have embraced and given birth. Hers is a message to the fallen; the eternal priestess is never absolved from her vows. Today the priestesses of Isis are nuns. Oh, Isis — Isis!" The sentences fell unexpectedly into my empty inner space, and I shuddered and leaned closer to read more from her lips. But now her cold mouth was an eternally closed gate and her body a ruin the dweller had abandoned.

And yet — my heart pounded wildly. There was a flash from under one of her eyelids. Her soul, receding to purer planes, looked back at me and waved goodbye with an encouraging, almost cheerful, smile. "Francesco, I am really alive. I always have been alive and I shall live forever!"

This blessed promise thawed the icy horror within me and changed it into an incomprehensible hope. And only then was I finally able to weep the tears that would not come during the three days of darkness.

14

Reflected Light

The brief moment of spiritual communication passed and then came all the rites of death. My father became a sick, weeping old man. His mind became confused; it could not accept my mother's death. With sinking heart I would watch him get up from his seat under the cypress tree and wave to me with a sweet, gentle smile.

"Bring me the key, Francesco, boy! Your mother will be back from church soon." He would wait for me impatiently. "Hurry, son! Mother can't get in."

I would give him the key and he would grab it eagerly, limp to the gate, open it, and wait. Sometimes he would look down the street with an intent smile, waiting for her to come; then he would go out into the street. When my worry led me to follow him, he would smile encouragingly, but it was obvious his mind was already clearing.

"She will turn the corner soon," he would say.

And so the two of us would stand there, and he would lean on me as his troubled legs began to ache and he began to feel hopeless. I never dared say anything, for these memory lapses always ended the same way. Suddenly the smile would be replaced by an old man's tragedy. "Let's go inside," he would say softly. "My poor boy!" Then he would let me help him back into his chair in the garden.

A pedantic, religious old spinster named Maria Dora came to look after us. She was an aunt of my mother's, one of those women who always play second fiddle in life. She took care of the dying and nursed the newborn. Then after the little ones grew old enough to leave the nest, she would complain forever about how ungrateful they were when they refused to let her meddle in their private affairs. She was a good and self-sacrificing woman, but somehow she made the qualities irritating and became a burden to the people she smothered with her loving care. She had to have someone to pamper, someone she could urge to eat, drink, or rest when he didn't want to. To top it off, she had the unfortunate knack of being tactless without meaning to be or realizing it. I believe this trait really came from her secret need to suffer various indignities so she could cry over the results of her peremptory good deeds.

Our family trouble came at an opportune time for this professional caretaker of family troubles. She took the delirious, helpless old man and the skinny, motherless boy under her wing, cooing and flitting about in her eagerness. I appreciated her but she irritated me too, especially by the maladroit way she handled my father. For Maria Dora was as inflexible as iron. How could she understand my father's unbearable sorrow which led him into realms of insane hope and grim despair? How could she sense the struggle in his hazy mind? She could feed, clothe, and bathe him and apply poultices and compresses, but when he wandered in the dimensions of time she punctured his fancies patently.

"Now, Giuseppe, you know perfectly well that Marietta is dead. She died in childbirth. She won't be coming home from church or anywhere else. Now calm down! You know she's never coming back." She was always surprised when her reassurance put her gentle patient into a towering rage.

"Get away from me, you shameless hussy! You won't let her see me; you're keeping her from getting in! She's out at the gate, cold and tired, and you have stolen all her belongings. Marietta! Please help me, dearest!"

My father didn't live but a year after my mother died.

★

My new guardian was my father's half-brother, an old and overworked silk weaver who was glad to hand me over to Maria Dora. I saw him briefly at the funeral. He was a restless man with yellow-stained fingers and a preoccupied stare. He could hardly sit still through the reading of the will. The minute it was over, he jumped up and came over to us. Maria Dora, the triumphant queen of bereavement, was embracing my shoulders, holding me in front of her like a shield. She was in her element; not even the black veil and tear-stained face could hide her elation. My guardian, on the other hand, looked at me as though I were some spoiled food he had to eat.

"Well, that's that," he said sourly. "Giuseppe always was careless. When he was a kid, he'd exchange his piece of plum cake for a green frog. Then he had to marry, at his age, and now there's this boy . . ."

"Don't you go worrying your head about him! Just you provide what's coming to him and I'll do the rest!" Maria Dora's attack was so vehement that my guardian blinked.

"Hmmmm. Well, of course, it doesn't really matter . . ." So they left it at that. He paid his cash obligation every month and never darkened our door.

Fortunately, Maria Dora liked our roomy old house so we stayed there amid the beautiful, gloomy memories. We had no material worries; my parents had left a small estate that was rented to cover our modest expenses. I have never spent a more interesting and sheltered youth than that one in Milano by the Catarana Canal, amid my tactful and tender ghosts. It was easy enough to handle Maria Dora. I quickly learned and catered to all her weaknesses so that she thought she controlled the house while actually dancing on my string. For the first time in her life she was really happy.

When I remember how much she thought of me, I can't help but be ashamed of my behavior. She believed — and I made her believe — that I was totally virtuous, composed in equal parts of kindness, gratitude, fear of God, and diligence. And she thought I was a superior intelligence as well, especially when Fra Niccolo started singing my praises. Fra Niccolo was one of the teaching monks from the monastery of San Marco; I had accepted him as a teacher so I would not be hounded to get an education. Of course the narrow-minded little priest was astonished at how fast I learned to read, write, and do arithmetic. I only had to put up with him a couple of hours a day; the rest of the time I could really study, researching in books and performing experiments in my father's modest workshop.

When I began my studies, my only asset was an avid and desperate diligence. I swiftly learned to my dismay just how ill-informed I was. I didn't know where to start or what paths to pursue. The essence of alchemy seemed like a tangled mass of thread that I could unravel by pulling the end — if only I could find the end. I knew a great deal about the outer manifestations of the science and its visible effects, of course. I had known and served the Magus, admired, and finally killed him. I had drunk the stolen Essence and now I possessed seeing eyes and lived in two worlds simultaneously. I had performed a transmutation in a dilettante's workshop and summoned the Initiate between the four green mirrors at Dreisesselberg. I had consciously passed twice through the gates of life and death. But I still didn't understand any of these things. I had just used these mysterious, powerful forces as a layman uses electricity today, with some knowledge of their habits but not of their inner rules and dangers. Thus the forces reacted differently from my expectations every time. They kept turning against me to crush me, acting on some unknown law that controlled them.

15

Homonculus

It would take too long to tell how I finally managed to gain a partial understanding of the symbolic language of alchemy. I say partial solution because I was still far from deriving any benefit from it. Every time I thought I had found the solution, my experiments would end in lamentable fiascoes. You can well imagine how dispirited I became when I sat down alone and unprepared to read Raymundus Lullus' description of the preparation of the Philosopher's Stone.

"You prepare the stone thus," Raymundus Lullus wrote. "You catch the sap of moon-grass and extract its essence over a small, gentle fire. Then you will have what we call a quicksilver in the form of a white liquid, which is for washing and purifying the whole nature of our stone. This is one of the most important secrets; it is the first gate. The great dragon must be cleansed in this liquid and cast out of the Arabian desert; it would drown in the Great Sea.

"Turn it around and send it back to its birthplace in Ethiopia. We say that if it is not sent back and replaced on its own soil it will depart for another region. And you should know that every other region and climate will certainly kill our stone to hide it from those who are ignorant and incompetent." Then another alchemist, Basilius Valentinus, speaks of driving the Red Lion through the gray wolf three times.

The thing was made harder by the fact that each great alchemist used different animal and natural names to symbolize the various chemical substances and processes. They also had a hundred different names for the Prima Materia — for example, Leo viridis, Venenum, Nutrix, Chaos, Azoth, Draco devorans caudam suam, and even Mercuris Philosophorum. I found the most lucid references in the writing of Cornelius Agrippa von Nettesheim.

My first step was to make up a dictionary of chemical substances and processes and put down beside them the cover names used by the various masters. Thus I learned what was meant by cineration, putrefaction, currupcio, ablification, and resurrection. But I still could not find the base of the Prima Materia.

How many years I chased the phantom of Prima Materia! How many different places I looked for it — in blood, fire, water, semen, excrement, and air. Then when Homonculus finally helped me find the terrifyingly simple solution, my insane joy was tragically premature. "Terra virginea" — that was another name for the Prima Materia.

I freely admit I would never have found it without the aid of Homonculus, but it is discouraging to try to talk about him. That was one of the craziest adventures of my life. How can I possibly describe this pitiable, horrible phantom who inspired the mad experiments of obsessed alchemists and burdened the sleep of many more? It was the demon Homonculus who squatted behind all the infamous medieval experiments with artificial people. He was trying to get a body for himself, since the laws of the Universe denied him legitimate birth. But even his best mediums could contact him only "through the wall," that is, through the "overhearing" of uncertain dreams. None of them could see him and he made no alliance with anyone — except me.

This unfortunate creature had been searching for millennia until he finally found me, another prisoner, whom he could contact directly and use. For Homonculus' situation was like mine, only much worse. I was merely a captive in the physical and astral realms where the whirling eruptions of emotion rolled and swept me through alternations of life and death toward the calmer waters of consequences. He was frozen in the barren, sterile intellect beyond the astral plane and this side of the mental — a mid-realm of "outer darkness." He couldn't connect anywhere for he was as dry and unemotional as an empty sophism. He was never attracted by lust and never moved by temper. The astral vortex repelled him as a too-complex force field with alien vibrations, and the majestic abstraction of the mental plane could not accept him. This plane could not accept him because he was a mass of theoretical dead letters that were jumbled, undigested, and frozen by the chill of his total separation. He was literally the "nihil" living in no man's land between existence and latency.

Once he had been a human being during the peak period of the ancient, magical civilization. He created a masterpiece, an apparently irrefutable theory that denied the existence of his own soul. Thus he closed the third eye, spiritual sight, from the world of men. To replace this seeing eye, man developed the central brain, which acts like the groping fingers of the blind.

Man could not see the truth promptly and tangibly anymore; he had to grope after it piece by piece, working from cause and effect. Homonculus celebrated his dark deed by constructing a labyrinthine ghost castle where the corridors led the wandering soul to the coffin from which there is no resurrection.

The magical civilization declined and was destroyed by cataclysms, and the beings who were a part of it went to live on planets with denser physical atmospheres. But Homonculus, who had trapped so many souls like birds in his mental snare, was damned to remain in the fiction of death.

Now it was his monomania to deny life and all that was a part of it. He dissected and trampled all concepts of heat, light, motion, and faith but could provide himself no support or refuge to take their place. By persisting in this beyond conceivable limits, he killed his internal physical and astral planes. For if the slightest trace of these two lower planes had remained in him, he would have sunk to the lowest physical level and become a rock. But now he lingered like a tangled, rusty bed frame of intellect from which the cover and stuffing had fallen away. He had no fluids or intense forces, none of the passions or sufferings of the two planes. Thus he became an outcast, perpetually haunting the closed gate of spiritual resurrection.

During one of our strange and disquieting sessions, I managed to get him to explain how he came to abandon the artificial human body fiasco and realize that simultaneous transmutation on all three levels was his only hope of liberation. Obviously he had discovered something else too: only a *human being* can perform that experiment; never Homonculus, the paralyzed phantom.

My solitary contemplations and my single lamp in the dusty alchemical workshop were what attracted the eternally alert, damned entity. He watched me for a long time before he ever tried to reach me.

I still remember the shattering experience that was our first meeting. I had just arrived at another impasse after several months of hard work. I had been experimenting with blood, which involved my overcoming my horror of it and sustaining increased attacks from my demons. The passionate legions were strengthened and intoxicated by the smell. But though I had filtered, heated, condensed, thinned, frozen, dried, and evaporated blood, all I had gained was an increase in their attacks.

I was completely exhausted and hollow with the emptiness of failure. Already I was beyond rebellion and despair; I was lethargic. I had just cleaned the bloody test tubes because the activity gave me a few moments' peace from the astral wolves. They usually quieted down somewhat in the bleak night atmosphere of the forbidding room, just like carnival drunks do on Ash

Wednesday. Now I felt sick and began to notice my aching back and burning eyes, to which I had been oblivious while I was working. Misery literally overpowered me. I was cold; I didn't have enough blood to warm me because I had used my own for my experiments. My abject condition was ideal for Homonculus; it enabled him to throw the first rope of the bridge he wanted to build between us. It might have been an hour past midnight.

The first thing I noticed was the dimming of my lamp. I thought it had merely run out of oil or that the wick was sooty and adjusted it automatically. There was no real reason for me to be staying up; I just didn't feel strong enough to walk to my bed. I just sat there with my aching back bent over my scattered notes. Despite my open eyes and discomfort, I fell into the sort of half-trance in which the soul wanders defenselessly in the dark.

The lamp darkened again. This prompted a few stray thoughts — I had just filled it and I had cut and pulled up the wick — but still the light was smothered by the damp cold.

Now the flame narrowed, sputtered, and smoked. Slowly I realized it was not casting its light in a normal circle; the light stretched to the left corner of the wall and seemed to wash it away into infinity. And at the end of the yellow beam, magnified in horrifying immensity, something was waiting — or someone.

It is almost impossible to describe the outer form of Homonculus as I saw him that night. His existence is a negative one, his form the color and substance of extinct cosmic nebulae, so black that no outline can be discerned — and yet I saw menacing chasms and hell-bound tunnels within him. His blackness was of many shades, but he was easily distinguishable from ordinary darkness.

Homonculus stood there, an enormous, Chinese-ink shadow beyond the material and astral forms. He looked like a bizarre cave entrance painted by a Chinese artist except that his outline was constantly changing. Peaks, hooks, and tentacles would shoot out from him at unnerving, unexpected points. The figure would elongate and then crash down to condense in a whirling spiral. This phenomenon was actually his thought forms, for he was possessed of motion like every other living being. I became dully absorbed in just watching him. Presently I felt a pressure to listen to an alien voice that pounded in my brain.

"Can you see me?" It was like a shout in an empty hall. The sound seemed to come from inside me, but I knew it was the voice of the titanic spirit I saw whirling in the distance.

"Yes!" My raspy voice broke the spell. Suddenly my astral rabble screamed around me like frightened vultures. My heart pounded wildly and I broke out in a cold sweat. Somehow I managed to stumble to bed and bury myself, still fully clothed, under the covers.

What had that presence been? I couldn't stop shaking. Homonculus' paralyzing shadow shook me more than anything else I had ever experienced. He was the very antithesis of Light, while there is a spark in even the most horrible astral demon. Homonculus absorbed and annihilated light. He was darkness itself — the Devil.

★

It was weeks before Homonculus managed to contact me again. His desire for contact weighed continuously on me in the meantime, howling through me like a ghastly autumn draft. Whenever I was scared or tired, I was especially conscious of his efforts. Then I was almost grateful for my astral whirlpool; it shielded me from him like a hellish armor.

Now it was December, with colorless days that swiftly gave way to long, gloomy nights. The very walls radiated winter. A pan of embers hardly warmed more than three feet of floor area. Winds blew through the corridors, wailed in the chimney, and cut into my bones.

Presently I took to my bed with a severe cold. I was ravaged by fevers but my temperature fell at last. My body, cooled and weakened by profuse sweating, was again in a condition in which Homonculus could appear. And there he was again, as always at the end of a long beam of light. His deep, sepulchral voice reverberated in my brain.

"Can you see me?"

"Yes." This time I answered with a silent, shivering thought. "What do you want?"

"To ally myself with you."

Fierce protests rushed into my brain from my every reason and instinct. Homonculus' imperious voice calmly broke through the raging flood.

"Think a minute, you fool! Do you think you'll ever find the Prima Materia messing around with blood and excrement? You'll never find it by yourself — only with the aid of Homonculus!"

That established the bridge between us. My entire being had been long concentrated on the Prima Materia and everything else had been secondary. I ignored the warning signals of my senses and reason. The magic words glowed between us — *The Prima Materia!*

This was the first step, the foundation of the Cosmic Temple of Transmutation, the cradle of the Great Magisterium, the holy and ancient mother womb where I could find liberation. Now it was my own excitement that disrupted the connection. How hard I tried to get back in touch with that powerful entity of wide horizons who *knew* — while I had to grope like other human worms. He wanted to help me. He offered to ally himself with me, had chosen me for the purpose. Did he demand a price? No matter; I would gladly pay.

But the more I wanted another meeting the farther I was from achieving it. I began to realize that Homonculus required a peculiar condition of physical and emotional repose to make contact. I attempted to induce the half-trance that had led to our first meeting, but my disturbed thoughts and their hysterical companions barred my way. Only for a few seconds could I create an empty space within myself. Finally, after making strenuous efforts, I succeeded in getting a glimpse of him again and compiling from the fragmented words I could gather a method of establishing a permanent connection. I had to learn a special breathing exercise and a sitting position. Later on I used a special incense prepared to his recipe.

Even so it was almost a year before we established permanent contact. The silent, candlelit night hours were best for us. And these infernal seances produced a strange ferment in my intellect that drove me out of my peaceful harbor.

Homonculus acted on my intellect rather as a grinding wheel does on a knife. He taught me the abstract speculation that dissects everything layer by layer. I also learned the spell of destructive questions that kill every concept without arriving at any positive conclusion.

For Homonculus did not bother to deny God; he simply proved that He couldn't exist. In the same way he proved that eternal life is a fiction. His chain of syllogisms was unassailable and would have been impressive if he himself had not been living without a body for thousands of years — living in the cul-de-sac of a perfectly constructed theory that was refuted only by reality.

We had some immensely strange debates but they never lasted long. He would crush my arguments with his powerful, grinding logic just as a hungry lion crushes a mouse that has got into his cage by accident. I had always thought that vanity was a hot emotion that whips and kills, but in Homonculus I found it in a vastly different form, a sort of magic, mummified vanity that had been embalmed for thousands of years. This dried-up spectre of emotion hounded his tragic intellect. This thought monster had the compulsion to manifest himself and appear before men with all his frightening accomplishments.

Homonculus wouldn't tolerate having his work attributed to me. He demanded that I declare him; otherwise I would never have uttered a word about his presence. I was surprised at his sinister gloating over the enthrallment and astonishment we produced in human jackasses.

"I despise them," he told me, "but their admiration is my due, just as tax is a king's— except, of course, that the difference between ruler and subject is minuscule compared to that between myself and them!"

His theory was that the Universe is just a stupid, sluggish mortal body with a brain that is as unconscious of the suffering of its cells as that of any human jackass. The only difference is that its life cannot be measured in human time. This ignorant, blind Titan must be killed, he said, so that the suffering corpuscles could be freed to fall back into the peace of eternal nothingness. And he, Homonculus, was to be the liberator — the Savior of Eternal Death. The murderous dagger was to be his implement of transmutation.

A white magician, he explained, possessing the Great Magisterium builds up the life of the organism by becoming a finer cell, a brain cell, which he nurtures to the status of God and manifests through himself. Then the power of Homonculus can open the main artery he has enlarged, and the blood of this cruel and senseless Macrocosmos will be drained. The Titan will die, motion will cease, matter will be dissolved and annihilated, and with it will go the materia and the essence of an invisible substance — the fiction of the human soul.

★

No one knew the makeup of matter better than Homonculus. He was like a surgeon except that the matter he reduced to its basic components was infinitely more subtle. He knew the secrets of the function of that chemical laboratory, the human body, from the glands to the circulation of the blood, from the genes to the mechanism of the astral body. He taught me things in 1633 that contemporary medical science knew nothing about.

When he had discovered that he had to transmute himself on all three levels to be liberated, he began his Sisyphean experiments with artificial human bodies, influencing alchemists to work for him. According to him these experiments failed because of "contaminated, low-grade brain filters" that distorted his instructions. He finally discarded the idea altogether because he saw an easier solution by using me. My constitution could experiment on all three levels; he had only to use his own genius to get through the gate to the other world I had pried open by my mystical transgression. We were perfectly united now, having established a permanent and direct connection.

Now Homonculus decided he had to "repolish" me before we could begin. He had to establish "order" in my mind and "clean out" muddy concepts to hone my reasoning ability like the finest of blades. This was the purpose of our debates. He did thorough work and it began to affect my everyday life. His implanted skepticism destroyed the metaphysical conglomeration of emotions built by my experience and made me arrogant, impatient, and provoking.

Obviously I couldn't tolerate Maria Dora's pious dogmatism anymore; I had to argue with her and mock her. Fra Niccolo, that obtuse and timid little priest, became frightened of me, though all my questions about God, creation, sin, free will, and the fall of man were just feeble echoes of those of Homonculus. Still they made him break out in a sweat and, after stammering pitiably, he would cry, "*Apage, Satanas!*" and cross himself fearfully. These same questions came up again during the period of antireligious materialism in the nineteenth century, and the people who raised them believed, even as I had, that they had finally chopped off all the heads of the "hydra of metaphysical lies."

Of course I wasn't behaving very prudently, but I was overcome by the fervor of my new convictions. This sort of thing happens even now to a person suddenly converted to new beliefs. Today we realize that atheism and materialism are just as passionate and dogmatic as their opposites.

★

My transformation made old Maria Dora almost physically ill. When Fra Niccolo told her he wouldn't teach me any longer for anything under the sun, she cried and begged me to come to my senses before I endangered not only my soul's salvation but my health. Already the city was alive with rumors that I had sold my soul to the devil and that my dead mother was really a witch who had arranged the transaction. Obviously such a contract would involve my taking a stand against the church and disturbing the pious flock as much as possible to divert the lambs from the righteous path. My satanic, cunning questions were obvious proof that this was my intention; if they had not been spawned in hell, an honest religious man could have answered them. Only the devil spun such snares for God's gullible doves.

I knew that most of this insidious gossip was coming from the monastery of San Marco and that it meant grave danger. I would have been glad enough to leave, but Homonculus wanted me to stay a little longer and complete my studies. I would have to leave before too much longer in any case because my father's workshop was not properly equipped for the great experiment. Money and patronage would be no problem; Homonculus knew the levers that would move human stupidity and gullibility.

★

As it happened, I had to leave sooner than Homonculus wanted me to. Maria Dora's loving concern brought on the catastrophe as was often the case when she tried to help people. Not even Fra Niccolo's hurt piety and pride spread the news of my godlessness faster than she as she told her tale of woe to old women, nuns, and horrified priests.

We didn't have to wait long for the results. The sentence was pronounced; the devil must be driven out of me.

Now exorcism is a great and solemn ceremony, and people crowd around with holy fear and curiosity as the divine expert swings his censer, sprinkles holy water, and uses the flaming sword of sacred words against the Evil One. But my devil wouldn't cooperate. It didn't scream when sprinkled with holy water and the incense just made it sneeze. I found the whole spectacle both humorous and revolting — the women pressed together in religious horror, Maria Dora red with weeping, Fra Niccolo's gloomy, monkey face, and the dirty little kid who had gotten in somehow and picked his nose through the whole affair. All these burst in on me in my peaceful workshop. They tore Trismosin's *Aureum Vellus* from my hand, burned it, and threw water on it like it was a dead rat. Then they sprinkled me but to no effect. My devil did not leave; in fact he began to laugh and jest and have a high old time. He proceeded to argue more cunningly than ever and wound up by chasing the entire company out of the house. I was lucky to get away with simply being banished, and the only reason they contented themselves with that was the fact that I was long gone when they tried to catch up with me.

I began to realize in those last hours just how strong were the ties I had to the lovely old house. Memories of my mother's gentle, blue-clad figure followed me from room to room. Old whispers permeated the walls, and the furniture retained the curves of long vanished forms. As I bade my macabre farewells, the past seemed to waver on the threshold of the present. I felt I had only to call and my father would come shuffling into the room. The blankets on the bed took form as though someone lay sleeping under them. I was again haunted by those screams and the smells of bloody birth and the frightful desolation that followed. My soul was filled with loneliness and tender mourning. The objects in the house reached out to me and spoke of the thoughts and feelings of many years. The great dusty cypress outside spoke to me of unspeakable things. The black and white flagstones, the faded curtains, the time-stained pictures, the fragrance of the wardrobes and cabinets all hurt, each on its separate nerve end. I had not realized how attached to them I was.

I left hurriedly at dusk with only a small package, pursued by Maria Dora's sobs and my own desolate feelings. For a long time I didn't dare look back; I stared intently at the wet, withered leaves under my feet. A nervous October wind rippled the puddles formed by the afternoon rain. I thought about visiting my parents' graves but decided against it immediately. Why should I? They weren't there. Empty shells crumbled within them — ruined castles, just like that old house.

It was anno Domini 1636 and I was twenty years old. I stopped on the Viale dei Colli and looked back at the house. It lay with extinguished eyes under an overcast sky, deserted forever. I burst into tears. Suddenly I was certain I was lost without my mother.

We wandered over half of Europe in the years following my banishment. During this time we had many adventures, turbulent, amusing, and sad, but we accomplished very little useful work. However, since Homonculus was my accomplice, I gained considerable fame as an alchemist, sorcerer, and miracle doctor without suffering any evil consequences. Whenever a situation became perilous, Homonculus would tell me to leave and off I would go, sometimes afoot, sometimes on horseback, and occasionally in a four-horse carriage with finely trimmed horses. It all depended on who had been my latest victim or how generous my latest patron had been. Homonculus knew how to make gold but he chose to make it wholly from human stupidity.

My methods of convincing the most cynical doubters were not charlatanism. They were based on an exact recognition of the logic of events and a deep-seated knowledge of the relationships and laws of nature. Of course it was Homonculus who knew these things, not I. He could predict weather changes, floods, earthquakes, and even political tensions and wars, and he made me use these predictions as threats. Plagues and animal diseases always happened just as he had said, and he was always right about the point at which any disease turned for the better or the worse. His diagnoses were infallible, and he was never wrong about the hour of death. As I have said, he was proud of his abilities in a dry and ghostly way but he would never let me spread myths about him.

"This is just acquired knowledge deduced from observations through thousands of years," he said. "I've been able to pry out even the most hidden characteristics of matter and I didn't begin as a specialist. I started from the synthesis of the Macrocosmos as an integral whole. For instance, I know how tiny cells on earth will react to spots on the sun; I also know, like any physician worth his salt, that kidney malfunction will cause the legs to swell."

Homonculus was completely right about everything that related to the physical world and its component parts, even down to their most complex functions. Yet he erred gravely and fundamentally about the essence of these things. It was for naught that his calculations were exact and unassailable; his mathematics might be perfect but the Mystical Life eluded him. But more of this later.

16

The Woman-Man

At last I found both a patron and a place where I could perform thorough, interesting experiments — in Hasenburg under the patronage of Christina, Queen of Sweden.

Much has been written about this strange woman-man. She has been characterized as a romantic, a tragic genius, a madwoman, a perverted and debased personality, and a saint. Actually she wasn't any of these and yet was a little of all of them.

Undoubtedly she was really a man, a man whose eager, clever, and perverted curiosity had trapped him in a woman's body — the body he adored so much that he wanted union with it not only during the short swoon of passion but for an extended time. He wanted to be inside the organism and listen to its nervous system, brain, emotions, and flesh. He wanted to live through her moods and concealed dreams, her malice and eccentric goodness as no man has ever lived with a woman. It was in vain that he was torn from his mother's womb, suckled by his nurse, and pleasured by his concubine. The other pole was still an alien planet, light-years away. He wanted to *be* a woman.

This strange duality was the origin of that extraordinary schizophrenia that was so incomprehensible to the world. Christina possessed a male psyche and the peculiar instincts of woman at one and the same time, though they alternated in strength.

As a man she was a serious scholar searching for knowledge and a skeptical, self-tormenting ascetic, though at other times she was a poet, lover, full-bodied drinking partner, and gourmet of spicy foods and sultry women. As a woman she was a high-strung, whimsical creature who went to church and prayed. But most of the time she was an unpredictable, hysterical, and cruel creature who routinely yielded to all of her passions.

You never knew which entity would surface at what moment. What one built up, the other tore down. What one loved, the other hated. What one was ashamed of, the other boasted about. I have never seen a more tragic duality headed toward a more certain downfall than Queen Christina.

Her weaker, feminine nature desired power, yet power and responsibility seemed to choke her masculine impulses. The man within her rebelled and cried out for freedom but the superstitious, vain, and hedonistic woman wanted gold, merely for the sake of power.

Christina needed gold, and Homonculus and I needed a workshop, a library, and freedom to work. Thus Hasenburg became the scene of our exciting experiments. The Queen had to fight fierce battles for our sake, for her envious courtiers were threatened by my influence over her. But the fever took Christina just as it had taken me. Every researcher who goes into unexplored territory knows the feeling. She was lured by gold but sometimes the other experiments intrigued her as well. As for myself I was still struggling with my redemption and Homonculus' monomania; I wasn't in the least interested in gold.

We spent many afternoons and nights together in the giant hall with its colored slate floor. Expensive spirit lamps hanging from the beams threw their strong light on a chaos of fired clay crucibles, water cauldrons, storage pits, mixers, fire tongs, containers of acid, pots of iron power and cinnabar, steam pipes, and bellows. They were all over the massive table and piled on the shelves around the walls.

We worked several perpetually burning furnaces at the same time, being careful to keep an even flame. We also used manure — which had been outmoded since Valentinus — because it generated heat through the decaying process. Crucibles filled with salt, sulphur, and mercury that had been purified by complicated processes and embedded in virgin earth lined the broad, iron-covered brick furnaces like embryos in the mother womb.

Each crucible was coated with wet steer manure, and the filtered heat of the evenly burning charcoal came up to it through a hollow brick dividing wall. We were trying to recreate the nursing warmth of the sun that filters down to the seeds in the soil. Each crucible contained a substance that was different in composition and preparation and was being maintained at a different temperature. The substances were to be born in thirteen months.

The Queen turned out to be an astonishingly tireless famulus. She wanted to participate in everything, even the manual labor of lifting the tubs and working the bellows. Her strength and skill at these operations overjoyed her, and she tended the furnaces with an almost maternal devotion.

Homonculus only allowed the Queen to know about what was absolutely necessary, only the crude operation on the physical level. She had no idea of the importance of the timing of each "conception" so it would take place under the proper cosmic influences and constellations. She didn't suspect that there was a relationship between my vegetarian asceticism and the operation I was performing. She knew nothing of the difficult concentration exercises I performed every morning at sunrise in my solitary room, working under Homonculus' direction.

Her restless and intelligent spirit sensed that I was concealing things from her and she was full of questions. I never completely satisfied her with my answers, but she submitted to the restrictions I imposed as conditions for her participation in my work.

How much hope we had of each conception! How much excitement glowed around those red furnaces! We relieved the stage fright of those thirteen dragging months by tending the thousand details of the workshop, puttering around with the fire, the manure, and the bellows. After the conceptions had taken place, we relaxed silently and extinguished the intricate, frightfully expensive spirit lamps. We watched the dark silk, star-dusted sky cling to the arched windows and felt the melancholy North cold that struggled with the heat from the furnaces. The new moon appeared in the window under the arch. It waxed full and waned slowly. One month had passed.

During these first serious experiments Homonculus' confidence rubbed off on me. It seemed impossible that the "divine child" should not be born in one of the crucibles, just like it was impossible that spring wouldn't follow winter. Homonculus had made the calculations, investigated the possibilities, and narrowed them down to four by the process of elimination. And these four alternatives were fermenting inside our four furnaces. One of them had to be the real solution.

★

We weren't disappointed when we opened the first crucible. After all, why should it hide in the first one? When the second one also proved barren four months and two days later, I was a little anxious. But Homonculus was undaunted.

"There isn't a single argument in the Universe to refute me!" He radiated dark certainty. "We shall reach our goal in the next four to eight months."

But we didn't. There may not have been any argument in the Universe to refute Homonculus, but there certainly wasn't any transmutation either. The factors just didn't merge and transform as they do so effortlessly in nature's furnace; they stubbornly remained separate and unresponsive. Apparently the Universe was built on something other than thesis, antithesis, and synthesis; there was something we hadn't taken into account.

Yet in spite of all our disappointments, the only problem must be some missing element, something we didn't know about yet but would discover. Well, we would search for it with tenacious and astute analysis. It could only be some missing nuance, some negligible but irritatingly important hairspring of construction. So we had wasted twenty-four months. So what? We would start over.

And we did.

★

Of course our experiments were costly, and people are seldom patient of failure. Queen Christina held out fairly long, considering her internal and external problems. She was always surrounded by slander and the scheming of her abundant enemies, some secret and some open. The man in her fought them haughtily, but the woman was scared and tried to bribe them with hasty gifts. Somehow the levelheaded ruler could never balance out the unbridled woman. Although successful wars enlarged her country by rich new territories and huge war indemnities poured into the treasury, it was always empty. And of course the scapegoat for these problems wasn't hard to find — the infamous Burrhus and his tame devil.

Finally the state council delivered an ultimatum to the Queen through the mouths of an incited mob. "Down with the sorcerer!" they screamed. The three-cornered fight went on for years — Oxenstierna and the people on one side and the Queen on the other. Finally the atmosphere became so charged that Homonculus advised me to leave to avoid physical violence.

The Queen bitterly accused me of plundering and abandoning her, but she was really glad to be able to end the conflict. She had wanted to settle it for a long time but felt she could not retreat without losing face. She was already disheartened about ever getting positive results; the crucibles had deceived us again and again. Only distrust was conceived in their wombs, not redemption. No process at all took place in them; we couldn't even get the first phase, the so-called black body or "caput corvi" in Hasenburg.

"It's the atmosphere of Sweden; it cools and enervates," Homonculus intoned with hypnotic conviction. "It is full of inhibitions and radiations that are inimical to the astral forces.

"We'll have to go somewhere else. The circle's narrowing but we need more conducive circumstances. Then we will try adding saltpeter and alum and using a different sublimation. We won't leave out the purified gold foils this time either. Besides," he continued, "we need a man in a man's body — someone rich and powerful enough to give us full protection. It is also vital that we acquire the unconditional obedience and blind faith of such a man in case we're slow getting results."

All these conditions were fulfilled by Frederick III, King of Denmark.

17

The King's Friend

My semi-escape from the Swedish court was welcome enough for me with the Danes. They were always, and recently disastrously, at war with Sweden and were willing to give me shelter. My relationship with the Swedish queen had been a topic of gossip in Europe for a long time. It had been thoroughly twisted out of proportion, of course, and a number of scandalous details had been invented around our simple and impersonal relationship.

Denmark was fermenting just then with the decadence of the impotent loser. The Danes had lost their land beyond the Sund to Sweden under the peace treaties of Roeskilde and Copenhagen. Since they couldn't win, they hatched plots and schemed and made accusations and generally wasted their energy in squabbling.

The whole country was divided into various factions that snarled at one another, as is characteristic of decadent societies. The loss of Schleswig had triggered the formation of anti-German secret societies, and the majority of the people seemed to live in a state of white hatred against the Swedes. Meanwhile the nobility, especially the younger generation, took to aping Swedish customs. They proclaimed that their own ideas were truly liberal and cosmopolitan and that there was an individual freedom that transcended national boundaries. What they really meant was that they would make no sacrifices for the common good. They were contemptuous of both the King and themselves, and their inner restlessness led them to indulge in all kinds of unnatural revelries, exaggerated fits of asceticism, and heretical religious extravagancies. Thus they roused the wrath of both the citizenry and the clergy.

Finally the general indignation produced a coalition that took action, that action being the Royal Law or "Lex Regia" of November 14, 1665. This law stated that the luckless and feeble ruler who had let most of the Danish empire slip through his fingers was bound only by the Lutheran religion, the Royal Law, and the obligation to maintain national unity. Otherwise he was accountable only to God. The Imperial Diet was abolished, and the government-dependent, the bureaucratic hierarchy, and the standing army became the base of an absolute monarchy. Thus Frederick III became absolute King of an absolute kingdom, accountable only to God.

★

I frequently thought that Frederick was an atrociously bad actor whom a wealthy patron had forced into the major role of a great drama, much to everyone's chagrin. He would gesture and sweat in his loose, overdecorated costume, making all the proper moves without the slightest belief in his ability to perform them. Even an indecisive commoner has a torturous time of it when he has to make a definite decision, and Frederick III had to make decisions and act on them all the time. Unfortunately he could do neither; he couldn't even decide what to wear. He had numerous advisors, minions, astrologers, philosophers, scientists, and impostors around him all the time, and he listened to them all. Then he could not bring himself to accept the advice of any of them.

Frederick III was an unfortunate and petty man. His monumental distrust of himself and everyone else was combined with boundless ambition and pathological sensitivity. Even before he was plagued with ill luck, he was a damaged soul and his frequent humiliations had practically turned him into a madman. He regarded every word as an intended sarcasm and every smile as supercilious and rushed to forestall the suspected injury by saying the wounding words first. He drove his whole court nearly mad by speaking for them and expressing disparaging thoughts he supposed they had. Naturally their concerned protests sounded exaggerated or came out in nervous stammers, and this upset the King still more. He seemed to have a thousand eyes flashing in a thousand different directions, and sometimes he was frighteningly acute. Thus he continually sought out ways to hurt himself — and these wounds never healed. Although it hurt him, he wanted to see that he was a monster in other people's eyes. The end result was that he was emotionally dependent on the very people he fought.

He "owed something" to every living being in his retinue, and that total "debt" would have made a Mount Everest. He was always going to "pay them back" all at once and crush all disdain for him throughout the kingdom. Naturally he wanted to be a wealthy, conquering King, a famous and infamous giant of history about whom heroic poems could be sung.

Thus Frederick III wanted the power of the Magus as well as gold. The fiascoes caused by his clashes with reality had pushed him slowly into the world of fantasy; it was obvious why Homonculus had chosen him as both victim, patron, and patient. And although indeed we profited from the strange relationship, we gave him something in return — purpose. We made his unbearable life bearable and he was finally enabled to do what he had never done before — trust, hope, and believe. He trusted until the very hour of his death.

The three of us worked together wholeheartedly and seriously with no intent on the part of any of us to deceive one another. My demon and I gave that pitiful, self-crucifying madman many priceless hours of forgetfulness, and Homonculus allowed Frederick to know much more about him than he had allowed Christina. Once the King was allowed to see him after a period of intense preparation. The experience made him ill, but it made his faith absolute. He trusted us and our ability to succeed blindly.

Long afterward I realized why Homonculus had such a beneficial effect on the King. The man was but a pale, soft shadow of the demon; they were identical at the core. Both had intellects like descending spirals, denying everything and creating nothing. These traits in the King had destroyed all love, friendship, family relationships, and loyalty around him; he had poisoned all he touched with his malice and suspicion. Finally there was nothing left for him in the whole world but the devil — Homonculus — and I.

★

The person who best understood the King was a perverted old scoundrel named Hyacinthus. He had been thrown out of every major European country and had been in a dozen different jails for every crime from stealing to sex abuse. With scornful and malicious masochism, Frederick III had given him asylum.

It was Hyacinthus' custom to tell all the weaknesses and bedroom secrets of the most powerful people in Europe, always in the filthiest possible way. His inner rottenness was a secret delight to the King. The fellow called himself a seer and a philosopher, but I suspected he was barely literate. He said his entire philosophical works were "in one volume in his head."

Physically he was medium-sized and heavy, with feminine breasts and a sallow complexion. His thinning hair was fluffed out from a sloping head, and his face was marked with the signs of excess dissipation. He spoke in a falsetto, and his clammy hands marked everything he touched. Everything about him was utterly disgusting, especially his boundless arrogance.

But sometimes he could be astonishingly original. Hyacinthus knew human nature; he openly did the mocking the King believed others did in private. He knew that he might dare it, that it was a sure way to dominate the more tactful and worried courtiers. It was what the King pitifully urged all his courtiers to do, but they all realized rightly that he didn't really want such things from them. What he really wanted was for them to tell him his self-concept was wrong. The end result was that he behaved like a jealous madman who tortures his mistress to make her reveal the name of her lover and yet is scared to death she will tell him.

Hyacinthus did tell him just that, and the King hated him mortally. But still he kept him at court and gave him a fine reward for every public impertinence. One such impertinence was a story he spread about the reason the King didn't kiss women. The first woman he had kissed, the old lecher said, had closed her eyes in disgust, the second had stared in repulsion, and the third had blinked in horror. But all three had lied in unison and said it felt good. They all loved the King, but he interrogated them day and night until they confessed in exhaustion. Then he cried and raged and chased them away, declaring he was done with women forever. This tale was told in the King's presence, and the monarch managed to force a laugh.

"Very good! I only wish I knew which one of those innocent lillies paid you to defend her before me — or maybe you got something from them all, you old pimp!"

"That's about the size of it, Your Majesty." Hyacinthus insolently looked the King in the eye.

His words fell into an embarrassed silence. The atmosphere became almost tangibly clammy, for everyone knew the three ladies who had ruled the King's heart for various periods and then vanished permanently from the court.

"But you ladies and gentlemen mustn't let me shock you." Hyacinthus turned to the hostile group that was too horrified even to make a pretense of subdued conversation. "The ladies I'm talking about bear only a superficial resemblance to real people. You see, I am merely talking about three aspects of our lord the King. You will understand presently; let me explain.

"Our most gracious ruler, who is subject only to God, is really like a powerful spirit that permeates not only his own domain but also the souls of his subjects, admirers, and friends. Thus he can see himself through everyone's eyes and think about himself through everyone's mind. No matter what we poor worms say, he knows what we really mean, for he is inside us, crowding out our own spirits. How else could he speak for us and refute our words of devotion? He says what he thinks, feels, and sees by looking out from inside our souls. You see, the ladies really loved and desired the King, but our most majestic lord looked at himself through their eyes and was unable to feel love or desire. He has only one true enemy, a relentless and treacherous one — himself. Of course it is superfluous for me to state that our most wise and gracious lord is the sun of my own spiritual and material existence," he added unctuously. "And may God preserve him to save us all!"

★

Meanwhile our work went on slowly, thoroughly, and expensively, but we didn't have to worry about opposition. The King covered our expenses generously, for we had become the focal point of his life. Homonculus knew well how to fling him some appeasing tidbit to reconcile him to the repetitiveness of our labors. His bedroom and study became littered with painted mottoes written in prominent letters, things like "Don't look at yourself from the outside. Get on the inside and look out!" "Opinions of others are worthless." "He who would rise above all is alone and true only to himself. He uses everyone and trusts no one."

Such phrases kept the King's disintegrating personality together. He would stare at them for hours, wrinkling his forehead in concentration. Then he would sleep as exhaustedly as though he had done hard manual labor. Often he fell asleep in front of the mottoes and dreamed, and then I had to interpret the dreams. They were always nightmares in which he was being chased. He would hide in archways, climb endless spiral stairs, and crawl in chimneys. When he did this last, someone always lit a fire under him. He had only one pleasant dream that recurred frequently. He would be lying helpless but calm in a cradle, and a buxom woman dressed in dark clothes and smelling of milk would rock the cradle. Sometimes she would lean over and cover him with a blanket.

Only the mystic powers knew why this poor, mediocre man was born to be King, for his responsibilities were far beyond his abilities. Until Homonculus and I entered his life, he was so tormented by inner conflict that he was headed for mental imbalance and suicide. The two of us relaxed his tension, bolstered his confidence a little, and gave him a soothing sense of mental superiority. The poor man certainly had known no happiness from mistresses, friends, or family. We were the only ones who made him happy, giving him special exercises, studies, or manual chores that "only he" could do for us. He would putter around for weeks at these trivialities and forget his deeply scared self in the nirvana of healing, impersonal work.

★

Homonculus decided our workshop should be some distance from the palace. We were given a bleak, uncomfortable house surrounded by a thirteen-foot wall that was six-feet thick. The first floor and cellar were better equipped than anything we had ever had, for the King gave us huge sums of money and countless workers. My previous experiences had led me to avoid being seen in court; I came only when the King specifically commanded it or when he was ill. I didn't want to be around those prying, hateful eyes, but as time went on I couldn't avoid it. The King became heavily dependent on me and involved me in his daily affairs to a much greater degree than I desired.

But those first three years I led a pleasant and secluded life with Homonculus in our little fortress far from the city. Only the King was allowed to see us. He usually came over in his coach at dusk and made his retinue wait outside, to their great dismay. He gave me an old couple from among his own servants, and they performed their duties with about as much curiosity as the stones in the yard.

My living quarters in the cold, dank rooms of the second floor were furnished from the royal stores, but their heavy luxury could not relieve the severity of the huge chambers. Even the fireplaces looked like little rooms. Huge woodpiles could blaze in them without providing any heat, because the wind sucked it all up through the monumental chimneys.

My windows, set with fine, expensive stained glass by orders of his royal highness, gave on the unkempt park. My two old servants couldn't garden, and I didn't want anyone else prying around my workshop. So the grass ran wild and the knobby trees leaned over weed-covered paths.

That was when I began to see that these frozen figures were really like the moving forces of the astral world. I suddenly realized that the same symbols exist in our physical life too, if only we could decipher their meaning. Now I began to see and hear the same intense emotions and imploring wails in the curving branches and trunks of trees that I saw and heard among my internal astral demons. The difference was that the trees were mysteriously frozen on this earth, damned by the shackles of physical existence in time and space. And when they died physically, they would yet continue their emotional rage. Ever since then, mute nature has been audible to me.

Now I truly understand trees. Some are muscular young rebels and some are inordinately joyous, shouting odes to the sun. Some are indecisive and have a poor self-concept and some are beggars that stretch their branches humbly for alms of light. There are also devious tricksters and snarling backbiters, tyrants who deliberately blot all light from others, haughty puritans, and gentle, maternal protectors. Some trees are penitent hermits who eschew all decoration and some are amorous and poetic. Some are peaceful, contemplative sages who understand and forgive everything. There are prosperous burgesses who produce a fine fruit crop, heavyset peasants, and gloomy, cynical old men.

I began also to understand the expressions on multicolored flower faces and the faces of the waters, the chasms, and the grim rocks that lie along the road. I found revelations in crystals whose splits are occult designs; they talked to me through their facets. Observation of these facets told me all about them — what they were and what they had suffered, just as today handwriting tells a graphologist.

★

The elaborate workshop produced a series of elaborate fiascoes. It was only the obstinate monomania of Homonculus that kept me trying. Not that I am lacking in tenacity. I was just beginning to feel that Homonculus was caught in a rut and that we were never going to get anywhere using the same old methods. Of course I had no logical arguments to advance against my clever ally; I just had a "hunch," what is politely called intuition.

So I kept working under Homonculus' instructions. I did every experiment with precision but with waning conviction. As time went on I became more and more certain that I was performing useless work, wasting my time, and changing the King's fortune into smoke that went up the chimney. Also my body began to react adversely to my damp, cold quarters. I caught a cold, and bronchitis and rheumatism began to torture me. I was already over fifty-four. But the King wasn't young either, and his unshakeable perseverance moved me. He no longer patronized me for the sake of the gold I couldn't produce; he needed me because he trusted me, and of course he was grateful for his relative physical improvement. He knew most of the credit for that really belonged to Homonculus, but the demon merely frightened him; he loved me. I reciprocated his friendship sincerely, for I felt sorry for his tragic loneliness.

My illness scared the King and he pathetically begged me to take care of myself. He gave me to understand that he wanted me to outlive him and refused to leave my bedside. Presently he too began to sneeze and suffer from a swollen nose and cold feet, and I jokingly told him to leave before he shared my fate. Immediately he accused himself of causing my illness and began to take action.

This was the famous and infamous affair of 1670. Homonculus would allow us to move only if our workshop remained intact, so the King literally had the house lifted and brought close to the palace where I was able to have a well-heated suite. There was a corridor from my rooms to the laboratory. This move kept many master builders occupied for months and cost a fortune.

You can imagine what the hostile nobility, puritan citizenry, and outraged priesthood thought about all this. Every court in Europe sneered, and lampoons were circulated all over the continent. I personally detested the whole affair. I felt ashamed for the King and I would have loved to walk out on the whole business. But I would not let down the man who had a pathological fear of being ridiculed and yet risked it to please us. The remaining years I spent with this kind, unfortunate man were spent there as an act of charity inspired by this consideration. I knew I would be through in Copenhagen the moment the King breathed his last.

★

I finally left at dusk, just as I had left Milan, and once again the weather had magically conjured up a wet, windy October day. A slow rain drizzled, conveying that dark hopelessness northern rains always produce.

The King's feeble hand had been scrabbling at my arm just a few hours earlier as he begged the assembled court dignitaries for mercy in that stifling death chamber.

"Please — don't harm him. He's been everything to me — more than everything. I don't want — I command you . . ." he had gasped. Poor man. Even when he was healthy no one had taken him seriously.

His relatives and the nobility who had been summoned watched his death agony with calm curiosity. They listened to his labored breathing and wondered when the doctor would pronounce him dead. No one felt any pity or love for the dying King. He was already superfluous; they looked to the new power. The room was full of people, but he knew he was alone with me so he turned his face toward me, who had understood and loved him, and spoke in a feeble whisper. I had to read his lips as he formed the words.

"Leave now. I can't protect you any longer. Quick!" Suddenly an awed, alien expression appeared in his eyes. He seemed to see my abysmal inner hell with preterhuman vision. And he spoke clearly one last time, his voice piercing and urgent. "*Get away from him! You've got to get away from him! Find out his name — his real name! God help you!*"

★

I took those words with me into the rain-darkened streets. For the two humble, old servants who had tended me did their final service to their dead master by rescuing me. There were troops waiting to arrest me at the main gate, the side entrances, and the laboratory; the death chamber, after all, was hardly the place to effect an arrest. I knew what they were there for, but it didn't matter to me. The King's death and those shocking last words were so emotionally overwhelming that I didn't care about the future.

Now I simply felt old and tired. I had wasted my whole life without getting any closer to my goal. If anything, I was further than ever. The body of Francesco Borri felt too worn out to start again, and I now realized that my alliance with Homonculus was simply a terrible burden that impeded my progress. It was of him the King had spoken; I was sure of that. But how could I get away from a demon who needed me, whose tool I was? The bridge was firmly established; I was his slave. "Find out his name — his *real* name!" I heard the dying man's words time and again. Undoubtedly a glimpse of the all-knowing had been granted him.

My steps echoed treacherously behind me in the broad corridors. "Those conceited busybodies are waiting out at that gate to throw me in prison," I thought, "but it doesn't really matter. Even if I'm free as air, I'm really in a worse prison than they could devise . . ."

"Find out his name — his *real* name." But I did know his name. Surely it was . . .

A stooped, skinny figure appeared from the shadows of the first column of the colonnade. He waved and I followed him. We went down into the inferno of the palace, past the prison where my enemies had planned to drag me. The musty odor and noise of rats scurrying among the old stones brought back memories of another prison . . . I finally emerged from the subterranean corridor that wound right to the very limits of the city and for a few moments I was happy, in spite of the rain.

18

The House Without a Gate

Now I wanted to go to Turkey — or rather Homonculus did. I had plenty of money, for the King had given me gifts that could easily be converted to large amounts of ready cash. My destination was changed abruptly by an irritating incident. These were the days of the Nádasdy-Frangepán conspiracy, and its repercussions swept me up in Vienna.

In those days everybody was suspicious of everybody, especially foreign travelers, because so many diverse people had been involved in this tragic affair — ardent patriots, dreamers, fanatics, and opportunists. I was mistaken for a courier of the conspirators and taken into Vienna under armed escort. When investigation revealed my identity, I was treated to a sour apology. Meanwhile Homonculus made another of his master strokes. He told me about Count Sinzendorf, the Minister of Treasury, who was a secret believer in alchemy. I obtained an audience, and he took me into his service.

Homonculus was pleased with this new arrangement but I wasn't. I was beginning to abhor alchemical workshops and the repetition of barren experiments under the direction of an avaricious potentate and a mono-maniacal phantom. I had had enough. Now I was becoming impatient and desperate. How could I get out of this trap? Death itself would not free me of Homonculus. I had to find another way.

Meanwhile Homonculus was watching me carefully. He knew what I was feeling but it didn't worry him. He was sure of his power over me. I worked slowly and listlessly and finally he was moved to remonstrate. When I resisted, he threatened me.

"What will happen if I just quit?" I demanded bitterly.

"You will obey me," he intoned. "I am stronger than that astral horde around you. You are my creation; your entire intellect and concepts are mine — *mine*! My hook is deep within you. You are my slave and, when this body of yours crumbles, I'll just jerk the line and have you forever." Then I fathomed the depths of my misery.

Homonculus left me for a while after that — left me alone with my misery to bring me into submission. He wanted me to grasp the full force of my bondage; there was no return. I had pushed myself away from the shore of normalcy and now I must either sink or swim in the dark river of mystery.

★

It was while I was in this miserable and discouraged state of mind that the unexpected happened again and ruined all of Homonculus' calculations by redirecting my life. It was always this invisible, illogical factor that he denounced so bitterly that tripped up his irrefutable genius.

For Rome, which had been watching my activities for a long time, finally caught up with me in Vienna. Count von Sinzendorf fought for me for nearly a year, but the Papal Nuncio interceded and I was extradited to the Pope.

I went to Rome under armed escort. I knew nothing good awaited me there but I wasn't afraid. I was a broken old man and thoroughly miserable anyway. What was the threat of prison, torture, or death compared to the heavy shadow of Homonculus?

I was locked in the Castel Sant'Angelo and left alone and unquestioned for some time. I had heard about the customs of the place, and I was prepared for a long and monotonous captivity. The forced idleness was much to my liking, though my solitude allowed the other world to become very real to me again. I spent weeks in a nightmarish dream whirlpool, surrounded by distorted faces, apocalyptic monsters, and images of passion. My desire to be rid of Homonculus loosened the dam I had constructed against them, and their onrushing dirty mass blocked the bridge between us. Only occasionally did the dark shape break through the astral foam, summoning and commanding. I was reluctant to perform the exercises that would strengthen our bond, so he began straining toward me quietly, ripping through the shell of senses that surrounded me.

So I surrendered. By all means let's continue the experiments, I told him, but where? I was a prisoner, and after my trial they might well kill me.

He reassured me on the latter score, and soon I realized that he was not remaining inactive. The result was a visitor in the night. When he threw back his cowl, I saw he was a high-ranking church dignitary. And his name, when he gave it, was not unknown. He was considered the most skillful diplomat of the papal court, a man with a mind both cautious and curious. This man could cover himself verbally in every direction. His speeches dazzled the masses, but those who analyzed them realized he had used a lot of splendid words without telling them anything. He knew no personal loyalties, only conformity to what was demanded at the moment. He could wriggle around obstacles like an eel darting about in the dangerous waters of power politics.

This cold, clever, and worthless man became my new patron. As I became aware of his inner motivations, I realized he was interested in me largely because a person of much higher standing than himself was. And the privileges I was given were otherwise unthinkable in that infamous prison. I was given a decent bed, good food, freedom of movement, and even a laboratory — a luxuriously equipped alchemical workshop.

So I began again performing the familiar processes I had grown so tired of, automatically performing the duties Homonculus assigned. I blended various combinations of materials, fed the fire under the false womb, and knew there would be no conception. Still this new patron and workshop were the path to my redemption from Homonculus. The event approached quietly, as all great events begin — a drop of water forming with others to start a tidal wave.

★

I was given a famulus to carry coal and water, rinse pots, sweep, and take care of the lamps. He had a thirteen-year-old daughter whom everyone considered retarded, but she was the apple of his eye. Her mother had died in childbirth.

I frequently worked late into the night, and Alessandro had to remain available in case I needed him. When this happened, little Marietta brought him his dinner. She would creep in quietly as a mouse, and I didn't even know about her for a long time because Alessandro had to stay in the storage room while I was working.

One night — it must have been after ten o'clock — Marietta walked into the workshop. At first I thought she was just curious, wanting to watch the fire shadows flicker on the walls as I worked over a spirit lamp evaporating water from twelve times washed sand. It was a while before I noticed her; she just stood quietly and watched me work. Alessandro had fallen asleep after a heavy supper, and I had simply forgotten to close the door; that was how she was able to walk in. Her gentle, childish voice interrupted me suddenly.

"This is hell, isn't it, Signore Burrhus?"

Her hair was in dark braids going down to her shoulders, and the tight bodice of her long blue dress revealed she was frighteningly thin and under-developed. Her cheeks were hollow and old-looking, but her large blue eyes shone with an inner light. Hands clasped modestly in front of her, she waited for my answer. I was speechless with surprise. Something about her scared and touched me. I put down the crucible and turned the spirit lamp in her direction.

"Who in the world are you? How did you get in here?"

"I am Marietta — Alessandro Combatti's Marietta — you know, your servant."

"Oh! Alessandro's little daughter!"

"Yes, I came to bring him his supper. I've wanted to come in for a long time because I've got to talk to you, but my father won't let me. He's asleep now."

I sat down and pulled her to me so the light shone on her peculiar face. She made no attempt to resist but stood between my knees looking at me solemnly.

Marietta — the name contracted my heart. It had been my mother's name, and the memory of it began to bleed within me like a reopened wound. This little girl didn't look at all like her; she only had the same name. Yet memories flooded my heart with sorrow and hopeless longing.

"Yes," I said softly, "you're right, Marietta. This is hell. What did you want to tell me?"

"I can't tell you here. It's a message. Since you came, it's been the strongest of my voices."

"What voices?"

"The ones I hear," she said quietly. "A Madonna made me promise to deliver a message to Signore Francesco Borri, now called Burrhus. But not near hell; we could both get into trouble with the devil who guards his power over you."

Just then Alessandro's frightened face appeared in the door, and he rushed in to jerk the girl away. "Marietta! I've *told* you not to! Forgive me, Signore. I swear to the Holy Virgin it won't happen again. My poor little girl is demented; she has no idea what she is doing."

"Calm down, Alessandro! It's all right. I didn't know you had such a smart little daughter; we're getting along very well together. You can go on back to sleep," I added jokingly. I was shivering inside at the possibility that something would keep her from giving me that message, that message so important it shook my whole being. For I heard my mother's whisper in it, felt her continued desire to help, to rescue me from the brimstone precipice over which I dangled. She had used the weak, pure body of little Marietta to speak to me. What tenacious, radiant love, ready to make any sacrifice to fight a way through to me!

When Alessandro had left, I took the little girl's hand. "Let's go outside, Marietta. You'll have to tell me right now; you may not get another chance." Already the lamps were turning yellow, and the workshop grew alarmingly cold despite its hot furnaces. A beam of light was already stretching to the corner, and I felt the approach of the monster in my whole being. I jerked open the door to the yard.

Marietta was trembling. I lifted her slight body and brought her mouth close to my ear. "Tell me now, child. Don't be afraid! The Madonna is watching over you."

And Marietta whispered my mother's message.

★

I sent the little girl home with Alessandro and returned to the workshop.

My mother's gentle voice, wafted from beyond the grave, filled me with light and prayer, throwing a magic cloak around me to give me the strength to reenter that silent room of red and black shadows where Homonculus waited for the reckoning in deadly anger. His hostile presence thickened and chilled the air. Terror tore into me with sharp talons, the terror that can crush a man who merely glimpses it.

Homonculus was concentrating all his power and will to subdue me with his evil knowledge. The fires in the furnace darkened and spewed heavy smoke, and although the night was balmy outside, the heated workshop was covered in frost from deadly cold. The cold curled around me like a slippery reptile, clinging to my face, slipping inside my clothes, and attacking my bones. I felt the penetrating cold paralyzing me, dimming the flame of my mother's message. If that light were extinguished, I would be overcome with panic and lost. I knew I had to withstand it with the whole force of my faith and memory.

I leaned forward over the table. My voice echoed sharply from the walls as I spoke to that infinite light beam that stretched toward the corner. "I know who you are. You can't hurt me because I am not afraid of you!"

Suddenly the shrill scream of a hurricane wailed through the chamber, and the glass ball on the spirit lamp broke with a resounding crack and scattered shards all over the floor. Crucibles reeled and bumped into each other on the shelves, tottering as though they wished to flee. A mass of soot in one of the furnaces exploded with a muffled thump and I was covered in it. It blinded me and I could taste the stuff in my mouth. I was exhausted and miserable, but I turned against my pursuer with the rage of the hunted animal.

"*I know your real name! You are the house without a gate! I have nothing more to do with you! I dissolve the bond and deny the attraction. Leave me. Leviathan; leave me forever! I command it!*"

I bent forward and clutched the table. My loud, intent shouting had drained me physically. My knees began to buckle and I was sweating profusely. Slowly I slipped to the floor.

Gradually I stopped shaking. Terror streamed through my nerves as I tried to recover. I don't know how long I stayed like that. When my shaking had finally calmed and tears had washed the soot from my eyes, I noticed a change in the workshop. My skin was being soothed by a warm, gentle atmosphere, and the naked flame of the spirit lamp blazed cheerfully. The furnace glowed. A lullaby of crickets was being wafted in through the windows out of the star-dusted night.

In that moment, exhausted and filthy, I felt a brief moment of joy such as I had never felt before. I knelt and mumbled incoherent thanks to God and my mother. Then I staggered up, leaned out the window, and blessed the crickets.

★

I was free. What do I mean by that? Maybe someone who receives a last-minute pardon at the moment of execution would understand how I felt when the mystic curtain finally fell between me and Homonculus. Death itself is insignificant beside the unfathomable, hopeless misery of an eternity with Homonculus; where there is death, there is ultimately resurrection and salvation.

So the prison closed again on Homonculus and he was alone with his barren monomania for another millennia. Then I was so terrified I couldn't even pity him. Today I can.

★

Rare moments like this imbue even the most miserable being with vivid memories and an inexhaustible hope that he may yet arrive at his goal. The taste of these moments never passes. They are like the little grains of dust in the oyster that mature amid agony and tears to form a pearl. It doesn't matter how many lifetimes it takes or how many names, memories, and human labels appear to be involved. It is then that conception occurs. Everything that happens from then on is protective shell, guardian, and enhancer, the alchemical furnace of that small but immense essence.

I didn't have much time after my break with Homonculus. The great shock of the event hastened the death of the infamous Burrhus. I didn't even have much strength for my daily walks on the ramparts; I was not permitted to leave the castle. Otherwise I got whatever I wanted, including the privilege of receiving visitors. I didn't want to see anyone, though of course many people were curious about my long and adventurous life.

My patron frequently came to ask about my progress, and I didn't hesitate to tell him I had failed. I had no desire to lie anymore. He reproached me bitterly and expressed great dissatisfaction; things might have gone ill with me if I had not at about that time succeeded in healing the intestinal problems of an even higher potentate by prescribing a special diet.

Nobody bothered me after that, and to my great joy everyone forgot about me. Only Alessandro and Marietta stayed with me. When I became bedridden, my former famulus looked after me, and Marietta's strange, sweet presence would sometimes break the witches' ring around me for several hours.

Marietta stayed by me with touching concern, and I grew very fond of her and glad of her visits, though she never heard my mother's voice again. A rich flood of voices constantly surrounded her. She could not *see*; she could only *hear*. Bewildered souls in transition, musing souls with questions, helpless souls who foresaw danger, and others who wished to give help shouted across her peculiar horizon.

How hopeless was the task of that small window in the wall of the other world to enlighten the sleepwalkers of the flesh! Nobody bothered to look through it. They turned their heads, deaf and blind to the sobs, pleas, and warnings of their departed loved ones who called after them continually.

Everybody thought Marietta was crazy. Alessandro was the only one who guessed that she had been chosen, and he dared not tell anyone for fear she would be tried for witchcraft. So he diligently spread the story that she was hopelessly crazy and kept her away from people as much as he could. He was not afraid for me to know the truth anymore, and he was happy that his lonely, ridiculed child had found someone who understood and respected her strange talent.

I witnessed some strange and bizarre dialogues through Marietta. As she listened to her voices, she sometimes spelled out words in exotic languages I didn't understand. Sometimes she transmitted the evil railings of my own astral beings. This disturbed her.

"But they are bad. They are torturing you, Signore Burrhus. Why don't you chase them away?"

I confessed bitterly that I had no power over them and begged her to help me. Maybe she could hear a voice that would help me. But I got no answer to my request. Where would it have come from? Outside? I couldn't learn anything else about my predicament from outside; Amadeus Bahr had already told me everything. Still, with Marietta's help, I hoped to receive the secret of transmutation by an "act of grace."

Homonculus' efforts on the physical level had disappointed me and now, despite all my gratitude and love for her, Marietta proved a disappointment also. She did open the way to the long series of experiments I later performed in the dangerous astral kingdom of presentiments, premonitions, visions, and prophecies.

Without a doubt, she inoculated me with hope and curiosity about a new possibility. I took this with me when Francesco Borri's strange life finally ended after a few weeks in bed. I had spent seventy-nine years in that body, and it was a blessing to get rid of it.

I left my money and the jewels Frederick III had given me to Alessandro and Marietta. I know they mourned me bitterly. They were timid, sweet island dwellers cut off from the sea of humanity by their very differences.

Those who are called, when destiny brings them together, recognize and greet one another as brothers, and it was as such that Marietta and Alessandro mourned me.

★

Before I finally left the shadow of the Castel Sant'Angelo, I spent a little time at the tiny signal light of Marietta's open soul. Desperate, bodiless entities who wanted to call back to their loved ones or enemies thronged around her quiet and open refuge. But now she was calling me, summoning me with a tender, spiritual desire, calling me by my own name — not my earthly name but the one that is mine alone of all living beings. I do not know how she learned this mystery but she knew it at the time of my death. She had acquired power over the inner core of my soul and was exerting an irresistible attraction over me.

She didn't want to detain me long, just to have a short farewell before I went on my way. God only reveals His secrets to those who do not abuse them.

CRUCIBLE IN THE FIRE

*How those who are poured forth from the great World
Soul revolve through the Universe seeking one another!
They fall from planet to planet, and from the depths they
cry for their lost home.*

*These are your tears, O Dionysos . . . O Great Spirit,
divine liberator, restore your daughters again to the joy
of your light!*

(Orphic Fragment)

19

Louis de la Tourzel

My next rebirth occurred at the beginning of the eighteenth century and took place, as a result of my encounter with Marietta, in the midst of unusual and complicated circumstances. It was five years after my death in 1695 before I could connect with a viable body. My repeated efforts caused a great deal of trouble to the woman who finally brought me into the world and cared for me until her mind became completely deranged. This unfortunate woman aborted three times and gave birth to a stillborn child once before I finally came to stay, much to her concern. She was a creature of a thousand fears and premonitions, and she continued to struggle in their net until finally her mind gave way.

We lived in a dusty, placid French town called Varennes, which later became famous through the abortive flight of Louis XVI. My grandfather, David Pétion, whom I never knew, had grown up just outside the town. He was the illegitimate son of a nobleman and a clerk's daughter, and in that caste-conscious time this meant total social exclusion. He had no family connections and was soon made all too aware of his anomalous status. The peasants considered him an outsider and the nobility would have nothing to do with him.

Pétion was a cunning, selfish, and ingenious man. He realized that he had to choose one position or the other if he wished to make a place for himself in the world. The fact that he lived in the country awakened his ancestral feeling for the soil; he loved and understood the most blessed and difficult occupation of tending it. In the meantime his mother had made an advantageous marriage, and she was able to give him a respectable sum of money when he came of age. By now he had made his choice; he would be a peasant. But still he was well aware that his father's position could bring him many privileges. If, for example, his father legitimized him, there would be no limit to the amount of land he could acquire.

165

So he began a merciless fight to force his father to legitimize him. His father was in a precarious position, being heavily dependent on his marriage, and the son threatened and blackmailed him until he acceded to the demand — on the condition that the boy never use the name and title publicly. To this David Pétion agreed.

The young man bought a small estate in Varennes and managed it well. His wealth grew steadily, if not always ethically. Pétion was an eccentric and selfish misanthrope who took a special delight in making a profit from the financial difficulties of some noblemen. He was quick to scent such problems out, and in this way he acquired a lumber mill and a dairy farm, among other things.

Being a nobleman's son exempted him from the various taxes which were even then driving the peasantry into a ferment of rebellion. Hundreds were leaving their homes, villages, and land to live from hand to mouth as poachers, smugglers, or beggars. The third class was perishing irretrievably under the burden of feudal and state taxes they had been forced to carry alone. But David Pétion throve.

He married twice, and my mother was the child of the second marriage. She was sickly and imaginative and her father didn't care anything about her. His second marriage had been contracted wholly for profit; his wife brought a rich dowry. To judge by her portrait, that was the only way anyone would have had her.

The year my mother Sophie Pétion turned eighteen, Louis de la Tourzel came to Varennes to live with relatives. This was a highly expedient move, for he had piled up huge debts in Paris and become involved in a sordid gambling scandal. It was generally believed that he escaped with mere banishment only because he was distantly related to the influential Soubis family. Certainly he brought no baggage but the romantic velvet cloak, silk suit, lace frills, and silver-buckled shoes he was wearing. He was as big a burden on his relatives as the atmosphere of Varennes was on him. He had a reputation for vice, and the neighboring landowners rejected him for the sake of their wives' and daughters' virtue. His uncle and aunt told him plainly that they would provide him food and lodging but preferred to be without his company. The result was that the lanky, hook-nosed playboy who had already worn himself out in the debaucheries spent most of his time at the Good Ruler Tavern, where he played cards with traveling horse traders and the local merchants. He won with suspicious frequency.

Whatever others might have thought, de la Tourzel considered his banishment to Varennes simply as a passing accident, the result of "the intrigues of his enemies." He told everyone who would listen all about his life in Paris, how much money he had spent, how many duels he had fought, and who his mistresses had been. He talked about everything in the world except the affair that had brought him to Varennes. He was a cocky, loud-mouthed man, sensuous as a satyr, and the women were crazy about him. Men invariably despised him. Very few peasant girls or women escaped his advances, and the fame of his violence spread along with that of his sensuality. Many were secretly thrilled.

Sentimental, nervous Sophie Pétion, completely alone since her mother's death, was attracted to the "pale, banished nobleman" like a moth to flame. She was a slim, blonde girl then with unusually large and well-rounded breasts over a waspy waist. Her chin was graceful and heart-shaped, and she had high Slavic cheekbones and dark, slanting eyes — eyes that shone with overwrought sensuality. It was inevitable that these two derelict passions should meet head-on and burst the dam of convention.

Sophie glowed like a torch, stooping joyously under the sultry yoke of love. Even Tourzel's fickle fancy was caught for a while by her unconditional abandon. She submitted to all his perversities with innocence and ecstatic docility.

"You're quite a woman, Sophie!" Tourzel laughed one day as he lay sated beside her. "Even Madame Perault's institute can't produce a lover like you."

Sophie apprehensively asked what kind of institute Madame Perault had, and Tourzel explained insolently that it was Madame's business to teach the most beautiful and distinguished women in Paris how to be good wives.

In a few months Sophie was pregnant, a brutal fact that changed everything. Suddenly she became frighteningly aware of the danger of her actions, and the alien strength passion had lent to her will vanished like mist. Again she was weak and timid, restrained by the prejudices of her upbringing and the morals of a small town, and by these she judged herself guilty indeed. She lost weight and her skin grew yellow and blotchy. Her eyes were always swollen, for she cried secretly at night. She no longer met Tourzel with lustful kisses when they rendezvoused among the trees or in the hut of some bribed ranger. Now she met him with wild outbursts of reproach and demand. Tourzel responded by being harsh and rude; then he stopped seeing her altogether.

Sophie was stunned by the extent of her dilemma, and she wanted to commit suicide. Her plan was to go back to their rendezvous in the forest where she had first learned the "sin" and stab herself with Tourzel's dagger, which she had managed to confiscate during one of their quarrels. But then she wanted to say goodbye to somebody. At first she thought of her confessor, but she could already see his look of condemning scorn and she did not have the courage to face it. It was only then that she thought of her father, the reserved miser she only saw on Sundays when he walked silently with her to mass. After all, he was her father, the only person in the world to whom she had any tie.

So she went to her father's side of the house, yearning for a little love. Old Pétion's rooms were as isolated from the rest of the house as though they were on an alien planet, and Sophie could never recall having been there before. She had learned early in life that she was neither expected nor tolerated there, and she had not tried to force the issue while she was living in her pleasant dream fog. But now she needed him.

She wouldn't tell him what it was all about, of course; she would just go speak to him, say something nice. Then she would ask if he needed anything and if he would care about her a little, since she was very lonely. But, no, that sounded like an accusation and would make him angry. She'd just promise to be a good daughter and tell him that she loved him even if she had never shown it. Of course it was easier to imagine these things than to say them, especially to someone who had never done anything for her but beget her. And how could you talk of affection to someone with small, narrowed eyes and reproving lips?

The stale pipe smoke, awakening so many memories of childhood fears and rejections, almost made her turn back, but she kept on resolutely. It was getting dark, and the old man had not yet lit the lamp; he thought every drop of oil he saved would turn into money.

The room she entered looked like a large and disorderly workshop, for the old man repaired his own furniture, tools, and saddles. He even resoled his own boots. Since he never threw anything away, crates, boxes, broken bits of things, and crucibles of evil-smelling glue were scattered all over the room. When Sophie timidly opened the door, her father was sitting in his straight-backed chair beside a cold fireplace. The room was almost totally dark, for the tiny window let in very little of the pearl-gray sunset.

Sophie stepped closer to the motionless figure. Fear made a lump in her throat and she had to try several times before she could falter, "Good evening, father."

There was no answer. She was about to leave, relieved that she did not have to face his probable rejection. He was asleep. Then the presence of death coiled itself about her like a slimy serpent.

★

Possibly — probably — old Pétion, petrified in his selfishness, would have rejected Sophie's pathetic appeal. But the girl was tormented by a terrible enemy — the implacable *other* in her that could never recriminate enough. After Pétion's death, the nervous, unhappy creature became convinced she had committed an irreparable wrong. She virtually beatified her father to degrade herself further, berating herself for not having approached him sooner. He had probably been lonesome, longing for love. If he had lived in a pig pen, it had only been so that she could have more. And she, ungrateful and debauched woman, had been rolling around with her lover while some hidden disease killed her father. Who knew what he must have suffered there all alone? He had had no one to call to bring him water or to call a priest. Perhaps he was damned because she hadn't been there.

So Sophie fasted and prayed, paid for masses and performed penances in hysterical spasms of remorse.

Meanwhile it was discovered that old Pétion's fortune was much larger than anyone had thought. A tremendous amount of money was found under the floor in a chest. The old man had not trusted either banks or paper money. His treasure was a shower of gold coins, like a fairy tale.

Suddenly the world changed around Sophie, his sole heir. Even the young noblemen nearby suddenly found it was not beneath their dignity to ask for the hand of the dazed and awkward girl. Moreover there were rumors about Pétion's background that made them hope a thorough search might reveal a title to go with the gold.

Tourzel heard too and realized his time had come. He came a few weeks after the funeral and took charge as though he were already a member of the family. Sophie, flustered by the crowd of events, cried and protested his presence, but the cynical faun conquered her yet again.

"Why are you acting so silly?" he asked the sobbing girl when it was over. "You've always complained that I wouldn't marry you after getting you pregnant. Now I'm perfectly willing to make you Madame de la Tourzel and you act like you don't want the honor."

"Oh, yes, now you'll marry me," Sophie wailed. "For money!"

"But a nobleman can't listen only to his heart, my dear! I am fortunate in finding a girl suitable both to my heart and my position. And remember the child will be born in a few months; you want it to have a name. If we marry within the week, it will be considered merely a premature birth. Your pregnancy is beginning to show, and no decent man would marry you in that condition. If he did, he'd be contemptuous of you for the rest of your life. At least I love you, Sophie, and," here an evil grin crossed his features, "I have proof that I was your first lover and that the child is mine."

★

This was the background of my mother's marriage. She told me the whole thing in clinical detail as a means of doing penance. Poor woman, she was already half mad then.

So Sophie became Madame de la Tourzel. She was disillusioned with her husband and hated her weakness, but she was still drawn by craven sensuality. And their life together — if you could call it that — gave her nothing but worry, jealousy, and regret. Everything she had feared about Tourzel turned out to be true. He left for Paris just a few days after the wedding, paid off his debts with Pétion's money, rented a palace, bought a carriage, and used it for occasional visits to Varennes. He never offered to take Sophie to Paris and, when she hinted at it, he insisted it was impossible because of her condition.

"It's because of my condition I want you to stay awhile," Sophie would beg. "Here I am alone in this empty house and sometimes I have bad days."

"You must understand my position, my dear," Tourzel would reply calmly. "My pride won't let me live on your money. Now that my affairs are in order, I may be able to get a position worthy of my station. I'll have to attend court constantly to secure one."

"You must understand" was the refrain of all Tourzel's visits to Varennes, and soon he forgot to bother with the "my dear." The only reason he came at all was the humiliating fact that he still needed Sophie's signature to borrow large sums of money. Of course the much touted position was always just within reach; Tourzel was in hourly expectation of being appointed to a high position for years. And of course to get it he must circulate in the courts, the gambling halls, and the "distinguished parlors" of Paris' hot social bloodstream.

Sophie miscarried in her fourth month of pregnancy and sent a mounted message to inform Tourzel. He regretted that he could not come; he must not risk missing an important traveling personage on whom their joint future might depend. He turned up six weeks later and impregnated the still recovering woman yet again. Then in the course of after-dinner dalliance he coaxed a large sum of money from her and left. And what had happened to the important personage who had kept him from the sickbed of his wife? As it happened, they had missed each other and by the time Tourzel had tracked him down, someone else had the position. But it didn't really matter for he had a prospect of an even better position . . .

He was always talking about his supporters and how well they thought of him. And he told Sophie of all the untiring hands that moved here and there about his affairs. Of course these hands needed constant "greasing;" that was why he had to stay in Paris and have plenty of money. But as soon as he got his position he would bring Sophie to Paris and present her in court. After all, he would need to manage a big house and he couldn't do that without her. But in the meantime there was no sense in her being with him because he had to be on the go from morning till night. Often he would visit some lord on his estate and promote his affairs amid the friendly atmosphere of the dinner table with fine wines and spicy stories. He would drop so many names and titles that poor Sophie's head would spin, then repeat his refrain, "You must understand." In a few years Sophie indeed understood.

My father died when I was ten years old. He died as he had lived, involved in a whorehouse brawl. Several of his companions were suspected, and the lengthy investigation revealed only the facts of Tourzel's filthy life and the fact that no one person could be charged with the deed. Everyone involved had been paralytic drunk, and the knife had been Tourzel's own. Others had also been wounded in the affair. It had all started over a girl named Lolette who had recently come to the house. Tourzel had monopolized her, as was his custom with new flesh, and he had taken offense when other patrons wanted a share of the "public treasure."

So the Estates General condemned the whole lot to the galleys for life. They were all black sheep of noble families. It was a brash fate but it was the only way to save them from their own depravity. Their bodies might perish but their souls would have a chance at new life.

★

I had never seen my father except during his brief visits to Varennes, but the ravages of his debauched life were very evident to me. He always came with a hangover and poured out on us all the rancor of his evil disposition. A little drink would quickly make him cheerful, but by nightfall he was always in a foul temper again. He couldn't have lived long even if he hadn't been murdered, for both his nerves and his digestive system were shot.

My mother always considered these visits a merited punishment; she never grumbled or complained but she never gave him as much money as he asked for either, despite his threats.

"That money is for your son. He's not going to be a beggar just because you're a drunken bum."

"You dare say that to me, to *me?*" You could hear him all over the house. Then I would have to control my nausea as I listened to the sound of blows in the other room. There never were any screams; my mother bore it all in silence. Shortly she would come out with a quiet, frozen face and take my hand.

"Come . . ."

Finally I tremblingly planted my small body in front of her and interrupted. "He beats you; I heard him. I don't want him to beat you. I want to kill him!"

Her face broke. "You — you're like a little old man!"

"Throw him out!" I insisted. "He's nothing to do with us!"

"Yes, I'll make him leave; that's what I intend to do."

She led me into her bedroom, pulled the marble-topped washstand away from the niche where she kept her money and counted out a sum so he would leave us in peace.

Of course there was a special ceremony for this withdrawal. She was a superstitious woman and her superstitions ruled her life. She had a certain way to get out of bed, a particular shoe to put on first, and a rule about what hand to put on the doorknob. Her whole day would be ruined if she saw a black dog, a man with a ladder, a pregnant woman, a red-haired child, or a cripple in the morning.

Before she opened the money chest she would spit to the east and west, then to the north and south. When she took out the money she would spit on the first gold coin she removed and say, "Multiply and come back."

"Why do you do that?" I asked curiously.

"To bind it and make it come back."

There was a special ceremony when I got up and another when I went to bed. When I went to bed, my mother would put earthen jars of water on small tables at each side of my bed. Then she would bring in two hot coals in an iron skillet and drop one in each jar. As the coals went out with a hiss, she would declaim, "May witchcraft be extinguished likewise!" Then she would stand by the head of the bed and lament, "He's gone; can't you see? He is dead — dead. The swift-winged angels have taken his soul. There is only a shell here, empty and silent. Now shoo, avant, leave here!" Then she would spread a ring of white flour around the bed, but her soul was so full of anxious confusion that the spirits that fed on fear were left inside it. On St. Lucia's Day she would scatter a whole sack full of poppy seeds in front of my door, believing that witches couldn't approach me till they had picked up each individual seed.

Poor woman! She could not help me in my condition. In fact her unintentional black magic attracted the dark forces more than ever. These forces gradually came to control her for she was afraid and could not understand them. She didn't even know their real names.

I pitied my mother with a compassionate, helpless affection. She loved me desperately and blindly but she had none of the clear, constructive love with which Marietta of Milan had blessed me. Her high-strung, remorseful motherhood finally destroyed her. I would not have dreamed of telling her my secret. She could sense only a little of my unusual abilities and disabilities, and this little bit of knowledge drove her to do everything she could think of to appease God and all the devils in hell to keep them from taking me from her.

I couldn't even begin to lead her soul out of its destructive maze of superstition. Her inner commands became more and more tyrannical as time went on, forcing her into insane actions. The poor woman's mind was too weak to fight her two worst enemies — her unbridled sexual passions and her rigid, unforgiving Catholicism.

★

Sophie started having visions after my father's death. I tried vainly to explain to her that she formed these visions herself out of her own astral forces and that they were merely the result of her intense fear and remorse. She didn't understand.

First, old Pétion appeared one night before she lit the candles. He stood in the dark corridor to the kitchen and wore a long shroud. As she approached, he looked at her forbiddingly, his face saffron yellow. "Pray for your sins!" he intoned — as though he wouldn't have done better to pray for his own. Then he disappeared. I learned all this after the servants had thrown cold water on her to bring her around.

The whole thing made me angry, and I tried to explain to her that the whole phenomenon was caused by her irrational guilt.

"Oh, be quiet! No matter what you say, I know I saw him and he spoke to me. And I know he is troubled by my sins."

"Oh, come on, Mother! He ought to be more worried about his own.

You've told me how he got his money and how he mistreated my grandmother into an early grave."

"Stop, for God's sake! The dead hear if you abuse them, and they take revenge!" She paled and began the appropriate litany. "O ye white souls and ye black souls, ye dead who come back! My child is mad; you must not heed his words! He is a poor idiot boy and knows not what he says. Laugh, pity, and avant! I, his mother, will do reverence for him. Yes, I will do everything and more!" I couldn't do anything.

After old Pétion appeared, she started torturing herself. She would lock herself in her room and beat her naked body. She wore a spiked belt under her robe and fasted until she was her own shadow. She wouldn't even clean up. And nobody ever had more masses said for them than old Pétion did, at her expense. But none of this satisfied him. He came to the house more and more frequently and even took to bringing a guest — his son-in-law, my father, on an unexpected vacation from hell. The fact that the two men had never known each other in life didn't seem to make any difference.

My father did a magnificent job of collaborating with the old man to take the last shreds of my poor mother's sanity. The two of them took over the house, and Tourzel wasn't satisfied with just that. He had become overbearingly virtuous since being knifed into the next world, and he couldn't get enough of prayers and penances. No matter what his poor widow did, he still threatened her with the fires of hell. He had been repulsive enough as a person, but he was an unusually loathsome ghost.

I had to sit by and watch my mother's mind deteriorate as she was haunted by the creatures of her own imagination. But weren't we really in the same boat? I at least knew the names and natures of my rebellious forces, but I had no more power over them than she did over hers.

★

Finally the intolerable situation erupted.

My mother had become a ruin, talking aloud to herself and peering around like a hunted animal under her disheveled hair. She would make gestures to chase small demons off the furniture and complain to me that they were befouling her meals and shouting obscenities during her flagellations.

Finally one morning she jerked open her door at dawn and ran naked into the street, screaming at the top of her voice. The whole thing happened so suddenly I couldn't stop her; I had to throw on some clothes hastily and follow her.

Her screams and the sight of people gaping in windows enabled me to follow her to the church square. I ran as fast as I could and managed to catch up with her on the church steps just as she was about to rush in to early mass. She was truly a revolting spectacle, her flesh scarred and gray, and I tried to wrap her in a blanket someone threw me. She started struggling, scratching and biting and hitting me with the whip she used for flagellation. I was exhausted by the time it occurred to someone to help. We finally managed to overpower her and roll her, wriggling like a giant snake, into the blanket. She twisted with the sick strength of the insane and swore and wailed continually. A large crowd followed us back to the house, including the priest and Bayon, the nosy apothecary of whom I shall say more later.

Finally the poor woman calmed down. When we put her to bed, she lay on it rigid with her eyes wide open, and we thought she was dead. We finally found the doctor, who discovered that she still had a faint heartbeat.

So my mother had survived, but now her condition was public knowledge and thus began my hopeless fight against both church and state. The one attributed her condition to the devil and would have exacerbated it with their hocus-pocus; the other simply wanted to lock her up in the Salpétriére. The state won and my mother, who in the meantime had suffered increasingly severe fits, was bound and taken to the Salpétriére. The year was 1718.

20

Monsieur Bayon

Thus I was left alone in the house in Varennes with a few lazy, impertinent servants. I was seventeen. Though I bore my father's high-sounding name, his family wouldn't have anything to do with me. They would have preferred him to be childless.

The town aldermen, on the other hand, were all too solicitous. Bayon, the apothecary, magnanimously agreed to become my guardian and tend my body, soul, and estate until I came of age. I was lucky as far as the estate was concerned because he was downright conceited about his honesty. He was perpetually enchanted with the purity of his own ethics and performed every action on an imaginary stage before an enthralled audience.

He immediately decreed we should close down the Pétion house and get rid of the servants, which was perfectly all right with me. I had no pleasant memories of that cheerless barn. But I didn't particularly like moving in with the Bayons. They gave me a room stuffed with sacred pictures and its own prayer stool. The oven smoked in the winter and the windows wouldn't close completely, but I knew I had to be patient and wait for my freedom. By now I had sufficient experience to appreciate the regular, compliant processes that could ameliorate my strange and irregular fate. I could wait. I had plenty of time.

In addition in the Bayon home I had the diversion of watching a farce based on the family life of a smug, stupid tyrant. I learned that if a man strives only to be respected and acknowledged he will lose his natural dignity irretrievably and become the target of petulant ridicule, even in his own house.

Bayon had an unusually ugly wife who apparently treated him like a little tin god. Their only son, Etienne, appeared to listen in awed attention when Bayon began to sing me his aria of self-adulation. The boy would mumble

177

the prayers with his father and always addressed him as "my dear father." I winced at such perfection. Even the servants appeared to attend their master with admiring humility. His table was always spotless when he rose as head of the family to bless the bread.

In fact Bayon bombastically blessed everything he touched. His toothless, pointy-chinned wife would nod, then put her hand on his and practically thank him for being alive. Etienne also said, "Thank you, my dear father," like a puppet, and I winced again. Good heavens, what *was* all this?

Then I caught a glimpse of Etienne and couldn't believe I had seen right. What an impertinent, scornful look! I learned later that I had not been mistaken. The entire household was sneering at Bayon behind his back. Even the servants cast aspersions on his physical appearance and manners.

Next day Etienne, who was two years my junior, told me that he had caught his father reaching under the housemaid's skirt in the corridor one day. He had snickered in his high-pitched voice and, though they never discussed the matter, his father had ceased to "push him around" in private.

As for Madame, she was so full of bitterness and hurt that the slightest touch brought a full flood of scorn.

"Bayon always was a good-for-nothing scoundrel," she assured me. "It was I, Madame Bayon, who brought money, order, and prosperity into this house, and yet only three days after our wedding I caught him in the barnyard with a filthy gypsy woman! Imagine my humiliation! He's out all day chasing every skirt in the neighborhood and then has the gall to come home and preach morals to me even while he's on the chamber pot. I'd certainly like to know what he tells his confessor. He probably talks about how good he is till the priest absolves him of all past and future sins just to get rid of him.

"And as for his business — he's hardly ever at the pharmacy to look after it at all. If I didn't take care of it myself, we'd all have starved long ago. He's always visiting somebody gabbing; people have gotten so they run when they see him coming." Thus she exposed the whole truth of her marriage to me with spiteful thoroughness.

Once a week Madame Bayon had all her friends in to an afternoon weaving party. They would consume enormous quantities of Bayon's bread, honey cake, and milk while engaged in the hard labor of tearing him apart. They would imitate all his words and gestures brutally. Bayon didn't know about this and didn't want to know. He didn't even catch on to sarcastic remarks made in his presence; he had absolutely no sense of humor.

Etienne told me he had called Bayon "dear father" only ironically since the episode of the kitchen maid, but his father accepted it at face value. He had even once expounded on how much he deserved the endearment.

For a long time I didn't understand why Bayon's family performed their act of being devoted when even the money belonged to his wife. Then I found out. Bayon was capable of frightening violence when they omitted these attentions and thus forced him to look into the chasm of reality.

This experience of looking at two sides of human action made me the richer, not from observing the physical and astral planes, which were merely disgusting, but trying to look into the third plane for reason and solution. When I did this, I could find compassion even for a moron like Bayon.

One afternoon Bayon accidentally overheard one of his wife's afternoon parties. He had had to come home because he had forgotten the key to his safe. Had he sent his assistant as usual, he would never have learned the truth, but the two men had just quarreled and Bayon wouldn't ask him. I don't know what Bayon overheard through the bedroom door because I only heard the story afterward, but it isn't hard to guess. They said he suddenly appeared among the gossiping women, pale as death, and began to shove, kick, and beat them. He hit Etienne so hard, one side of his face swelled. But it was Madame Bayon he beat the worst, along with the servants who tried to save her from him.

There had been only three such outbursts during their married life to date, and each of these had increased Bayon's self-respect and disposed his household to maintain his illusion. He was like a large, fat snake, deaf and blind, that could be angered only from a safe distance.

The household was grimly silent after this latest scene, but I saw Madame Bayon looking at her husband with honest tenderness and admiration. Etienne's awed face showed no mockery now, and even the servants were eager and truly humble.

Thus Bayon had won his battle, but he didn't realize it. He felt he had lost everything. His outburst had filled him with remorse and shame. He spoke to no one, lost weight, and scurried through the streets like a branded thief. For he had just swallowed the bitterest pill of all — he had lost his role. He really wanted to be a magnificent and virtuous man who could command respect, and he had deceived himself into believing that he had already attained that goal. It was obvious, of course, that his soul had been inoculated with an ideal, and I knew that his future births' destiny would lead him to it. Someday, after immense suffering, he would be what he idealized. Of course only the magical emanation of true greatness of soul will win him the respect of others, but by the time he gets it that will not be his only goal.

21

The Ghost of Jose de Assis

I finally moved to my own house in Paris in 1724. When I had come of age and was financially independent, I liquidated all my assets, to Bayon's dismay, and cut all ties with Varennes.

My mother had died. The last visit I paid her shortly before her death is one of my darkest memories. I had managed to get a visitor's permit to the Salpétriére, where more than one hundred years would pass before Pinel struck the shackles from the unfortunate inmates. The history of psychiatry has a lurid chapter on this period but I, an eyewitness, can state that the reality was more horrible than any description.

Salpétriére at that time was called the Hospice de la Vieillesse and consisted of about forty-five buildings around a high-domed church. The enormous outer grounds were beautiful with trees and symmetrical lawns, but the further in one went the more their beauty was marred by forbidding, tragicomic instruments. There were artificial ponds spanned by tilting bridges that contained pagodalike cages used to shake patients out of their lethargy. There were rotating chairs where patients were spun to drive disturbing images from their heads, or at least food from their stomachs. There were treadmills and rotating wheels to activate depressed patients, and numerous other ill-made gadgets constructed by perplexed, impotent physicians. The whole place looked like an amusement park or county fair.

Inside the so-called "milder" patients were crowded into the day halls which were constantly filled with their screeching and indescribable attacks. The overworked personnel, infected with the general excitement, could not cope with the situation; indeed most of them were rough, ignorant women who were willing enough to vent their spite and anger on their charges. This could be done easily enough simply by not intervening as patients assaulted, wounded, or befouled one another. Public sexual outbursts turned the place into an infernal bacchanalia — and the worst of it was that deranged children suffered among them.

My mother was in a windowless cell two feet square. The air was foul. Her arms were chained to the wall, her feet to the floor, and a long chain ran from her waist to the ceiling. She sat on a bench firmly fastened to the floor, and the pointed end of the infamous mouth pear protruded from her mouth. The officious young doctor who took me in whispered with counterfeit sympathy that her condition had necessitated this "regrettable final restriction." I cried out in anger and pain and begged him to let her come home where I could take care of her and at least keep her clean. Criminals were better treated than this poor woman, whose only crime was being ill.

The prison sanitarium authorities were offended by my request, and my agitated demands and threats served only as oil on the flames. They finally removed me from the building by force.

I suffered from the memory of my mother's cell for years. Her outspread arms, sore-infested skin under the tattered clothing, and almost pupiless eyes haunted my sleep and ruined my appetite. I was relieved when I learned she was dead. It was as though my own fettered and wretched body had been released from that cell.

★

Paris was in smoldering turmoil in 1724. The Sun-King, who had only died in 1715, had filled the country with unrest, and the financial blunders and general depravity of Philip of Orleans' regency had tried the patience of the people so severely they could not bring themselves to trust the promising start of young Louis XV.

By this time the troubled country was already in the hands of Cardinal Fleury, a man whose policies were peaceful and clever and who knew how to make useful compromises. Of course he could not heal the rotten, outmoded system of which he himself was a part. He could only smooth over the surface while the poison fermented at the core and bred a revolution that sought only destruction and had nothing to do with negotiation. Cardinal Fleury merely gained time for the Bourbons, lengthening the sick man's coma and producing the illusion of health with rococo rouge and rice powder.

As yet the young King's personality had no definite outlines. His indolence and irresponsible lechery, insensitivity to urgent issues, unfeeling love of comfort, and the hauteur that would make him an absolute monarch were still hidden by the pliancy of youth and the skill of Cardinal Fleury.

Hope is immortal. Until a ruler actually proves himself as great a tyrant as his predecessor, the people will weave glorifying legends around him for their own sake. Never had there been greater hope for a reformer than there was then, and some ascribed this humanitarian role to young Louis XV, hoping that it would be he who would change and equalize the untenable state of society. But the majority watched suspiciously as the same old things continued to happen in court; the rich positions and estates continued to fall to "God's chosen ones," regardless of merit or ability.

★

I purchased my strange house with all its furnishings from the heirs of an eccentric Portuguese named Jose de Assis. It was in one of the small cul-de-sacs off Faubourg Saint-Germain which have since disappeared without a trace. The red brick building set behind ivy-covered stone walls greeted me like a friend at first sight; it is not only the past but also the future that touches familiar strings in the soul. This would be the setting for the inevitable.

In addition to the house, an old servant was included in the purchase price, a prim and eccentric man named Maurice. He belonged with the house just as much as the furniture in the walnut paneled rooms. Maurice watched me jealously to see if I would move anything from its accustomed place and, if I so much as absent-mindedly replaced a book on the wrong shelf, it was back in its former place the next day. This produced a stubborn and tacit struggle between us, but finally Maurice won. I had long since lost any zeal for the kind of fight which could only be important to an ephemeral human being. After all, I wouldn't try to rearrange a hotel room for I would know that after a day or a week I would move on. Thus I acceded gracefully to Maurice and was careful not to disturb the dogma de Assis had planted in him. The Portuguese whom he had served for thirty years had thoroughly indoctrinated him with the idea that he, de Assis, would remain consciously alive after his death and that he would return and give a message to Maurice. Of course the old servant wouldn't talk about this; he was the soul of loyalty and discretion.

In going through the library I managed to get some idea of my predecessor's character from the notes he had scrawled in the margins of his books. The library itself was interesting, full of works on theology and the occult. There was also a collection of erotica, and I was surprised to see a large number of volumes on the Inquisition. Sencia's *Fra Giorgio Da Casale,* written about the Inquisition of Pope Julius II, was thickly underscored almost throughout and dotted with exclamation points and question marks. In some places words had been feverishly crowded next to the texts, fragments of a flood of thought. With a little intuition and imagination these could be pieced together to reveal the inner workings of an original and distorted mind.

There was a portrait of Casale by an unknown artist on the frontispiece. It showed a pale, hollow-faced old man with heavy eyelids and a wicked mouth. De Assis had scrawled under it, "Yes, that's him all right. That's the way he used to look at me in the mirror. I remember that and I will remember even more when I've pried the gate open completely."

Further on he had annotated a passage on Casale's youth. "That's not true! How little people understand of others' actions! Giorgio did what he did because he was afraid not to. He was really a coward; it was fear that made him cruel. My Lord and God! Spring trees in Verona — a woman passing on the yellow road between the rows of blue trees — she wears velvet, and her breasts swell from the deep neckline of her dress. 'Giorgio, Giorgio!' — the music of her voice cuts his loins like a knife and yet — he is a grotesque, pimply adolescent, and wild images flock between the lines of his prayers. That image is sharp and clear — the large, red stone slates in the monastery corridor and the suffering, begrimed face of the crucified Christ on the cell wall. Yes, I remember! I remember for certain!"

Obviously de Assis was fighting for those memories that flash through everyone's awareness in the odd millisecond. He was systematically besieging the forbidden gate within him that shut out the past. Perhaps the especially strong recollections came to him or perhaps these were the discoveries of the solitary pensive man. Since these things exist in and around us, we have only to concentrate on them without distractions. We have only to ask; they will answer.

I found wavy lines of writing all over one of the pictures in a book of primitive erotica. It was a drawing of a shapely temptress posing in front of a mirror. "The flesh of evil women is cold and smells like frostbitten wild strawberries. They came only in my dreams, but they robbed me of my virility. Smooth-skinned succubi — beautiful and horrible — I remember them."

And on the last page of an ivory-bound parchment Old Testament, I found a note written in mirror writing. "Maurice will wait for me. He will receive a sign when I am ready. He was in Verona then too . . ."

★

The first person I met in Paris was Dr. Péloc, whom I called in over Maurice's protests to tend his respiratory problems. Péloc was a slovenly man of medium build who apparently was not conscious of the threadbare appearance of his blue velvet coat, the fact that his shirt looked like a used menu card, or that there were holes in his socks. He brought a fresh, friendly atmosphere wherever his bustling figure chanced to go. His hands were chapped from constant washing, and he had a habit of rubbing them together with such eager determination that the patient automatically felt he could conquer any ailment, however serious.

Péloc promptly won Maurice's devotion, not only because the incense he prescribed relieved his breathing but simply because one had to like Péloc. He was completely selfless and lived only for the needs and joys of others. Eating and sleeping were simply auxiliary matters, and he only wore a coat in the winter if somebody else thought to put it on him.

People sensed that he was that divine servant who bore burdens and listened sympathetically, and they clustered around him with their problems. I wondered how he managed to do all he did. People sent for him day and night, and many could not pay him. His more affluent patients paid him well — I always paid him generously — but the money never stayed in his pocket. He would get it one place and give it away the next if somebody needed it. This rare type of person is always a magic center, for most people are so self-centered they have no room for even a little bit of anybody else's life. To me he provided the first link to help me understand what my new life was to be.

Péloc's shabby little figure became a part of many human destinies, bringing warmth to the slums, stale middle class homes, artists' hovels, and the mirror-lined palaces of the nobility. And he was just the same to all of them. In his eyes the frame was nothing; his concern was the human being who told him about the wounds of his body or soul. He utterly lacked the arrogance of the righteous revolutionary; he had mercy on peasant and nobleman alike.

Perhaps it was his total involvement that prevented me from being totally honest with this valuable friend. I wouldn't encumber him with my burden too. How tired he would be when he paused to spend the occasional half-hour at my fireplace! His eyes would keep closing in the warmth, but as soon as he snored he would always start awake and apologize. Then he would resume talking again.

"Poor Madame Lacroix! You know, the baker's wife I told you about. She started in labor at seven o'clock yesterday evening and at dawn I delivered dead twins. How she talked about them! I'll have to find some way to help her bridge the gap until she can get pregnant again. She has so much milk, and there's that empty cradle she embroidered the satin cover for . . . These times are terrible for women. What do you think, M. de la Tourzel? What if I got her a basket of kittens? Yes, yes, I think that would help a lot!" And already he was wide awake with care and compassion, forgetting his own fatigue.

Péloc was greatly interested in learning about the strange Jose de Assis, and he would complain of not having enough time to study him. Yet in spite of everything, he managed to read a good deal at night. His clear mind synthesized everything easily. He had a good overview of alchemy and he knew how to distinguish the reality from the fraud. He knew the importance of Paracelsus and had used his methods with great success.

Once I asked him if he thought de Assis had already sent his message to Maurice. I didn't dare ask directly, for Maurice didn't know I knew about the matter.

"No, it hasn't happened yet," Péloc replied.

"How do you know?" I asked curiously.

"Maurice told me."

This made me feel a trifle miffed, but the feeling quickly passed. After all, I myself was a mass of sinister problems, while Péloc held the master key that could open even the soul of old, withdrawn Maurice. The old servant pampered him like a mother. He would shuffle in unannounced and set a plate of food before the Doctor, then grumble if he didn't clean it.

"This little bit couldn't find a place in the Doctor's stomach because he's not used to eating. But drink that vegetable soup; it's all energy. Who heals the Doctor when he gets sick?"

Of course Maurice was fond of me too in a dry way and saw to it I had everything I needed, but he worshipped Péloc. No one could be distant with Péloc; he evaporated all tensions, and people unmasked their vulnerable souls to him.

Once Péloc pointed out a picture hanging over a glass cabinet. It was a sunny Italian landscape that seemed to have been put in a shady corner intentionally. I had tried to move it to a better place, but the next day it reappeared over the glass cabinet again.

"What's that a picture of? I can't see it very well," Péloc said.

"It's a landscape of Verona, Monsieur," Maurice replied.

"Has it always hung there?" I asked casually.

"No, it used to be on the other side of the room."

"Then why . . . ?" I stopped abruptly, for Maurice's mouth had hardened to a closed line. He waited a few moments for me to continue, then left.

★

Alchemy was already declining at the beginning of the eighteenth century, which was clearly aware of the obscurity, error, greed, and ignorance generally associated with its practice. Men were intoxicated with the new "enlightenment" and had never even guessed the secret essence of this millennia-old science. They were elated because they had managed to beat to death the first two letters of the ancient word with their new minor discoveries.

Modern chemistry had been born and the elements were rapidly being discovered. Both the Aristotelian concept of earth, water, fire, and air and the alchemical concept of mercury, sulphur, and salt were being assaulted by the results of experiments. Air and water turned out to be composite bodies with the quantities of their relative elements carefully calculated. Processes of chemical analysis were being refined and made sufficiently reliable for gold and silver to be distinguished from their alloys, thus eliminating both honest mistakes and deliberate frauds.

But it wasn't just the progress of science that brought alchemy into disrepute. Many people began researching its historical background in an effort to destroy even the roots of the "rotten tree" of alchemy. They heaped scorn and disdain on titans like Hermes Trismegistus, Geber, Basilius Valentinus, and Paracelsus. These youngsters were proud of their imaginary victory and really believed they had finally gotten rid of these magical sources of light, when actually they were just blocking the sun from their eyes with their hands.

Dr. Péloc watched this new, merciless religion dubiously. The two of us discussed the intellectual revolution at length, as befitted spectators watching the preparations for a bloody play of social and spiritual transformation.

"I can't criticize their discoveries," Péloc told me. "I've seen these magnificent chemical experiments myself and I know they're important. I also know that this chemistry will eventually transform the entire world. It's just the priggishness of these youngsters that makes me angry. They're at the beginning of a new science and they act like they're at the end. They think that since they've laid a new foundation for the future they can destroy the classical masterpieces of the past without even bothering to try to understand them. After all, a healthy present can only come from the past, just as a child can only come from his parents. Chemistry is on the point of committing patricide. Of course there have always been times when the past has been resolutely buried under the influence of revolutionary ideas; various physical and spiritual cataclysms have destroyed powerful and highly developed civilizations. Then the survivors and their conquerors invariably fall back into primitive darkness.

"For instance," Péloc continued, "how much do we know now about the superior astronomical and mathematical knowledge of Chaldea and Egypt? And about their traditions and philosophy that are hidden in those symbolic hieroglyphs? We are attracted by the lucid surface of the Greek intellect, but we are very far from understanding its profundity and the insights of Orpheus, Pythagoras, and the Eleusian mysteries.

"The true mission of alchemy is to guard this esoteric tradition, and the artificial obscurity that has been built up around it is simply a smoke screen to guard the sanctuary. You can't blame the Adepts for resorting to such measures. There are plenty of examples in history of the deadly perils of bigotry against which they had to protect themselves. The burning of the library at Alexandria and Savonarola's fanatical vandalism are clear examples of the fanaticism; be it religious or scientific, that is the worst enemy of eternally valid traditions.

"True science and tradition can be opposed only temporarily. The un-compromising scientist who traverses his path honestly simply makes a long detour before arriving at the realization that all roads lead to the mystery of the Creative Spirit. That's where the traditional initiate starts out.

"First science has to reduce matter to a system. Then it has to reduce the system still further until it becomes a spiritual principle. Chemistry has started this process and it has given the properties of matter easily understood names for the first time. True alchemy knew these properties just as well or even better, but it clothed them in figurative language. Chemistry is obtaining its results by experimentation and deals only with effects." He paused. "The great analogies of alchemy deal with the causes. You don't have to be an oracle to see that for the next few decades — or centuries — chemistry will not heal internal diseases so well as the alchemist Paracelsus did, despite its important and useful discoveries. Paracelsus paid attention to the whole organism, the structure of body and soul, then eliminated the causes. Our chemists will be merely specialists for some time to come; they'll prescribe medications for individual organs without realizing that what helps one may well poison another."

"So you believe in the Doctor Universalis, Péloc?" I asked.

"Absolutely. I believe chemistry, and the medical science that depends on it, will eventually return to Paracelsus and thus come to respect the old traditions."

22

The Messenger of the "Lambs"

It was Dr. Péloc who brought Jean Lepitre to me. Péloc didn't relish the role but he couldn't refuse the man's request. He confessed awkwardly that he had said something that had roused Lepitre's curiosity about my strange house and library, and now the man was insisting on coming to see it no matter what. Péloc had tried to discourage him but Lepitre had a thick skin. He had finally wrestled a promise from Péloc at least to mention his interest to me.

"What kind of a person is this Jean Lepitre?" I asked cautiously.

"Well, he's a bit daft, but basically he's all right. Maybe he's more rigid in his ideas than other people. He has a small shop on the Rue Saint-Honoré; he sells devotional articles, old books, and various kinds of manuscripts. He also lives with an older woman in some sort of theoretical soul union; there's no physical contact between them. The two of them pray a good deal and they've also founded a few Bible study groups where they give lectures. Their groups do good deeds for one another, call each other brother, are careless about their dress, abstain from meat, and generally live in delirious loftiness. They believe that they gradually pass through two stages of sainthood."

"Ooff! That's a complicated doctrine."

"Oh, don't worry. Their reality is quite different from the world concept they've dreamed up for themselves. I know them fairly well through treating Lepitre's tuberculosis, and in my opinion all they lack are thought and sincerity. You see," Péloc elaborated, "they first delude each other and then their followers. The highest human sainthood requires an ecstasy other than theirs. Lepitre and his Rosalie Bault are both too passionate and they won't admit it. It's dangerous to deny the existence of the bodily passions. Rosalie Bault was deeply in love with the hectic young Lepitre, and it was only later that she changed from passionate woman to devoted pupil. As for Lepitre himself,

189

he is fired by the fevers of tuberculosis. Both of them clamp the lid on their emotional fires, and I'm afraid someday there's going to be an explosion."

I laughed. "Well, at any rate you've aroused my interest, Doctor, even if I have to put up with a conversion attempt. When do they want to come?"

He sighed. "Sunday."

★

After what Péloc had told me I wasn't surprised to see Rosalie Bault as well as Lepitre Sunday afternoon. They were a strange couple. Lepitre wore an outmoded broadcloth coat that vaguely suggested the priesthood. He was tall, stringy, and stooped, and the tight-kneed breeches and wrinkled cotton stockings showed how pitifully thin the man's legs were. His black, woolly hair had obviously never enjoyed the services of a comb, and there was feverish color in his cheeks. His formless lips appeared to be forever on the verge of an enraptured smile, and he had a habit of holding his head back and regarding you with half-closed, glittering eyes.

Rosalie Bault's face was a worshipful reflection of the man's. I have never seen a more slovenly woman, and yet I came to find out that she was far better educated than her partner. Her tangled hair, flabby skin, and faded clothes were positively repulsive in the unforgiving light of day. In some godforsaken forest she might have passed for a hermit, but for a woman to look thus in Paris roused my suspicions. Any extreme fashion, be it luxurious or slovenly, indicates a desire to be superior to other people.

Lepitre grasped my hand as if I were a vision of heaven. Speaking in a subdued voice he told me he had longed to know me and considered it a privilege and a joy to be under my roof. I was both shocked and embarrassed by his manner and worked to pretend that such effusions were normal. His breath was hot and putrid, and I wished he would quit holding my hand. For one horrid moment I thought he was going to kiss me but he desisted. I was somewhat upset as I ushered them into the salon and more than a little put out with Péloc. What did he mean by saddling me with this kind of people? Later I realized he was only the means that directed the inevitable to me; it would have come about in any case.

Lepitre began by informing me that we were all children of God and therefore brothers. Basically I agreed with him but his flowery, sugarcoated imagery repulsed me. Sickeningly sweet religion has always been repulsive to me though I feel very close to Christ and respect the simple prayer uttered in solitude.

But Lepitre and Rosalie relished these mawkish sentiments like fine wine.

Purplish blotches of excitement appeared on the woman's face and neck, and she would lick her lips nervously when her voice faltered. Lepitre's confidence grew by the minute; soon he was telling me how he and Rosalie lived in chastity and enjoyed only spiritual intercourse. This, he said, frequently lasted for hours.

"Very interesting," I said dryly. "And how do you — um — manage this spiritual intercourse?"

He was willing enough to tell me. Their beds were at opposite ends of a room that was divided down the middle by a curtain. When they went to bed they would extinguish their lights, lie down on their backs, and think about each other until they shivered with the heavenly pleasure of a steadfast, ardent love. This spiritual wedding was frequently so intense that they moaned, wept, laughed, and prayed in their ecstasy. I glanced over at Péloc; he looked like he had accidentally sat down on a bed of nails but was too polite to mention the matter.

Suddenly Rosalie leaned forward and put her hand on mine. "But you must come to one of our meetings! You may be one of us and simply not have realized it as yet. You know that the Lord is gathering His lambs for eternal life and preparing destruction for the wolves. The gates of hell will open one day and pour out a rain of fire, plague, and agony, with floods, earthquakes, and other natural wonders. And all the fornicators, and the people who are so proud of their intellect, and those who pursue this new science and neglect prayer, and the agnostics, blasphemers, drunkards, heathens, heretics, and Jews will be thrown under a big mill wheel and have their sinful, lusting flesh ground to bloody pulp. They will be the food of Satan until the end of time and then they will suffer eternal damnation." Her voice trembled with an almost sensual pleasure and she practically smacked her lips over all this destruction. I was revulsed.

"We have done our duty by warning you," Lepitre assured me solemnly. "The lambs await your coming."

So that's their game, I thought. Lepitre was presenting me with a card containing their complete address. "I will certainly come and see you," I told them, heartily wishing them outside the front door. They rose to take their departure, a procedure reminiscent of a limpet reluctantly detaching itself from something.

"Forgive me," Péloc whispered as he rose to follow them.

"Never," I replied, but I smiled as I said it, for at that moment I had no intention of ever visiting the lambs at the home of the Marquise D'Anjou.

★

"How in the world do you stand them?" I asked Péloc when he dropped in as usual the next evening. "How do you keep them from herding you into their fold?"

"Oh, I asked for a deferment," Péloc replied with his raffish smile. "I promised to jump on the ark at the last minute and reminded them that I now have other matters to take up my time. I think they've been quietly interceding for me with their bloodthirsty lord ever since. They're really not the monsters they seem to you. There's something pitiful about their faith. They really want to do good, you know, and the slightest deviation terrifies them. And the god they believe in is not at all understanding. He's always scaring them and he absent-mindedly forgets their virtues and remembers their faults. To top it off, he's left them room for a thousand individual doubts and has managed to give each small branch of the group the impression that it's the only one that has the truth and the others are going straight to hell.

"You can't imagine the dissension in that group," he continued. "They argue like they were a fully authorized ecumenical council. Lepitre and Rosalie are very bitter about the fact that the groups they've started have elected independent preachers who interpret the Bible to suit themselves. Some of them even publicly doubt Lepitre's call and question the purity of his relationship with Rosalie. Some of them don't believe in the immaculate conception, and some don't believe in the resurrection of the body. The group is a total Babel of primitive minds. They can't agree on anything because of their obstinate distrust of intelligence and reliance on the emotions. They've taken over the ship, slain its captain, the mind, thrown the helmsman overboard, and started steering solely by the wind. Now siroccos of sensuality and passion keep blowing their glowing devotion off course. They rise to the crest of selflessness and then tumble down into petty bickering inside a minute. One minute it's all tearful enthusiasm, and then a single word puts them in a rage. The whole lot spy on each other and discuss each other's private lives in public. They're always ready to denounce somebody in a flaming sermon, and the brother they denounce is always ready to start a counteroffensive. It's like living with a bunch of petulant prophets who are forgivingly concerned over the souls of those who persecute them." He broke off as I began to laugh, and the thing was so amusing that he himself had to join in.

"I may laugh," he told me, "but I refuse to say their cause is ridiculous. Just think of the amount of trouble they must give God! They're the most difficult beings in his creation. The unbelievers' denial asserts Him, the tenacity of the doubter summons Him, the humility of the simple leads them to Him — but these people make Him a monstrous, anthropomorphic Lepitre.

"I've long believed," Péloc continued thoughtfully, "that the skeptic will get to heaven quicker than these commission agents who try to lure everybody in, in hopes they themselves can squeeze through in the crowd. I think we'll find quite a few of them have been preaching the devil's words. And that's not just a sophistry, either. A sectarian's soul is like a junk shop — full of massive, unpleasant idols. About the only things it doesn't have room for are God and truth!"

I stared at him. The man had always been fascinating and entertaining; now I decided to lead him to talk about that innermost human secret, whose privacy increases with its profundity.

"God — you speak of Him with such certainty, Péloc. I envy you the strength of your conviction. It makes me feel lost."

"I think it's easier to talk about any relationship in the world than the one with Him." Péloc stared straight ahead as he spoke. "One reason I never mention Him is that my concept of Him is in a constant state of flux. When I was little, my God was somewhere behind the starry stage props, sitting on a throne and wearing a long beard. I thought of Him as a boring, distant old gentleman with whom I was due to have a painful interview after I died. Then in the difficult hour of adolescence He closed in on me and became a dark and unfeeling accuser who left me without any escape. When I got through that crisis, He shrank into insignificance, and I pulled Him out and looked at Him only when I was feeling pious. I gave Him various characteristics, made a fetish of Him, and flattered his vanity. I prayed to bribe Him, but I still considered Him only a Notable to whom formal homage was necessary.

"Then in my early adulthood I became interested in finding out who He really was. So I felt Him, weighed Him, and discovered He looked just like me and was just as finite and impotent. This being so, I killed Him and He stayed dead a long time. Now He exists as a ghost; I can attribute no form or shape to Him. He wanders around inside of me, deep in my vitals and yet elusive. He doesn't have a voice, just impulses that reach up to the threshold of thought. And yet those impulses are more real than any other thought or word in the visible world around me. God is more than anything I know or even know about."

We sat silent for a moment. His words had recalled my own dead God, killed by the precision logic of Homonculus. Strangely I felt that despite my improbable circumstances, Péloc and I had had similar experiences. There was a short, embarrassed silence while we tried to find the road back from infinity.

"By the way, what kind of person is this Marquise D'Anjou?" I asked finally.

"Would you like to meet her?"

"God forbid! But I do like to hear about queer specimens."

"Oh, well, the Marquise D'Anjou is nothing like the alarming couple who visited you. She's a well-groomed, educated widow — it was her husband's death that herded her into the lambs' fold. Before that she was just another high-born woman, except that in the court's opinion she was scandalously faithful to her husband. He died young; they had been married just ten years. When he died, she felt that all the joy of life had gone with him, and she made persistent attempts to follow him. Since she was deeply religious, she wouldn't commit suicide directly, but she did the next best thing. She would sit naked after bathing with all the windows open to the winds of February. She would visit the plague houses and drink from the cups of the stricken, but she never got so much as a common cold. Finally a dream convinced her that she was wrong and that she had not only a duty to her children but also some mission that would appear in time.

"Not long after that she and her children and Jeanne Girard, their governess, were driven into a small shop on the Rue Saint-Honoré by a rainstorm. Jeanne incidentally was the one who had had that important dream. Thus Lepitre, opportunely surrounded by his devotional objects, landed his biggest fish. Really it was all that meddling Jeanne's doing.

"So now the Marquise D'Anjou is the lambs' financial prop and provides them with a base of operations. She is a little puzzled by the whole thing and a little reserved, but she serves them gratefully because she believes they are the cause to which God directed her. She sees it as a penance to prepare her to rejoin her lost husband forever."

"All this is very moving," I said skeptically, "but I don't see how a well-educated, sophisticated lady could fall for the well-meaning chatter of a servant who has too much imagination."

"The Marquise says there were things in the dream that only she and her husband knew about and that that proves it was a direct message from him."

"A shrewd servant can find out anything she wants to."

"True enough," Péloc replied, "but Jeanne wasn't hired until after the Marquise died five years ago; she never knew him in person. Yet in her dream she saw him in the moss green dress suit he wore to the reception at Versailles where the two first met and fell in love. The suit itself got lost before they even married; it was packed in a box that fell off the carriage into a river while the Marquis was traveling. Furthermore he had never been painted in it and it was not the type of suit he usually wore, though of course the Marquise cherishes her memory of it. Yet Jeanne described it in every detail — color, shape of buttons, the pattern of brocade on the doublet, and the type of lace on the collar.

"Jeanne saw the Marquis sitting on the curve of a fountain with one hand on his sword and his legs crossed. He was nervously shaking his foot, obviously waiting for someone. That had been a habit of the Marquis' but nobody had mentioned it since his death. Jeanne saw that there was a yellow paper boat in the fountain and that the Marquis impatiently threw pebbles at it till it sank. This was exactly the way the Marquise had seen him two days after they first met; this was the time and place where they had declared their love — which indeed seemed to have endured beyond the grave.

"In Jeanne's dream it was she who came out of the forest to meet the Marquis, who was understandably disappointed — she's a fat, pig-eyed female. He jumped up with a despairing gesture. 'She didn't come this time either! For God's sake, tell her not to cry so much! I can't get in contact with her because of her despair.' He then made those comments about the children's need of her and her coming mission."

"It's really interesting," I mused.

"It is. But if you knew Jeanne . . ."

"What about her?"

"Well, I can think of better mailboxes for messages from beyond, but then man's ways are not God's ways. The Marquise swears by her, of course. She asks her advice about everything, keeps anxious tabs on her dreams, and showers her with presents. Aside from her strange gift, Jeanne is just a cunning, selfish woman who knows how to exploit a good thing. She craves applause like a ballerina, and everything she does is obviously premeditated."

"You think the woman's a fraud, Péloc?"

"Well . . . partially. Boundaries are awfully indistinct in this area. Jeanne has some talents that are worthy of notice, but talents like these always manifest themselves rarely and unexpectedly. You can't order or direct them. That's where most people who have them usually fall down. But Jeanne knows the art of filling in the intermissions of her revelations with tales spun to fit the foibles of human nature; she's been very successful that way with her mistress and the lambs. The only people more numerous than the fraudulent are the gullible. Her dreams are all the rage; she has a whole court of admirers. There's a fellow on the Territorial Council named Cortey who stakes his life on her. He'd impale anybody who dared to doubt her divine mission. Of course he's just a cantankerous half-wit who trails around after her like a drunken dog, but she has lots of people dancing to her tune. The Marquise pampers her outrageously to keep her in her employ."

"So who takes care of the children?"

"Well, Corinna is fifteen and she manages to look after her six-year-old brother through all the turmoil."

I laughed. "Well, now I don't need to meet them, Péloc. You've given me such a word picture I couldn't learn more if I knew them for years."

"Oh, I doubt it. Pictures of women are always incomplete, you know; their images are as numerous as the men who reflect them."

"You're an expert on women too?" I could not forbear to tease. "I haven't seen that side of you."

A gentle, ironic smile touched the thin face. "*Apage, Satanas!* I know enough about them to stay away from 'em. I am simply their friend who hears the miserable and often hair-raising secrets of their bedrooms. I pity and heal them, but otherwise — there are some bottles that should be left corked."

"Anybody who's got that bad an opinion of women usually has a great deal of experience."

"I'm not about to tell you any ribald adventures, young man," Péloc replied promptly. "I have much the same opinion of men. The whole drama of men and women is a poor, ugly thing if you aren't drunk with nature's wine. Somehow or another I don't seem to have any in my blood. I'm stone cold sober in a drunken world. I find my flushed fellow creatures a little peculiar but I understand their condition. It's my job to hold their heads when they need to vomit. That's all."

Maurice shuffled into the den, the flame of his candle throwing his wrinkled face into sharp relief. One by one he lit the candles so that the book bindings and polished furniture shone. Péloc yawned.

"All the same, I'm sorry you haven't met the Marquise D'Anjou."

"Is she so beautiful then?"

"Beautiful? More motherly and comforting really. The daughter, on the other hand . . ."

"What about her?" I prodded.

"A strange little bit of Eros. Right now she's like an excitingly talented sketch, but later — she'll cause some turmoil, I think."

After Péloc had left, I sat for a long time thinking about the widowed Marquise, her prophetess Jeanne, and the girl Corinna, who was destined to cause romantic turmoil. I had no idea the girl would begin with me.

23

Astral Waves

The minute Péloc came in, I knew he was trying to keep from telling me something. He seemed excited and troubled, clearing his throat and pacing until I felt downright sorry for him.

"Get it off your chest, Doctor, and you'll feel better."

He stopped and stared at me. "Why do you say that?"

"Is it that puzzling?"

"No, that is . . ." He blinked guiltily. "I don't really want to get you mixed up in all this. I told them definitely I wouldn't relay the message . . ."

I couldn't help smiling at this. "Lepitre?"

"No, no!" He shook his head vehemently. "It's Jeanne. She's had a dream about you. I'm awfully sorry . . ."

I burst out laughing. "For goodness sake! No one can direct dreams!"

He made a face at me. "Jeanne can."

This stirred my curiosity. "What did she dream?"

"Well, it's a long story, and getting any meaning out of Jeanne's dreams is like fishing for cherries barehanded in a tub of syrup. To begin, she saw a large seaport from which two ships were about to sail. Naturally one was black and the other white. The decks of both ships were crowded with people. On the black ship hairy black devils — Jeanne's imagination is definitely artistic — were leaning over the bulwarks, embracing lewd, naked white women with glistening bodies. The lambs were on the white ship clothed in white garments naturally. The Marquise D'Anjou was at the head of this group. They were also at the bulwarks looking anxiously at the shore. And from both ships came the cry, 'Louis de la Tourzel, come and join us!' A thin, pale man stood on the shore wrapped in a dark cloak. He appeared to hesitate, trying to choose which ship to board. Just then a woman in a light blue silk cloak and hood stepped up to him. Jeanne couldn't see her face but she saw her take the man's arm and point toward the white ship. The woman spoke. 'Why are you running away from your destiny?' The man appeared surprised. 'I was waiting for a third ship, a blue one, but if you say this is the one I should take, heavenly messenger . . .' " He broke off, realizing that I could hardly contain my laughter; he was making all this bombast irresistibly funny. "Wait! This is a touching scene and I haven't finished yet. The tall man allowed the woman to lead him to the white ship, whose occupants sang psalms of triumph at the sight. The demons on the black ship yelled curses after him but the white ship set sail almost immediately after he boarded. It glided through the water for an instant, then took to the air with the wings of a dove. The black ship naturally burst into flames and sank into the maelstrom amid the wailing of all aboard."

"A nice subject for a moronic church painter," I said approvingly. "I see Lepitre has told Jeanne all he knows of my body and soul."

"No, what he mentioned was your social and financial status. Jeanne has a weakness for the nobility, especially rich nobility. They're the only ones she really wants to serve; she prefers to dream for them too whenever possible. Commoners and civilians are just tools to her. I think she hopes to lead one of her noble followers from the ethereal to the earthly and gain the marriage contract that could make her a permanent fixture where she is now only guest performer. And her followers are so blind she'll probably achieve it. Cortey is already being drawn in; he'd love to have her for a house oracle. He's taken to coming in and sitting on the edge of her bed every morning to hear her night's revelations before anybody else does. Jeanne is certainly skillful enough to bridge the short distance from the edge of the bed, divert his ecstasy into a more profitable channel, and then show the discomfited Joseph the only gentlemanly solution." He paused. "But I forgot to tell you something about that dream. As the white ship flew to heaven and the black one sank, the woman in the blue cloak threw back her hood, and Jeanne saw that it was the Marquise's daughter Corinna, her nominal charge. She rushed over and spoke to her. 'How ever did you get here, Corinna darling? Let me walk you home.' The girl looked at Jeanne like she had never seen her before. 'I'm afraid I don't know you, and my name is not Corinna. It's Marietta.' Then she turned and left hurriedly."

★

You can imagine the sudden excitement that surged through me. How had the name of that woman — my mother and liberator, the person to whom I felt closest and whom I saw as the solution to my life — gotten involved in that vulgar, contrived farce? Jeanne had seen her in blue silk, the pure azure of the spirit, the color that meant her . . . Why had she sent a message by that fraudulent woman? How was Jeanne a better tool than my own yearning soul? I couldn't understand, but I heard a joyous peal of bells within me. Corinna — Marietta. Marietta — Corinna!

★

The Marquise D'Anjou received me that Friday. The D'Anjou palace had been built only fifteen years before and, like all of its period, was pompous, massive, and ornate. It was just like the rococo lady — glittering with silk and jewels and totally unwashed. Its seventy-foot halls were walled with brocade and mirrors and its floors were inlaid. The rooms were decked with dreamy Gobelins, filmy Chinese vases, slim, curving ottomans, small tables of pure silver, chairs whose backs formed Aeolian harps, silk pouffes, decorative porcelain fireplaces, silver candelabra — and there wasn't a bathroom in the house. I later found out that Corinna had managed, after a terrific struggle, to get herself a hip bath. This stood in a corner of her dressing room, covered with a blanket as though it were indecent. The delicately ornamented chamber pots, of course, were highly visible.

The lambs met in a large room paneled in creamy damask. When Péloc and I got there, only a few people were present but rows of chairs indicated that more were expected. I looked around the gathering and found that, as I had suspected, they were a strange lot. They were conversing together in small groups, but those who were looking toward the door stopped and stared at me, the "new soul" in their midst. Abruptly they parted to make way for Lepitre's enraptured figure to float over to me. He had his hands folded in front of him like a priest, and he held his head piously on one side. Rosalie, still in her rags, trotted behind him like an ancillary limb. I thought about ducking out but it was too late.

"Our dear brother! At last you come to us!" I was only slightly mollified by the fact that at this point he tripped over the carpet and regained his balance only after some rather unpriestlike and turbulent flailing.

Somehow I managed to get through the eager greetings and questions of this odd group. They praised me to the skies and declared they knew I would be a munificent contributor to their cause. Finally I was able to join Péloc in the alcove from which he had been shamelessly enjoying my ordeal.

"You know you're going to hell for this," I muttered.

"Maybe so," he replied unrepentantly, "but the expression on your face during Lepitre's speech was worth it."

"But where are our hostess and her daughter and their prophetess?"

"Oh, the Marquise and Jeanne will come in when everyone has arrived. Corinna doesn't come to these meetings at all. Jeanne and the Marquise insist that she is still too young to be interested in such things, but personally I believe religion bores her. She seeks another type of entertainment."

I was disappointed because I had thought I could talk to Corinna at once, and Péloc's remarks merely added to my emotional confusion. This Corinna didn't sound like a tender, pure Marietta. Yet I determined to stay, no matter what, and learn why the dream goblin had lured me here. I spoke abruptly. "I really want to meet Corinna though. That's why I'm here."

Péloc instantly covered his surprise with a tactful neutrality. "Well, there's nothing to keep you from meeting her. There's always a point at these meetings at which it is possible — nay, wise — to leave unnoticed. Corinna is always glad to see me, and she will welcome you as my friend."

I laughed at the sharpness of his glance. "No, Péloc, I'm not a lecher or a sentimental jackass. The only reason I'm interested in Corinna is Jeanne's dream. You see, there really *were* two cherries in the tub of syrup. There were two incidents in that dream that have made me very curious about the blue-cloaked woman Jeanne thought was Corinna."

"Damn the woman!" Péloc grumbled. "She keeps confusing me. Every time I finally decide she's a fraud, she produces a genuine phenomenon." Just then a tall, ascetic man with a tousled white mane entered the room. Péloc poked me. "There's one of the counterprophets, the painter Frederic Boisson. Lepitre and Rosalie call him a spy of the Antichrist. They'd love to throw him out of the fold, but he has too many followers. He's a better speaker than Lepitre and he lives alone in poverty. Since he's really talented, he can express his monomania the better, and the Marquise and Jeanne like him. That effectively ties Lepitre and Rosalie's hands."

"Why do they hate him so much?" I asked, watching him step into the group to be surrounded immediately by followers.

"Boisson's pet subjects are the creation, the Book of Revelations, and the end of the world. He has his own arbitrary explanations of these things and they are diametrically opposed to Lepitre's arbitrary explanations. The two of them can make quite a scene but actually they live for each other. Each studies, writes, and speaks primarily to refute the other." He pointed to another group just coming in. "There's George Duflin and his disciples," he said. "They don't believe in the immaculate conception, and this upsets Lepitre just as much as if they didn't believe in his own virtue, which they don't."

Duflin proved to be a small, thickset albino with a wide nose and sugary smile. His complexion was ruddy, in contrast to most of the people there, and I was to learn later that he could quickly fly into a rage. He spoke with a slobbering hiss and constantly rubbed his hands together like a merchant just making a good deal. His walruslike wife had borne him ten children; she must have known all about immaculate conception. Their oldest children, fidgety girls who seemed to be all hands and feet, accompanied them.

Professionally Duflin was a goldsmith. He was one of the rising stars of the new order, made a citizen by Louis XV, and he had attended the university, patronized the arts, bought books, and amassed a fortune in industry. It was his type that was later satirized by Molière as Monsieur Jourdain, the "bourgeois gentilhomme." Péloc said it was a desire to hobnob with the aristocracy that had brought him to the Marquise's salon to begin with, but he quickly discovered that the lambs provided rich soil for his priggish vanity. Since he was better educated than most, he soon discovered a calling as a hair-splitting preacher; he was a positive gourmet of shallow and pompous words. His small mind budded with joy as he became convinced he was called to teach the world, and he welcomed conflict as a young dog does. Heaven was indeed a profitable investment, he discovered, because he could collect the interest here on earth.

Of course no one could be a greater contrast to Lepitre and Rosalie. They quarreled quite frequently, Duflin's annihilating sarcasm against Lepitre's piping assaults. Boisson always retreated into complacent superiority on these occasions until somebody took a verbal swipe at him, at which point he would enter the lists with his fiery verbal flailing.

The next person to come in looked like a gypsy, with the shadow of a beard around his lips. There were ugly scabs on his chin and forehead and his feet were surprisingly small. "That's Martin Allais," Péloc told me. "He's half Spanish and totally scoundrel. Came to Paris not too long ago. He's supposed to be a physician. I've heard he trained to be a priest but had to give up the cloth just before ordination because of a sex scandal. He's certainly a very learned theologian, but on the other hand nobody's ever seen his doctor's diploma. He advertises his celibacy, but somehow there always seem to be women around him. He plays on their sympathies by talking pathetically about his weak heart and numbered days. For a man who's dying, he's mighty cheerful. He's the only really evil man in the whole group. I'm sure he's just a charlatan who's found a happy hunting ground in the Marquise's salon, but his numerous followers are sure he can heal both their bodies and their souls. He lives very well indeed on their dazzled gratitude."

I watched Allais' priestly progress across the room. "Why don't you expose the fellow?" I asked.

"Well, for one thing," the doctor replied, "people would think I'm professionally jealous and afraid of losing my fees. Besides, I know these people. Logic just bounces off them like arrows off a stone wall. They see what they want to see and believe what they want to believe. Allais really is an excellent speaker and an original healer. You see, all these people live in an ill-defined morass of emotionalism, and they resent it when somebody tries to pull them out. One thing I've learned over many years is that you have to let people live their lives their own way. If you force them out of some experience they have to have, they just go find it somewhere else. Of course it takes a good deal of self-control to stand by and watch somebody run headlong into disaster despite the warnings of their friends — but after a while you get the knack."

The groups were beginning to take shape around their various leaders. I noticed that the group around Lepitre, men and women alike, looked bewildered and disordered. Their drab, untidy clothing was so uniform it looked almost like the garb of some obscure religious order. They talked, whispered, and clung to one another like adolescents about to go skinny-dipping.

Boisson's group was both more colorful and more grotesque. There were an elegantly dressed old lady whose face was lined with sorrow, an art student whose too-innocent eyes bore the marks of premature debauchery, a statuesque girl who was obviously a model and had probably got religion modeling for a puritan painter, a stern mother with a rigidly subdued daughter, an eccentric sporting beard and sandals, a hysterical old woman who laughed and cried by turns, and a youth who was no doubt trying to model himself on Boisson and was going crazy in the attempt. I later learned that one of the bizarre figures was a mad sculptor who was devoting his entire life to one work — which he refused to show to anybody.

Duflin's group was entirely different. They seemed to have achieved a compromise between body and soul and were lounging on the balconies of the ascetic movement in the firm conviction that they were taking part. The area around him was bright with the gaudy dresses of upstart women who obviously had a taste for rich foods. Madame Duflin was an imposing mountain of flesh with the vacant gaze of a ruminating cow. The men of the group were all like Duflin or tried to be. Some of them were his employees, overawed of both their master and their surroundings.

Duflin's two daughters were overflowing from two of the high-backed chairs like hippopotamuses, obviously greatly embarrassed by the noises the delicate things made under their weight. I was sure they were going to fall out of their chairs or collapse them sooner or later, and I must admit I rather looked forward to the event, though I pitied their adolescent agonies.

People were still arriving, and the air was filled with all the little murmurs and scrapings of a waiting crowd. Suddenly I noticed a dark, bearded newcomer who was dressed for all the world like a Hindu penitent. I found out from Péloc that he was a cabinetmaker named Charles Banet, a leading light among the lambs. He made his followers abstain from both meat and salt, holding that salt was the devil's essence. It was his theory that if all salt could be eliminated from the body, the soul would be free of sin. He was the antithesis of Duflin, rather than Lepitre, and it was his pleasure to call Duflin's followers carrion eaters, Pilates, and Pharisees. They retaliated by accusing him of secret gluttony, immorality, and drunkenness.

I was literally dizzy from watching this myriad crowd and absorbing its vibrations. I had never before been among so many unpleasant people.

At last the double doors from the interior of the house opened and a tall, dark-clad woman entered on the arm of a short woman with coarse features, obviously the Marquise D'Anjou and her fashionable prophetess. A tall, bony man of about fifty hovered protectively at Jeanne's side — Cortey, her spellbound council member. Jeanne's dreams were supposed to have healed him of a nasty social disease, and Péloc told me in a whisper that he was writing a book about this new Pythia that he planned to publish at his own expense.

The Marquise D'Anjou was still a beautiful woman. She was a trim brunette with a gentle, heart-shaped face, doelike eyes, and lips that were both sensitive and sensuous. Her speech was a fashionable drawl, but the predominant impression she left was one of goodwill, grief, and impressionability. She was one of those helpless beings who offer themselves humbly to any strong personality, a tacit invitation Jeanne Girard's ambitious soul understood very well.

The lambs surrounded their benefactress respectfully, but most of their attention was really directed to Jeanne, their favorite. Cortey, acting like a pouting child, tried to keep the crowd away from her; he feared they would "burden her sensitive soul with their bad emanations and drain her precious strength with their violent desires." The man was both offensive and slightly crazy, but his devotion to the thoroughly unworthy woman was touching.

Lepitre himself brought me to the Marquise, the crowd making way for us.

I leaned over her hand and kissed it. Seen up close, her face was marked with loneliness, and she was older than I had at first thought. She responded to my politenesses with a friendly, motherly smile and invited me to come to their meetings whenever I could. Behind her face I could see the irresolute core of a woman who lived on imagination and memories. When reality touched her, she started like a woman wakened from some dreams.

Jeanne was impatiently waiting to greet me, and I too looked forward to the event, despite her repulsive appearance and personality. She almost melted when I kissed her hand as though she were not merely a governess. She blushed, laughed a little, and most unnecessarily shook my hand, but soon her native cunning reasserted itself. Raising her head, she stared me full in the face, her own slowly assuming an expression of exaltation. Then she declaimed, "Yes! This is the man in my dream. This is Louis de la Tourzel!"

The crowd thrilled to her words, and Cortey got tears in his eyes. All watched me, obviously expecting an admission of humble conversion. Further I felt that in this crowd of fanatics I dared not avoid the issue or speak with cautious moderation. I had my cue and I took it. I bowed to Jeanne again.

"I confess myself greatly shaken by your dream, Mademoiselle; it has already brought significant changes in my life. I hope that the Marquise will honor me with a visit so I can have the pleasure of your company also."

Her response was so direct as to be positively crude. "But of course we'll come, Monsieur de la Tourzel! We've heard so much about your strange house and that magnificent library and your odd little butler." It was characteristic of her to speak for the Marquise, who sanctioned her silently.

The two women now went to sit on the podium, where Lepitre awaited them. In the first row of chairs Rosalie's face dreamed up at him with greasy light. Her eyes were wet with tears obviously waiting to flow, and she carefully mirrored her idol's expression as he looked over the assembly with lifted head and half-closed eyes.

The tattered Lepitreans gathered around Rosalie, and Boisson and his followers scornfully filled the next two rows. Rosalie overheard part of a remark from one of them and turned to deliver a mean, hissing response before resuming her saintlike position. The Duflins filled the rows behind the Boissons, the delicate chairs groaning under their robust figures. In the next row sat Martin Allais, surrounded by a tight group of women who leaned forward so as not to miss his slightest word. Charles Banet eschewed chairs altogether to sit on the floor, and his grim disciples followed him, looking proud and uncomfortable.

Finally Lepitre shook a silver bell, and the whole crowd stood and fell silent. Lepitre carefully replaced the bell on the table and pressed his finger-tips together. "Let us praise God," he intoned softly, then curved his neck like a rooster about to crow and launched into the hymn in a surprisingly high falsetto.

"Father of the Trinity,
Our Beloved Father,
Wrathful and Most Glorious God,
Ever Hallelujah."

The assembly joined in gradually and arrived at such a frightful outburst on the hallelujah that I felt quite uncomfortable. This sounded like a war cry. There were about ten verses to the thing, all saccharine until they came to the bit about punishing sinners. All the diverse elements in the hall appeared unified in their pious emotions.

I looked around at the happy, intense faces. There was a touching simplic-ity about the whole thing; could such people really snarl and fight with each other? It hardly seemed possible as they boomed out their heavenly passion. The scene that followed exceeded my wildest imaginings.

Lepitre began what was apparently his usual monthly introduction from which I learned that "It is now the fourth year that the Lord has herded us into this dear and blessed pen." I glanced sideways at the Marquise to see what she thought of this reference to her mansion, but she was merely smiling placidly. It was obvious she was present in body only and was really enjoying a secret, ethereal rendezvous with her departed lover.

Suddenly this gentle still life animated only by Lepitre's droning burst into the most awful witches' orgy I had ever witnessed outside the astral world. I had been dozing and could not imagine what had upset everyone so much. Panicked by all the shrieking, I was about to leave hurriedly when I saw Péloc smiling at me. He winked.

"What in the world happened?" I asked as best I could over the uproar.

"Oh, nothing much," he said calmly. "Lepitre just told them that the Holy Spirit had revealed through Rosalie the seven truths of attaining saint-hood, and Duflin remarked that next he would be claiming Rosalie was the prophet Isaiah. This upset Boisson, since his disciples have lately come to the conclusion that *he* is Isaiah, so . . ."

I sat down and put my head in my hands.

Rosalie's head rose like a Gorgon above the enraged mob. Her mouth worked but her words were inaudible, and she disappeared as though she had been pulled down. Lepitre, red-faced, was shouting and waving his arms.

He grabbed his bell and shook it, but this only increased the confusion. Suddenly Boisson's bass clove the din.

"You have seen him and known him not. Woe unto ye, hypocritical Pharisees!"

"What's he talking about? Who have we seen? Who didn't we recognize?"

Boisson's face glowed with insane arrogance and rapture. "Isaiah!" he bellowed.

There was a silence, then Rosalie gasped, "But that's unthinkable!"

A chorus of sneers rose from Duflin's followers.

"The hour of your trial draws nigh!" Boisson boomed. "Thus the Lord spake to me. Repent ye, for the trumpets of the Last Judgment even now are sounding. The gates of heaven and hell gape open . . ."

"Enough! Silence!" Banet's followers were yelling and stamping in fury. I later learned that Banet had decided he was John the Baptist and was therefore jealous of anyone else claiming to be a prophet.

"Antichrist! Down with the Antichrist! Drive the wolf away from the lambs! We mustn't tolerate tares among our wheat!"

A pale old woman dressed in black stood up, hands raised in horror. "Peace, brethren! Lambs should not quarrel with one another!"

"The Lord drove the moneychangers from the temple!" Duflin yelled.

"Amazing how quickly every violently inclined person lights on that story," Péloc murmured.

I took the hint. We left.

24

The Black Eros

The noise diminished gradually as we walked down the winding, mirrored corridors. By the time Péloc led me into a small, apple-green parlor, it was only a slight murmur. The sun had already set but the silvery twilight that peered in at the window was still tinged with it. Beyond the window a well-groomed park looked trim and bored.

Corinna sat drawn up over a sketch pad and Christian, the little boy, was lying on his stomach looking at a massive folio of pictures. Just above the ottoman where Corinna sat was a Gobelin of the naked Diana hunting. When we came in, the children looked up in delight but they became timid as wild creatures when they saw me behind Péloc.

It's hard to recall the first moment I saw Corinna. "First" isn't accurate either. The slightly angular curves of her boyish body and her awkward yet coquettish charm filled me with a deep, unconscious desire. Love had never meant much to me in the walking hell that was my life. The episode with Charlotte Bruggendorf had left me nauseated and unfulfilled and had served only to convince me to avoid the astral world of the senses. I had always been partnerless, a loner, a grim traveler with first a transcendental ambition and later a dark secret.

My avid quest for the Elixir and then my efforts to escape from the effects of it had consumed all my strength and left me with no time to lust for women. This region slumbered latent, a blank spot on my personal map. I did not know the mad, altruistic desire to dissolve into another being or the torments of jealousy, the subservience that makes you despise yourself, or the violent passion that might just as well be hate that comes when the loved person turns out to be viciously different from what you'd believed but still fatally indispensable. I didn't know the million faces of tenderness or the blazing desire that distorts everything into either feverish beauty or unbearable pain. None of these things I knew until I met Corinna, the hypnotically beautiful, unconsciously wicked, debased tool of the dark side of Eros.

When she straightened up on the ottoman and smiled that timid, bold smile, wild excitement pulsed through me. I felt like a gawky child before her, though she was still as undeveloped as a Malay boy, with long limbs, narrow hips, broad shoulders, and velvety Creole skin. Her thick, dark hair was tied with a green ribbon and framed the narrow, charming face with curls. Her eyebrows curved like an Oriental's, and she had sparkling, slanted green eyes. Those eyes were inexpressibly tender; they radiated a soft light that begged for affection. Her very glance felt like a shivering caress. She had slightly protruding cheekbones, a short, tilted nose, and full red lips that curved ever so slightly downward. When she was serious, her face looked sad and sweet. When she laughed, her snow-white teeth sparkled and her expression became mocking and shamelessly provoking. Midway between these two faces she had a gentle and infinitely attractive child's smile, with tiny dimples. And she had as many other alluring faces as nature itself.

And how hungry she was! How insatiably hungry for the diverse varieties of lovemaking and all the little games that could be played with them. How frighteningly docile and how ingenious she was, while being totally without conscience or scruples. For her there were no boundaries and obstacles, and no shade of guilt plagued her soul. She simply played and enjoyed. It didn't matter who was set aflame by her glance or how much misery she caused. There was something less than human about her sensuous insensitivity and that careless, carefree laughter.

The nymphs that titter in the fantasies of the astral plane are like she was; they are the prompting demons of the nymphomaniacs who throw scorn on the gentle, Isis-like mother and her followers, those faithful women who are the eternal bearers, nurses, and grief-sharers of men. These demons give the fornicators a cheap victory because they have the horrible key — a lack of scruples or sympathy. And yet, though they don't mean to be, they are our teachers, as are all things that cause great pleasure or horrible pain. Thus Corinna became my teacher.

I didn't even notice Christian for a while. From the moment I met Corinna, I saw everything else through a haze for many months — until a series of brutal shocks restored me to normal vision. When I finally saw him, I noticed that he was a serious-faced little boy and remembered suddenly that his mother had been carrying him when her husband died.

I was still groping for words when Corinna, stimulated by the presence of a man, dropped her shyness like a cloak. Later she told me she had fallen in love with me then, and like a stupid fool I rejoiced over the matter. I didn't know how sincere and thorough was her desire nor how brief, nor how changeable were its objects. Considering her other adventures, she was faithful to me for an astonishingly long period and even continued to return to me after gross infidelity. I meant more to her than most of the men she ruined, but that was cold comfort.

But now she was speaking with a curious, provocative charm. "Louis de la Tourzel, I presume?" I bowed wordlessly and took her outstretched hand, making her burst into a peal of laughter. "My, but poor Jeanne had to work hard to get you up here. She described you quite well in her dream — tall, pale, and romantic." Her voice was mocking.

"Mademoiselle flatters me."

Corinna winked like an accomplice. "Well, you see, I was awfully curious about you," she blurted out thoughtlessly.

I could hardly speak for the pounding of my heart. "Why?"

"Why Dr. Péloc has told me so many interesting things about you."

"I'm sorry," Péloc was embarrassed, "but Mademoiselle insisted." I could have embraced him for arousing the girl's interest in me. Now she was looking at me with calculated coquetry.

"You will show me your lovely old house, won't you? And all the weird books and your butler and all?" Her body arched toward me like an affectionate cat. I stuttered as I told her I would be delighted if she could visit me when her mother and Jeanne did. Then I reached for the drawing she had been working on, but she put it behind her back. "No, it's no good. Besides . . ." Then suddenly she turned and showed it to us. It was a childish drawing of a big-bosomed nude lying in bed with a lanky, horse-faced man leaning over her. "Don't you recognize them?" I shook my head. She wrote in large letters "Jeanne and Cortey." Then she burst into mischievous laughter and danced around the table.

★

My encounter with Corinna left me feeling like any other lovesick fool. I stared broodingly at Louis de la Tourzel's gangling figure in the mirror. I had inherited my father's pale complexion and long frame, but I was also touched with Sophie Pétion's sensuous sentimentality.

For centuries my body had only been a changing, hostile shadow seen in various mirrors; my conscious mind had concentrated on my internal torture chamber. Suddenly I discovered that Louis de la Tourzel's body could be a tool of ecstasy, something to be proud of, a thing that could give pleasure mounting to unbearable pain.

So I had fashionable clothes made and bought wigs from the court hairdresser. I bought a fine ornamental equipage with thoroughbred Arab stallions and learned to ride. All this occupied a few weeks, while the magic thread of desire became thicker and thicker. There were only a few, brief encounters; I would send flowers and poems secretly, and she would wave from behind the curtains when I took long walks under her window.

Finally the Marquise D'Anjou, or rather Jeanne Girard, decided to visit me. It wasn't difficult to insure that Corinna came too, and the rest of my plan was already arranged. If Corinna loved me, all I needed to do was sue for Jeanne's favor with presents, money, and flattery. Then she would smoothly dream our marriage.

They came on a strange, end-of-April day, on an afternoon that seemed filled with restless, fragmented melodies. The sun was performing a whimsical veil dance with fluffy white clouds, and the wind stirred up the smells of dust and distant flowers. Yet there was still a touch of ice in the air.

The sun lit up my house, which was decorated for a rich banquet, and struck glittering shafts through the long-stemmed roses I had paid a small fortune for at the greenhouse. Maurice was arranging things with smooth efficiency, directing the temporary help with barely veiled disgust.

When the visitors came, the serious, old-faced Christian was with them. The Marquise apologized for bringing him; he had cried, she said, and insisted on coming. I assured her I was delighted to see him. Of course I was delighted; I was drunk and delirious. Corinna was close to me, in my house.

Already her velvety, almond-shaped eyes were immersed longingly in mine as she flashed me a shy, dimpled smile. Her slender, pliant body was set off by a scarlet velvet dress trimmed in antique lace, and a real pearl sparkled in the calyx of a golden lily pinned over her breast. She was so beautiful, so mysterious, so unreachable — I was quivering inwardly with desire and could hardly control my hand as I bowed over the ladies. As my burning lips branded Corinna's wrist, I saw her naked arm shiver just a little.

Péloc, dear, good Péloc, was there to help me overcome my confusion. He had managed to rearrange his busy schedule just to be present at my reception. He knew how I felt about Corinna and that I intended to marry her as soon as possible. And as a dazed lover I didn't listen to his veiled warnings and hints.

"I don't want to meddle," he told me, "but I wish you'd think things over before taking such an important step. Above all, use that keen observation of yours to examine the object of your affections." He was obviously searching carefully for just the right word as he continued. "It's always a good idea for someone in love to get to know his partner before the wedding. A person might have an outstanding personality and still not be suited to the proposed partner. Desire alone can only justify an alliance for a very short period of time."

I paid little attention to his cautious advice, but finally I got irritated at his persistence in discouraging my affection for Corinna. "For God's sake, Doctor, what's your objection to the girl? She's high-born and well-educated, and a baby couldn't be purer!"

"You think so, Monsieur?" His smile was resigned. "Remember, I've known and cared for Corinna for a long time. I should say I've known and pitied her. Now I'm afraid for her, for her chance to save herself from herself. And I will be frank with you, my friend. I'm afraid for you. I'd like to save you from her, even from the innocent, inexperienced child she is today."

"What in the world are you talking about, Péloc?"

"Remember how I described her from the first? I promise you I won't mention this again, but I think I owe it to myself to warn you that marrying Corinna can bring you both danger and misery. Corinna will never be a faithful wife. She's adventure, excitement, and lust personified, and she will be faithful only to the moment and only to herself. All her actions, even her toys, reflect this whimsical flame that will die after it has set everyone else ablaze and flare up again somewhere else entirely. Corinna's just a child now, but within her lies an ancient, debased magic element, something satanic under that dangerously attractive cover, an element that brings ruin and tragedy wherever it goes. Whoever is sucked into the vortex will perish or at least be crippled, and she, the vortex, will continue unperturbed and irresponsible until some cataclysm destroys her."

Strangely Péloc's words merely tantalized me and fanned the fire within me; the dark allusions were a sweet pain to my senses. "I love her," I repeated stubbornly, "and if I knew I were to be impaled for it tomorrow I would still love her. Corinna's turned you into a poet, at any rate; those are eloquent jeremiads. Maybe you are telling me God's truth or maybe just the results of something you've successfully repressed; whichever it is doesn't concern me. I may be on the rim of a vortex that will destroy me, but I have to continue toward it, burn my way through it if necessary. I can't avoid it. When I first saw Corinna, I knew I couldn't escape my fate."

We stared at each other; both of us realized I had unconsciously echoed the blue-clad woman of Jeanne's dream. But what connection was there between the ethereal Marietta and Corinna? What profound mystery had intermingled them in a dream message?

At last Péloc turned his gaze, looking sad and worried. Then he spoke softly. "In that case — well, I'll help you in any way I can if you care to accept my help."

I assured him that I was counting on him. I knew he had given me good advice, I told him, but he mustn't be upset if I didn't accept it.

But now the salon's polished mirrors reflected the light of the great silver candelabra, and Corinna's eyes, hazy from the heavy wine, blazed like the fire. Péloc was assiduously entertaining the Marquise and Jeanne, and Christian found ample amusement in my Indian ivory chess set.

Now Corinna and I played a delicious, secret game. I was showing her all my drawings, engravings, and books just so I could bend over her and touch her. She knew well enough what I was about, and I felt her long, slender leg press mine under the table. Presently she jumped up and announced in a smothered voice that she must hear again the musical clock in the dining room; she had forgotten the melody.

I followed her with trembling knees. As soon as we were in the dark corridor, she snuggled close against me, strong as a liana vine, and I embraced the strong body that pressed shamelessly into every curve of my own. I kissed her open mouth, then groaned with a tension I could no longer endure.

"You, you . . ." I stammered. "Look, you've got to leave. I'll hurt you, Corinna; you don't know the misery I can cause . . ."

But she was clutching my neck, gasping, "Kiss me again, more . . ."

I dove blindly into the deep red vortex. I kissed her ever more eager mouth and her neck and shoulders where her dress had slipped down. Then somebody slammed a door somewhere and we jumped apart and hurried into the dining room. Here she adjusted her dress and smoothed her hair; it was frightening how quickly she could compose herself while I still shook with the amorous fire. I stepped up behind her and slid my hand down her neck and shoulder to her waist.

"I love you, Corinna. My God, how I love you!"

She turned her head to face me. "Yes," she replied softly, "I love you too. Ever since I first saw you I've wished you would kiss me."

So we went back into the salon, and Corinna immediately attracted everyone's attention by beginning the clock's minuet in a clear, ringing voice. "I've finally got it!" she exclaimed, then continued singing.

I retreated into a window recess to hide my agitation. Outside it was beginning to blow up a storm; tiny pebbles were being hurled against the glass. I rang for Maurice to come and draw the curtains. As he passed the seven-branched candelabra, I noticed how drawn and tired he looked. Poor old man, I thought compassionately; the evening's almost been too much for him.

Suddenly the child Christian's voice broke the silence caused by the servant's entry. "Is it true that only those who want to die will die, Mama?" For a few seconds nobody answered this startling query, and Maurice turned from his work to stare at the boy. There was a strange tension in the air. For the first time, I really looked at the small Creole face with the dull, dark eyes. It was an ageless face — serious and almost grim.

"Wherever did you get that idea, son?" The Marquise sounded alarmed.

"Everyone dies, Christian," Jeanne Girard said unctuously, "but pure souls rise again."

The boy's face set in an obstinate expression, and he raised his voice. "I don't want to die, Mama, and I'm not going to." At this point he looked up, and I thought he was looking at Maurice, who stared at him unwinkingly, but I saw he was looking over the old servant's head at the picture above the glass cabinet. "I have always lived," Christian muttered stubbornly.

The Marquise D'Anjou stood up suddenly. "This child scares me."

I wanted to say something to reassure her, but I too was overcome by the ominous tension in the air. "You yourself speak often on the subject, Madame," I offered.

"But what can a child understand about all that, Monsieur de la Tourzel?" She took his hand to lead him somewhere to amuse himself, but the boy wouldn't move.

"Raise the candle, Mama, so I can see that picture," he demanded.

"Christian, you promised. You said you'd play quietly if I let you come."

Maurice shuffled forward, supporting his old body against the furniture, and lifted one of the heavy candlesticks. The picture over the cabinet seemed breathlessly alive in the flashing light, and Christian looked up at it and laughed.

"Look, Corinna!" he said, pointing. "It's Spring in Verona. I recognize it."

There was a loud crash. Maurice had fallen face forward onto the carpet. The candlestick had dropped from his limp hand, and the flames began to eat at the carpet. Péloc quickly ran and turned the butler over on his back, while the practical Jeanne helped me stamp out the fire. The Marquise and Corinna stood paralyzed, and Christian clung to his mother, whimpering. Then Péloc stood up.

"Get the boy out of here," he said softly.

"Is Maurice dead?" I whispered.

Péloc nodded.

Corinna told me later that there was a colored plate of that particular painting in an album Christian looked at frequently; she had often read him the text under the picture. It was obvious what had happened, yet — the fact that all of the links of the chain had been formed to convey the message to the old, tired servant was more than chance. I don't know if Christian really was de Assis, freed for a moment from the forgetfulness of childhood, or if his spirit merely temporarily assumed control of the child's sensitive nervous system. I only knew the boy's aura had shone with an occult glow in that sinister moment, and the shadow of a powerful being could be seen behind him. Certainly Maurice received his message and thus was at liberty to die.

★

I sincerely mourned this strange and eccentric person of whom I had become so fond. By the laws of similarity I have always been attracted to the unusual, the lonely, and the introverted. "The crowd" is more alien to me than are fish and insects. Yet I had to admit Maurice's death solved a sensitive problem, for I was determined to marry, and I knew that by Corinna's sparkling, luxurious standards Maurice would seem an intolerable old vulture. Nor could I imagine him controlling a household of maids. It was strange that he had accompanied me right to the threshold of my solitary cell.

★

The intuitive and servile Jeanne quickly divined my intent; looking back, it was probably what she'd been aiming for all along. Certainly my lavish gifts proved a great inspiration to her. The roll of brocade and jeweled rings produced beautiful and colorful dreams and when I slipped a pearl necklace into her hand, she immediately proceeded to dream that the Marquise D'Anjou agreed to give me the hand of her daughter. Though I was willing to use Jeanne for my purposes, the whole transaction disgusted me. I knew too that she was playing with forces that would eventually turn against her, but in my blind passion I didn't care. The daily secret meetings I had with Corinna inflamed my desire until it completely dulled my conscience.

We celebrated our engagement quietly at the Marquise's palace, and I requested permission to have the wedding a month to the day after the announcement. There were to be only a few friends present, chiefly Péloc. Of course we would have to put up with Cortey.

The lambs presented a knottier problem. We would have to invite all or none, else there would be a bloody revolution. Jeanne managed the whole thing skillfully by inviting the entire congregation "to sanction and bless this union born of a blessed and holy dream." By an ironic twist, our marriage was blessed and holy in exact ratio to the reality of the lambs' religion.

★

I completely renovated my house. The brooding spirit of old de Assis remained only in the library; the rest was playful, powdered Paris, the depraved and debauched city of Louis XV. The paneling was replaced by glittering mirrors and brocade; Corinna knew well how to select the shades that would complement her beauty. She was a tireless shopper, and I was proud to please her. She bought wrought silver salon trimmings and carriages from an exiled aristocrat and added to them Gobelines, vases, fine rugs, and heavy fabrics. For herself she bought fine lace lingerie worthy of a hetaera, pointed shoes encrusted with gems, multitiered wigs, jewel cases, perfumes, and incense. Her virtuous, absent-minded mother prepared her an elegant and proper trousseau at home but Corinna, with Jeanne at her side, reveled in the shops. This shopping and the necessity of concealing it from her mother distracted her temporarily from her amorous pursuits; she hardly had time for me.

As for me, I was fighting evil premonitions, deliberately closing my mind to my own uneasiness and Péloc's warnings. "She's still just a child," I told myself. "Her body may be ripe but her soul is still dormant. It is up to me to awaken it. When the first fires have subsided . . ." But I could think no further than that. I was engulfed in the flame and nothing else mattered.

The hectic month passed quickly and the long-awaited day dawned. Since the Marquise had gone into seclusion when her husband died, she was out of touch with most of the aristocracy, so most of our wedding guests turned out to be the lambs. They filled the small chapel on the Rue Saint Michel and then proceeded to the Marquise's sumptuous reception.

I can only remember a few foggy flashes of the whole affair, through which I moved like a sleepwalker. The images were wavering and unreal, and they kept approaching and withdrawing, just like the shapes in my astral world. Sometimes I would get a clear image of a familiar face among the gaudy, unkempt lambs, and I could feel Corinna's glove on my arm. I looked at the daring, enchanting profile that sometimes seemed so unfamiliar.

Suddenly I realized that I would have her naked in my arms that night. Somehow against the solemn notes of the organ this seemed terribly sinful and yet overwhelmingly desirable. I noticed nothing more until the tear-stained Marquise kissed me in a motherly way and the lambs flocked round to greet us.

Corinna squeezed my arm and whispered, "Rosalie's sweating even worse than usual today, and now she's going to kiss me. Do you think she ever kissed Lepitre?"

I had to choke back my amusement. "Only their souls kiss," I whispered back.

Corinna grimaced. "Now if Rosalie were a little prettier . . ." Then she put on an angelic expression and offered her forehead for the greasy old woman to kiss.

Just then Lepitre came toward me looking alarmingly exalted, so I quickly grabbed Péloc and shoved him between us so that he got the passionate kiss intended for me. Corinna had to press her face into her lace handkerchief to stifle a giggle, and Jeanne rushed up to her with motherly concern.

"You go right ahead and cry, dear. A crying bride is a happy woman." This promptly caused Cortey to start crying, and Corinna started shaking so badly with suppressed laughter that she had to lean against Jeanne. When she finally looked up, her face was as tear-stained as though she *had* been crying.

At the reception the lambs sang psalms and ate the fine food as though its presence were an affront. They all appeared to be keeping an account of what the others were eating so they could accuse each other of greed. Jeanne had been careful that none of the leaders should be asked to offer a toast, but her efforts to avoid quarrels were of no avail for they quickly became sufficiently exalted in champagne to quarrel anyway.

Duflin and his family were the only people uninhibitedly enjoying the food; they managed to put away awe-inspiring proportions with methodical teamwork. The two girls had been our bridesmaids and in honor of the occasion were corseted so tightly their eyes protruded. They were eating heartily, even though the waists of their silk dresses were stretched to their limits. Suddenly Duflin made some sarcastic remark about Banet that made one of the girls laugh, and her corset and dress exploded with a loud pop, while her poor, smothered body escaped in all directions. Madame Duflin rushed her out in the midst of a chaos of laughter, shrieks, and sobs; she was still trying to stuff her back into the dress as they disappeared.

This time Corinna couldn't control her laughter, so I led her into the yellow salon where she leaned against me laughing. I kissed her to stop her and continued the business until her passion responded.

"Come on," she said breathlessly. "Let's go home — to you."

★

It was Corinna's erotic genius that made me her enthralled slave; her instinct never faltered. I have seldom met a lover who didn't admit that his longed-for first night had been an embarrassing disappointment, but with Corinna I had no such problem. Her ingenuity stretched the seconds to hours. She was the dark priestess of lust, the lewd, astral religion.

The next day she immersed herself in de Assis' pornography and read the erotic sexual lore like someone at last admitted to a longed-for paradise.

Since it was I who broke the seal on this dangerous bottle and let out the demon that took possession of her, I atoned most severely and suffered most from the astral density of the demonic passion. She sharpened her weapons on me; I was the guinea pig of her orgiastic exercises. She was the teacher and I the pupil of this intense, unrestrained magic.

Corinna's undeveloped nubile charm soon gave way to the feverish sensuality of a perpetually hungry, unrestrained woman. Every curve, every movement was a lewd promise. She cared for her body as the truly great hetaerae once had, bewildering the servants by bathing twice a day. Both body and hair were soaked with perfumes, and her clear, blooming skin was always powdered. She wore her own light, fragrant hair, using wigs only when we went out to the theater or some ball — and later when she began sneaking out for secret adventures.

Corinna had a passion for masks. She had a whole collection of them and she used them at every opportunity. One of her favorite tricks was to slip into my room at night attired only in a lacy silk mask and her splendid nakedness. Pretending to be seeking refuge, she would hold a candle over her head and greet me in a disguised voice.

"For God's sake, Monsieur! Forgive my intrusion; I had no choice! Hide me, I beg you, please hide me. They are coming for me . . ."

I always went along with the game. "But who are you, Madame, and how did you find your way to my room dressed only in a mask?"

"Don't ask; there isn't time. I hear them coming. Where can I hide?"

"Well, you can get in my bed, if you like . . ."

"Anywhere!" Then she would jump in beside me. She would act like she was trying to avoid me, but the arch of her back and hips always offered themselves to me. Thus she became mine every night, always in a different guise.

Corinna's hungry young body never tired of making love but I, who was set aflame over and over, began to be drained by my Messalina. I started losing weight, got pains in my back, broke out in sweats, and got dizzy when I walked. My condition would have become really serious if Péloc hadn't intervened.

When he first suggested a trip to restore my health, I wouldn't hear of being separated from Corinna. She herself snuggled against me like a frightened little girl after Péloc had told her about the matter and asked me if it was true that she was making me ill with her love. What could I tell her? I told her she was my life, health, and happiness, and this quickly calmed her. Then she claimed her pleasure yet again. It wasn't until I had fainted after an orgasm that she began to encourage me to go to the seashore. She joined forces with Péloc, and both besieged me with arguments.

"If you love Corinna and want to live with her for years to come, you've got to be cured of that incipient lung disease. You owe it to her."

Corinna joined in vehemently; if I should die, she couldn't live another minute. "It's terrible to be separated for a few months," she told me, "but it's better than being separated forever."

I was troubled suddenly, for I realized she was lying to me, but at the time I simply thought Péloc had scared her. Her turbulent emanations were scored with waves of sensuality, and I flattered myself they were directed at me. So I listened as she talked about her mother's bitter fate and begged me not to condemn her to the same thing. I was moved, fascinated, and — convinced.

I didn't know then that the person I really should have thanked for saving my life was a handsome, muscular, curly-haired stableboy whom Corinna hired just after I left. He brought her the cynical, coarse sensuality of the Paris underworld. She should have seen that this inane, befuddled youth was a future blackmailer, but Corinna's perceptions of people were apparently different from mine. To her, Marcel was a new variation of pleasure, and he was sufficiently robust to endure her tireless passion.

Corinna never felt any remorse or repentance. She simply took up with anyone her appetite desired as instinctively and naturally as a young animal. When I began to demand explanations, she lied exasperatedly, as though she were placating a child who made impossible demands. At first she was amazed that I should be so angry. What was the matter with me? Had I really imagined she would be content with just one man? She loved me and I was an important support to her, but I had not been able to satisfy her. Her beautiful body and erotic art demanded infinite variety. This was her nourishment and life breath. I could possess and enjoy her but I could never own her. I realized then that she embodied all the lustful demons of the astral world; she was a machine of gratification that understood no moral cordon. Instinct reigned supreme in her.

So Corinna lied without flinching, repeated banal promises, assured me of her fidelity, and demanded my trust even in the most scandalous situation. She was slippery as an eel, elusive and unwavering in her purpose.

We had been married just a year when I left Corinna alone for the first time to go to Corsica, miserable in body and in mind. I rented a primitive cottage close to the rocky seashore in the Porto Vecchio area where the fiery sun could burn the disease from my body.

If I hadn't been impaled by my passion, I could have been blissfully happy in my new retreat. I slept on the open porch to get the foul air of the city completely out of my lungs. That had been Homonculus' method, I remembered.

I loved to watch the interplay of sky and sea, these masterpieces of whimsical and powerful artists who forever brought new variations to their work. There was the pearl gray curtain of dawn, then the royal disc of the sun glided forth with a different entourage of color each day. It would change in front of my eyes from a blood-red lamp to a white fireball that heated the air like a furnace. And the sea, that wide feminine eye, mirrored the heavenly mystery. It always grew cooler at sunset, and the clouds dropped their borrowed tiara of gold, red, and violet. A cool wind would blow from the sea, which became sullen and restless and gave off its salty odors.

Now the animals would come out after their sleep during the heat of the day. The stars would come out in the bluestone sky, and Clara, the gentle peasant woman who looked after me, would begin to sing in the kitchen. She always sang an ancient, sweet love song of the type only found in the Mediterranean. Then the treacherous fever would rack my body as I began to remember Corinna. The memory of holding that painfully desired body drained me like a succubus. It was no good being away from her; she was still with me.

I wrote long letters of longing, and she answered with brief scribbles like an obedient schoolgirl. I got a special messenger to take our messages back and forth; I spared no expense. Even then I was nearly crazy at the time he took.

In addition I told the messenger, a self-important, stupid fellow named Vernier, to observe everything. Did Madame look well? What did she talk about? Did she send any verbal messages? What was she wearing? Did the servants say she was sad when she was alone? The poor, stupid fellow wanted to give me my money's worth, so he would always tell me that Corinna was in the best of health, that she went out a good deal in the afternoon and evening, always accompanied by Jeanne Girard, that she dressed gorgeously, was never sad, and giggled a great deal with her pert maid Josette. No matter how late she had been up, she always got up early and rode with Marcel, the new stableboy. The only verbal messages were that I was to take care of myself, not to rush the cure, and come back to her completely healed.

In spite of my agonies of love, the fresh air and sunshine were gradually restoring my sick lungs and blood. Sea baths and long swims improved my appetite and revived my spirits, and Clara's full, simple meals began to fill out my bony frame. Long walks in the sun and wind bronzed my skin, and I began to swim farther and farther out to sea. The restoration of my health cheered me, and the passionate love I still bore for Corinna after four months' absence was not so stressing as before. A rested, well-fed man who has peaceful dreams gets rid of his jealous fantasies easier than one who is physically depleted.

For a long time I didn't want to be aware of my gnawing jealousy. When it finally reached the threshold of awareness as a painful doubt, I shoved it from me hurriedly. My astral torturers drew back and watched me, waiting for the inevitable to happen, just as they had done in Straubing when my vanity had made me the captive of Anton Bruggendorf.

My inner conflict kept me from going home as soon as I could have. I hesitated, torn between the desire to embrace Corinna with renewed strength and fear of learning something I didn't want to know. Finally cowardice won out. I decided to minimize my risk by sending Vernier ahead to tell Corinna I was coming.

The ruse didn't work. I managed to get home before Vernier, and my arrival was completely unexpected. Vernier had been assaulted and robbed on the way to Toulon and was unconscious in a hospital, unable to tell anyone anything. It was futile of me to try to avert what fate intended. I would have found out the truth even if Vernier had gotten there before me. It wasn't even disguised. Not the affair with Marcel, no, though I learned all about that. Marcel was snarling against Corinna like a rabid dog, sending her threatening letters that she threw into the fire with a laugh. Naturally he came to me when I returned.

It wasn't just desire for money that led this blackmailer to tell me every detail of their perverted, sordid affair; it was a jealous revenge that drove him. No male ever got away from Corinna without a mortal wound. I had the cynical satisfaction of seeing what had become of the "beautiful" Marcel with his bulging muscles and sweet perfumes. Now he had the baggy eyes and trembling hands caused by many nights of hard drinking. He had turned to alcohol, the narcotic of primitive man, to burn the memory of Corinna's naked fragrance from his body and brain. She had just played with him for a few weeks, but now his clothing hung on a stooped frame and he obviously didn't bother to wash. Naturally I ordered him out and had him thrown out when he became insistent. I found out later that he was finally executed for murder. I often wondered why the crude, vindictive spade had not murdered Corinna, who had led him to his downfall. He had watched her careless, unguarded moves for months and even followed her on her masked nightly escapades, but he had never dared to talk to her. Once he had staggered up in front of her among the trees of the Bois de Boulogne, but Corinna just laughed and looked straight at him as she asked him what he wanted, and he couldn't manage to utter a word. He slunk away like a hypnotized wild beast.

★

It was not Marcel I found in Corinna's bed the warm October night I returned from Corsica. It was a sixth-rate actor named Alfred le Coeur, an hysterical pink monkey who nearly fainted when he saw me. He ran distractedly around the room holding his red silk trousers in front of him, unable to locate the door. But I was more confused than he. I stood speechless, barely conscious of what I witnessed.

It was Corinna who remained cool. She sharply told her whimpering lover that the exit was on the right and to get the hell out of there before I killed him. Then she got up without even bothering to conceal her nakedness and approached me with quiet defiance.

"You think I've betrayed you, don't you? You've thought that all along; that's why you sneaked home unannounced at night, just so you could get some proof to support your suspicions. You should have stayed here with me like a proper husband, to protect me from temptation and embrace me when I hungered for it! You went off and left me to sleep alone with my fierce desires. Oh, don't make excuses; you could have been back long ago," she said accusingly. Then her tone changed. "You're strong and healthy, and you stayed away for months while I longed for you." She pressed closer to me.

"I was hungry. I relived every moment I spent in your arms — and still you didn't come. Men kept following me and whispering suggestions; I couldn't bear it any longer. As for that eunuch, I just wanted to tantalize him with my nakedness without actually giving him anything. I read to him from those books until he lay whining beside me. That torture alone pleased me enough so that I didn't commit the sin of infidelity . . ."

I slapped her. I didn't realize it until I felt my hand swing and jerk like a whip. Then I jerked open the door in disgust and despair, determined to run away from this foul, disgraced bedroom and the astral demons who mocked me. But Corinna thwarted me with those naked arms that twined about me like lianas. I cursed her and beat at her, trying to free myself from those arms and thighs, but she clung to me with surprising strength.

"I love you," she gasped. "I love the hand that beats me. You — how strong you've gotten! Your skin is brown and smooth now. I've never wanted you so much, and I won't let you go. Come to me; you were my first and only . . ."

I glanced down into the hopeless inferno that was her soul. I knew she was lying and I knew what would become of me if I stayed with her. But that violent passion overpowered both outrage and self-respect; she set me aflame again. We fell onto the bed, and I let the red vortex carry me away . . .

★

I should have put Corinna away, banished her. Nobody who has never been overpowered against his better judgment will ever understand why I did not do just that. Part of me longed to be free but the other part was a slave. My violent, trembling passion made me a prisoner on the astral plane, bound by Corinna's bewitching loins. In the same manner Francesco Giuseppe Borri had been imprisoned on the deepest plane of matter by the alliance with Homonculus.

I can't even say that I believed Corinna when we acted out our farce of a reconciliation with tears and promises. No, I knew and understood what was happening in and around her, and I despised her. But though I could not leave her, I could not keep myself from striking her time and again in my futile anger. I beat her and dragged her around by the hair, I who had never before imagined I could hit a woman. But the more I beat her, the more humbly she crept back to me and the more she conquered me with her body. Nothing made her happier than to force a man to succumb to her against his will and take her in a blind passion of lust.

It was the dark side of Eros that took possession of her now. She no longer sought the straightforward pleasure of strong, young bodies. What attracted her was the depraved and bizarre, the rotten and perverse, the tragic and the dangerous. I saw what was happening to her and knew I could not save her. I lived in a state of constant worry about both of us; our fights and reconciliations were becoming more frequent all the time.

I would leave her and find I had to hurry back. I would rush into brothels to barricade the memory of her body with other women — only to find that in the instant of climax I called her name. Her fragrance, nuances, the delicate shaping of every part of her body, the stir of her movements, and the bright whip of her laughter had invaded my very being. It was only her body that made my senses glow and racked me with lust.

The more often and more deeply I fell, the more indestructible was her demon's power over me, despite what I knew about her. Not only did it control my physical reality but my astral world as well, where my passion made it even more powerful. The composite being created by my astral passion did not even have Corinna's lying beauty; it was an obese reptile with bulging eyes, covered with the slime of self-centered lust. Only the perversion of sexual excitement could make it desirable even for a few minutes. Yet the monster grew continuously from our sinful gushing of sperm and tainted blood from which no life could be born. For Corinna's womb was barren.

People don't really understand the mystery of blood and sperm. They think that when this awesome oil of the lamp of carnal pleasure is expended on a barren, goading passion it overflows the circle of the obsessed lovers without consequence. Actually a dark life springs from each dark ecstasy. The diseased and debauched loins produce succubi and incubi — those elemental, astral vampires who visit the lonely beds of troubled adolescents, frightened virgins, longing widows, and perverts, and drain their strength in the hours of sleep and loneliness.

The priests of the black masses knew this. It is said that one of them performed the infamous "sperm mass" for Diane de Poitiers, conjuring a hideous demon who was bound to obey his parent and conjurer. This is supposed to account for the young Henry II's obsessive love of a woman old enough to be his mother.

★

Corinna's maid Josette married, and Corinna hired a haggard, domineering woman as a replacement. She had met this woman, Germaine Regnier, at a secret gambling house she had taken to frequenting without my knowledge.

Germaine Regnier was no chambermaid; rather she was her mistress' friend and confidante. She had a supercilious manner and was always talking about her aristocratic and pontifical connections and intimated she knew things that "could unhinge even the royal palace." She herself, she hinted, came from high origins she kept sacred "for very good reasons." Actually she was an intrepid, talented confidence woman and she used her talent to organize Corinna's disordered depravity. In addition, her masculine manner and incongruous clothing revealed her true inclination; she reminded me of Christina of Sweden.

This woman now became both slave and ruler of Corinna's bedroom — from which I was artfully excluded. I raged at Corinna and threatened her; I revealed Germaine's true sexual proclivities and demanded that she dismiss her. She cried and smiled that childlike smile at me and told me I was accusing her of things she didn't even understand.

"Germaine is a highborn woman fallen on hard times," she would say, "and she has come to me for help. I would rather join her in her poverty than remove her from her station. You've got such a dirty mind; you see evil everywhere," she complained once. "You've made my life hell. Already your jealousy has broken my spirit, and now I'm even scared to sleep with you, when I used to want to so much. But the real reason I've not let you into the bedroom is that recently I dreamed my father came and urged me to become a nun. He made me promise to be chaste for two months and go to church." Truly Corinna was an able pupil of Jeanne Girard; she had even learned to dream what suited her.

I was suddenly consumed by such violent anger I was afraid I would crush her skull. The intensity of the feeling terrified me; I ran. When I came back, the bedroom door was locked again and Corinna begged me to leave her alone because she had a headache. I knew Germaine was in bed with her; I kicked the door and left.

Péloc, to whom I revealed my total misery, did his best to help. He gave me excellent advice on how to break my emotional slavery. He told me I could turn my convulsive emotions to calm indifference if I continuously used conscious autosuggestion. I should concentrate on everything that was hateful about Corinna and on the repulsive bodily functions she shared with all humankind. He suggested that I remember the Hindu teaching that "Woman is only a vessel filled with urine and feces."

I tried to do this but I couldn't. Things that were repulsive in any other circumstances were exciting in connection with Corinna, or else I simply could not associate the ugly thing with her.

Meanwhile Germaine brought her insatiable mistress every imaginable pleasure, and Corinna's astral surroundings became increasingly horrible. Every debauchery brought a new demon to join the legion of depravity. Already she had begun to attend the black mass. She was just twenty-one and had been my wife for five horrible years.

★

At last Jeanne managed to get Cortey to marry her, and I met Lepitre and Rosalie again at the wedding. Lepitre was more haggard and feverish than ever, and Rosalie was even more exalted and slovenly. During the ceremony I noticed that Corinna's perverse imagination was being fascinated by the tuberculous prophet. He was a veritable bonfire of unsatiated sensuality, and he positively radiated the murderous hunger of asceticism. Corinna and her invisible demons were naturally struck by this unsuspecting bundle of energy who was suppressed by self-reproach and embalmed in penances. And then there was the amusement of robbing the love-struck old Rosalie of her one and only god. Here indeed was a tasty assortment of masochistic and sadistic lust, danger, and tragedy to enjoy!

I knew Lepitre didn't stand a chance; he couldn't escape Corinna's sexual magic. If he had really been pure and saintly, of course, the temptation would have bounced off him like a child's arrow off a stone wall. But his astral surrounding was infected, and his unresolved relationship with Rosalie kept his senses and sentimentality in constant turmoil.

Jeanne Girard's preposterous, tragicomic wedding reminded me of my own marriage when Corinna was wreathed in orange blossoms and surrounded with a halo of veils. What a trap it had been! To what extremes she had carried me, this diabolical virgin through whose embrace I had hoped to find heaven!

Jeanne's flat, powdered face looked coarse in her exaltation, and her towering white wig merely accented her essential vulgarity. The jewels her "dreams" had brought her looked like cheap stage jewelry on her puffy breasts and fleshy fingers. Her loud manner with its mixture of servility and arrogant familiarity was already changing to the condescending reservation of the socially established woman. Now at last, after years of elbowing and lying, she had reached her goal of respectability, and she looked dazed and a trifle tired, like someone reaching fulfillment of any goal. It is always a moment mixed with disappointment and resignation.

Cortey glowed with the simple happiness of the idiot child. He was happy, and Jeanne was happy, but what different things the word meant to each of them! I had never been so aware of the limitation of words; they conceal reality rather than reflect it.

Meanwhile my mother-in-law, the Marquise D'Anjou, had become more preoccupied and absent-minded. The gap between reality and her private world had widened, and she looked over at the people on the other side with an uncertain smile, hardly aware of their presence. She had besieged God in prayer and he gave her beautiful dreams, caressing this faithful and gentle child who had waded so unsuspectingly through the dangerous tideland of Jeanne's visions and the perilous swamps of the lambs' beliefs. Now she met her husband every night, thus being compensated for the loss of Jeanne. She lived her days in a dream and knew reality only at night in her husband's arms. This introverted creature had not the slightest doubt about Corinna's fidelity or the happiness of our marriage, and I wouldn't have jarred her world with the truth even if I could have.

Corinna wore a pale green brocade dress to the wedding. It had a deep, rectangular neckline and a small waist that exposed the twin mounds of her pointed breasts. She was wearing a heavy, sweet, oriental perfume she had bought for a pretty penny from an old Turkish eunuch in some mysterious exile in Paris. This perfume always disturbed me, filling me with bitter anger and a piercing desire. And of course she was spreading it all around her with the movement of her black Venetian lace fan.

After the ceremony I happened into the small reading room that opened off the yellow salon. There I found Corinna standing in the window recess with Lepitre. My footsteps made no sound on the soft carpet and they were unaware of my presence, indeed seeming to be in a trance. Corinna's face and posture and the glowing red vortex around them immediately told me what was going on. Lepitre, his eyes half-closed and feverish spots burning in his cheeks, talked in a subdued, passionate tone, and Corinna was listening. I knew well enough how she was listening. That mild, childlike smile conveyed devout attention, but in reality she was searching his words to find some revealing echo of her own passion. She was measuring him, imagining him in the moment of climax, and subtly managing to strip both him and herself under the cover of her trite phrases. I sat down in a high-backed armchair and watched.

Lepitre was evangelizing Corinna, and it didn't occur to him that he was being unusually emotional. He didn't realize that his words had a new flavor and that blood was coursing through his veins. He thought the flame he felt was a reflection from heaven, when really it was being heated by the demons of suppressed instincts well below the level of his awareness.

Corinna, fascinated and oblivious to her surroundings, moved her naked breasts and stirring fragrance closer to Lepitre. She leaned forward as though she would drink the word straight from his lips. I am sure Lepitre never dreamed of kissing her and would have repudiated the thought had it occurred to him, but suddenly in the middle of his loftiest sentence her lips crashed down on his and there she was, embracing him. Her body clung to him like a muscular octopus, exciting his senses, and he groaned like a wounded animal before they parted abruptly.

Lepitre stared at her with horror. Then he stammered a few inarticulate words and incontinently ran. Corinna merely smoothed her dress and pulled up a shoulder strap that had slipped. Then she turned to leave and saw me sitting there in the chair like a statue of misery. She didn't lose her composure; she never lost her composure. She just laughed.

"Did you see that?" She winked like a mischievous gamine. "Some prophet! Right in the middle of his sermon — shame Rosalie didn't see. I thought he was going to bite my head off. If the whole thing wasn't so funny, I'd raise a scandal." She pulled a lace handkerchief from her bosom to dry her tears of laughter. Then she noticed that I had remained silent. "Well, why don't you say something? Why do you keep looking at me like an executioner? Are you blaming me for this too? There I was listening to his sermon, and all of a sudden he jumped at me like a wild animal. And you watched!" Suddenly her voice became accusing. "You didn't defend me, slap his face! Why he could have raped me right in front of you for all you care, you . . ." I stood up, and she drew back. "Oh, yes, you can hit *me* well enough; I know all about you!" She turned and ran out of the room.

★

Rosalie may have noticed the change in Lepitre, but it may also be that the shaken man confessed his sin to her, beating his breast and begging her to help him overcome this great temptation. Péloc remained in the confidence of these two tragic people, and he told me their full story in an effort to perform psychological surgery. He wanted to free me from the monster of passion by showing me the extent and result of Corinna's depravity. Poor Péloc!

At any rate Rosalie may have absolved Lepitre verbally, but the incident started a revolt in her. Her idol had in failing become a living flesh and blood entity to her, and her distorted heavenly love instantly changed into a jealous, demanding physical passion. Lepitre was hers, whether in the greatness of his purity or the covetousness of his desire. No one could take him from her;

they were mated in heaven and hell. If they had soared together to heaven, they could burn together in hell.

She offered him her own body to sate the dark desire that had taken hold of him. After all, this would be a much lesser sin than committing the act with another man's wife. Then later they could repent together. After all, they need only do it once. But Lepitre was repelled by her desire and the sudden realization of how ugly, slovenly, and old she was as she bared her breasts to him in wild generosity. He had been poisoned by Corinna's fragrant beauty, the flavor of her lips, and the memory of her body.

Then Rosalie understood the reality and became envenomed with hatred for Lepitre, Corinna — and herself. She was totally deranged by the events that crashed down around her. She and Lepitre stayed at home so that the lambs and their counter-prophets could not learn their ugly secret. They lived together like wild animals; one would hide and the other would watch and listen suspiciously to every move. Their beds were changed from cradles of heavenly pleasure into torture racks, and the magic bridge they had built for themselves during those spiritual intercourses became a path for transmitting repulsion, suspicion, accusations, and contempt.

I knew Corinna would arrange to meet Lepitre again and she did. When Jeanne and her new husband paid us the customary visit after their marriage, she mentioned that Corinna had made her a wedding present of some valuable old books from Lepitre's shop. Corinna didn't bat an eye; she simply changed the subject casually. As for me, I acted like I hadn't noticed. What could I have said? She had no capacity for compassion and understanding. She was just a blank page, a merciless astral entity in a body who had no experience of suffering. And I was living beside her like a prisoner who keeps lengthening his sentence by committing some new crime.

When I was away from that enchanting body, I hated her, but I could not stay away too long though I never lowered myself to the extent of going to her bedroom. But I despised myself when I found myself trembling with desire for the moment she would want intercourse with me again, when she would break into my room in her shameless nakedness, challenge me, infuriate me, and finally degrade me into a rutting animal with the magic of her body. She still needed me from time to time to get the sadistic gratification of having absolute power over my whole moral being. It was this desire that gave birth to her campaign against Lepitre and Rosalie, and the demonic forces beyond her body incited the urge constantly.

The unfortunate Lepitre and Rosalie were ripe for some astral hell; their pious self-deception had done that for them. The whole affair was blowing up for an explosion, and I felt sorry for them; yet when I could pull myself out of my own obsession in the matter I could see that Corinna was only a tool to destroy something erroneous and blind in them so they could become their true selves. When I thought of this, I began to realize dimly that my own current anguish had meaning and resolution somewhere. This was just something I had to go through, like a novice has to stumble blindfold through dark corridors at the time of his initiation.

But it was only occasionally that I was able to feel like this. My days and nights and weeks and months were like a spider's web of gray despair in which I struggled fitfully. The very air felt filthy around me and there was a muddy film in my lungs. I always felt sticky with sweat and grime, and baths in our green marble bathroom that was a vestibule for fornication never seemed to get me clean. I began to have difficulty in breathing, and my strength began to dwindle as the tuberculosis took hold of me again. I developed a wracking cough and began having fevers at night. Then in the spring of 1736 I began to spit blood, and poor old Péloc used superhuman perseverance to get me to leave and take a cure.

This time I went to the snowcapped mountains of Switzerland where the dawn glitters on the ice-laden trees. The fiery sun merely preceded the grim, snowy twilight, and the whole scene reminded me intensely of Dreisesselberg Castle and the strange colors and mists I had witnessed in the tower chambers. Even the stars looked the same from the window of the small hunting lodge where I was staying. I had been in a similar condition then too with physical and astral diseases that never left me.

I hadn't said goodbye to Corinna. She hadn't been home for two days; that made the whole thing easier. My flaming indignation could only flare in her presence; else it drained me physically. I left a few lines for her; that was our farewell. Really my trip was just an escape from her. I wanted to shed the worn body of Louis de la Tourzel, hoping my bondage would be shed with it. And I wanted to die alone. The giant alchemical furnace of the mountain sun couldn't heal me, for one important ingredient was missing — my will to live.

I wearily loosened all the forces of decay within me and lay quietly in the crucible of the nights, dissolving in sweat and blood. But I still wasn't free of Corinna. My astral rabble fed me Borgia memories like fanatical terrorists. They conjured up the odor of her sweet perfume and her words and gestures during intercourse and painted her naked body on the canvas of my closed eyelids. Now they were celebrating their full power over my tubercular passions, dancing about my desires like night insects.

In spite of all this I sent Péloc optimistic letters and asked that he tell me everything that was happening to Corinna. She herself wouldn't bother to write. Sometimes if a messenger was available she would send a whimsical note, sweet or sarcastic according to her mood.

Péloc wrote that Germaine was manager of the household, bossing the servants and arranging receptions for playing high stake card games, Corinna's growing passion. Nor were these evenings confined to persons of our own social scale; anyone Germaine found interesting was invited. Thus every night aristocratic idlers, cardsharps, actors, demimondaines, and perverts rubbed elbows in the green salon next to Corinna's bedroom. Here she had set up a fully equipped game room. The result naturally was a series of fights, scandals, thefts, and swindles of such magnitude that they caused Corinna's high-ranking police official lovers considerable difficulty in hushing them up. There was also a nightly buffet where virtually anyone could drop in for a good meal at my expense. Of course Péloc told me the whole truth intentionally. He hoped thus to cure me of Corinna. Yet hate is merely the other side of love. Only if I had become indifferent toward her could I have freed myself, if I could have managed not to care in how much filth she indulged herself.

Three months after I left, Rosalie murdered Lepitre and committed suicide. Her method of murder was as insane as the passion that raged in her old body — she hacked her idol to pieces. He must have been dead after the first few blows, but the obsessed woman wanted to pay him for all her misery. She would fulfill herself just once after all these years of suppressed desires, psychic masturbations, and the floods of tears after his humiliating fall. So she bathed in his blood, since he had not let her embrace him, because she had loved him so much and been so bitterly disappointed. Then she opened her own major arteries and lay down beside the corpse, convulsively giving him the only embrace she would ever enjoy.

Péloc wrote me the whole story — it was he who had found the horrifying bodies. The day of the funeral, Corinna gave a gala house concert for Rene Gillet, a newly famous harpist. She had also taken up with the charlatan Martin Allais and appointed him her physician.

When I read the letter, I simply stopped trying to make the effort to get up. What was the use? I was coughing up chunks of lung and losing weight steadily. The diseased passion within me was destroying the remnants of my strength.

I wrote one more letter to Péloc and thanked him for his friendship, the only thing that had been precious in my miserable life — but my last breath held Corinna's name. I had lived only thirty-six years in the passionate, overly sentimental body of Louis de la Tourzel.

25

The Green Window

The next part of my journey was the strangest and the least easily told. I can try to describe it in words, but words are too rigid to hold the endless colors and terrifying intensity of the lower reaches of the astral world, the seat of passions and suppressed instincts. Later I will tell about the higher planes of the astral world where intelligence calls to art and the great masterpieces are born.

The instant I died, my whole being flew back to Corinna as though it were flung from a suddenly released spring. I was chained to her by every desire of my lacerated body. The being imprisoned on this astral plane is subjected to a sensual hunger far above the capacity of any human physique. Each sense is a high-tension wire carrying more voltage than can be borne by any human system. The astral body remains forever unfulfilled and feeds on the tiniest scraps of the finite world.

★

Now I was chained to the legion of demons which surrounded Corinna's glowing body, helping to fuel her desires and sharing the pleasures she grasped. I saw her live her whole life and could not turn away for an instant, although I was revulsed with horror. The whole demon pack of my thoughts, desires, and sins revolved about me as I watched.

I had many companions at this black witches' carnival. I recognized the handsome Marcel, who had been squeezed out of his body by a noose, and Lepitre and Rosalie revolving like moons of endless despair.

Corinna's fate unfolded on the vast stage of life before us just like a pornographic thriller. She dressed and undressed, put on and took off masks, laughed and screamed, lied and destroyed, made love, gambled, and drank, grasping pleasures from every depraved passion, but it was really the demons who controlled her. As time went on, their technique in handling their puppet became ever more flawless, and her tough body tolerated the debaucheries well, for her soul was still asleep. Her wealth was not so fortunate; it dwindled rapidly in her mad card games, regardless of how generous her lovers were. She continued completely barren, her womb barricaded to new life, and her years continued to burn out like straw.

Martin Allais was with her constantly, and she tolerated his presence with equanimity for she sensed her kin in his intrepid depravity. He never had intercourse with her but always witnessed the act, and his bulging eyes burning with the red haze began to excite Corinna more than anything else. She drew him into her vilest bacchanalias and would tempt him by getting him alone in her bedroom, stripping, and reciting de Assis' pornographic verse. But Allais remained steadfast; this gourmet of evil who had produced an especially destructive theory about the beauty and redeeming necessity of sin resisted her siege like a castle. He simply offered flattery, encouragement, criticism, and advice as required, blackmailed her, and stayed with her. When she bathed, he would improvise cynical but provocative verses about every part of her body. At last Corinna became more interested in him than she was in anybody else.

Allais was a terribly clever scoundrel. He was willing to put in tedious years to gain the whole prize. He disciplined his Latin temper, suppressed his desire, and conquered his vindictive jealousy. Finally he got what he wanted. It was an imposing accomplishment, even if it was an accomplishment of evil.

And Corinna fell into the trap. The starved and bewitched woman thought there must be some exotic joy in Allais' embrace, so she obeyed him and threw out Germaine, that less dangerous evil spirit who was faithful in her own way. She began to live with Allais publicly and gave him the keys of her bedroom and strongbox.

Allais didn't wait too long to let Corinna know the truth. He knew he had caged a beautiful beast of prey who would soon want to break loose into freer hunting grounds. So now he systematically imprisoned her. He locked up her money and clothing and turned out all her friends. If she rebelled or escaped briefly, he beat her so brutally she had to stay in bed for days, secretly charmed by the experience. For Allais had no illusions about her; he knew that no one man, regardless of how passionate and sophisticated his technique of lovemaking, could possibly satisfy Corinna. So he dragged her into perversions so ugly she began crying and begging for mercy.

But the more painful surprise for Corinna was the infection of her blood.

Allais' ugly blemishes had meant nothing to one unaccustomed to observing with her brain. It was the syphilis that cracked the callowness of her soul. She was forty when the disease became visible. Her insane debaucheries had aged her faster than most women, but while she had had her health she had been able to fight the ravages of time. Now her skin became slack and she was troubled with rashes. The dark shadows under her eyes became blue bags. The breasts of which she had been so proud grew flabby. Now the eyes that had once glittered with conscious beauty were dull and confused with fright. Her teeth began falling from the inflamed gums and her voice grew raspy. The shiny black hair that had sparkled with life became a dull gray. About the same time she lost all her money.

Allais, now toothless and bald from his disease, took the rest of her jewels and money and left her alone with her blind panic. Nor was he the only one who left this shell stripped of beauty, wealth, and health. Even her demons left her. No one wanted Corinna any longer. People shunned the staggering beggar woman with the raspy voice. She looked ninety and she wasn't even fifty.

The spirits of Lepitre and Rosalie were freed from their bondage around her; they began to make their search for repentance in new bodies. Only the handsome Marcel remained; something bound his soul to this decaying form.

And as for me, the experience was shattering and — I wish I could convey the full meaning of the word — majestic. The only similar experience I had had was my liberation from Homonculus, and this had been a longer process, lasting years by human reckoning. As Corinna's sensual beauty disintegrated, so did the ties between us and I was no longer bound by blind passion. It wasn't just that she had lost her charm, but what had happened to her had marked me like the bluestone brand of the old Greek initiation mysteries.

I had been shocked out of my astral daze by witnessing the transitory form and inevitable disintegration of even the most triumphant beauty. Now I understand that carnal pleasure and self-centered lust were all hopeless illusions and that those fireworks of emotion and sentiment were satanic in essence, carrying deadly peril in their wake. I understand — but the word is too feeble; it means something different to everybody. *What I mean is that I understand it with my feelings, so that I was free of a bondage that could hold me only while I believed it could. I might have resisted its force and been frightened of it before, but I had believed in it more than I believed in God. Now I didn't.*

This cool gust of knowledge tore the burning Fata Morgana to bits, for I saw that all suffering, bondage, affection, terror, misery, sickness, and death are merely illusions. *They have no power until we give it to them with our belief.* When I recognized this truth, I uttered the real name of the astral passion just as I had once uttered Homonculus' real name to get mastery over him.

Now I was free of the bonds of the inferior physical and astral planes. In Corinna's body, the lowest point on the astral plane, I untied the knot on which every man must stumble.

True experience can come only from within. We must become one with each experience to free ourselves of all its dangers. Anyone who has passed through the nether world has been delivered from hell, and anyone who thinks he can stroll across the abyss on a narrow plank will invariably fall in. All the lambs — Lepitre, Rosalie, Banet, and the others — stood on this bridge dizzy but blustering and thought they could go straight to heaven. But they turned out to be wrong; Lepitre and Rosalie had fallen headlong into the hottest caldron. I was moved with compassion as I thought of the experiences they would have to undergo to find their way out.

I was not in the enchanting moment of grace of which human beings have such ridiculous and erroneous notions. Grace is really the law that turns evil into medicine and makes the nadir of sin and death the beginning of illumination. Not even God can take a single step for a man or cancel any of his debts or remove a burden from his shoulders as an act of favoritism. Then the unfinished experience would remain terra incognita on the map of the soul and leave a dangerous gap which darkness could penetrate at any time.

Now I had two of the keys of Hermes, but I needed the third.

Now the demons of the astral world couldn't frighten or subdue me any longer because I wasn't afraid of them. I knew they depended on me for existence; I had created them and I was their master. I could simply confront them and make them vanish like mist.

I had come the long way around, but it had been worth the trouble. I couldn't have avoided it anyway; it had been inevitable ever since my journey began by Rochard's crushed skull.

Being afraid of something makes you a magnet for that of which you are afraid; if you stop being afraid, the magnetic attraction ceases.

★

I stayed with Corinna a little longer out of compassion, but then I realized that her suffering and fear were simply the labor pains of her rebirth from a miserable demon into a human being who could be enlightened by suffering. This freed me from my useless hesitancy and I left her quietly, for I could not help her yet.

Now I needed an inconspicuous, contemplative life to rest from the depths to which I had finally descended and gather my forces to conquer the most difficult plane of all — the mental plane. Now I was nothing but ashes and exhaustion, an astral body covered with barely healed burns. My new task was to ignite this almost extinguished alchemist furnace to a white hot glow for a different type of catharsis with a different fire . . .

★

Before I move on I must say a few words about Jeanne Girard, for her fate is a notable example of the dangers of dilettantes experimenting with the dark forces.

I was able to observe her later life through the Green Window just as I did Corinna's and to see much more of it than I could have in my physical body, even possessed of the dubious advantage of the third eye of Atlantean man. My body had tied me to time and place and now these did not trouble me. If I wanted to learn something about Jeanne Girard — Madame Cortey — she was revealed to me immediately in her total internal and external environment, just like an exotic fish in an x-rayed bowl.

The woman really did possess occult abilities, but her self-propagating lies had dragged her down into a low, dense layer of existence. Lying in the deep waters of the astral region, she became an illuminated passageway for electric flounders and deadly cold monsters. In the deep, the light turns into irresistible but destructive heat — a sad, faraway reflection of the divine brilliance. This is why even wild beasts prowl longingly yet fearfully around fires; these are their mute, desperate prayers.

Thus Jeanne's soul became filled with elemental monsters. They penetrated the witch's kitchen that was her body and soul and broke into the indescribably delicate mechanism of life. Every lever was pulled by a different talon until yet a stronger pushed it aside. In modern medical terms, what Jeanne suffered was a singularly severe case of schizophrenia. She shattered into innumerable personalities and spoke in diverse and terrifying voices. Hostile and alien beings gave tongue through her mouth.

The conflicting voices she heard caused her to do numerous inappropriate things. Once she stood facing the wall for hours without accepting food or cleaning herself. Another time she hid everything she could lay her hands on in a variety of unlikely places and then could not remember where she had put them. Frequently she alarmed the servants and confused Cortey with disgusting, perverted propositions.

When the couple had still been active socially, her demon had caused her to utter obscene blasphemies and confess to vile crimes. As her condition became more acute, she began to set fires and smash things; then she tried to strangle poor Cortey, who was barely able to save himself. She wound up where my poor mother had — the Salpétriére.

Once Jeanne recognized me in a rare moment of lucidity. She was in a stupor, but she raised her arms shakily toward me and muttered, "And you, Louis — Monsieur de la Tourzel? — You want me to give a message to little Corinna? — I won't tell her how scarred and gray you look — I'll tell her something nice — to make her glad —" Suddenly she shuddered and screamed, aware of her own misery. "Monsieur, for the mercy of God, please help me! You aren't one of them; they've been blocked out a few minutes. They're stealing my life — tearing me apart! Please stop them before it's too late! Please extinguish that lamp!" Then her reason was swept away and she burst into hoarse laughter.

THE PHOENIX SOARS

Blind Soul! Arm thyself with the torch of the Mysteries and thou canst find, even in the night of the Earth, that shining, other body — thy divine Soul!

Follow this heavenly guide! Let it be thy genius, for it holds the key of thy past and future embodiments.

(The appeal to initiates from *The Egyptian Book of the Dead*)

★

Turn your attention within and glance into the infinity of time and space! The song of the stars, the speech of numbers, and the harmony of the spheres all have their origins there. Every sun is a thought of God and every planet the thought's expression.

Ascend and descend, O souls, the path of the seven planets, and in the seven skies of these seven planets shall ye recognize the divine thoughts.

What do the stars sing? What do numbers talk about? What do the spheres reveal?

O, ye lost or redeemed souls, these stars, numbers, and spheres are revealing your fate.

(A fragment attributed to Hermes)

26

The Sign of Aquarius

The woman whose body could accept my soul with its new goal was gentle and even-tempered, just like a true alchemist furnace.

I was born on the gray dawn of February 27, 1760, in a place permeated with the mystic radiation of the secret sciences. My father, Cornelius von Grotte, was court musician and confidante to the Landgrave Karl, Prince of Hesse-Cassel, and the two were members of the same mystic Order.

My father was a very skillful painter and writer, but his glowing artistry was directed to only one end — the accomplishment of the Great Work that becomes steadily more obscure to the outer world as it nears completion. His works were not for this world; they are guarded in the secret library of the Order, and only those who understand the three levels of symbolism can see them.

The castle of Grotte stood in the middle of the dense, murmuring Forest of Hawks, and the windows of its square towers overlooked the river Fulda. The north windows overlooked the icy mountains of Karls Rue Park and the silhouette of the Orangerie Castle and its marble pools. Within the castle was the silence of meditation, which made it seem austere as a monastery. Even our few guests instinctively walked on tiptoe so as not to disturb the gentle, euphoric spell. Not even the hushed conversations in the evenings or the massive tones of the great organ disturbed it; they merely seemed to add art to the serenity.

My mother was a tall, Gothic woman with improbably slender fingers, a transparent face, and a high, noble forehead. She was the most taciturn woman I met in my whole life journey, but hers was the silence of accommodation, peaceful and expressive. People who talked to her never felt she was indifferent or reserved; her smiling eyes and compassionate silence prompted even the timid and introverted to communicate. Hers was a power of silence.

She was well-educated and unusually intelligent, and she quietly graduated through the grades of the Order with my father. She was always first to read and criticize his writings, and her marginal notes show her intuition. Her intense energy was always channeled into some important work, and my father who, like most artistic, rhapsodic geniuses, was frequently discouraged, received tremendous help from her emotional balance. Words cannot express what she came to mean to me.

She was well prepared for my coming; this time my parents knew who was to be born to them. They knew more about me than I knew myself, for my third eye had been reopened only by the Elixir I had acquired by murder. The Order had kept track of my path for a long time — a few millennia — and expected me to be born among them in the sign of Aquarius. I had neither to hide nor to tell anything.

During my infancy my new body couldn't transmit my spirit completely and my parents communicated with me accordingly, but by the time I was ten or eleven they treated me like any other junior in the Order — as an uninitiated adult. They knew my goal and knew that it was their task to lead me toward it. Both they and their friends had expected me, and they loved me and awaited my birth with more joy than ordinary parents, for they knew what I had done and the depths of hell from which I had climbed. The prodigal son was returning to them, tattered and wounded, but past his crisis.

A person who has been an initiate and falls away loses the Ancient Memory. He has some obscure presentiment of this great loss; it burns in him as he wanders the labyrinths, a consuming sense of loss that stays unsated for thousands of years. He strives to reach the occult light again, though he is dazed and blinded like a moth. He will burn and fall only to try again in a new body, obeying the mystical tenet, "Burn thy body with the fire of thy thoughts." The body will always burn during this futile experiment but it will burn with astral desires, which are strengthened and awakened by the experience. Yet this flaming seed only produces a mortal body. It was beside Corinna's disintegrating body that the transcendental light of thought flared within me. For Corinna had encompassed and consumed all of my astral restlessness and egotistical, lewd attraction to beauty of form; she sucked them all into her flesh and blood and enchained them on the chain of her forms. When the magic of her body was shattered, all my desire for the spectral world of astral swamps went with it. My impassioned, sidereal second body was burned by the fire of thought, and my third one appeared — numb, dormant, ignorant, and inexperienced — a Junior ready for awakening, realization, and illumination.

I didn't participate in the Order's gatherings while my body and brain were developing. Instead my parents introduced me to mental exercises. They forced me to do organized work regardless of how difficult I found it. During certain hours of the day, with no exceptions, I had to perform various assigned tasks — writing, translating difficult texts from French to German or, most arduous, I had to memorize portions of books whose unknown oriental language had been notated in Latin characters. Later I studied Hebrew, Egyptian, Urdu, Sanskrit, Tibetan, and Chinese, and learned all their strange characters. These tasks strengthened my restless and quickly-distracted mind and compelled me to concentrate and persist diligently even when the task itself was unrewarding. Boring though they seemed, they were still the only way to learn, and I was richly rewarded for these dry hours by the hours when my parents worked to waken my mystical senses and train the delicate feelers of intuition which seek out the truths of etheric Akasha beyond thought, time, and space. My bedtime stories were occult music and poetry, which filled me with the thrilling moonlight of mysteries and taught me the meaning of symbols.

27

The Temple of the Moon

For many peaceful years the same silvery night seemed to fall on my father's study as though it had stopped in time. The same highlights shone on the gigantic, copper-colored organ pipes, and the triple rows of keys responded in the same way to my father's agile fingers. This huge instrument was the channel through which I experienced the exalted beauty of transcendental poetry, just as Orpheus, that most blessed and misunderstood interpreter of the divine art, was able to recreate the Elusian nights.

My father always established the atmosphere for his story with the strange, sonorous colors of the organ. He would play bewitching, mystical chords that flowed together without resolution; these evoked wonderful, luminous colors to the seeing eye and told the tale in living symbols that needed only to be translated into words. And the first story he told me was this:

"Once long ago there lived in the city of Ur, where the people wore the gentle moonmask of the nightborn, a Princess named Bel-Shalti-Nannar, the daughter of King Nabuniad. Now all this took place during the last days of Abraham's city of Ur, after the death of the great Nebuchadnezzar. The eyes of this Princess shone like the pure lines of the Moon Temple and their depths were like the shadows of moonlit nights. Though Bel-Shalti-Nannar was beautiful, she was a stranger to all mankind. Her female companions shunned her, for they sensed that she was much older than they, and the men avoided her, for they saw behind her purity not the hungry fire they expected but the ashes of horrible fires long dead. Thus Bel-Shalti-Nannar became a priestess of the temple of the Moongod and Nin-gal, the Moon-goddess — a temple that lay beside the stepped Ziggurat and was lit by the bright moon disc.

"Bel-Shalti-Nannar knew and loved the traditions of the ancients and searched tirelessly for knowledge concerning the glorious, sacred past of the city of Ur. Like her father Nabuniad, she read the secret messages of the ancients upon their statues and stone tablets. She had a contemplative and questing mind and a bold spirit, for she did not shrink to take her questions to Nannar the Moongod and his radiant mate Nin-gal. She besieged them continually with questions, for she wished not merely to believe but to understand.

"The nine old priests would smile wisely as they watched her tall, slender figure follow the moon over the Holy Road and turn into the Corridor of the Nine Columns. Then they would retire silently to the Lesser Sanctuary and light the four oil lamps around the throne of Nin-gal, the veiled Goddess.

"Bel-Shalti-Nannar would ascend the four sets of seven steps and stand upon the square tower of the stargazers in the face of the full moon. And lo her blue garment shone in the light that threw deep shadows behind her. Then would she address the disc of light.

" 'Behold, I am here. Thou didst call and I have answered Thee. My face shines with Thy radiance, even as Thine cloth shine with the brilliance of the Sun. But lo there is deep shadow behind me and Thee, a shadow that cloudeth both heaven and earth. The very communion between us casteth a shadow upon heaven and earth. For this cause I, who am slave to Thy chain of light, serve Thee weeping, for I can in no wise understand either Thy nature or mine own.'

"Thus spake Bel-Shalti-Nannar unto the full moon for seven years, and for seven years the moon answered not. It spake only with the silent tongue of the oceans, the blood, and the humors. But Bel-Shalti-Nannar did not falter nor was she discouraged in her quest. Nor did she seek wisdom of the nine old priests who lit the four lamps around the throne of Nin-gal in the Lesser Sanctuary. She knew that their knowledge could sustain and rejuvenate only those who drew from the secret fountain which they did visit in secret.

"And in the seventh month of the seventh year, the full moon spoke to Bel-Shalti-Nannar.

> Those who persist in asking have ever received an answer, but mortals seldom wait until their question is fully formed and condensed into an arrow that can break the seal of silence. Because thou hast waited, even so thou shalt receive an answer. Hear ye it and lock it within thee and allow no one who is unworthy to learn the words thereof.
>
> Verily there is no limit to Him who is boundless, infinite, perfect, and eternal. Thus everything that existeth — truth, infinity, and even eternity itself — hath also its opposite. If this were not so, He would not be truly free.
>
> Hence the Tree of Knowledge, which is even a great analogy, could have

stood in front of Him who was free without harm, for it is the work of the Everlasting Emanated Being. The evil and deadly, attractive and beautiful thing could have stood before Him to awaken the desires of the flesh against which the Everlasting warned but did not make impossible.

Therefore no mortal can give unto the inexperienced child his life experience, either in this world or the world above. For lo the pattern must be repeated continuously, even as the ripples when a stone is thrown into the water.

For the mortal must needs experience the evil form, the world of death, in order that he might know of a certainty that He is the right Way and that redemption proceedeth only from Him.

The Eternal and Nin-gal, his reverse potential, are the divine duality. For the veiled Goddess already ruled the Lesser Sanctuary in the sunken, ancient Homeland. She who hath been and will be worshipped and venerated by the nations of the earth, even she is the ruler of all the blessed and sinful women of the earth. She ruleth also over me, her humble servant, pronouncing my secret name, Shin, and is even the mediator who ruleth over the planets, stars, and the very Universe. Her veil is the Milky Way and the vast covering of the stars. She it was who was the Goddess of your forefathers, the resplendent Ishtar of their sunken, ancient Homeland, the Atlantean Isis.

And, behold, desire slumbered in Nin-gal, the temptress, and the desire of procreation flared within her.

The Everlasting was the Begetter, and Nin-gal, the Great Mother from whose womb the third, the Mortal Being, came forth burdened with Nin-gal's mortal desire and uplifted by that recognition of the Everlasting that conquereth death.

It was His Word that spoke Nin-gal into being, but He Himself is unmanifested.

So Nin-gal's progeny, the Mortal Being, began his journey.

And lo the Great Law also began: as it is below, so is it above.

The Mortal Being, like the great Mother and Father, was split in twain by desire and by the curiosity for the separate way. And this sundering born of desire and curiosity gave birth to the twin forces of attraction and repulsion. And from these were born a third, and the third followed the example of its parents. Thus an infinite number of mortal beings came forth from the womb of Nin-gal, and each was a repetition, a widening circle of the wondrous God-drama above.

And the Everlasting consented unto this, for the cure for desire is gratification and the cure for evil is suffering. Where desire slumbereth slumbereth danger also, danger that is averted only by the total fulfillment of the ripples of the Omniverse.

Though He is unmanifested, yet is He a part of every being, an invisible substance that cannot be destroyed.

For the Everlasting needs no experience. He is unchanging and is Lord over death.

Behold, Nin-gal desired, she burned with the pleasure of conception; she brought forth her progeny in sweat, exulting in the illusion dance of time. She tried without ceasing to form eternal beauty from the temporal matter, but her labor was in vain, like one who maketh images in the snow.

Nin-gal indeed experienced the pleasures of time and, behold, she found them to be nothing, a bubble in the wind. She suffered and perished often in the drama of existence, always striving to return unto Him who is patient, silent, omniscient, and eternal. To this end she endured the fiery furnace of pain to make complete her surrender. But this cannot be accomplished until the three become two and the two become One.

And the Mortal Being returneth continually unto Nin-gal, and Nin-gal doth return continually unto him.

Since the inner essence of every being is the omniscient and patient Divine Ego, in each and every being there liveth not only the figure of coming into existence but also the desire of Nin-gal, born of her bitter disappointment and knowledge, to return unto her Divine Partner.

This is the meditation, knowledge, and disillusionment of the more mature Nin-gal as she ascends toward the Unique, Unmanifested, and Everlasting.

Nin-gal's cry of desire and wail of repentance echo through the Omniverse even unto this day.

The cry of lust descendeth into the lower paths of existence.

In every bride, the veiled Nin-gal hasteneth with lustful excitement into dangerous desires and the illusive joy of creation.

In every priestess, Nin-gal taketh the vow of chastity and resisteth those desires and passions that bring suffering.

Every womb holdeth Nin-gal's new hope, her new invention.

So also in every tomb lieth Nin-gal's bitter failure, from which is born repentance and recognition.

For lo a thing must needs die and decay ere it shall rise.

If Nin-gal would rise unto Him forever, first she and the Beings to whom she gave birth must know death and decay.

As it is above, even so is it below.

"Bel-Shalti-Nannar stood erect in the square tower of the stargazers and faced the disc of the moon that began sinking below the sand dunes. She breathed deeply as the pale, mysterious face of Shin disappeared, dragging her long, milky veil behind her to make way for the dawn.

"But Bel-Shalti-Nannar did not await the sun, that lamp of red joys. She returned down the four sets of seven steps and hurried along the Corridor of the Nine Columns, with the light of the sun reaching longingly after her. But the Princess would not turn away after it; instead she walked swiftly past the nine old priests who stood in ceremonial order before the door of the Lesser Sanctuary. As she approached, they drew open the curtains unto her.

"So Bel-Shalti-Nannar entered into the sanctuary and approached the base of the throne where the four oil lamps enveloped the veiled Goddess in shimmering light. She knelt before the throne making an obeisance, then sprinkled incense into the vessel prepared for it and lit it from one of the oil lamps. This done, she began to gaze intently through the blue smoke at the veiled face of the Goddess. And lo the silence of ecstasy reigned within the Sanctuary, and only the vigilant priests numbered the days and the hours thereof.

"And lo the veils began to drop from Nin-gal's figure quietly and without the seeming of motion. On the fourth day, after the fourth test, Bel-Shalti-Nannar discerned the soft contours of Her knees, waist, and arms. Upon the fifth day, she saw Her hands which held the key of life. And upon the sixth day, the last veil fell and she beheld the face of the Goddess — and, behold, it was as though she looked into a mirror.

"Then did Bel-Shalti-Nannar understand the illusion of all things, even that delusion condensed into matter divides That Which Is One. She understood the tragedy of living beings and her own tragedy within it. Redemption and liberation were also made known unto her in this moment, but lo they were afar off, at the very end of the Days of the Earth, and she was consumed with bitterness and dejection after all her fastings and sacrifices. She spake unto the Goddess.

Oh, Thou silent and disappointed Mother, Thou wretched Mother of the World. Alas we must remain in this dark world until the last desire hath been burnt from the Cosmos, until the Pharos of the last emotion dieth out and the last question of mankind becometh ashes, until the bubble of the last death bursts upon the Eternal River. Alack, we must wait and dance the dance of the Great Spiral, the endless ring dance piped by the flutes of our own bones. . . .

"And Bel-Shalti-Nannar wept bitter tears as she gazed upon the uncovered visage of the Goddess on which her tears were mirrored.

"Then a seventh time she filled the lamps at the four corners of the throne and threw fresh incense into the censer.

"And lo after the endless night, the seventh day dawned and the tears of the Goddess were dry. She smiled as a bride who journeyeth unto the bridal chamber. And, behold, the door behind her, even the door of the Greater

Sanctuary, was opened, and the eldest of the priests awaited her upon the threshold, his robes embroidered with the pale green and gold sign that signifieth Aquarius. He stretched out his hand unto her, and she arose and followed him. And Bel-Shalti-Nannar smiled with the hopeful smile of the Goddess as she entered unto the Greater Sanctuary."

28

The Greater Sanctuary

As another dusk turned into evening, my father continued his story.

"Inside the Greater Sanctuary reigned a darkness as deep as the velvet inner spaces of the deepest meditation. It clung to the opened eyes of Bel-Shalti-Nannar as a heavy sheath. Stretching forth her hand to feel her way, the Princess continued forward on her quest. The Sanctuary was a long room and the floor thereof began to slope. And lo the passage became narrower also. The ground beneath her feet waxed difficult and uncertain, and she was compelled to bow her head beneath the roof. The very air stank with a damp, evil odor.

"Then were the ears of Bel-Shalti-Nannar smitten by a dull, throbbing noise, a sound which had no form or shape but yet was infinitely menacing. And, behold, the roof was now so low that the regal Princess must needs crawl upon her knees, moving among Things that impeded her progress. A great anguish fell upon her, like unto a black owl that hunteth its prey. She felt the whirl of its wings upon her, and tiny pearls of horror started from her fair form. Already she felt she could go no farther, for now she lay flat in a tunnel, scratching at its walls with her fingers to pull herself along.

"And lo suddenly she came upon two points of light, lights that glowed with green, evil gleam. She stared as one in a trance, and the icy serpent of horror coiled itself around her heart. For the points of light were set in a face; they resolved themselves as two scornful eyes.

" 'Stop!' These eyes commanded. As Bel-Shalti-Nannar gazed upon the face, its features appeared in the greenish light. Behold, the skin was scaly and repulsive and glowed with decay, the large imprint of the nose barely visible in the decaying substance. A third, dead eye sat in the middle of its forehead, and within its gaping mouth shining worms whirled in voracious hunger. And yet the head glowed with evil life. Bel-Shalti-Nannar felt its presence suffocating her soul, and its contemptuous doubt boiled about her spirit, to drag it into the depths of the astral reptiles, the misery of an animal existence. 'Look at me!' the face commanded her.

"Then was the heart of the Princess Bel-Shalti-Nannar smitten with unutterable memories and feelings. And the Head spoke.

" 'Dost thou not know me after these tens of thousands of years? Dost thou not know me, whom thou didst deny, abort, and slay, from whom thou fleddest behind the seven veils of matter? It was to escape me that thou didst pour into thine ears the hot lead of human voices and did blind thine eyes with the glittering treasures of the earth. Yea, thou didst run and shout, drink and go in unto men, and throw thyself at the feet of alien gods whose temples resounded with the sistra, the flute, and the gong, all to drive out the memory of my face and put away from thee the moment when we should meet again, thou and I — the murderer and the victim.

" 'Hadst thou known that it was I, even I, who lured thee through the chamber of the Lesser Sanctuary into the trap that is the Greater One, that it was I who awaited thee at the end of this horrible tunnel instead of the illumination and redemption thou desirest, then wouldst thou have hurled thyself from the summit of the Ziggurat onto the stones below. But thou wist it not. This is the consequence of thy sin of forgetfulness. Behold, thou art here, weakened and thirsty from eternal want, delivered into the hands of Him who hath waxed strong through hatred and waiting. And even thine own fear, the fruit of thine own sweat and tears, contendeth with thee for its freedom, striving to gain power over thee.'

"Slowly the vapors of memory arose within Bel-Shalti-Nannar, and she perceived the name of this three-eyed monster. It was the faith she had betrayed, even the holiness she had defiled and then discarded secretly, as a woman leaveth her ill-gotten babe upon the stranger's doorstep. This had all befallen long ago in the Ancient Homeland before the Time of the Destruction when the Titans, ruled by the Third Eye, lived in the Paradise of Three Worlds and knew no death. For lo the third eye in a man's forehead is the gateway of mystic sight and power. When the Titans sinned and turned their strength one against another, it became the entry unto the hell of deadly hate. And, behold, the Serpent of Wisdom left their minds and did slither into their loins, there to become the passion of the lower world of instinct.

"And the feverish passion bore its fruit of selfishness, discrimination, pain, violence, and destruction. For though the Titans knew the world of the spirit, they knew naught of the lusts of the tempting earth that is poisoned by death; they were as newborn babes and thus were lost. The forces they drew from the Cosmos through their mystic eyes waxed exceedingly dark and destructive, for they had to pierce the defenses of others as powerful as themselves to take what their envious senses did desire. Thus the pure light of the Sun turned its face from the earth, and the evil emanations of the gutted ghost planets were drawn into the world through these transcendental eyes.

"And lo the initiated priestesses also turned away in this time of mystic storm, and the pure temple in her soul sank within her to be overgrown with weeds. Yea, the very key thereof was lost, and the betrayed Idea in the sunken sanctuary became a bitter ghost, an evil demon on the threshold.

"And, behold, the judges of the Cosmos made an end to this hellish drama. A small moon crashed upon the earth, and it was cleansed with fire and water. And the rebellious Titans were driven forth from Eternal Paradise, and the third eye was taken from them. There remained unto them only a tiny, mysterious gland behind the forehead, a center of dim presentiments and warnings. And lo the Titans became men. They learned the secrets of sin and suffering and strove to develop their understandings, struggling with the hieroglyphs of nature to grasp with their mortal minds the great Cause they could no longer divine.

"And the heavens closed against the men and the fear of death oppressed them. They searched the dark void with their minds and hearts, pitiful and helpless. The gods their fear created were naught but threatening tyrants; lo they could neither comfort nor heal. Thus blinded mankind perceived only the prison walls of cradle and grave, and the serpent of passion within their loins demanded yet more bloody sacrifices and sensual delights. So blind and damned mankind begat blind children unto damnation.

"The stricken Titan Gilgamesh wrote the words of his horror which he had felt as he mourned over the body of his friend who had become mortal.

> Enkidu, thou friend of mine heart,
> thou panther of the meadows,
> Lo together we had reached the Gates of Truth,
> Our feet had trod the Great Mountain,
> even the peaks thereof.
> We had conquered the Heavenly Ram and broken
> the pride of Humbala of the Cedar Forest.
> What dream hath now seized thee?
> Thy face is dark, and thou hearest not my voice,
> Nay, neither do thine eyes regard me!

★

He laid his hand upon the heart of Enkidu,
but lo it was still.
Then did the faithful friend cover the silent body
as though it had been his bride.
And he cried out like the lion,
even as the lioness robbed of her cub,
And he threw himself upon the body of his friend
And tore his hair in agony.

(Fragment from The Gilgamesh Epic)

"Yet the Forgotten Temple still waited silently, deep beneath the waters of remembrance, sunk into the depths of the waters. And the key thereof had been lost, and its dead god haunted its sanctuary as a monster.

"Now Bel-Shalti-Nannar understood that she was within the Forgotten Temple once more. She had found the corridor leading back to the past where she had once walked, ere the very memory of it had been wiped from her soul by the hand of the judges. Thus she stood at the door of the sanctuary prison and was confronted by the demon of the faith she had repudiated and disgraced.

"And Bel-Shalti-Nannar was exceedingly afraid. As her fear waxed into terror, the Guardian of the Threshold waxed increasingly strong. Then as her terror was like to become insanity, a vision appeared before her like unto a shipwreck that riseth from the deep. Behold, she saw upon a column of the temple a picture of the Guardian and a priest overcoming him by shining the light of a lamp upon him, which light pierced him like a dagger.

"Now Bel-Shalti-Nannar knew what she must do. Her fear was changed into purpose. And lo the light of the lamp spread throughout the place and the monster face began to fade. Then did the inner voice of Bel-Shalti-Nannar speak into the mournful gloom, words that were as daggers before the demon's face.

" 'How shalt thou overcome me, unhappy shadow? Wouldst thou overcome thy creator? For thou art indeed that which I have created and would save. Thou art part of my own being, made unclean by mine own ancient sin, and now I would redeem and purify thee. This desire is within myself, not from any other source or against my will. I shall redeem thee, Guardian, not by hating thee but by having compassion. I shall not turn away but shall embrace thee, touching thy wounds and washing thy festering sores to disperse clotted time into infinity. Yea, come unto me.'

"And lo the face faded away before her and became as ashes in the light of the lamp. The accusing eyes dimmed. The bony skull disintegrated in the dusty air and, behold, a small light stood in its place. And reverent joy filled the heart of Bel-Shalti-Nannar, for the only flame in the Greater Sanctuary is upon the altar, even the Eternal Fire in the alabaster chalice, and it did beckon unto her. Now she could stand erect, and her astonished eyes beheld immense columns rising unto the starry firmament.

"And lo she did walk through eight spacious halls, each larger than the last. And in the eighth hall there was an altar upon which stood an alabaster chalice holding a single flame. Behind it lay the boundless space of infinity. But lo as she became accustomed to the dim light she saw a coffin, even an open coffin, before her. The healthy young body of Bel-Shalti-Nannar shuddered as she touched the cold, deadly stone and smelled in memory the stench of reopened graves. She felt every part of her body scream within her, rebelling in the fear of death. Her will to live arose and essayed to push her away from the coffin, but Bel-Shalti-Nannar stood firm. She freed her pure spiritual awareness from the tempters and commanded them to be silent from the height of the Holy Goal.

"And, behold, the clamor ceased and there was silence, and Bel-Shalti-Nannar laid herself in the coffin, stretching out between its icy stone arms. And lo her body began to cool and harden. Her eyes closed and opened a few times with a strange clicking noise, then remained open, gazing at infinity. Her consciousness remained unto her while her jaw slackened, and then suddenly she began falling inward at great speed. The consciousness she clung to so desperately now left her, and darkness rushed over her as waves over a drowning man. She knew she must not lose herself, so she set her thoughts in the present upon the light on the altar. And the vast inner spaces became as a funnel beneath her, a tight-throated funnel through which she fell head first. Her awareness contracted into a tiny point and lo she slipped through the narrow space into which she had been led.

"Then did Bel-Shalti-Nannar enter the bloodstream of the vast, ringing, rushing, radiating, whirling, and revolving Universe, the infernal Cosmos in which the planets, suns, galaxies, and nebulae did dance the unceasing dance of death and rebirth. And she was filled with unimaginable pleasure, the intoxicating lust of power as her awareness grew and she realized that these suns, stars, and planets were her own, moved by her own power. For all these creations danced, died, and were reborn in, through, and around her. She was the synthesis of their being, the Titan, the God of the Universe. It was she who gave them meaning. The majestic chords of contentment and pride resounded through her being, accompanied by the jubilant music of the spheres.

"So Bel-Shalti-Nannar sat enthroned in majesty above the physical Universe, and she looked down and felt what was told of old of the day after Creation, 'And lo it was very good.' Thus the endless revolutions of the Universe flamed and glowed and whirled around her — and slowly, after endless Time and repetition, the Princess waxed weary. And her weariness became apathy, and apathy became boredom. No longer was she the triumphant ruler but rather a prisoner chained by the bondage of iron laws. For since she was the total consciousness of the entire Universe, she was completely alone.

"Thus in her bleak isolation Bel-Shalti-Nannar drew unto herself her own inner Universe searching for some companion. And immediately the harmonious creation over which she had presided exploded. Everywhere she looked were beings in her own image who ran from one another, collided, fought, loved, prayed, cursed, procreated, became ill and died. And lo all that they created died also. And she beheld her own inner conflicts played out in them as theirs were played out in their offspring in perpetuity. Then was Bel-Shalti-Nannar shaken with horror and helpless agony, for she perceived that matter itself is a trap both above and below. And with her entire being she longed for freedom. But could there be such freedom? Could she escape this circle of the serpent devouring its own tail?

"As her desire for liberation grew stronger, the mind of Bel-Shalti-Nannar became concentrated as a single, tiny wand of light, and lo her whole spirit became this wand. Its dagger point sought and found the hidden opening through which she might escape from the labyrinth into meaning.

"And lo she came unto the Antechamber of the Messiahs."

29

The Antechamber of the Messiahs

"The Antechamber of the Messiahs was a place without form, glimmering in transition, for this is the place of the Immaculate Conception by which the Unmanifested seeketh to make Himself known. It is even the Gate of the Word, where the Essence of Truth floweth before it is dressed in the material Word in the world of Nin-gal. Here did Bel-Shalti-Nannar learn the secret of full knowledge and liberation. And from hence she returned by the Secret Path one last time, for everyone must return from the Antechamber of the Messiahs when he has become impregnated with the Word.

"When Bel-Shalti-Nannar arose from her coffin in front of the altar of the Greater Sanctuary, the nine old priests awaited her with their ninety disciples and all those whose souls belonged to the True Temple. And they awaited her word to learn why she had returned to them.

"The eldest priest bowed and spoke unto her, calling her by her true name. 'Then you have returned unto us, O Bel-Shalti-Nannar.'

" 'I have,' she who was called by her divine name answered quietly. 'I have returned to speak unto you and, behold, the words which I speak must not be recorded, neither shall they be preserved in pictures, for the words I speak are the Path itself, the Action and the End of All Action. I shall speak of the Final Step. To hear these words is to do them, to submerge into the separateness that in the end leads to the liberation of Unity. For lo I have returned not from a place but from the ending of every place. The very word 'end' hath no meaning there, nor can the thread of speech reach beyond its threshold.' And she pronounced the Word unto them.

> Man himself is the secret of liberation. For lo he is the image of God.
> He mirroreth the image of Nin-gal. But he hath the Everlasting within him.
> Behold, Nin-gal may be liberated only at the Great Dusk, the time when the

last of the fruit of her womb shall be returned to her. But Man may walk a separate path. Man can redeem himself.

For lo we have a Way, even God, the Begetter, the Unmanifested.

Watch ye for the Messiah, the Avatar who cometh again and yet again to play out the mystery.

He walketh upon the road and calleth unto Man to follow Him into freedom.

He walketh upon the road for a while, then turneth into the Hidden Path which leadeth to the Secret Gate. Watch ye!

Behold, a woman conceiveth. And in every country among every race and kindred there runneth one legend: Immaculate Conception.

And lo it was immaculate conception, even as life was conceived in the womb of Nin-gal by the Word of God.

And when the Divine Child appeareth, the Earth is fearful and dark.

Then are the planets in oppressive, murderous conjunction; they fill the world with horror. Evil emanates from the fixed stars. And lo the comets plough the sky, and sunspots and magnetic storms shake the net of the earth and waters. Strife erupts in the Earth, and illness becometh mortal, mania turneth to madness, and quarrels become wars that anoint the Earth with blood.

Shaken and aroused by strange happenings, the three blood-stained planes of the microcosmos await with trembling as He cometh.

Then the Child becometh a Man. For a time he walketh like unto other men, remembering and preparing, but already is his enemy stirred, watching and opposing Him. For lo their senses recognize danger and the presence of a Being greater and more destructive than any other. Within Him lieth a cold loneliness, the enemy to the hot current of life. He is as one who carryeth smuggled merchandise, yea, even that which disintegrateth matter. The matter hindereth Him, torturing His body, senses, and feelings.

Its weapons are the ridicule of man, obstacles insurmountable, slanders, hunger, want and sickness, even doubt, beauty, and the many colors of pleasure. But even these trials bring purification and strength unto Him, and the Messiah proceedeth upon His path.

Now His step quickeneth as He turneth unto His own path, following in the ways of others no more. He marketh His path and declareth Himself.

And lo the spiteful whisper as they watch the lone figure; they know it is He. The feet of the feeble begin to follow, for they recognize Him.

The winds of the world move them with wild force; they would sweep away the mortal hands that cling to Him, dissolve in flood the roads in front of Him, and reshape the very earth around Him. The Powers turn the spinning wheel of life to stun and delude Him and those who would follow Him. But lo the shadowy walls of matter part before the Messiah and He crosses the torrent in safety.

Then for one moment is the path filled with light before all the three worlds and the Gate appears. It is in vain that matter seeketh to deny His words and put Him aside. For the cruel death of the Messiah is even martyrdom, and His martyrdom becometh the key of the Gate of Liberation.

Thus the Mysterium cometh to pass before the eyes of men.

The revelation hath come and the Word hath been spoken.

Lo the light shineth and bright footsteps show the Way — the Way to Salvation through suffering and death.

"When she had done, a silence fell upon the hall, and the slender figure of Bel-Shalti-Nannar grew paler and ever paler in the blue moonlight. And who shall explain her disappearance? For it was unfathomable.

"And lo the eldest priest vanished even as she had done, yea, and the other eight and their ninety disciples, and all those who were of the True Temple, the secret priests, cultivators of the Holy Science, the dreamers and sages.

"Thus it came to pass that in the day when the fate of Ur was fulfilled, the temple of Nannar lay empty for the soul had gone out of it. And lo its hall was silent; neither were the hymns of Nannar and his divine mate heard more within its precincts. The colorful procession of the holy emblems with the sound of harp and lute emerged no more.

"And the storm that had long been forming in the East broke mightily soon after the spiritual force had gone from Ur. Belshazzar, the brother of Bel-Shalti-Nannar, even he who acted the regent for his father, was slain by the Persian invaders. And Nabunaid himself was made captive. Then was the kingdom of Babylon delivered unto the great Cyrus.

"And, behold, the people who dwelt in childlike ignorance near the temple began to quake, for they felt that the power of the empty temple had deserted them. Thus they wandered away seeking new light like unto a swarm of insects.

"And the slow-grinding mills of Time worked their will upon the temple. The Persian Kings also, who followed Zoroaster's religion, cast down its images and hastened the total destruction of the city. Only a heap of ruins remained; its very name was forgotten. Wild beasts sheltered within its terraces and Bedouins camped in its shadow, never knowing that beneath their feet lay buried the Sanctuary from which the Liberated had begun their journey unto the Antechamber of the Messiahs."

30

He, Who Never Dies

When I was eighteen I was made a Practitioner, the third grade of the Order. The laboratory work I began to perform under my father's guidance was completely new and entertaining. During those quiet, absorbed hours, I learned the true characteristics of nature and the great laws of the divine life force that work behind them. Poor blind Burrhus! He had simply played with these phenomena like a child playing with dynamite. And all the vast knowledge of Homonculus was miserably small beside the knowledge of a single functioning cell, for it is filled with life's secret and performs a transmutation every second.

The members of my Order have been variously called Rosicrucians, Templars, and Trinosophians, but in essence the Order was simply a continuation of those ancient communities which guarded the traditions of the most profound philosophy. The school of Pythagoras performed this sacred chore to the same extent as did the Essenes of Judea among whom Jesus prepared Himself for His mission. I have intentionally omitted the Masonic Lodge from this group for it has deviated into worldly affairs.

In the eighteenth century the centers of the Order were the castle of Karl von Hesse and the mystical school in Louisenland in Schleswig. Its leader was the Count Saint-Germain, a friend of Karl von Hesse, who was revered by the Brotherhood, misunderstood and admired by the nobility, and execrated by the masses, who referred to him as "the man who has never died." He was the quintessential wizard, scientist, and artist — the Magus. He had been the eyewitness of millennia, this enigmatic emissary of the Secret Brotherhood.

The Hermetic Order itself was basically Egyptian in origin but it also embodied the Christian mysticism of Christian Rosenkreuz. This Rosenkreuz had been born in 1388 into the German nobility and reared in a monastery. During a pilgrimage in the Holy Land he was initiated into the mysteries of the Secret Sciences by some erudite Arabs in Damascus. After three years in Damascus he went to Fez in Africa where he learned more about magic and the relationship of the macrocosmos and the microcosmos. Then he returned to Germany by way of Spain. Once home he founded the monastery community of Sanctus Spiritus where he retired to continue his studies. Later he accepted some of the monks, from the monastery where he had been reared, as disciples and thus formed the first Rosicrucian society. These monks wrote the results of their researches in books still available to Rosicrucians today.

Rosenkreuz's tomb wasn't discovered until 120 years after his death. It was an underground vault reached by a staircase, and there was an inscription on the door that read "Post annos CXX patebo." Inside the vault a light was burning, but it was extinguished the moment someone entered. The vault had seven sides and seven corners, and each side was five feet long and eight feet high. The ceiling, which symbolized heaven, was quartered in triangles; the floor symbolized the earth.

In the midst of the mystic chamber was an altar. There was a copper plate on it engraved with the initials A.C.R.C., and chiseled below it were the words *"Hoc Universi Compendium vivus mihi Sepulchurum feci."* Four figures surrounded this altar. Each of them was inscribed, and the inscriptions taken together read:

Nequam Vacuum
Legis Jugum
Libertas Evangelii
Dei Gloria Intacta.

Rosenkreuz's body was under the altar; it showed no signs of decay. His hand held a scroll on which an illuminated "T" was visible. The members of the Rosicrucian Order took a vow of secrecy about this matter.

Really Rosenkreuz was fulfilling a mission and doing the work of his distant masters who saw that the time was ripe to establish "spiritual embassies." Today the history of the "Fraternitas Rosae Crusis" is well enough known not to require further discussion.

Saint-Germain, however, was more conjectural. The public part of his life was so astonishing and his personality so fascinating and unusual that the average person could not understand him. He had traveled widely, was wealthy without visible means of support, and had a penetrating intellect; these things all aroused suspicion. People who had to have a label for everybody called him an impostor, but no one ever caught him in a swindle. Instead he was highly esteemed by rulers, philosophers, scientists, and artists.

I was twenty when Saint-Germain paid an unexpected visit to the Castle of Grotte. I had heard a good deal about him, of course, and I had been granted entry to the secret place that housed his famous occult library and rare manuscripts. His secular friends also knew about this library and they tried without success to find it after his supposed death. I had also seen his paintings, whose colors were mixed so brilliantly they dazzled the viewer. It was a well-known fact that the French painter Vanloo had asked to learn the secret of this mixture and had been refused. And I knew that Saint-Germain was in the habit of giving violin concerts, conducting symphonies without the score, and composing both lieder and operas.

Many of the powerful personalities who knew Saint-Germain — Frederick the Great, Voltaire, Madame de Pompadour, Rousseau, the Earl of Chatham, and Sir Robert Walpole — had tried to find out something about his origins. The most common theory was that he was the son of Rakoczi, the Prince of Transylvania. Later the Theosophists declared that he was Ferenc Rakoczi himself and that someone else had been buried in the great man's place. Other people believed that he had appeared in various countries under different names: the Marquis de Montferrat in Venice; Chevalier Schvening in Pisa; Chevalier Weldon in Milan and Leipsiz; Comte Soltikoff in Genoa and Leghorn; Graf Tzarogy in Schwalbach and Triesdorf; Rackoczi in Dresden; and Saint-Germain in Paris, The Haag, and St. Petersburg. Some of the mystic writers connected him with the mysterious Comte de Gabalais who came to the Abbé Villiers and gave him some essays on submundane spirits. Others were sure he was the Signor Gualdi of whom Hargrave Jennings had written in his book on the Rosicrucians. They also suspected that he was really Count Hompesch, the last Grand Master of the Knights of Malta.

All of this was understandable in view of Saint-Germain's widely varied life, but it is certain that he was not really all the people he was alleged to have been. In those days the world was still a huge place, and more than one adventurer, countries away from the original, took advantage of the prestige of his glistening personality. The same thing happened to another initiate, Count Cagliostro, a man of noble aspirations who became completely fused in the popular mind with the charlatan Joseph Balsamo. I myself obtained evidence that Cagliostro and Balsamo were two different men with widely disparate personalities.

But anyone who thought the multifaceted Count Saint-Germain was simply an adventurer out for material gain was thoroughly mistaken. He owned in his own right an unrivaled collection of paintings and precious stones, and Madame de Pompadour testified that he gave the King valuable Velasquezes and Murillos and presented her with the rarest and most valuable of her gems. For he was always the patron, never the patronized. He never betrayed confidence. Yet no one was ever able to determine the origin or extent of his wealth. He had no connections with any of the great banking houses but he appeared to have unlimited credit.

Currently Saint-Germain was friendly with Louis XV, whose whole court was fascinated by his knowledge of chemistry. At Louis' request he would remove flaws from diamonds and rubies right in front of everyone. He also achieved astonishing results in coloring precious stones with his own mixture of paint and crushed mother-of-pearl. The King lavished him with favors and he virtually turned the court upside down, bringing a new excitement and freshness to the rigid aristocracy. People began to look for miracles everywhere and could talk of nothing but alchemy and the occult and Saint-Germain's strange sayings.

The Count had a perfect knowledge of history that went back thousands of years. He talked about events at the court of Francis I as though he had been there himself, giving an intimate description of that King and even imitating his voice and manner. Furthermore he could give just as many confidential details about Babylon during the reign of Cyrus the Great. Naturally he dumbfounded people. Some branded him a compulsive liar and sensation-seeking charlatan, but even they had to admit that his facts were always accurate and were presented naturally rather than being introduced artificially. Saint-Germain had the genius to comprehend the entire European situation at any given time; he parried his political enemies with the greatest of ease.

The Count always seemed to have letters of recommendation that opened the highest doors in Europe. He had lived in Russia during the reign of Peter the Great, and he had been the honored guest of the Shah of Persia between 1737 and 1742. It appeared he was known and respected all over the globe.

And beyond all this Saint-Germain had a supernatural command of languages. He could speak German, English, Italian, Portuguese, Spanish, Arabic, French, Greek, Latin, and Chinese so fluently that he was accepted as a native in all these countries. Only his French was slightly accented; he spoke it as do the Piedmontese. He was ambidextrous and could write the same text simultaneously with each hand, or a different text with each. Sometimes he wrote a sonnet and a mystic poem both at once.

Saint-Germain had performed public transmutations twice, and people always flocked to get his rejuvenating elixirs and medicines. Frankly, I didn't like what I heard. Undoubtedly he had the extraordinary abilities that should belong to a real Magus and initiate, but why did he display them so openly, almost blatantly? Why the dazzling fortune and the two valets and four lackeys in cream and gold lace livery? Why should an Adept have a wardrobe like a courtesan, fresh jewels for every week, and a new name for every year?

I voiced my doubts to my father and he smiled.

"Saint-Germain doesn't need those trappings any more than you or I. His real home is the hermitage in the Himalayas from which he came and to which he will return when he has completed the mission assigned him by the higher forces. I myself can swear that he never eats at the rich tables to which he is invited; he eats a meager, meatless diet that is prepared to his own recipe. Every morning he does esoteric oriental concentration and meditation exercises without fail, and he refrains from having intimate relations with women. Since he can make stones into gems and base metal into gold, it is easy enough for him to put on this character which the world accepts more readily than the yellow robe and shaven head. Those diverse abilities are nothing but the toys a doctor uses to captivate a sick child while he examines its ills, slips a dose of bitter medicine into its mouth, or cuts out a dangerous abscess.

"You know yourself that this sick, fermenting world that has deviated so completely from the source of all spiritual health would never understand the Magus in his true form. Our sophisticated, monomaniac Universe is drifting toward a crisis, and Saint-Germain has been sent out into a quaking world already facing a grim sunset to establish first-aid stations for souls. But the things he must do to attract their attention! They are so blinded and deafened by matter that he must ring all the bells and show them marvelous colors and phenomena. He has to be a king among kings, a Croesus among the rich, and a Magus among philosophers. He has to understand everyone's tongue, see through everyone's eyes, and at the same time hear the secret voices behind the visible actions. He even has to penetrate walls," my father concluded with a sigh.

"But who is he really? How long has he lived in one body?"

My father gave me a gentle, understanding glance. "I asked Saint-Germain the same questions many years ago when I was a Practitioner."

"What was his answer?"

"He said the Secret Science was his father and the Mysteries his mother."

"Did that satisfy you?" I was disappointed.

"Not then. But later I realized that is all a true Adept can ever say about himself."

One evening I went into my father's study just as it was growing dark. I had been in the park all afternoon practicing my nature and symbol understanding exercises. A creek hurried along under the old trees there and I had collected from its bed strangely colored, polished pebbles whose delicate, translucent bodies were veined with lines like ancient hieroglyphs. These lines were mute screams of pain and yearning; you only had to read them.

I had also spent some time watching a teeming anthill near a huge linden tree. The ants scurried to and fro about the base of the trunk. This was a real ant metropolis, totally absorbed in its industrious, fascinating work. Yet the little insects were prisoners of their communal instinct. Watching them I realized that the experiment of collectivism must always be a fiasco. It locks itself into a circular cage of slavery to achieve the outward appearance of liberation, sustaining a lifestyle that leads nowhere. The society grinds without seeds, makes strenuous efforts with no meaning, refines its operations to masterly precision — all going nowhere until the fragmented group consciousness rouses itself to break out of the swirling hell of this ingenious and terrible society and forms into unique, self-aware individuals.

This September evening as always I reported my results to my father, putting my prize pebbles on his desk. He had just finished writing and was waiting for me. He listened to my observations and then added his own remarks, which often helped me to get entire thought complexes into focus. When he had finished, I got up to leave and prepare for supper but he restrained me.

"Wait. We're going to have a visitor."

"A visitor?" I was surprised. So far as I knew we'd had neither letter nor messenger that day. "Who is it?"

The room had grown dark. Suddenly I felt a presence that had not been there moments earlier. My father also felt this, for he stood up. Following his gaze, I turned around.

The newcomer stood in the glimmering gray rectangle of the window. Now he came forward. "Perhaps we might light the lamp now, Cornelius." He had a pleasant voice and his speech was polished and attractive.

"Welcome!" My father shook his hand with real joy.

Then I knew who the man was, and I felt a sudden stage fright that made me remain motionless while my father did the work of lighting the lamp. As the blue-white light poured through the room, Saint-Germain came over to me.

"So this is he!" he said, giving my father a friendly nod. Then the pressure of his strong, dry hand put me at ease. "At last — but not for the first time — good evening!" he said softly, staring into my eyes.

"Good evening." I returned his greeting, relaxed now and unselfconscious. I stared at this mysterious man. It wasn't the first time I had seen him; the memory of him slumbered deep within me. "At last — but not for the first time" — Oh, yes, he knew. He knew where it was we had met in the dim, distant past. Only the shadow of remembrance brushed me.

The man's eyes were dark and gentle, but there was intelligence and mystery there too. They seemed to see and understand everything. His face was oblong, with a delicate, slightly curved nose and a mouth where smiles seemed to lie in waiting. When he did smile, an expression of pure joy transfigured his face. For the rest, he had a slight tan and black hair and was wearing a simple, if finely woven, suit on his medium frame. I couldn't begin to estimate his age.

It was unusual that I was able to meet him, for generally the lower grades of the Order were not allowed to get acquainted with those on the higher levels except for the immediate next grade. There were nine grades in all: Juniors, Theoreticians, Practitioners, Philosophers, Minors, Majors, Adeptus Exemptus, Magisters, and finally the Magi. There were a good many members of the lower grades; membership diminished in proportion to the difficulty of the grade. Of course the ultimate rung on this ladder was God; he stood in the position of ten. This represents the duality: God equals one, World equals zero.

But my situation had been exceptional from birth. My father, who was my master and had directed me from my earliest exercises, was already a Magister, the second highest rank.

No one ever called Saint-Germain by his secular name, even when he made unexpected appearances at the Order's meetings in Retenburg. Each member of the Order had a fraternal name different from the one by which he was generally known, and his secular name was never used. Saint-Germain's fraternal name was "Tempio Aperto" — Open Temple. When he conducted the secret initiation ceremonies, he was called Hierophant.

Of course the exceptional opportunity to meet him was not a divine grace that had fallen into my lap; I had worked for this privilege once upon a time. I remembered it gradually later, during the silence of initiation. I had actually been a member of the Fraternity for many centuries before my fall and had gotten as far as the threshold of the final trials. But my talent, intellect, and discipline had been only on a human order, and during the convulsive crisis of conscious death and rebirth I had yielded to my weaknesses, fears caused by imperfect knowledge and passion caused by unresolved emotions. Still my ideals had ever been high, and I really understood a good deal of the theory of secret symbols and the truths of existence. My return had been a genuine joy to my fellow members and the Magi, who had never ceased to regard me as a member. Really my lapse, in spite of all the misery it had caused me, was simply a practical test of a tenet of faith laid down during my mystical initiation. I had had to learn and understand it thoroughly and make it a real part of me, despite the tangling chaos of material unreality.

Initiation always occurs twice. The first time is when an Entity has come to Earth but still has an undimmed awareness of the other world. Then he steps into the Temple of Mysteries. During the trials he is alone in the silence of condensed time and shrunken space, and an indelible sketch is etched upon his soul in a few sure marks. The trials themselves are symbols of all the temptations, possibilities, and dangers to be undergone later and of the true meaning of existence. This sketch once made is guarded by the soul, and its lines are still visible through the thickest body dress, even though their meaning has been forgotten. It is the burning urge that appears in our restless dreams and drives us to and fro from experience to experience in the barricaded physical world. It is the source of the eternal discontent that causes us to reach forward for ephemeral goals. For behind these goals is the Chimera, the sacred riddle, that lures us on even through the midst of passion, ambition, intellectual attainments, death, and birth. No matter how far we stray, we are still on the prescribed path and will return to our beginnings.

Then there is the second, final initiation that takes place at the end of the road, after the fires of passion are burned out and human experience has been endured. The theory becomes a living reality, and the gate of the first mystery swings open. But once you have passed the first gate, you cannot leave until you have trod the entire maze.

★

Saint-Germain's arrival caused a real change in my life, for my father told me I was to accompany the Count to Paris. I could tell he was watching intently to see how I would react. Would I reveal joy, immature excitement, or anxiety?

I confronted myself honestly, facing the ashes of dead fires the name conjured in me. I knew that I must go where I was sent, that every course set before me was a part of my personal task. Knowing this, I submitted obediently. "What will my duties be in Paris?" I asked quietly.

"You are to be the Count's secretary and famulus, to learn from him and obey his instructions."

"How long will I be in this post?" I suddenly felt sad at the thought of leaving my parents and this beautiful, peaceful park where I had spent so many wonderful days.

"Until your work is finished." My father was firm. I was ashamed of having been so immature.

My mother came up to me, encouragement in her every feature. I embraced her. "Distance means nothing to the soul," she whispered. "You have to check your knowledge before every important examination, you know. Go in peace, Cornelius."

31

The First Messenger from the Past

I thoroughly enjoyed my journey with the witty and amiable Count Saint-Germain. The Count's famous thoroughbreds drew our luxurious carriage, and inside were all kinds of ingenious mechanisms to add to our comfort. Our trip itself was so well organized that his own rested horses and servants awaited us at every relay. It was in Saint-Germain's carriage that I first saw a drop-leaf table, a small refrigerator for food, a water tank, and a heating device that enabled Yidam, the Count's mute Tibetan servant, to make coffee or tea. There were even push-button censers for incense that either refreshed or tranquilized with no aftereffects.

"Do you like my little toys?" Saint-Germain smiled at my bewilderment.

"They astound me," I admitted.

"Louis XV thought they were devilish, but he wanted them so much he tried to steal them. Really this wizardry is just a little loan from the future. Such things will become commonplace. People will acquire these comforts only to find they do not solve their problems. The evolution of man is headed in that direction, but right now it is hard to believe it will ever come about. Nevertheless the framework of life will expand alarmingly and the classes will become better equalized. The masses will begin to live more like the privileged few and to share their problems."

"Aren't you talking about a revolution?"

"*Revolutions*," he revised. "Many of them — external and internal. They will erupt periodically for centuries." The Count stared pensively into the distance. "The first will come soon," he added softly.

★

Before we went to Paris we spent a month in strictest seclusion in Ghent.

Saint-Germain never even set foot outside our quarters; I was his link with the outside world.

The old town of Ghent seemed to have stagnated in time; its ancient houses with their narrow windows, arcades, and ornamental carvings and the cobblestones underfoot reminded me of Nuremberg, where I had also walked with a Magus. I was again serving the same man, of course, though he had a different body and face. But I was completely different from the persecuted, obsessed Hans Burgner.

Saint-Germain kept a strict diet during his seclusion and fasted periodically. I supervised the preparation of his meals, not because Yidam needed my oversight — he executed his master's thought commands perfectly — but to teach me about nutrition. The main ingredient in his menu was oat flour; Yidam used a small handmill to grind it to varying consistencies. He didn't use much salt but did much of his seasoning with honey, milk, and lemon. Everything was cooked in pure vegetable oil. Fresh butter and fruit completed the menu. I was glad to share this repast; I had become accustomed to such meals in my parents' home.

I dwell on this to point out how much the old alchemists knew about the necessity of a proper diet and the importance of vitamins. They taught even then that diet was decisive in preventing or healing most diseases. Two hundred and thirty years before, Rochard had kept a vegetarian diet and prescribed the same for his patients.

In addition to maintaining a strict diet, Saint-Germain, like Paracelsus, Trismosin, Albertus Magnus, Sendivogius, and Rochard, used a medication that strengthened the human organism and improved its resistance — the essence of nature's healing power. This secret of regeneration they had gained from profound knowledge and intuition.

I was only allowed to see the Count for one hour every evening. He was always serious and taciturn, very different from the worldly, vibrant cavalier. There was an abstract, noble simplicity about him; he was regenerating those energies that he must pour on the world so that a very few of the millions of possible seeds on the barren soil might take root. He would listen to my summary of his mail and dictate brief replies.

These letters came from almost every important personality in Europe and brought him all the latest news, usually with requests for advice. Thus he saw events before their birth and was sometimes able to change them — unfortunately not often enough to make the world picture a saner one.

While we were in Ghent, Saint-Germain intervened to give me a strange and important experience.

One morning two of our servants — one permanent and one temporary — were walking the Count's thoroughbreds in front of our lodgings. I was just coming back from my early morning walk, and I noticed a man eyeing the horses with approval. Soon he began striking up a conversation with the servants. He was a conspicuous man in foreign clothing, with an olive complexion, dark, burning eyes, a large aquiline nose, and a strong jaw — obviously of Latin origin. I estimated that he was about forty-five or fifty, though his tall figure was still muscular and youthful.

Yet it wasn't his appearance that caught my attention; it was a certainty that I knew the man from somewhere and had forgotten his name. I stepped back under the arcade and watched his animated features and broad gestures. He was asking the servants what nobleman it was who owned such rare, beautiful animals.

Our regular stableboy was too discreet to reply, but the other took it upon himself to declare that the horses were the property of the Count Saint-Germain. He added further that the Count had been in residence for a month and would see no one, despite many entreaties.

The foreigner immediately responded eagerly. "Why I know Saint-Germain — know him well. Announce me immediately. He'll see *me*."

The servants, scared and apologetic, refused. I was annoyed by the importunity of this aggressive man, but I was more certain than ever that I knew him, and it worried me.

"Well, I'll write him." The man cut off their argument with the arrogant gesture of a man performing before an audience. And then I recognized him — Louis de la Tourzel, that drunken satyr who had been my father in my previous life before he got killed in a brothel brawl. I watched his retreating figure; he had kept the feline movements of his previous life. His body was obviously still merely a vessel of passion, but there was more intelligence and complexity in it.

Saint-Germain noticed my brooding immediately that evening. When he asked, I told him what had happened. Before I could even finish, a rock with a letter attached to it crashed through the window. "That's just like him," I said resignedly. Somehow I still felt I had to apologize for him. I went over and picked up the note, which proved to be both aggressive and theatrical. His writing was bold and coarse, but the note was admittedly witty and original.

My dear Count! You won't keep me from communicating with an old friend, even if you have a seven-headed dragon at the door. When would it be convenient for you to see another master of the art of living? I burn to shake your hand. I'll be round tomorrow evening to collect your answer in person.

Your Casanova

The signature made me gasp with surprise. "Casanova! Well! This *is* progress."

"No," Saint-Germain contradicted quietly, "fulfillment. It is the logical end of a lifeline that is going in the wrong direction; it contains the decline within itself."

"He seems to be exaggerating when he calls you an old friend," I prompted, unable to resist the temptation to learn more about this enigma.

"There is such a thing as a one-sided friendship, Cornelius. I have run into him a few times on the stage where we both play a role."

"You obviously play thoroughly contrasting roles," I replied.

"We do. For that very reason they are complementary."

"Like light and shadow, you mean."

"In the material world one can't exist without the other."

"He arouses strange feelings in me," I admitted thoughtfully. "I'd really like to do something for him. He repels me but I pity him. I feel responsible for him, just as if he were still my father. I'm ashamed of him but he interests me. Are you going to receive him tomorrow?"

Saint-Germain said nothing for a moment, staring at me steadily. "I think I'll have to so you can understand him and get him out of your system, Cornelius. You need to realize that neither one of us can do anything for him right now. God himself does not interfere, you know, but merely allows him to continue to live and experience."

★

I awaited Casanova's visit with a troubled excitement I had not felt in a long time. The Count was once more the man of the world for the occasion. His dark suit and doublet bore jeweled buttons worth a fortune, his hair was powdered, and a huge, clear sapphire sparkled on his finger.

"Tonight you will have the opportunity to understand something important, Cornelius. You can't become a Master until you learn the real nature of things, including the law that a person can be reached only at his own level and only to the extent of his capacity. When there is no capacity to understand, you cannot force even the greatest and most wonderful treasures on a person. A prophet who keeps on preaching the Word to a rock is undoubtedly a lunatic."

Just then a servant came in and announced, "Jacques de Casanova de Seingalt."

Saint-Germain stood up and went to greet his guest, while I remained in the background, a mere observer. I enjoyed the advantages of this position many times during the years I was with him. Scores of candles were burning in the room, but the window arch was shadowed so I withdrew to watch this renowned and infamous man of whom so little was known and yet so much discussed. I was a part of his past, the past that was only a dim presentiment to him.

He had changed a good deal. I don't mean his features; of course they were different, though it was easy to distinguish traits of Louis de la Tourzel. But Casanova's face was darker and more passionate, yet with more cunning and experience. He was debauched but not a drunkard. His eyes glittered with intensity and distrust — the adventurer who sought and shaped his own destiny. There was just a trace of sardonic humor about him — a bitter, skeptical humor which was now only the ashes of fatigue, nausea, and old age. Yet it was a humanizing element by which his spirit had begun to grow. His exaggerated and expensive clothes invariably aroused antipathy in men, but you couldn't deny that the man had a presence. He maintained eye contact with whomever he was speaking, virtually leaning toward them physically and overwhelming them with the force of his voice. This technique swept over the weak and thoughtless of both sexes like a tidal wave.

Saint-Germain just smiled at Casanova's fulsome compliments and pledges of friendship. "You were good enough to write, my friend, that we are both masters of the art of living. Why don't we put aside the flattery we both reserve for the seduction of the masses? Let's allow ourselves the luxury of pure frankness tonight."

"Now, by God, there's a tempting offer!" Casanova was enthusiastic. "Dressing gown and slippers then?"

"My dear Casanova! Complete nudity."

The other man's face was perplexed; then he hooded his eyes in watchful caution. "As you will. Will you disrobe first?"

"Naturally," Saint-Germain replied sonorously as he bowed his guest to the table. Yidam appeared quietly with a heavily-laden tray. He laid out rich, spicy dishes and poured Casanova some wine, leaving the Count's glass empty. Then he left silently. "Help yourself," Saint-Germain said cordially. "You may want the strength for this unusual performance."

"I observe you're not eating the same food I am," Casanova remarked, "and your glass is empty. What proof have I that Europe's greatest sorcerer doesn't wish to poison me?"

"True." The Count nodded. "I see you've begun to disrobe first after all. Cornelius!"

I stepped out of the window arch. My appearance definitely deflated Casanova. Startled, he just sat staring at me.

"Where the devil did he spring from?"

"I've been here all along, sir." I spoke politely and bowed. "Cornelius von Grotte at your service."

"He's my famulus, my shadow, if you will," Saint-Germain explained. "You need take no note of him. He will remain but not as a factor in our conversation. Cornelius, taste our friend's food and drink some of his wine."

"That won't be necessary!" Casanova grabbed the glass and drained it at one draught. The Count had reckoned correctly, of course. I had been alarmed, since I never took alcohol or meat, but a mere doubt of the man's death-defying bravado would make him take still greater risks for vanity's sake. I sat down at the table.

"Does it bother you to have Cornelius here?" Saint-Germain asked.

"No, why should it? There's just something damned strange . . ."

"What do you mean?"

Casanova turned directly to me. "Tell me, boy, haven't we met before?"

I looked at Saint-Germain and he replied for me. "You have, in a way. He was once the only legitimate son you ever had, Casanova — not now, of course, but in a previous life."

"That is so, my lord," I affirmed.

It was obvious that the man was greatly disquieted and did not want to admit it. Finally he laughed aloud. "Your imagination is unrivaled, Saint-Germain! But why try your tricks on an old skeptic like me?"

"You are wrong, my friend; I am being entirely honest."

"Then I will be too. I think this whole thing is a fraud," Casanova retorted crudely. "But I'll go along with it. Continue your disrobing. Where did you get that black cook?"

"I brought him back from Tibet."

"And when were you in Tibet?"

"Eighty-five years ago."

"So that makes him . . ."

"Yidam is one hundred and twenty."

"One hundred and — oh, all right. How old are you?"

"Ageless."

"Foul! You're evading."

"Only by your narrow definition. But if you want to know, I have existed ever since the material world has existed."

"And you remember all this?"

"Yes."

"All right, tell me some nice gossip about Cleopatra."

"I found her fairly commonplace. She was really just a muddled, lustful woman maddened by reflections of ancient glory, a cow resting on the throne of departed eagles. She had nothing in common with the real soul of Egypt or the ancient Pharaoh-Priests who had possessed the Great Truth. Even her fabled beauty was exaggerated; she was no prettier than a young slave girl. It was only the splendor of her position that made her desirable. She was simply willful, incapable of the creative concentration that forms destiny. That's why she fell."

"Oh, come off it. You're interesting enough but you're cheating."

"I deny that."

"I don't want to insult you, but I am continuing to go naked."

"By all means."

"So I may continue to question the conjurer?"

"Of course."

"And you'll answer anything and tell me all your secrets?"

"I repeat, I will be frank."

"And what precisely do you mean by frankness?"

"You spoke of secrets, Casanova. True, I have them, just as nature does, but disclosing them is not just a matter of desiring to. Nature keeps no secrets, you know. She answers all questions in her own language. To understand the answer, you must understand the language."

"So now I'm stupid too."

"No, you are just a man who has studied different types of languages."

A satisfied, lecherous smile stole over Casanova's face. "Certainly there are some languages I know very well indeed. But you speak them nearly as well as I do. Your mysterious ways are just as effective with women as my notorious reputation. I've envied you more than once — the way you can bring a shadow of youth back into the face of a woman who fears she is losing her charms."

"Why do you envy that?"

"Because it's the key that opens every door."

"Perhaps so, but I have never used it as such."

Casanova's eyes showed cynical scorn. "You mean you're not interested in making love?"

"I'm interested in everything, even that."

"Then why your previous remark? Haven't you ever taken advantage of your opportunities?"

"Perhaps I have used them differently than you have, but I've always been satisfied."

Casanova laughed sarcastically. "How about the ladies, my dear Count? Were *they* satisfied?"

"I think so. I was honored with their continued friendship and, more important, they were grateful that they did not have to feel nausea and regret."

"Then they left your bed untouched, my friend!"

"Untouched bodily, yes."

"So you celebrated a soul wedding with them? I would have thought that an impeccable cavalier like Saint-Germain would be more afraid of ridicule than of feeding the host to a hungry woman."

"There, my dear Casanova, we come to one of the secrets it would be useless to explain to you. The only rapture you understand is the rapture of pleasure, which lasts only until the wick of the candle of the spinal column is used up. By the way, you had better start being thrifty with it! My ecstasy doesn't consume my energy. The longer it burns, the greater its vitality, and those with whom I share it never feel the fatigue of its burning out."

"Oh, I've heard the myth of eternal pleasure before — and I don't believe a word of it. I myself have gone through every hell and byway of pleasure and *I* haven't found it. I've had dark, insatiable Asian bitches who had learned their art in the holy books and could prolong for hours what passes in seconds in the west. I've had Sappho's descendants in Greece who could make love-making a long, deadly ceremony of beauty. I've had Italian women right beside the bedrooms of their old husbands, and I've had Spanish women who wore their chastity like a fiery cross. I've known the cold and determined art of the French courtesans that is more maddening than all the others combined. But all the ecstasies led to fatigue, and the lamp of pleasure burnt out. There's simply no pleasure without the body, and the pleasure always ends sooner or later because the body's strength is finite."

"No, the body's strength is infinite, like any other force. It simply eludes those who don't know how to retain and renew it," retorted Saint-Germain.

"You mean your famous nostrum, the Atho-ether?"

"Partially. That of course is only a symbol of the universal spirit."

"Would you show me some?"

"Certainly." To my surprise Saint-Germain rose, took a carefully sealed crystal vial from his cabinet and handed it to Casanova, who took it eagerly. There was a milky fluid in the vial that glistened and tilted with the movement of the bottle. "This fluid, like the human body, contains condensed, undiscovered forces," the Count explained quietly. "You can see it and weigh it. Shake it a bit and let the light shine through it. I warn you though if you or anybody else who does not know the secret should desire it, it will vanish like vapor right before his eyes. Do you believe me?"

"No."

"Well, here's a pin. Puncture the wax. If you can swallow just a single drop of that fluid, you'll renew your virility for years."

Casanova grasped the pin impatiently, punctured the wax, and held the vial next to the candle. The light shone through the transparent crystal; of the milky fluid there was no sign. "What happened to it?" he burst out.

"What happens to the energy of youth? Where is the vigor of our seed scattered in dreams? What happens to life in an instant when it flows from the bloody stump of a severed head?"

"How should I know? I can ask unanswerable questions as well as you can."

"But the answer is in your very hand. You just don't understand its language."

"You needn't rub it in. Me, I believe in what I can see, feel, touch, and comprehend in this world. I've no inclination to go back to the school bench, but I must confess that this idea of rejuvenated virility strikes close to home. I don't know the secret of it; you say you do. Then allow some of your vanishing Atho-ether to enter my system, and I'll be eternally grateful to you for lengthening the one thing that means anything to me."

"I cannot do it, my friend; it would merely delay your growth. But I will be glad to heal your gout. Fifteen of my pills will heal your pain in three days and you'll regain your elasticity."

"To hell with your pills!" Casanova exploded rudely. "There's a catch to them, just like your rejuvenating medicine. Then you would explain that they didn't work because I thought of a limping jackass when I took them. Show me some material results, something I can touch like a wine goblet or a woman. Give me something that warms me and gives me energy, something I can taste before devouring."

"Do you have a large silver coin?" Saint-Germain cut in smoothly.

"As it happens, I do. Why?"

"Lend it to me awhile and I promise you it will bring you interest before you leave this room."

Casanova handed him a silver twelve-sou piece. Immediately the door opened and Yidam brought in a portable iron furnace. He put a thin sheet of steel on the floor, placed the furnace down on top of it, and set about making up the fire.

"Excellent teamwork!" Casanova applauded ironically. "You've got it down pat. Your mute servant enters at exactly the right moment and carries out your prearranged orders."

"I gave Yidam the orders in your presence," Saint-Germain replied simply.

"How? I didn't hear anything."

"But Yidam did. He hears differently than you do, for he knows the language."

"Why do you keep saying that? To make me feel stupid?"

"I haven't repeated myself. I'm just stating facts. Anyone can learn what he does not know, if he wants to and has the interest to persevere."

"Well, I don't. Furthermore I don't believe there's anything to learn. I've no desire to be considered a Superman, as you do."

"I know you don't believe that there is anything to believe or that I can tempt you. That's all right. Would you like to examine this crucible before I close it?" He passed it over to Casanova, who turned it upside down and then tapped its sides inch by inch with his ring. Then Saint-Germain put the twelve-sou piece into it, fastened the lid, and put the crucible on the fire.

Yidam turned the sandglass on the table. Casanova and Saint-Germain watched him silently as he performed his tasks. The room was silent save for the hiss of the bellows; yet it was filled with the sound of Casanova's nervous restlessness. I could see his dense waves of protest and instinctive resistance swirling around Saint-Germain, who stood watching the fire with crossed arms.

The last grain of sand dripped to the bottom of the glass. Yidam nodded and set aside the bellows, then unscrewed the lid of the crucible with wooden pliers. Saint-Germain held his hand over it and dropped in a soft ball of wax. Then Yidam replaced the lid, turned the sandals, and applied himself again to the bellows.

The heat grew almost unbearable, just as it once had in the workshop of Anton Bruggendorf, but Casanova would not budge from his seat beside the furnace. The heavy meal and his conflicting emotions added to the heat he was feeling, and beads of sweat glistened from under his wig. His face was flushed, and I could see a nerve beating in his forehead.

At last the time was up. Yidam opened the crucible, then submerged it in water. The pure, yellow gold was cooled in minutes, and Saint-Germain pried it loose and handed it to Casanova.

"Have it examined by a goldsmith tomorrow. Get him to weigh a twelve-sou silver piece and compare weights — I promised you it would be equal."

But now Casanova's blind temper erupted. "It's a cheat! Just a mean, ordinary cheat!" He almost choked on his hatred. "I stood there and watched you smuggle the gold into the crucible!"

Saint-Germain remained impassive. "I believe that after that it is unnecessary for us to continue this evening." He bowed slightly, and Yidam opened the door. Casanova threw down the gold, flung on his cloak, and stormed down the stairs. We could hear him cursing on the way down.

"Lousy hypocrites! Trying to cheat *me*! Conceited charlatan!" His voice faded into the night.

I turned back to Saint-Germain who was opening the window to clear the dense, hostile odors with the cool autumn air. Yidam had already left. I quietly extinguished the candles until only one was left burning. Then I went to the window and thanked the Count for the mystery he had showed me.

32

Paris 1780

It felt strange to return to the city after so many years. I could feel and almost touch the progress of its disease, the loosening of its fibers as decomposition became imminent. The lava that would erupt into the streets was being heated most vigorously by those who danced atop the volcano — the majority of the nobility. For this was the era in which Versailles and the Trianon were virtually two hostile fortresses with the weak-willed King swaying between them like a limp bell clapper.

Yet despite the lampooning poems and scurrilous slanders, the people in general would have been willing to make their peace with Marie Antoinette. In spite of the inflammation of their chronic dissatisfaction, they were still spellbound by the magic of the throne. It was Versailles, deserted and mocked by the careless Queen, that howled for vengeance.

We got to Paris at the end of October. The Count did not go to court immediately but remained at home in his own palace. It was tucked away behind the Saint-Roch Church and sat in its own large park. There was a small building in front that camouflaged it nicely; what you could see through the trees looked gray and insignificant.

The same duality was found in the house; it was a true reflection of Saint-Germain himself. If one entered through the main gate, he went through a tropical greenhouse filled with exotic vines and flowers and decorated by artificial lotus pools. Then he came to the splendid halls within. The walls were covered in brocade and damask, and the upholstery, curtains, Venetian mirrors, porcelain fireplaces, carpets, chandeliers, tapestries, and artworks overshadowed Versailles itself.

But on the second floor, where Saint-Germain really lived, there was no such luxury. His bedroom was like a monk's cell. There was an enthralling painting of Christ over his narrow iron bed; he had painted it himself with those colors that glowed in the dark. The only other ornament was an ivory statue of Buddha that was fully half a meter high and had a green gem in the middle of its forehead. It stood on an ebony pedestal set in a small niche, and a lotus-shaped sanctuary lamp burned in front of it.

There were two rooms off this cubicle. One was a well-equipped bathroom and dressing chamber; the other was a small, almost empty room whose windows were covered by a heavy curtain. A rush mat was on the floor, and the walls were hung with large colored prints of twenty-two hieroglyphs. The only furniture was a long, narrow table which held a large skyglobe and two seven-branched candelabra. Both star-map and hieroglyphs glowed in the dark as did the portrait of Christ. The laboratory and library opened from this meditation room. I occupied a section similar to the Count's, and we shared the laboratory and library. My cell wall was decorated with a cross.

As I came to know Saint-Germain, all my doubts and suspicions vanished, and I admired and trusted him absolutely.

Every day we got up at dawn, bathed, and put on long, dark robes like monks' cowls. Then we each went into our meditation rooms to perform meditation exercises. In addition to animating hieroglyphs, I also worked on my telepathic ability. At a predetermined time after our basic exercises, Saint-Germain would send me telepathic messages from the other wing of the palace — geometrical symbols, letters, and finally whole sentences I had to write down verbatim. During this exercise I wore an Egyptian headband with a gold serpent in the middle.

After these exercises we would stroll in the park for an hour, then break-fast on porridge and fresh fruits. Generally we spent the morning working together in the laboratory. After lunch I read and made notes while Saint-Germain worked on his principal book, *La Trés Sainte Trinosophie — The Most Holy Trinosophy.*

This book is a work of unparalleled significance. It is really the diary of a soul's coming of age and may be seen merely as a description of Saint-Germain's own initiation and progress in the Mystical Brotherhood. The purpose of the book is to teach disciples who already know the terminology. The text begins with all the allegorical details of the ceremonies of the classic age, and symbolic language is used throughout. Thus the work seems incomprehensible on initial reading, but deeper analysis will show the hidden significance of each detail.

The book is written in twelve parts and each has a sketch that supplies the explanation of it. The first parts deal with the so-called Memphis ceremony of the Neo-Egyptian tradition, and the tests applied to the aspirant are related to the four elements — earth, water, fire, and air. Its basic pattern is the powerful one of the twelve houses of the Zodiac.

For the Zodiac is the great cycle of the soul, and it was by watching the sun's orbit across its signs that the ancient priesthood developed the idea of the sacred cycle. They believed the first sign was the beginning and the last was the end of all human wisdom.

Saint-Germain constructed this book of the Three-Layered Wisdom in alchemical symbols for the most part. What he was really describing, of course, was not the real chemical knowledge since he, like all other great alchemists, regarded gold-making as only a very small part of knowledge. He was writing about the spiritual process of man toward Adepthood.

During the afternoon I would take care of the mail and then walk for two or three hours. I roamed the streets of Paris freely but felt no desire to return to the scenes of my memories. Still I remembered my mother's parting injunction and decided not to avoid them. I would settle the matter — thumb through my old theses and see if there was indeed a gap in my knowledge.

First I went to the little shop on the Rue Saint-Honoré. It didn't seem to have changed at all; there were the religious relics crowded on the rough wood shelf by the cellar door, just as they had been in Lepitre's time. There was a musty odor about the place which immediately conjured up the image of the ravaged, slovenly Rosalie.

It was still a bookshop, just as before. The bell over the door sounded so familiar that my heart skipped a beat. There was a small, ugly girl squatting in the moth-eaten silence; her hollow face lit up as she jumped up to serve me.

"Can I help you, Monsieur? I'll light a candle for you. You go right on and browse." I watched her light the candle, lost in my memories. The girl, mistaking my silence for hesitancy, hastened to reassure me. "My father's out for the day but I can get you anything you wish — absolutely anything, Monsieur."

I was sure from her voice that she was offering some of the secret literature so much in demand those days. "*Anything?*" I prodded.

She nodded, disappeared behind a tattered curtain, and returned with a little yellow pamphlet. "The latest!" she whispered.

I leaned toward the candle and opened the pamphlet.

Chacun se demande tout bas;
Le Roi pent-il? Ne pent-il pas?
La triste Reine en désepére . . .

It was a satirical poem against the Queen. As I continued to read, the girl became agitated.

"Please, Monsieur! Someone might come in!"

To quiet her, I put the dangerous merchandise in my pocket, paid, and bade her farewell. Then I hurried to get home through the darkening streets. Voices rumbled out of the darkness; laughs, snatches of curses, and the sound of running feet filled the air around me. Somewhere someone was mockingly reciting the banned poem I had just bought, extracting the maximum laughter from the erotic details.

That evening at supper I showed the booklet to Saint-Germain and told him how I had acquired it and later heard it recited in the Paris streets.

"This is another poison that has overflowed from the palace into the sewers," the Count remarked as he leafed through it. "Fools! Don't they realize these attacks on the throne are deliberately undermining the only system that supports their own privileges? They're paying these poets to write their own death warrants!"

I shuddered at his ominous words; I too had felt this premonition ever since we had come to Paris. "They say terrible things about the Queen. You know her; is she really as bad as all that?"

"She's no better and no worse than the others; she just doesn't pretend. She isn't really evil, just extravagant — a curious, hedonistic, and superficial woman with all the amiable characteristics of a self-assured child. But this child doesn't realize she's playing with explosives."

"Maybe you could warn her," I ventured.

"I haven't even tried. Words bore her if they're not the most transparent rococo lace. Her soul has all the depth of the ornamental pool at the Trianon. Fate always chooses the best tool to fulfill itself. It will take searing events to change Marie Antoinette and burn the dross from her. But you'll soon meet her for yourself, Cornelius."

"Really? How's that?"

"Oh, she'll need me," he replied evasively.

33

The Bloody Crystal

I decided to make a pilgrimage to my old home. All that stood on the site was a small shack. The garden was overgrown with weeds and only the stumps of the fence were left. What in the world had happened, I wondered. Time hadn't done all that in just a few decades.

As I approached, an old beggar crawled out of the shack and studied me suspiciously. I decided to ask him to explain the mystery. "There was a brick palace here some years ago," I began.

"Maybe there was," he replied tersely.

"Who owns this property now?"

Now he became positively hostile. "It's not for sale. Belongs to the city." With that he crawled back into his hovel.

Curious, I started making inquiries at nearby houses and shops. Finally an old woman told me the house had burned down in 1750. A fire had started in a locked room and they could not find the key in time. A fitting fate for a house whose occupants had been destroyed by inner fires.

★

The Marquise D'Anjou's palace, where the "lambs" had met, was still unchanged. It had changed owners during the time of the spendthrift Corinna. She had been the sole heir of the D'Anjou fortune, for her sickly brother Christian had died young, but palace, jewels, and all had disappeared under the ministrations of Germaine and Martin Allais. The palace became the property of the Polignac family in 1780, and a distant member of the clan now occupied it. Saint-Germain's name would have gotten me in, of course, but I had no desire to revisit those pompous old rooms. The only person I felt any nostalgia for was the kindly Dr. Péloc.

★

Maria Theresa, Empress of Austria and mother of the French Queen, died without seeing the birth of a Dauphin, an event for which she had longed. She had hoped that production of an heir would solidify her daughter's position and bring her emotional maturity. Now Marie Antoinette was completely alone. The Empress' ambassador Mercy no longer had any influence with her now that his mistress was dead.

The death of her mother terrified the thoughtless Marie Antoinette. Maria Theresa had scolded her like a naughty child, but she had cared for her, even though it was from a distance. Now the Queen felt she had lost her only rear guard, the only person she could count on to support her against the world and even against herself. She found herself surrounded by selfish, frivolous friends, a weak and indifferent husband, and a world that watched her with suspicion. She was overcome with anxiety, and her only true friend, the little Lamballe, could only weep with her. Her other confidante, the Countess Polignac, was ill and could not come to court. Dark premonitions tormented her.

One evening in early December I returned from my evening walk to find our lower halls brilliantly lit. Deducing that we had company of high rank, I circled the house and went up to my room the back way. Here Yidam was waiting for me with a message; I was to don full evening dress in honor of our exalted guest, the Queen of France.

I was both curious and self-conscious as I made my way into the salon. I found two young women in deep mourning: the Princess de Lamballe and the troubled Marie Antoinette, whose eyes were red with weeping. The Queen received my introduction informally, almost absent-mindedly, and impatiently told Saint-Germain to begin his experiment.

The Count led his guests into the ornate study we never used for that purpose. A crystal ball stood on the desk, glittering in the light of the multitudinous candles. Obeying Saint-Germain's mute command, I extinguished all save the ones at either end of his desk. After seating the women in comfortable chairs, he sat down before the ball. I lit the censer and soon a soothing, comforting fragrance filled the room.

The Princess de Lamballe uneasily moved closer to the Queen and glanced fearfully at the Count who was absorbed in the crystal ball. Soon she also was mesmerized by the sparkling crystal.

During this hypnotic silence, I stealthily watched this woman who was the most envied and hated person in all France. Marie Antoinette stared motionlessly in front of her, a mask of sorrow. Her regular, delicate features could not compete with the childlike beauty of her companion, but a certain vibrant restlessness made her the more striking. Even now she exuded willful, haughty impatience, and those sensitive, sensuous lips revealed great potential for rash words, irrevocable insults, and irretrievable silences. The curve of her nostrils mirrored her insatiable demand for new and different entertainments and her total disregard for everyone else in the world. There was no depth to those clear, flashing eyes; she looked to the external world for her light. Just now her sorrow had unleashed forgotten perceptions from the death chamber of dormant abilities where both her past and her future awaited her.

Having deciphered this hieroglyph, I turned my attention to the ball. It was already clouded, coming to life. A whitish mist swirled with darker patches in the midst of it, just like the mute, crowded jostling of astral matter. Slowly the delicate face of the little Lamballe emerged through the murk — but it was the face of a dead woman. The mist about her began to glow blood- red, and parts of her naked body floated to the surface as if spewed up by an ocean of blood. The flesh of those begrimed limbs was decayed and corpselike . . .

I was aroused by a scream. The Princess de Lamballe was screaming wildly, her cries interspersed with gasps of horror. She pressed her hands to her eyes and gabbled hysterically. "Sweet Jesus, help me! Let me get away! I can't bear it! I won't look any more — lead us not into temptation . . . It's too horrible!"

The Queen quickly knelt before her, stroking and comforting her. Saint-Germain mixed a tranquilizer in a glass of wine and forced it between her trembling lips. Finally she became somewhat calmer but refused to tell the Queen what it was that had frightened her.

"It was nothing to do with Your Majesty, just me — I'd kill myself here and now if you commanded it, but I can't tell what I saw in that crystal. Please don't be angry; don't ask me to do it. I can't even bear to think about it. It's too horrible." Her lips began to tremble again and she broke into quiet sobs. The Queen, pitying her, did not ask any further but turned to Saint-Germain.

"Well, can't you say something consoling?" She spoke with the reproach of a spoiled child.

"The near future is like a sunset, Your Majesty; it shows a dark night coming upon us. But if you are satisfied with the light of a few years . . ."

"Well, what is it?" Marie Antoinette's voice snapped with fear and tension.

"One year from today, the Dauphin will be born."

A small sigh arose from the Queen's lips and the joyous smile of the mother spread over her face. "The Dauphin — My Lord and God! If only it were true!"

"It is already a fact, Your Majesty. This part of the future awaits us like a refuge — let's say in Varennes. We have only to travel there on the carriage of time."

The Queen positively glowed at the thought. "You don't know — you can't possibly know — how much that would mean to me, how many of my problems it would solve."

"It will solve many problems, Your Majesty, but it won't silence those you expect it to. They will become even louder, for the birth of the Dauphin will thwart many plans."

"Then I could care less about them!" This careless comment epitomized the Queen's attitude up until the tragedy struck. "What can they do to me if I produce a legitimate heir to the throne?"

"I have a humble request of Your Majesty." Saint-Germain spoke quietly.

"But what, Magister?" Marie Antoinette spoke jestingly, all attention and generosity. "You know I take care of my friends."

"If the heir is born as I said, will you give some thought to some advice I add to my prophecy?"

"Speak, Saint-Germain. Tonight I will even listen to advice."

"Will you follow it if . . .?"

"If the Crown Prince is born? Well — maybe. Assuming you don't advise something contrary to my nature or something that would bore or humiliate me."

"Maybe I didn't use the right word, Your Majesty." Saint-Germain's face was grave. "This is not advice; it's a warning. It may well bore and humiliate Your Majesty in your present mood. What I ask is that you make a short trip to Versailles after the Dauphin is born. Build a bridge between yourself and the nobility and another between yourself and the people. This would resolve and rescue everything."

"I'll have to think about that," the Queen replied, leaning back in her chair. "First let us see the prophecy fulfilled." Suddenly she made a mischievous face. "Have you ever met the King's sisters, Count Saint-Germain, or that old tombstone Madame de Noailles? I can't even think about them without yawning or laughing. They just want to take out their aborted lives on me. I believe they would send me to the stake if they could take my youth and the few free moments I snatch by doing so. I wish I knew why they get so mad because I want to breathe fresh air and enjoy myself like any other simple Frenchwoman!"

"Unfortunately Your Majesty was not born a simple Frenchwoman. You sit upon the French throne at a critical period. Your country is threatened by danger both within and without. Its throne must be a living, fighting symbol; it must fight the greatest battle in history for the trust and love of its people. Your Majesty must give birth not only to a Dauphin but to a fuller idea of the kingdom, an idea that can survive the dangerous currents that have been building up since the time of the Sun King." Saint-Germain's voice took on a more urgent, persuasive note. "Your Majesty is bold enough to take a stand against old prejudices, make war on the traditions of Versailles, and scorn the hate of the nobility — just to gain a little freedom and light-hearted pleasure. Won't you do the same thing, just once, for the good of the people? Try to understand and remedy their ills, acknowledge that they are in an untenable situation; thus you can make an alliance with them. No one on earth can fight two enemies at once with any hope of success; you have to align yourself with one or the other to survive. You do not wish to ally yourself with the past; make an alliance with the future. Let there be a bloodless revolution of long-awaited reforms; these things will eventually come to pass with or without Your Majesty."

The Queen listened to Saint-Germain's quiet voice with growing discomfort and gradually her face hardened into rigid rejection. "I prefer not to understand what you have just told me, Count Saint-Germain," she said coldly. "If I had chosen to understand it, I would have called it a threat rather than a warning. The kingdom, thank God, is still strong enough to put rebels in their proper place. It is the King's province to govern and handle the problems of the people. I never interfere in that area. His Majesty certainly does everything he can; no outsider can judge a leader truly. And you are greatly mistaken if you believe my personal quarrels and the petty intrigues against me mean I am rebelling against our past traditions. I believe unreservedly in the God-given power of the King and in the ancient, unshakable superiority of the throne. After all, good times and bad come to everybody. The people become discontented from time to time and sing rude, satirical songs, but they always rally around the throne when crisis comes to the nation. I'm not afraid of my people and I do not find it necessary to make alliances with them, for I am their Queen. And the hostility among some of the nobility is just the bitterness of a neglected lover; they know that any revenge they might take would shake the throne and destroy themselves. No, the nobility can never endanger the Queen." She spoke with proud stubbornness, drawn up to her full height as though the armchair were her throne. Poor, blind woman! She was both pitiful and majestic at that moment.

Abruptly she leaned back as though exhausted. "You are mistaken, my lord; you are merely exaggerating trifles. I hope your prophecy is more accurate!"

"Well, we'll soon know, Your Majesty," Saint-Germain responded equably. "I have only a year to prove it."

★

After the women had left, I told Saint-Germain the horror I had seen in the crystal. He nodded.

"The crystal was swimming in blood, Cornelius. It showed the future so clearly that even the frightened, childish Princess de Lamballe saw it. That's why she was so upset. Poor little Princess! What an end!"

34

The Trianon

The Dauphin was born in 1781 on the very date predicted by Saint-Germain. Everywhere there were jubilant festivities, and it seemed as though all the suspicion and misunderstanding between the Queen and the people had evaporated. The nobility was silent for the moment, and glorifying odes replaced the slanderous poems addressed to the King's consort. She was the mother of the heir to the throne and was received enthusiastically everywhere.

To her credit, Marie Antoinette did not forget Saint-Germain in her victorious maternity. The Countess Polignac brought us her invitation to the Trianon in person. She was even pleased to mention my humble person. Since I had been present for the prophecy I should also be present for the fulfillment.

Thus we were invited to the Trianon, that small rococo palace that stubbornly isolated itself from the world. "There'll be just a few of the Queen's close friends there," the Countess told us, "just a few gay and entertaining people among whom the Queen desires to rest from the fatigues of her obligations."

Marie Antoinette worshipped this Countess Polignac and followed her smooth and tactful guidance blindly. Unfortunately the Countess was wed to her own family interests and was neither astute nor sympathetic enough to guide the reckless, sentimental Queen properly. If she had only realized the danger of that tiny fairytale palace that opposed Versailles and alienated Paris, she might have changed the Queen's fate when the blow did fall. But it was more important to her and her family that no one else have any influence upon Marie Antoinette, and they virtually isolated her in a vacuum. The Queen left her little citadel only to go to the seething, scandalized Versailles to get more money for the Polignacs, or else for the Trianon itself; it consumed vast amounts of money.

Physically the Countess was more beautiful even than the Princess de Lamballe. Her loveliness and grace misled the Queen and everyone else who could be deceived by skillful acting. Really the delicate, fragile figure with the narrow Madonna face and wide, innocent eyes were signs of a personality that needed constant attention and protection. Her entreating, tinkling voice could both flatter and evade, and there was incredible tenacity hidden in that graceful, transparent figure. She could instantly recognize both possible advantages and possible dangers, and her tongue was a light, lethal weapon to execute opponents.

It was entirely a different woman that I met that evening amid the pastel tapestries, musically curved furniture, and petallike porcelains. A thousand candles sparkled and multiplied in the mirrors, and she came tripping over the soft carpet like a reflection of their grace. There was no sign of the sorrowful, anxious person I had met the year before. Marie Antoinette was the very personification of rococo, a lovely, gracious, pink goddess who stretched out slender fingers to acknowledge our homage with generous gratitude.

"Come, my lord. I want to announce your marvelous wisdom and ability to the world." She took his arm and led him toward her gay, curious guests. There was an inimitable rhythm in her walk that evening. She seemed almost to float, totally unaffected, fresh, and vibrant. An atmosphere of joy and victory surrounded her, and even this second birth had not affected her figure. Her waist was still waspy over her blue brocade crinoline, and her naked, powdered arms and neck sparkled with jewels, as did her towering wig.

The guests were young, handsome, and richly dressed. There was only one withered and overpainted beldame among them — the spirited and wickedly witty Countess D'Adhemar. I understood later why she was accepted by this youthful elite; she was their court jester, a distorting glass who mirrored their carnival antics. But how hard she worked to maintain that position! What an effort it cost her to camouflage her age and looks under a barrage of ribald stories! They expected her to entertain them, and she bent all her talent and energy to do so.

Now the whole group crowded around Saint-Germain asking for prophecies, beauty preparations, and the "Elixir." They asked childish questions and said stupid, frequently insulting things. He bore it all with equanimity and provided an answer for everybody. Finally the Queen rescued him from this embarrassing situation. She came up with the Princess de Lamballe and the Countess Polignac and asked him to go into another room and give her some private medical advice.

Now my habit of being inconspicuous became useful. I simply withdrew into a small, ill-lit salon and watched the chattering groups through the open door. The Countess D'Adhemar soon dominated the conversation, announcing that she had some exclusive, inside information about Count Saint-Germain.

It seemed the Countess had been at a gathering during which the elderly Countess De Gergy had suddenly come face to face with the famous Magus. The old woman had stepped back in amazement.

"I met you in Venice," she told him, "fifty years ago when my husband was ambassador. You looked just like you do now, except now you look younger!"

The Count had bowed deeply. "You honor me by your recognition, Countess."

"But you called yourself the Marquis Baletti then."

Saint-Germain smiled. "The Countess De Gergy's memory is as good as it was fifty years ago."

"Well, I certainly wouldn't forget the man whose medications are responsible for both my memory and my health. I am happy to renew my acquaintance with one of the strangest men in the world, no matter what he calls himself."

"I hope the Marquis Baletti did not have a bad reputation."

"On the contrary!" the Countess responded eagerly.

Saint-Germain took her arm and escorted her to their hostess. As they left, he murmured over his shoulder to the Countess D'Adhemar. "In that case I gladly acknowledge my grandfather."

This incident came to the ears of the Marquise de Pompadour, and her curiosity was so great that she taxed Saint-Germain directly. The Countess D'Adhemar heard all about their subsequent conversation from Madame du Hausset, the Marquise's lady-in-waiting. It was known that Saint-Germain enjoyed the confidential friendship of both the King and the Marquise and could enter their suites freely at any time. He was very tactful about using this privilege and never came at the wrong moment. When he came, he was always expected and wanted. Thus it was after his meeting with the Countess De Gergy.

The Marquise de Pompadour was excitedly telling her lady-in-waiting about the incident when suddenly Saint-Germain appeared before them. They had not seen him come in, and Pompadour was truly frightened.

"This is witchcraft!" she burst out. "How did you get here just as we were talking about you?"

"It was natural enough, Madame. You called and I came."

"But I hadn't sent for you. I haven't even gotten out of my chair."

"But you were thinking about me and wanting to ask me some questions. Am I not right?"

"Yes, it's true enough."

"Then I am entirely at your service."

The Marquise just shook her head helplessly. "What am I to do with you? When I try to pin you down about something, you manage to evade me and say only what you want to. I suppose I must stifle my curiosity and put up with your mysterious ways. Sometimes I think you just enjoy being mysterious and are intentionally obscure, but at other times I am completely under your spell. I would swear you have supernatural powers, yet the only thing I am sure of is that your friendship and advice are indispensable."

"You have been sincere with me, Madame; I will be sincere with you."

"Did you really meet the Countess De Gergy in Venice fifty years ago?"

"Yes."

"But that would mean you're over a hundred years old!"

"Is that so impossible, Madame?"

"I should say so! You can't be more than forty."

"I cannot make you a liar, Marquise. The Countess De Gergy, though I respect her greatly, obviously must have talked nonsense."

"You're evading again, but this time I'll pin you down. I have no reason to doubt the Countess' story, however fantastic it may be. She also told me you gave her an Elixir that made her look no older than twenty-four for several years."

"That's possible."

"Well, did you or did you not give it to her?"

"I gave it to her, but the Countess has exaggerated its effects. It merely healed her indigestion and replaced certain natural substances in her system. This restored her beauty."

"Why can't you give the King a remedy like that?"

"The King doesn't need it."

"How can you say that! You know that some days he is dizzy and suffers tormenting headaches. Why could not he too be made fresh and young?"

"I have already given the King advice on that matter."

"And?"

"He won't follow it. You are such a charming creature, Madame, and the young ladies you so generously bring the King are so irresistible . . ."

"You mean to say he — abuses his strength?"

"You know it as well as I do. You also know that neither one of us can stop him; if you did not supply him, he would go to others."

"That's true," Pompadour replied sadly. Saint-Germain had touched her deeply. Her face became thoughtful and it was obvious she was thinking of something that troubled her greatly. She tried to conceal the tremor in her voice as she continued. "If I dared ask — but I will ask you. Count Saint-Germain, how long can I keep the King? And if I lose him, God forbid, what will happen to me then? No, don't answer! I don't have the courage to face it; it tortures me more and more as time goes on." She glanced uncertainly at Saint-Germain, whose face was gentle as he returned her gaze. Madame du Hausset said he seemed to be looking at the beautiful Pompadour with pity.

"Do not be frightened, Madame; I will not alarm you. Your star is still in the ascent. But stars, you know, are like people; they die and are reborn. Even the finest child is born under the sentence of death, and those who die in one place are reborn elsewhere. It is like the evening, when we sleep to wake in the realm of dreams. One chapter of life closes and an even more important one begins. Change is a law, Madame, but it is also a law that no change extinguishes life."

This was the story the Countess D'Adhemar had gotten from Madame du Hausset.

Now the Queen returned with Saint-Germain and her two friends. She was smiling and laughter bubbled beneath her voice. The curious Countess threw out an opening gambit.

"It seems the wonderful Count has brought Your Majesty more good news."

Marie Antoinette seated herself among her guests. "Perhaps."

"Is it a secret?" the Countess persisted.

"No!" The Queen's silvery laughter flooded the room. "He says I'll have two more children — two more children and inner stability as well."

"I can believe the two children," the Countess D'Adhemar responded dryly.

"Oh, stop laughing!" The Queen made a mischievous face at her. "I can grow up as well as anybody else."

"May we beg Your Majesty not to?" the Countess Polignac intervened. "Come, Count Saint-Germain! Can't you give the Queen an Elixir that would make her an irresistible child forever?"

Saint-Germain shook his head with a smile. "I'm sorry, Countess. God has ordained that children should grow up, and I can't work against Him."

"What a shame," the Countess Polignac responded. "Adults are so boring."

"Then perhaps you ladies do not know the tale of the Isle of the Children?"

Saint-Germain glanced around the eager group. They had not heard the tale and clamored for him to tell it.

"Many, many thousands of years ago," he began, "there were two emerald islands in the Mediterranean Sea. These islands were really the peaks of two mountains which had once been the landmarks of a sunken world empire. Millions had fled the terrible cataclysm, but only a few managed to reach these mountaintops that became the happy isles. When the storm was over and the angry vault of heaven was again a brilliant blue, the survivors organized themselves on one of the twin islands.

"Using the memories of their advanced culture, they built permanent homes, cultivated the soil, tamed wild animals for domestic purposes, and followed all the useful scientific pursuits. They recreated their culture's laws of peaceful coexistence, which were based on ancient revelations, and established a society that would be of benefit to their children.

"But the children in the meantime, while the adults labored, had roved unsupervised among the rocks and had become used to irresponsible freedom. They would plunder birds' nests and drink the raw eggs or kill small game with stones and share their prey. All this made them muscular and rough-skinned, and they became boastful and competitive because of their physical strength. They thought it was fun to fight and believed they could get anything they wanted by beating someone else. Their emotions were unbridled, and they had no patience.

"When the adults had completed their labors and believed it time for their children to take over, they called in these children to teach them their new duties and the law. Great was the sorrow of these wise and gentle people when they saw the feral herd that appeared before them. They became painfully aware of the fact that while they had labored, their children had been left to become wild. Their bodies were strong enough but they were mentally lazy, and their emotions were like unchecked weeds.

"The adults tried to enlighten the coarse minds and to teach self-control and consideration for others, but it was in vain. Their youngsters abhorred their efforts and in the stupid arrogance of their physical power revolted against the leadership of the elders. They went off to the other island to establish their own free child empire.

"The first thing they did was to build droll houses of branches whose roofs were decorated with flowers. These funny green tents were quite gay in the sun, but soon it was noticed that some were larger and more beautiful than others. These had been built by children who were physically weak but cleverer mentally than the others. The strong ones who excelled in fighting had not been able to produce anything but shapeless, ugly lean-tos, for their hands and minds were clumsy and unskilled.

"Immediately the strong forced the weak to leave their beautiful dwellings so they could have them. When they saw that the weak were easily intimidated, they became drunk with power. They compelled the weak to do all the drudgery while they occupied themselves with hunting, fishing, and dancing around the fire. In addition, they took all the best food and allowed the weaker children only scraps.

"Meanwhile the weak children, made weaker yet by hunger, hard labor, and abuse, became embittered. Their suffering and oppression produced growing enlightenment. The strong children, on the other hand, became fat and lazy from their intemperate eating. It did not take them very long to gather all the food they needed, so they spent most of the day eating, sleeping, and abusing their slaves.

"Nor did their violence stop there. The fat tyrants began to quarrel among themselves with increasing frequency. The slaves witnessed their daily outbursts and the way they abused each other over trifles. They watched the raging fights in which their masters bit and tore one another like wild beasts. They saw the defeated grovel in helpless rage — and the slaves began to think.

"Were the strong ones really as invulnerable as they had thought? After all, they died off steadily. Their bodies had grown fat and soft from luxurious living, and their reflexes were no longer swift. They slept until high noon, while fish teemed in the lakes, wild fruits hung ripe from the trees, and grain blown over from the other island made luscious wheat fields ripe for harvesting. The climate was so mild and beneficent that food in abundance could be gotten free. But the fat tyrants had become too lazy even to reach up and pick the fruit above their heads. The slaves had to do all this for them while they sprawled in the shade, and then they ate their fill before giving those slaves meager scraps. Why? Because they had made a mutual agreement? After all, the tyrants in power weren't even physically superior anymore. The slaves had become more agile and tenacious, for they had had to build the fires, fish, hunt, and tan hides. They knew too how to bear trouble and suffering. And they were in the majority.

"At first only a few thought like this, and they kept their magnificent, terrifying thoughts to themselves. Then some decided to change the rules. When they made a catch, they ate what they wanted first and then gave the scraps to their masters. The tyrants immediately responded by executing the rebels in front of the stony eyes of their comrades to deter them from committing similar improprieties. They tortured them to death in all the ways their inexhaustible ingenuity could invent. Some were flayed alive and had salt rubbed on their raw flesh. Some were cut to pieces as slowly as possible. Others were flogged to death or crushed beneath large rocks. Still others were immersed in water filled with leeches.

"Not surprisingly every such example multiplied the number of sinners. Soon there were intrepid bands instead of lone rebels. The machinery of execution came to be used almost every day; it stank of rotting blood.

"Meanwhile the weather had become oppressively hot and the air was filled with the tension that precedes a rainstorm. The fat tyrants were preparing a new festival of execution. They had managed to drive crowds of escaped slaves out of the caves and expected to get the rest later. The noise of rats they heard with increasing frequency, the crude signs on the cave walls, and the red flowers that were put on their houses every morning didn't bother them. The heat increased their impatience and restlessness; they were eager to work out their own tensions on the bodies of the tortured slaves.

"But the slaves were also awaiting the festival. They knew they were in the majority; the magic word had been spoken, like the sinister tolling of the death bell. Now they spoke other words as well; they talked about the diminished strength of their masters and their own new-found strength. They talked about the injustices they had suffered, nor did they forget to repeat the slanderous accusations their masters had shouted at each other in their rages nor to tell the staggering secret they had learned during these fights. Their masters had bodies as vulnerable as their own and blood just as red.

"The adults who had continued their meditative life on the other island learned what was happening on the Isle of the Children, and they were deeply saddened. They held a council and decided to send emissaries to both sides in an effort to keep the tension below the breaking point. But the emissaries could do no good. Emotions had flared too high. The tyrants were unwilling to give up their lives of luxury; they buried their heads in the sand like ostriches and pretended nothing was wrong. As for the embittered and starving slaves, they had become obsessed with choking hatred for their masters. They were already a force ready to strike; all that was needed was a moment of ignition. Realizing the situation, the emissaries returned hastily to their own island before the holocaust and reported to the council that their mission was hopeless. The group was overcome with compassion and sorrow but their leader, who was the oldest and wisest adult, remained calm.

" 'Why are you so upset because the law of nature is also the law on the Isle of the Children?' he asked them. 'The forces must be balanced everywhere. No weight can be carried properly unless it is distributed properly. If it is not, by the law of reaction it crushes the one who pushes it too far. How can these children learn this? From words? Words don't mean anything to them; they are simply symbols of reality. The children must experience the reality themselves before it means anything to them.

" 'Our emissaries have not really been ineffective. Their warning will lie dormant until after the flood of passionate events fulfills it. Then when the passions abate, it will come to life and have living consequences. You know that flesh and blood that may be butchered are not identical to life.'

"Then the peace of understanding came to the members of the council. They returned to their work and meditation and awaited the calm that would follow the storm."

Now only a few candles crackled in the salon at the Trianon. As Saint-Germain's voice died away, silence reigned unbroken. His hearers sat quietly, overwhelmed by their feelings. The bird of gaiety had flown. The Queen's lips were pressed tightly together and her face was pale as she stared at the floor. Even the ever-watchful eyes of the Countess Polignac were turned inwards where troubled presentiments swirled in her thoughts. The Princess de Lamballe seemed completely withdrawn, her hands clasped as though desperately praying. The ugly, birdlike face of the Countess D'Adhemar seemed suddenly old and tired.

Two servants came in and put fresh candles in the chandeliers. This broke the spell.

"What happened on the other island?" the Countess D'Adhemar asked hoarsely.

"On the Isle of the Children?" Saint-Germain turned and looked at her gravely. "It happened just as the adults had foreseen. The festival was turned into a bloodbath; the slaves massacred their masters. And when they had killed all of them, they turned on the slaves who had been faithful to their masters, then on those who had been indifferent to the struggle, and finally on those who had not been sufficiently brutal in their murdering. The lovely island became a slaughterhouse in which no one could be sure that his turn would not come next." Saint-Germain's voice was soft but his audience was spellbound. "No one thought of gathering food or carrying on the normal tasks of life. Everyone was celebrating the victory that had turned into a holocaust. Starvation was general now and epidemics began to break out. On top of all this, a tropical storm washed away their crude houses which had sheltered their dark lust for murder. Shivering and sick, they finally had to face their true situation."

"And then they must have remembered the adults," murmured the Countess D'Adhemar.

"Not yet, Madame. That was still far in the future. The time I speak of was just a lull, not a resolution. There was much more strife yet to come, for the children did not yet understand the law of balance. There was always one individual or a small group who pushed the burden onto others before it came back to crush them."

"That — that was a horrid story," the Queen broke in angrily. "If I had known what it was about, I wouldn't have let you tell it. How could you do this to me?" Her voice choked with resentment. "I was so happy this evening!"

"It was only a story," Saint-Germain responded. "Did Your Majesty imagine there was some other meaning to it?"

"I can readily imagine what you meant by telling it!" The Queen stared at him coldly. "I know very well, and all I can say of the matter is that it is only a stupid, brutal nursery tale!" She rose and turned her back on Saint-Germain.

The ladies lingered a little while longer, but the Queen did not speak further to the Count. She soon retired, pleading fatigue.

35

Two Letters

Two days later Saint-Germain got a letter from the Countess
D'Adhemar. I still have this letter, along with the Count's reply. The Count-
ess was a witty, observant woman and a talented chronicler of her own time.
Her letter ran like this:

Dear Count Saint-Germain:
 Ever since that strange evening at the Trianon, which unfortunately ended
in your disgrace, I have been filled with increasing uneasiness. I am an old
woman; I have seen much and experienced much, and I think I can say I've
lived my life with my eyes open. My perpetual interest in people and social
connections has not persisted just to gain superficial success, though that has
had its part; it has been a secret passion. Despite my weaknesses, I am
truthful with myself. This has been both a burden and a blessing, but I assure
you my opinions on serious affairs are constant, even though I conceal them
for opportunistic reasons — or out of cowardice. I am telling you this so you
will know why I am writing.
 The grave truth in your nursery tale disturbed me greatly, for
you verbalized problems of which I have been aware for a long time. I truly
love the Queen and her carefree friends. Their youth is both electrifying and
charming, and their cultured beauty fills me with nostalgia. Alas, I am still
vain in my old age and still love my pleasures. Nevertheless I am not blind
to the fatal mistake that happy, artificial empire is making by neglecting the
convulsive questions of our time. I know well enough the stubborn faults of
that old-fashioned circle at Versailles and the weaknesses of our poor King in a
time that demands bold, courageous action.
 As for myself I confess that I adore this graceful, elegant, decayed old
world; I am part of it. I was born to it, I was young among its traps and
pleasures, and I am thankful that I grew old with it and won't have to live to
watch its fall. But I pity these young people. My heart is heavy when I think

301

of the future awaiting these carefree infants who play as though they lived in
the dawn of an era rather than a bloody sunset. I feel helpless and grieve like
those adult council members in your story. I keep trying to think what I can do.
It would be so terrible for all this beautifully sculptured charm to suffer
the brutal consequences of the sins of people now moldering in tombs.
Marie Antoinette's crime is one of omission only, and the King himself
is a harmless, well-meaning man — although I know well how dangerous it
is for the government to be in such weak hands during this critical time. I am
confused and in despair. Perhaps you can tell me what I can do and what I
must do. I can already feel the approaching catastrophe in my bones. Please
help me!

Your sincere admirer,
Countess D'Adhemar

Saint-Germain's reply, preserved among the Countess' papers, ran thus:

My Dear Lady,
    Your worries are the same as my own. My transparent little allegory was
intended to reveal rather than conceal the dangers into which the royal couple,
the nobility, and the "old regime" itself have drifted. Truly the time will come
when thoughtless France, which once could have protected herself, will be in
a state like the hell Dante envisioned. The scepter, the censer, the scales, the
spires and coats of arms, even the White Flag itself, will fall. I can not only
feel this future, Countess; I have already seen it. I am still enthralled by the
horror of what I have seen. There were rivers of blood flowing from every city,
a cacophony of human screeches, and screams of pain as courage vanished.
The word of the council meant death — and, great God, who could answer
such murderous judges! You do not know what it looks like when the axe falls.
But who will listen to the cry "veto" today? I knew when I told the Queen that
parable I risked expulsion from the Trianon; I would have risked even more.
Nor was this the first time I have tried to avert the disaster. But eyes are blind
and ears are deaf, dear lady, for the time must be fulfilled. You and I can do
nothing more. But be at peace within yourself; the storm will not reach you.
You will escape, but I fear that is all I can offer in the way of consolation.

Yours,
Saint-Germain

    After this exchange of letters the Countess asked Saint-Germain to meet
her yet again. This last, most significant meeting took place in the Recollets
Church during the evening mass. Saint-Germain supplied me with the details
of their dialogue at my request.
    The Countess was both agitated and crushed. She begged Saint-Germain

to try to reason with the Queen once more. A meeting could be arranged, she told him; the Princess de Lamballe, who was also troubled, would see to that. The Count refused, telling her it was already too late for warnings.

"What do you mean?" the Countess D'Adhemar asked fearfully. "Do you know of some conspiracy?"

"No, Madame. The Queen has simply missed the moment when she could have changed her fate. She should have acted immediately after the Dauphin was born, when the people's faith was reignited and they reached out in trust and longing once more. Instead she turned her back on them and went back to the Trianon. Even the maturity gained by her multiple motherhood won't help her — they won't trust her anymore. She has sown the wind and will reap the whirlwind. Even now the forces have moved to pronounce judgment on her."

"And their sentence?" The old woman stared at him fearfully.

"Death."

The Countess reeled, and Saint-Germain had to support her. "It's horrible," she whispered. "I wish I could deny what you say — laugh at you — but I can't. It's just as you say; I can see it. But what do they want of her? What will be the charges against her?"

"The charges, Madame? Every playful, innocent pastime will be turned against her; every lampoon and slander will be treated as a serious charge. And what do they want? The utter ruin of the Bourbons. The royal family will be driven off every throne they occupy; within a hundred years, the survivors will return to France as simple citizens. France itself will be shaken and tormented by all manner of governments — kingdoms, republics, and empires. Noble tyrants will be replaced by ambitious and unworthy ones."

The Countess D'Adhemar buried her face in her old hands and prayed for a long time. Then she stared up at Saint-Germain with tears rolling down her cheeks. "If you knew how much I love life — and yet I'm happy you said I'll die before the eruption," she whispered. He would have demurred, but she waved him down. "I know well enough what the last part of your letter meant. How much longer will you remain in Paris?"

"Perhaps a year."

"I see. 'The emissaries returned hastily to their own island before the holocaust . . .' "

Saint-Germain was silent.

36

Cagliostro's Double

I was glad when Saint-Germain told me that we would only be in Paris another year. It was not that I wanted to leave Saint-Germain; on the contrary, I was thankful for every second I could spend with him. He had taught me a great deal and led me into important experiences. It was Paris, this restless, unhealthy city, that was alien to me. The city reminded me irresistibly of a man whose fatal illness has temporarily regressed.

Saint-Germain avoided both Versailles and the Trianon but he received many visits from the nobility. He was also visited by artists, scientists, simple citizens, and even dubious and bizarre charlatans. One of the latter was Giuseppe Balsamo, who frequently impersonated the Count Cagliostro. Like every cheat, Balsamo was a skeptic and he hoped to find in Saint-Germain a less skillful but more fortunate colleague. The Count was willing to receive him and even asked him to bring along his wife, who was his medium.

And thus I again met Martin Allais. The smooth old scoundrel in a new body was more polished and dangerous than ever. His dark experiences, though he did not remember them, were concentrated like the hypnotic powers of a snake on every weakness that could become his prey. Physically he had changed surprisingly little, though his features were sharper and more refined. His hard, oily black eyes were overlaid with thick, tangled brows, and his lips were again thick and bluish, though firmer than before. His fingers were now longer and narrower. Altogether he was more articulate; the voice was softer, the speech more soothing and dazzling. In his desire to impress people, he had managed to acquire for himself a tall figure but even now it was beginning to fill out with the sensuous corpulence of Martin Allais. An evil aura streamed from him, repulsive and attacking.

I realized with a shock that his wife and medium was Jeanne Girard, now superficially young and beautiful. Her name was now Lorenza Feliciani and she vaguely resembled the shining, irresistible Corinna. How that confused, greedy creature must have longed for Corinna's marvelous and destructive beauty! How she must have admired and envied, to burn the idea into her soul so that she could carry it with her even through the maelstrom of rebirth! Alas, the same thing had happened to her that happens to any chubby woman who wants a slender, noble figure. She managed to put one on, but it looked completely different on her. There was no lustful, enthralling power of the dark Eros in those slanted black eyes, just a lurking cunning. Her forehead receded and her shining hair was coarse and stiff. The mouth was a little too large, the nose a little too stubby, and she was already becoming thick and stocky. Undoubtedly she was a beautiful woman, though perhaps more desirable to a low and sensuous appetite. A more refined taste would have been repelled by her obvious vulgarity.

Now she was Balsamo's victim, whom he had shaped into a blind instrument — one can imagine how. This was the man who had broken and chained Corinna's demonic strength, and he turned this hysterical, obsessed woman with her dim, inchoate memories into pliant wax. The demons who had possessed her previously were gone, driven out by a more concentrated power. Balsamo frequently hypnotized Lorenza. He had this ability, though he didn't understand it fully, and he used and misused it whenever possible. Now the poor woman was possessed by an embodied demon rather than indecisive astral ones. Balsamo exuded great strength and uninhibited will. He practiced black magic, although he didn't believe in it.

It was strange that Italian-born Lorenza-Jeanne and the Sicilian Balsamo should have drifted back to the scenes of their former lives. They were instinctively attracted, as though they had left something undone there. Of course they called the phenomenon another name and entertained firm, if dubious, plans for their stay. These would have to be tried out in more virgin territory to succeed; yet they were drawn back to the magic center of Paris again and again.

Saint-Germain received the couple in the workroom on the ground floor. Their self-assured skill as they entered was admirable; you could almost see the many thresholds they had crossed prepared for anything. Balsamo had the adaptive ability of a hunting and hunted animal and he had imparted it to Lorenza. Now they promptly adapted themselves to the splendor and refined elegance of their surroundings, but they couldn't fathom Saint-Germain. His real being was incomprehensible to them.

Thus the tone of the encounter was elegant and the gestures deliberately languid. Balsamo began by fulsomely flattering the amused Saint-Germain.

Encouraged by her host's smile, Lorenza, after a graceful wave of her black lace handkerchief, admired his sapphire ring. He promptly took it off so she could look at it.

"You shame me, Madame! Certainly Monsieur Balsamo must make better stones to enhance his wife's beauty than my own humble work."

For a second, Lorenza stared at him stupidly. "Isn't it real?"

"Why shouldn't it be? A jeweler offered me a fortune after appraising it. Madame pretends not to know what I'm talking about, but you're among friends here. After all, who can tell transmuted gold from natural gold? Nobody; there's no difference. Isn't that so, Monsieur Balsamo?"

The man narrowed his eyes like someone reacting to a quick blow, then addressed himself to Lorenza. "You don't have to pretend here, my dear. His lordship the Count knows all about it." He turned to Saint-Germain. "My wife is an ecstatic partner in my enterprises rather than a conscious one."

"I understand perfectly. If Madame desires it, you may keep this ring that has aroused your fancy as a memento of our little visit."

Lorenza looked at Balsamo, eager yet hesitant. "You cannot insult his lordship the Count by refusing," he said, rather too quickly.

"You honor me." The woman trembled with excitement as she put the ring on her finger; she was so moved by so fine a gift that she could not hide her feelings. Balsamo noticed that I was watching her and promptly glared at the unfortunate woman. It was a terrible flash that froze her completely. Her eyes dimmed and she put her other hand over the one where the ring sparkled.

Meanwhile the two men continued exchanging mutual courtesies. Balsamo was feeling his way cautiously, adroitly offering his various gambits. But now he was dealing with someone who saw clearly with the third eye. Saint-Germain, while appearing perfectly straightforward, answered his overtures evasively. The result was that sometimes Balsamo was sure he was addressing an overconfident cavalier whose belief in his own shrewdness was a veritable treasure trove; then suddenly he would sense the hidden scorn and frightening intelligence in his host's eyes. Occasionally his fine criminal instinct sensed danger and he would retreat, but his greed was greater than his caution and he continued to play. Finally Saint-Germain asked him to demonstrate the experiments he did with Lorenza.

Balsamo obviously wanted to avoid this without flatly refusing. "I myself would be happy to oblige you, Count Saint-Germain," he said politely, "but the matter is not entirely in my hands. Lorenza is not always in the proper state for such demonstrations, and I believe that she is a little bit indisposed today." He turned to her expectantly, waiting for her to confirm his wishes, but she was staring at the ring and did not notice him. He favored her with his piercing glance but even this did not rouse her. When he spoke to her, she did not start like a terrified child, as she usually did.

"Yes." Her voice was calm, her eyes distant.

"I was just saying that you are not in a proper state for me to perform an experiment today." Balsamo's voice was subtly threatening. "Remember, you had a bad headache last night."

"You're wrong, Giuseppe." Her soft voice was mechanical. "I feel perfectly all right." She lifted her hand and stared at the sparkling ring, oblivious of all else. Then she continued in a rather dazed tone. "This blue stone has such an interesting thread; look at it, Giuseppe! But how could the Count give it to me when it is a part of himself."

"I believe Madame's condition is ideal for an experiment," Saint-Germain remarked. "Perhaps we could start now, Monsieur Balsamo." Balsamo got up reluctantly and stood fidgeting. "If you need help, Cornelius is at your service." Saint-Germain leaned back in his chair as though awaiting an experience of interest.

"I can manage!" Balsamo said roughly. He advanced to his wife. "Lorenza!" He spoke commandingly. "Look at me, Lorenza!"

The woman did not respond. She sat spellbound by the glistening stone which almost seemed to live. Suddenly her expression became one of wonder, then of fear and unspeakable horror. She jerked upright and clasped her arms convulsively to her body, raising her head as though she were suffocating. "Help me! The blue snake is strangling me. Order it back into the ring — quickly!"

Balsamo leaned over Lorenza, yanked the ring from her convulsed finger, and threw it into Saint-Germain's lap. "So there's your ring. Now wake her up — this instant!" He was hoarse with rage.

"I will awaken her soon, Monsieur Balsamo." Saint-Germain spoke calmly, without moving. "I admit I have borrowed your superb instrument temporarily. Lorenza Feliciani is truly an excellent medium."

"What do you want of her?" Balsamo thrust forward, a face distorted with anger.

"Calm down, my friend! She is in less danger now than she is during one of your experiments. Soon she will wake up and be livelier and prettier than ever. I just want you to hear something from her, something you should take to heart."

Lorenza meanwhile sat erect and motionless, an expression of horror still on her face. Saint-Germain got up and stood in front of her; involuntarily, Balsamo stepped back.

"Do you hear me, Madame?" Saint-Germain's voice was gentle.

"Yes," she answered mechanically.

"Who am I?"

"The friend and comrade of Count Cagliostro in the Secret Brotherhood." Balsamo's face drained of all color.

"And who is Giuseppe Balsamo?"

The woman pressed her lips tight and shut her eyes, not willing to reply. Balsamo leaned toward her, his lips forming urgent demands for silence.

Then Saint-Germain spoke again. And what a voice he had! Quiet, but firm as a diamond. "You must answer me, Madame. You are not afraid now and you will not remember anything I do not wish. You are unfettered now, completely free and calm." Lorenza's face cleared magically.

"This is intolerable, Count!" Balsamo rushed to his wife and tried to lift her, but he could not move her. She seemed to be anchored to the chair. Balsamo was red with his exertion, but in his rage he tried again. He grabbed her arms and pulled until Saint-Germain was moved to intervene.

"If you keep on, you'll injure your medium. Sit down, Balsamo, and be quiet. Believe me, there is nothing else you can do." The Count spoke again to Lorenza. "You heard my question, Madame. Who is Giuseppe Balsamo?"

Now she replied smoothly, in a mechanical singsong. "He is the Count Cagliostro's shadow, forever one step behind him. Should the Count turn around, he disappears. The two are of the same name and sign — the sign of Gemini. They were born of a month and look alike; they are even of the same blood, but their souls are as different as daylight and dark. The shadow crawls upon the ground and dances on the walls — weightless, with no life of its own. It is merely a phantom, a slave of light. Giuseppe Balsamo cheats others, but he cheats himself worst of all. He does not know that a stolen name can become a tunic of Nessus to a usurper, that it is a dark fate as well as a bright shield. The fate of a shadow is always dark. Now Balsamo enjoys the riches of Cagliostro's palace. Therefore Cagliostro's earthly Karma will be fulfilled on him rather than on the Count, who has stepped aside. Cagliostro has liberated himself from his past actions; the bloodhounds of Karma have run on below him. But there on the ground is the shadow, a prisoner of that name. Cagliostro-Balsamo. One is above mortal consequences, unreachable. But the other, here below, is the target of those consequences. Balsamo-Cagliostro. Poor Balsamo!"

"Thank you, Madame." Saint-Germain leaned over her and gently placed the palm of his hand on her forehead. Lorenza opened her eyes and gazed about wonderingly. Then she looked timidly over at the agitated Balsamo.

"Did you put me to sleep, Giuseppe? I didn't even notice it."

Balsamo did not answer; it took all of his willpower to cover his confusion. But soon his uninhibited cynicism triumphed and he looked over at Saint-Germain with scornful superiority. "You didn't have to be so theatrical, my dear Count, about telling me you know about my little business. After all, I'm of the same craft myself and it's hard to dazzle me. I use poses, certainly, but I hate them and shed them gladly when I don't need them. We have the same philosophy, you and I. A painter is paid for his pictures, a musician for his music, a writer for his lies — why not pay the swindler, who gives better and happier illusions than any of them? People really want to be cheated; they're too credulous and stupid to face the fact that the ideas of good and evil, God and the devil, are simply lies invented by a clever clique of swindlers to serve their own interests and console morons. The lies are always unveiled for the initiate, who is strong and brave enough to face them. Why should we fight each other? You don't really expect me to believe you produced all this enormous wealth from your alchemist's crucible. I have a false-bottomed crucible myself, and a very cunning stirring spoon. We both change stupidity into gold, my dear Count. You might as well come down from Mt. Olympus and tell me what you meant by that little charade."

Saint-Germain leaned back cheerfully in his chair. "You have a remarkable philosophy, my dear Balsamo, and I won't deny I find it amusing."

Balsamo smiled a victorious and self-satisfied smile and winked at Saint-Germain. "I thought we could come to an understanding. You have your territory and I have mine. After all, there's more than enough for both of us. About the name Cagliostro, I have a reason for using it that I'm not going to tell you or anybody else. I may have a better right to it than you think. At any rate, it's a name with proven value and I like it. It suits me. And, believe me, I've worked harder for it and deserve it more than the man who legitimately owns it. I've put a good deal of my own work and energy into it and it's worth a substantial amount of money to me. Why do you want to take it away?"

"I don't, Balsamo. And the Count himself doesn't particularly care either. I'm just advising you not to use the name. Get rid of it before it's too late — for your own sake."

"Now don't play Dodonian Oracle with me! I know you're used to using that pose but I want a straight answer. Why do you advise me to stop using the name if it doesn't matter to you or Cagliostro?"

"I'm simply warning you — you expose yourself to danger by doing this. If you live as Cagliostro, you may also have to die as Cagliostro."

Balsamo threw himself back in his chair and laughed. "I thought the Count Saint-Germain was a better student of human nature than that! I quit wearing swaddling clothes a long time ago. Living itself is dangerous, and I was fully aware of the hazards when I chose this route. I also knew that only fools die when they get into difficulties; there is no prison that doesn't have at least one crack if you only know the magic spell. And I know it. I've gotten out of hell itself with my incantations. I don't really care either whether they bury me as Balsamo or Cagliostro, so long as I live to a ripe old age."

"I cannot withhold the facts," Saint-Germain continued unperturbed. "Your continued use of the name Cagliostro means death by torture in the prison of the Inquisition in Rome. It will be quite impossible for you to die of old age."

"Why do you keep up this ominous blather?" Balsamo broke in angrily. "Do you really think you can scare me? Why don't you come on out and admit you don't want me to use Cagliostro's name? Then I could give you a straight answer — that I will never stop using it under any circumstances."

"I've already told you it doesn't matter to me," Saint-Germain explained patiently. "I'm not asking you to do it or threatening you if you don't. I'm just giving advice that you can accept or reject. To be exact, I'm informing you of the risk you are running using Cagliostro's name. If you continue to do it, it's your responsibility, not mine. Nor will the Count Cagliostro, in whose stead you will have to die a horrible death, be responsible. Soon you won't be able to free yourself of his name by any means. There will be no one to prove you are two different people. The two will become one — in suffering, danger, and death. Cagliostro and I will both be far away and, when you are dead, he will be rid of his dangerous name forever."

"Oh, this is absurd!" Balsamo interrupted angrily, but Saint-Germain silenced him.

"Wait! I haven't finished yet. I'm going to interpret Madame Lorenza's trance. Cagliostro's name is in the path of forces which cannot reach him anymore, for he has risen above them. You, however, cannot dodge these dark forces if you lock yourself into Cagliostro's name."

"I don't know what you're trying to do, Count, but I know what you've done," Balsamo burst out. "You've confirmed me in the use of the name I've yearned for, hated, and fought to gain for years. Now I find it more desirable and exciting than ever; in fact, it is essential. I will cling to it as I do to my life."

"Even if it means death by torture?"

"I don't believe that fairy tale!"

"Answer me, Balsamo!"

"Don't be so melodramatic; you make me laugh!"

"Laugh all you like, but answer me."

"All right, I will. Yes, even if it means death by torture — assuming I'm stupid enough to get caught."

We heard a strange whimpering behind us and turned to took at Lorenza, whose presence we had all forgotten. Tears were pouring down her face, and she seemed to look at some horrid scene far beyond us.

"You have said it, Giuseppe!" The woman was trembling. "You have said what he wanted. The circle has been closed and the judgment pronounced. No knife can free you; no word can absolve you. The judgment is final."

"Be quiet, you stupid hen!" Balsamo spat.

Lorenza came to with a convulsive jerk and started sobbing hysterically.

"Stop that!" her husband snapped. "You know I won't tolerate bawling!"

"Be patient with me," she gasped. "I — can't stop."

Moved with compassion, I spoke involuntarily. "Please calm down, Madame. I'm sure Monsieur Balsamo will stop using Cagliostro's name if you ask him."

"I will not!" Balsamo retorted. "The name is mine. I have more right to it than that effeminate bastard who had it thrown in his lap by chance."

"Of course he won't stop using it, Cornelius," Saint-Germain said calmly. "Balsamo cannot discard the name now. It is already grafted to him, whether he likes it or not — and he must wear it until he dies." The finality of those words seemed to fill the whole room; even the skeptical charlatan was shaken.

"What do you mean — whether I like it or not?" Balsamo asked.

"The name has come to life and will follow you for the rest of your days, ruling and shaping your destiny. If you stop using it, you will be addressed by it. If you deny it, people will swear that it is your identity. If you throw it away, it will return like a boomerang. If you drive it away, it will slink back like a dog. It is a tenacious, merciless executioner, a magic robe that clings to your flesh."

"Let's go, Lorenza!" Balsamo said hoarsely. Recovering his poise, he added rudely, "I am bored with his lordship the Count's pompous theatrics. I am disappointed with the results of this meeting, Saint-Germain."

"I'm not, Balsamo." The Count spoke with friendly courtesy as he escorted his guests to the door.

37

Anna Müller

We started back to Cassel in the spring of 1784. I was relieved when we passed the French border; it was like getting out of an overheated room.

As for Saint-Germain, he was quiet and introspective. I didn't like to disturb him with questions, though I really wanted to know how long he was going to stay in Cassel. He had been so good to me that I hated to be separated from him, and not even the thought of reunion with my parents compensated for the loss. I dwelt hopefully on the idea that we were only going back to Cassel on a visit and might then go somewhere else as his mission called him. He didn't talk about the near future and I had been trained to curb my curiosity.

Nevertheless a link had been formed between us when I learned to obey his unspoken commands, and it transmitted my inner turmoil. He answered my questions without my having to put them into words.

"Don't be uneasy about the future, Cornelius," he said. "You are at the beginning of a productive period. And I will remain for a few months to prepare you for the examinations that you, like all mortals, must face alone."

When we had crossed into Cassel, we ran into a violent storm. High winds drove huge masses of water upon us. The carriage was impervious, but we turned into the nearest village inn to spare the servants and horses. Then the storm ended as quickly as it had begun, and the bright sun swept a green and pink landscape sparkling as with diamonds. Even the puddles glistened on the ground, bright with the petals that had been blown into them.

As we were leaving, a maidservant came up balancing buckets of rainwater on a pole over her shoulder. Her skirt was pinned up over pillarlike legs muddy to the knees and her wet, matted hair hung straight down her back. She was obviously pregnant. She looked at me with dull eyes, murmured a greeting, and went on to the squalid servants' quarters next to the pigsties.

I watched her sluggish, stout figure as she stooped to enter the low wooden door. Brown water and rotting straw seeped out from under the sties, and I could see the black noses of the snuffling hogs. The very fowls in the yard looked wet and filthy. For some reason I couldn't leave this miserable scene.

Then the maidservant came back out with a feeding bowl. She glanced at me, then stopped to look more closely. She took a few uncertain steps toward me and asked if I wanted anything.

"No, thank you," I replied. "I don't need anything." But then I asked her name.

"Anna Müller," she responded, startled. Her peasant accent was very apparent. I pushed some money into her hand and joined Saint-Germain in the carriage.

"Was it she?" he asked quietly when we were underway.

I nodded. "Corinna." Strangely, I had recognized her more quickly than in the deceptive body in which I had known her. That had been an artificial costume made by demons. Now she was unveiled, massive, and ugly in her strong primitive instincts that she satisfied like an animal. She belonged in this world of evil smelling barns, pigpens, and chicken coops. Her station as a drudge befitted her spiritual development. The dainty beauty and complex perversions had all been sloughed off in the peasant womb her drifting soul had found. All that was not a real part of her was gone; she was no longer a demonic genius. Now Corinna was herself, an ignorant and immature beggar at the beginning of her journey.

I was still mulling over this illuminating meeting when I returned home to the quiet and permanent Castle of Grotte. My parents did not meet me at the door; rightly they waited upstairs. Our relationship was not one which required emotional outbursts. I met them again in my father's dim study — tall, slender figures wearing identical smiles. And again I felt the inner warmth of deep peace and gratitude that had kindled within me the spark of the burned-out alchemist's furnace.

38

The Coffin

My father had advanced to the highest grade of the Order during my absence, and I also had progressed appreciably during the nearly four years I had spent with Saint-Germain. I had passed the fourth, fifth, and sixth grades and begun the studies for "Adeptus Exemptus." I was now familiar with the various magics and Kabalas and practiced many exercises of Indian and Tibetan Yoga. I also learned the mystery of the secret Sutras at a time when these spiritual treasures were still undiscovered by the white race.

In November of 1784, we were invited to Rotenburg at a different time from our usual monthly meeting. At this time we hadn't seen Saint-Germain for a week, and our last conversation, a deep and intimate one, had left me with a strong premonition. Under his guidance I had made out a long work program that would last me for years to come. I had sensed a farewell in his manner — and something which forbade me to question. My emotional reaction could not bind him who was already free, and such feelings were also unworthy of the student. For us, change, separation, and distance were just illusions of the matter-bound personality which still suffers from such things. No matter where he went, Saint-Germain was still my master and the head of my Order.

★

Karl von Hesse was one of the pillars of our Order, not only because of his immense interest in the occult but also because of his mental abilities and high ethics. He was one of the most cultured men of his age and astute enough not to scheme for political power and glory. Living modestly and contentedly, he was thankful that his desire for a secluded, introspective life accorded with the wishes of the ruling Prince. Thus he could raise his son

315

Victor Amadeus, born in 1779, as he wished — not as a member of an elite striving for earthly power but as a humble novitiate of the spirit.

When our carriage turned into the stone court of Rotenburg that fall afternoon, I was surprised to see a black flag fluttering at the entrance. Then I noticed that the flag on the tower was flying at half-mast, and the servants who came to meet us were in mourning. Discomfited, I had turned to question a servant when I felt my father's hand on my shoulder. He motioned me to silence, his face curiously peaceful.

We walked up the long stairway under tall mirrors swarthed in black. The very bouquets in the oriental vases were draped with black veils. Passing the huge, silent library, we went into the hall of the Order. In the center of the hall stood a coffin covered with a funeral pall on which a single, exquisite gold rose glittered in the light of four surrounding candles.

The coffin stood on a platform reached by seven stairs. Only seven candles burned in the room besides those by the catafalque. These were placed in wall brackets under seven frescoes which Saint-Germain had painted in his deep, living colors. They seemed to glow with light from some hidden source. The scarlets looked like burgundy by firelight and the greens were like the tender buds in May.

The first fresco showed a padlocked gate which an angel was trying to open. Its golden caption ran "Signatur ne perdatur." The second showed a lovely green island emerging from the sea in the clear light of sunrise and was inscribed "Aurora ab lacrymis." On the third were the twelve signs of the Zodiac, with the sun passing through Virgo. This one was captioned "Iam mitius ardet." The fourth showed lions, eagles, and bats warming themselves in the sun and was captioned "Non possen ibus offert." The fifth was two stringed instruments, one of which was being plucked by a delicate, ethereal hand. Its inscription was "Unam tetigis se sat est." The sixth showed Noah's dove bearing its olive branch over an immense expanse of sky and water; its caption ran "Emergere muntiat orbem." In the triumphant seventh fresco, a bird flew out of a nest and its inscription was "Ad sidera sursum."

★

Three people stood behind the catafalque. Saint-Germain, wearing a long, white shroud, stood in the middle with Karl Von Hesse on one side and someone I had never met on the other. Yet the third man looked familiar. He was tall and powerful, brown as an Indian, and had serious eyes under his domed forehead. His thin lips were set in an expression of resignation. Since he looked amazingly like Giuseppe Balsamo, I realized this could only be the Count Cagliostro.

The two men had been born under the same sign — Gemini — but there were quite a few centuries of development between them. Cagliostro's purified, utopian being was a future state for the ignorant Balsamo, who was racked by passions and still languished in the tower of the dark forces. Obviously there was a blood relationship between them; this was indicated not only by their common birthplace and physical resemblance but by the way their earthly fates were entwined.

I later found out that Balsamo was a natural child of Cagliostro's uncle and a Sicilian peasant girl. This debauched nobleman had spawned numerous children among the peasant huts, and he cared about them quite as much as a tomcat would. Thus Balsamo could hope for no name or help from his father and had to bear his embittering secret within the very shadow of the walls of his paternal castle. He managed to fight his way out of his peasant environment, but it was easy to see how his rebellious, envious hate became the driving force in that passionate personality and why he used Cagliostro's name. Giuseppe Balsamo had hated and longed for that name which he felt to be his by right and yet had caused him so many humiliations. It had made him an outcast, neither peasant nor nobleman. Now I understood his mingled pride and shame when he had discussed his imposture with Saint-Germain.

But now the tall, bearded Karl von Hesse stood looking solemn and serious, and Saint-Germain wore the contemplative Hierophant face the world has never known. My father pulled aside the curtains of an alcove on the ground floor where there were an organ and some chairs. We went in and sat down. The curtains on the tiers of alcoves around the hall rustled, and I could feel the presence of other people.

Saint-Germain mounted the seven steps and stood at the head of the coffin, his radiant face illuminated by the faint gold light. "My friends and associates in the Brotherhood," that quiet, even voice filled the great hall, "I have completed my mission and received the call. Now the world must hear the news of my death.

"I have already set our Great Work in motion, and the waters have begun to spring from the secret wells. Guard the source of this water and keep it pure. I have appointed a successor to be visible head of our Order, but my death does not mean I shall leave the unfortunate land of the West. Certain events must take place first. You will hear news of me from time to time, and I will send you a last greeting before my final departure. I will also visit personally some to whom I have something to say. But before I turn to depart on my new Road, I leave you these cardinal precepts: the Eleven Rules of the Order, the Six Duties of the Order, and the Sixteen Secret Signs of the Order. These Thirty-Three Formulae are the very foundation of our Order.

The Eleven Rules

Love God above all else.
Use your time to develop your soul.
Be completely unselfish.
Be sober, humble, active, and silent.
Learn the origins of the 'metals' in you.
Beware of charlatans and liars.
Constantly revere the highest Good.
Learn the theory before you try to practice.
Practice charity toward all beings.
Read the ancient books of wisdom.
Strive to understand their secret meaning.

The Six Duties

Heal the sick and relieve the suffering without thought of reward.
Conform to the customs of the country in which you live.
Meet with your fellow members in a pre-set place once a year.
Select your own successor.
Remember the letters R.C., symbols of the Brotherhood.
Keep the existence of our Order secret for one hundred years.

The Sixteen Secret Signs

A member of the Order is patient.
He is compassionate.
He is incapable of envy.
He is not a braggart.
He is not proud.
He is not debauched.
He is not greedy.
He is not easily roused to anger.
He thinks no evil of others.
He loves righteousness.
He loves Truth.
He knows how to remain silent.
He believes what he has learned.
His hope does not fail.
He does not falter during suffering.
He will always be a member of the Brotherhood."

There was a great silence as he finished, while the candles cried their slow tears of wax. I could hear the soft footfalls as von Hesse and Cagliostro lifted the coffin cover to reveal the snowy lace interior.

Saint-Germain lay down in the coffin and clasped his hands over his chest. His eyes remained open, but already he smiled the serene, undecipherable smile of the dead. Cagliostro pulled the face cloth over him, and the two men replaced the lid and nailed it shut. The hammering sounded disquietingly violent in the icy stillness of the hall.

Suddenly dark-clothed figures appeared and lifted the coffin to their shoulders. "Go with them, Cornelius," my father whispered. "Take a candle and follow." He himself sat down at the organ, whose deep consonances flowed over us like the silvery light of the moon. They spoke not of mourning but of resurrection and the secret joy of recognition.

I became aware of more people joining the procession; I could hear the solemn shuffle of many feet. I did not look back to see faces, but I felt a powerful current of affinity. We went through a long corridor to the chapel, with the organ's pealing following us like a distant benediction. Presently it stopped, but as the crypt was opened it burst forth anew from the chapel balcony. This was a composition my father had written especially for this occasion; he never played it again.

Now the coffin was laid in its deep stone bed, and the procession silently left the crypt. Saint-Germain lay alone in his coffin. The iron-sheathed door rolled noiselessly back into place, and Karl von Hesse refastened it with the elaborate seal in which the letters R.C. glowed.

We went back to the huge, darkened hall, and the mute figures disappeared through the draperies one by one. My father was already waiting in our alcove, and we went out the side door together.

Three messengers were riding ahead of our carriage with a written announcement.

"The Count Saint-Germain, the Magus and greatest wizard of all Europe, friend of emperors, poets, and scientists, died at Rotenburg in the province of Cassel and was buried at the castle of Karl Emanuel von Hesse on September 7, 1784."

39

The Ghost

It was a Russian chronicler who reported Saint-Germain's first appearance after his death. He reported that sometime during the winter of 1785-86 the Count had had an important discussion with the Czarina.

The second report came from Count Chalons, who had just returned from his assignment as ambassador to Venice. He told his friends how he had seen Saint-Germain on the Piazza San Marco the evening before he left. Saint-Germain had seemed youthful and alert and had laughed over the news of his own death.

"He who is buried many times lives forever," he said smiling. Then he proceeded to tell Count Chalons the most intimate news about his family and distant relatives. His information surprised the ambassador greatly.

"To tell you the truth, I didn't believe him," Count Chalons related, "and I thought he was being unspeakably vain to use such means to get an effect. But when I got home I found out he was telling the truth, even though changes had taken place that no outsider could readily have learned. Of course the most interesting thing was that none of the family had talked to Saint-Germain or even seen him in years."

The third appearance was in 1789, five years after his death, to the Countess D'Adhemar, who related the incident in her memoirs though she only told a little about their conversation. It occurred again in the Recollets Church during the morning mass. Suddenly she saw Saint-Germain's dark-clothed figure beside her. He gave her a friendly nod.

"His presence was so natural and serene," the Countess wrote, "that I was not the least bit frightened. It was just like continuing a conversation that had been interrupted the moment before. He spoke and I answered like a sleepwalker, though I was more intensely aware of my surroundings than I have ever been.

"Then the news of your death was false," I said joyfully. "I should have known."

"To the world the news is true, Madame," he replied gently, "but those who do not believe in death know that all such news is basically erroneous."

"I can't thank you enough for the hope you've given an old woman heading for the grave. Thank God I can see you again. You know my faith is as weak as my character, and I am prey to destructive doubts. I'm afraid to die and long for certainty, but I always kill the most soothing arguments with the poison of doubt. I dread the thought of annihilation in the cold, frozen darkness; my elements are heat, light, and motion. My body is a disobedient wreck but my soul is alive with curiosity and energy."

"You will live many times, Madame," he responded, "simply because you wish to live. Your soul is a vigorous young tree. The state of your body is only an autumn. Who can say the tree is dead when winter comes? Many new springs will bring it buds and flowers, and many summers will bring it thick foliage and fruit."

"I wished our conversation could have lasted forever," the Countess related. "After mass I asked him to see me to my coach. He took my arm to support me, for my legs were weak and arthritic. Once we got outside, I noticed how young and healthy he looked. His arm was like steel beneath mine, and he walked with a springy step. When he saw how I clung to him, he got into the coach and drove home with me. We drove slowly, and I even told the coachman to make a detour just so I could talk to him a little longer.

"There were so many things to talk about. I told him how all his predictions about the Queen were proving horribly true. Marie Antoinette stands alone within an icy cordon of enemies, even though she has matured a great deal since the birth of her four children. I told him that she could really be a good mother and Queen if time would only allow it. She sees her danger and is trying desperately to make amends, but no one will believe her.

"Then we discussed other matters, strange things that exalted me and strengthened my faith, but I promised Saint-Germain I would write nothing of these. It was with a regretful but renewed soul that I bade farewell to this brilliant man whom all believed dead. To me, everyone else was dead and lifeless in comparison . . ."

Saint-Germain appeared again to the Princess de Lamballe as she was being torn to pieces. He also stood beside Jeanne DuBarry at her execution, a noble, reserved figure amidst the screaming mob. These details come from Grosley, who also tells how Saint-Germain disappeared from prison.

During the Terror, he wrote, the police arrested a foreigner who was always present at the executions and showed a marked sympathy for the victims. Saint-Germain, for it was he, went with them without resistance. He found a great many friends and acquaintances among the captive nobles and strengthened them by his calm and tranquility. "When he was speaking," Grosley related, "the horror of death vanished from their faces like snow under the spring sun." His name was on the list to be executed and he even lined up with the others, but he was not there when they got on the tumbrel. The guards didn't notice his disappearance until they were making their tallies at the end of the day, when they all ran around shouting. "But that whole day he had stood by the guillotine," the chronicler added, "a tall, calm figure amidst the raging mob. His face was the last thing seen by the condemned, and his smile lingered on theirs — a smile of serenity on bloody, severed heads."

40

The Kyilkhor

In 1793, Karl von Hesse entrusted to me the education of his son Victor Amadeus. The boy, who was amiable and brilliant, had just turned fourteen, but there was an old spirit in that young body. He was keenly interested in the occult and followed every path of learning thirstily. His knowledge was like the counterweighted lid of a treasure box; it sprang open at the first touch. It was as though I were merely reminding him of blurred memories. There was no trace of self-interest left in the boy; his ascetic life cost him neither strain, repression, nor self-deception. He was simply indifferent to the temptations of the flesh.

Working with Victor Amadeus was a beautiful and easy task. He not only walked obediently, he flew without effort and his soaring intuition often left me behind. Soon I realized he was to be the great missionary of the future and began preparing him for this mission.

I was also gradually taking over the correspondence of the Order, a very important activity in such a far-flung organization. I learned the secret roster of members and was soon in contact with virtually every country that could be reached by mail.

My personal studies were also moving satisfactorily. At this time I was preoccupied with animating symbols. Both alchemists and oriental mystics use magic scripts to learn how to create certain symbolic beings; thus they understand and experience the process of creation. This mystery is a small repetition of the Great Creation. Unlike the blind process of procreation and conception, this is conscious, immaculate conception, conception of the spirit. It is the conception of an Idea that can, with the help of the spiritual principle and the will, create Karma and concentrate matter about itself. The original mystics perform this not by projection or transmutation but by creating thought forces. They use certain diagrams, like paintings of gods and demons, as the basis of their work. This is the Tibetan *Prima Materia,* a diagram they call *Kyilkhor.* Saint-Germain had given me one of these figures to animate so I could recognize and conquer my forces in this field.

Every color, form, and spatial distribution within a Kyilkhor is important. This mystic creature sits or stands in the middle of a diagram made up of symbols expressing its individuality. The animation of the diagram corresponds to transmutation. It is the custom of the Tibetan mystics to give some sort of magic assignment to their animated Kyilkhor and to judge by the way it is executed whether and to what extent they have succeeded in conceiving the idea and implanting it. If this operation is executed properly, the spirit or demon of the Kyilkhor becomes truly alive and performs assigned tasks without fail.

★

My Kyilkhor was a life-size statue of a Tibetan sorcerer. Saint-Germain had sculpted it from clay and painted it; it was a startlingly lifelike statue of a Tibetan sitting in the lotus position. There was a strange, withdrawn smile on the thin lips under the high cheekbones and slanted dark eyes. My first task was to conquer the feeling of repulsion it aroused in me. The more I looked at the figure and concentrated on it, the more malicious its expression seemed. The eyes seemed to stare at me dully, evilly. Slowly I became convinced that this sorcerer must have been a black magician in his native Tibet; the forces of destruction seemed concentrated in him. I didn't understand why my Master had chosen him, but I could not decline the assignment. I eliminated my repulsion.

It was thirteen months before that rigid clay first quivered with the breath of life and another nine weeks before he was breathing regularly. There he sat on the rush mat opposite me, warmed by my radiated heat and pulsating with my force in his veins, but he was still mute and motionless.

I will not dwell on the bizarre and startling details of this huge experiment. It required the total concentration of my forces and abilities and involved disheartening relapses. When the life force is put to such deadly strain and concentrated on a single object, it keeps trying to slip away, and mysterious short circuits happen. Then the lifeless matter, which has begun to live in the mystic excitement of creation, promptly dies.

Nor will I give the details of the tiring but stimulating watch that must be kept on the life-flame, for this can be understood only after long study and experiment. I will merely say that this experience is a milestone, one of the ultimate and more dangerous trials. There are now a good many Tibetan works on the Kyilkhor available in European languages for those who are interested.

It was two years before the Kyilkhor's eyes showed signs of awareness. It was three years before his body and limbs began to move. Now the way he held his head changed, and his eyes began to follow me as I walked about in the room. Observing this, I called to him and he got up and began to follow me with slow, unsteady steps. He would creep behind me throughout the castle, then follow me back into the meditation room and sit down automatically in his place. He grew stronger every day.

Now it was time for him to learn his name. "Lu-gyat-kahn!" (This means "Eight Serpents.") I repeated it countless times in front of him.

"Lu-gyat-kahn, Lama of the Red Sect, who dwells in Mithong-gat-kha, the invisible mountain top . . ."

"Lu-gyat-kahn." His mouth had moved. He quiveringly tried to repeat the name but no sound came from his throat. His mute lips began forming the name more and more definitely, then a soft, hissing sound erupted from him. "Lu-gyat-kahn!" It was a muffled whisper, now growing stronger and stronger as it vibrated through living vocal chords. The word was hoarse and unmodulated but fully understandable.

Again and again I repeated, "You are Lu-gyat-kahn."

"You — you are Lu-gyat-kahn," he would repeat automatically. Then one day he said what I had been waiting for. "I am — I am Lu-gyat-kahn."

It was not imitation. It was his own thought from his own animated personality. I was elated with unspeakable jubilation. At last I had arrived at the peak of my creative powers and acquired the Key of Life that Isis, the Great Mother, holds in Her left hand.

I was mistaken. This was only half the task. For Saint-Germain had had a reason for choosing that particular statue.

★

Spring was approaching and the whole world seemed filled with its swelling life force. The branches were still bare but the bark shone with renascent sap. Even the apparently dead humus poured out disquieting fragrances that disturbed the sleep of young animals.

By now the Kyilkhor was moving about without me and performing the chores I assigned. At night he would sit in my room and guard me with watchful eyes while I slept.

One unusually warm March night during full moon, I was aroused suddenly by hearing my name called.

"Cornelius." It became louder. "Cornelius!"

I sat up and saw the Kyilkhor standing beside my bed, looking at me strangely. Knowing that the anxiety that came upon me was the most terrible danger of my practice, I did not allow it to overcome me. Calmly I ordered him to leave, but he wouldn't.

"Cornelius," he began, leaning closer to me. Abruptly his voice was raised in malevolent joy. "Are you afraid, Cornelius?" He raised his right hand, and I felt his reptilian touch on my chest above my open nightgown. The fingers groped upward convulsively, then found a grip on my throat. I didn't move or let my panic-stricken life instinct cause me to struggle or cry for help. Instead I looked straight into his eyes, blocking the fear that rose up within me. I felt the pressure of the cold fingers and the pulsation of my bursting veins. The pounding of my heart seemed to fill the Universe, but I looked him in the eye.

"Let me go free." He spoke practically in my face.

I did not answer. He relaxed his grip slightly, and a subtly imploring note came into his voice.

"Let me be free to go out into the moonlit garden, where the animals are wailing in the pain of lust and the buds are bursting through the branches. Let me go out the gate and walk along the highways among the people with their warm colors and odors. Cut the umbilical cord and let me be a separate individual. I promise you will never hear of me again. Let me live and you also will live."

I did not answer. Slowly his grip relaxed until his hand slid off me. He straightened up and began cursing me in a sorrowful mumble.

"Unlawful creator — be damned!" He was walking away from the bed now, but his disturbing plaints continued. "What kind of joy can I have? What kind of life? No heat can warm me, no light can comfort me. No one can vouch for me or liberate me; I don't even have anybody to pray for me! No one strengthens me or defends me against this tyrant. Who could break down this prison? Why was I aroused to be aborted alive?"

The wailing, yearning voice was beginning to sap my internal resolve. Aching pity began to seep through the dam I had erected against every disturbing feeling. I found myself pitying my own materialized thoughts that I had formed into a fictitious being who was now rebelling to have his own way. I knew the situation was absurd and these temptations dangerous, but still I faltered. I genuinely felt sorry for this projected part of my ego.

While doubt and remorse were surging through me, the Kyilkhor suddenly stopped and turned around. Again I saw the evil in his yearning face. Then the current of my waning force rushed into him, and a single leap brought him back to my bedside.

"Now — give me your whole being! Your veins are open, and the blood is flowing — blood, heat, and life — all flowing into me — you will be drained, and I shall have the power. Power!" He became incoherent with intoxicated lust. Suddenly he grasped the heavy marble lamp from the bedside and wielded it over my head.

I resigned myself and waited quietly for the inevitable. I was not afraid, but I felt no more pity for him. My emotional storm had ceased. The lamp fell with a thud to the pillow beside me, cutting my forehead slightly as it dropped from weak, hesitant fingers. My forces had returned to me with my inner balance. As the oil poured out on the bed, the Kyilkhor began staggering, fell to his knees, then fell on the floor.

I got up and lit a candle, then turned him over and felt his heart. His heartbeat was very weak. I lifted him and put him on the bed. As I moved, a drop of blood fell from my wound onto his face. He started convulsively and opened his eyes. "Thank you," he murmured. Then his eyes closed again.

As for me, I was totally exhausted from my terrible struggle. I had to sit down because my knees were shaking. Meanwhile the phantom I had conjured up and for the time being defeated lay on my oil-soaked bed. Finally I got up and went to the room beside the laboratory to rest on a rush mat — the mat across from the stand from which the Kyilkhor had descended. I rolled up in a few blankets and fell into a deep sleep.

I was awakened at dawn by a feeling that someone was watching me. Then I saw that the stand was no longer empty. Apparently the Kyilkhor was back in his place, peacefully meditating.

"Here we go again," I thought wearily. "Here we go again, and who knows how many times I'm going to have to endure it before it consumes me." Internally I groaned for Saint-Germain, the Magus, who had given me a test that seemed beyond my abilities. Then my eyes cleared and I almost cried out. It was Yidam who sat on the stand.

Seeing I was awake, he rose and bowed to me, then handed me a letter. Then he left without speaking. The sight of the letter fired me with such hope that I didn't try to stop him. I thought I could see him before he left, but he left before I could see him. Now I tore open the letter.

"Kill him, Cornelius!" The words flashed from the page. Saint-Germain hadn't bothered with a greeting. "If you bring a demon to life without being able to kill him, you face a greater, more complex danger than death. The Kyilkhor you have created and named is a cameo of the dark powers. It has brought back a mummified black cult that existed beyond your memory, though you yourself nurtured it at one time. It is the Guardian of the Threshold at the gate of your personal sanctuary and represents the most ancient bondage. You must dissolve that bondage.

"A Kyilkhor must always be killed, else he becomes a tyrant. There is profound meaning in this construction and destruction process — the Divine Truth that the world is your creation. It was you who brought it into existence. You must learn to break it down and dissolve it or you will never be free of its control. A Kyilkhor must be killed, be it saint, messiah, or god. You have forced him into matter and woven a body of death and illusion around him.

"The world itself in all its darkness and demonic chaos is nothing but an unconsciously created Kyilkhor. The entities which created it lost their keys, and that is why they were defeated. Their Kyilkhor became stronger than they, and it tormented them. Their own lewdness and greed produced depraved images, and their uncontrolled imaginations filled these things with the Elixir of life. The demons began to live, became independent, and made their creators their slaves. For a Kyilkhor must be served not only until the decay of one's current body but even after death and through future incarnations. It is a Moloch of passion and is insatiable. Weakness and fear have created a Kyilkhor of fear, sickness, and death, a monster that sucks up the most precious creative forces and uses them against trapped human beings.

"If you learn the key to creating and destroying the Kyilkhor, you will have the key to your own liberation and victory over the world.

"Now I leave you to your own counsel. You are alone; you have begun to travel a separate road. Alone you created and alone you must return your creation to its original elements. The disciple is alone during every crisis and every solution.

"Be careful, strong, and brave, and persevere in your efforts. Remember you cannot turn back. You are in the middle of the sea of mysteries and must reach the other shore. You may reach this shore in years, months, or centuries — it all depends on you. But beware of killing the Kyilkhor. This demon is even more terrible when he is invisible. To rid yourself of him, your dagger must pierce all three of his bodies; you must burn him with a fire that will consume him in all three worlds.

"If you can annihilate the Kyilkhor, you will receive more powerful forces than you have ever had during your earthly life, and these forces will serve you obediently. But if you fail, you will not see me for a long time. You can summon me only by solving your problem. Then I will come and initiate the Magister."

Now I heard shuffling steps approaching. I turned to the door, which was opening slowly. The Kyilkhor stumbled in like a sleepwalker, my dried blood still daubing his forehead. He sat down on the stand, breathing heavily. Occasionally a shudder wracked his frame.

"Give me some warm food — I'm cold," he mumbled.

His misery filled me with premature hope. I had forgotten that it was my strength and emotions that fed him. My warm joy was his sweet drink, and my hope was his medicine. His face turned a healthier color and his eyes opened. His breathing cleared and he sighed with pleasure.

"Ah, that's what I needed. That's good."

The weeks that followed were both difficult and terrifying. Vainly I tried to block his ability to feed on my forces. I could not succeed. If I destroyed part of him with days of grueling effort, he would rebuild it in a few hours by tapping my forces when I relaxed. If I began to hope he was getting weaker, the hope would strengthen him. If I felt discouraged by his renewed strength, he grew yet stronger. It was a Sisyphean task, and as the months passed I reached the point where I no longer cared about any changes in his condition.

Thus for a long time we were at an impasse. He lived and moved beside me like a mirror image, and my concentrated efforts couldn't diminish his vital force. I was depressed by this tenacity and thus had to fight a battle within and without. If I succumbed either to my creature or my own despair, I was lost.

My health was beginning to suffer. The constant tension made me lose my appetite and I lost weight. The outside world ceased to exist for me; the Kyilkhor became a hateful monomania. The land about me, the castle, the quiet figures of my parents — none were real except he. My parents of course knew about the dark waves that threatened to drown me, but they could do nothing.

How many ways I tried to cut myself off from the Kyilkhor, to keep him from draining me spiritually! Nothing worked. I would painfully restore my balance of indifference only to find it immediately threatened with upset. Irritation and anger pried at my defenses, and I felt I could not hold them off much longer.

What I feared most was that my murderous hate would overcome me and I would kill him. I wanted to stick a knife into that breathing, vigorous body, even if it meant my own death. The insane desire pulsed through my emaciated body and shaken nerves — Finish him off! Squeeze out his life or beat him to death! I was close to emotional collapse; naturally this made him stronger and even more self-confident. I saw I would have to give up. I could not find the connection that linked us. The current flowed between us, no matter what I did.

I had to face the fact that I would lose. I was overcome with shame and misery when I thought of all the trials I had gone through and what my future would be. My parents and Saint-Germain would be so disappointed in me. I had failed the great trial and now I would again suffer the dark, bitter fate of the fallen novice. The Kyilkhor had simply gotten the better of me, and he would fulfill his murderous passion and evil desire for autonomy. He would kill me so he could live, and I would lose my body, the fruitful environment of the Castle, my parents — and my memory. I would have to start all over again, groping blindly, and everything the Kyilkhor did in the meantime would be my responsibility.

For I had conjured up and loosed a monster on the world. I had given a form, name, and personality to a blind, inexperienced force complex which now sought the crude experiences of life because I had not given him my intellect. All he had was a life-filled body and an elemental spirit, a demon whose avid will was bent on the emotions and passions.

But if I killed him instead of waiting for him to kill me, the situation was even worse, for he would then possess me. This demon would force me to do his will, use my body for his debauchery, and drive me to death or madness — and I still would not be free of him. I was in the worst trap I had been in since my alliance with Homonculus.

When I realized I was well and truly defeated, my anger vanished. I decided I would never raise a hand against my creature, regardless of the consequences. I would rather be the victim.

Now I decided to end the tension of waiting; I would confront the inevitable. I did not bid my parents farewell, for I felt I had lost that right. I simply locked myself in the meditation room with the Kyilkhor.

I sat down on the bulrush mat not afraid but simply very weary. There was the Kyilkhor sitting across from me. I could feel his burning glance but I didn't look at him. I wasn't interested in him; I was looking inside myself. I knew there could be no help from anyone else.

My inner space was filled with still, gray water, dark and rejecting. It would take effort to penetrate it and I could not — did not want to — make that effort. I didn't even struggle as sleepiness overcame me and my inner landscape blurred into darkness. My awareness slipped imperceptibly into the dark waters like a corpse.

A strange dream came to me in this deep sleep. I saw the meditation room and its image reflected in a mirror. The room itself was dark, but its mirror image shone with clear light. I saw myself sitting wearily in the shadowed room; my head hung down in sleep. But the mirror image showed me bolt upright, shining with the ecstasy of meditation. The Kyilkhor sat on his stand in the dark room, positively glowing with health, and he watched me like a tiger. But the stand in the mirror image was quite empty, and I was astonished.

Now the Kyilkhor in the dark room got up and approached the sleeper on the rush mat with curved fingers. I was frightened and would have shouted to wake the victim, but the meditator in the other room turned and put his finger to his lips.

"But he'll kill him in his sleep!" I wanted to shout this aloud, but I was in the grip of a helpless paralysis. The meditator shook his head, then pointed to the empty stand. "He may not be there," I responded desperately, "but he's certainly here!"

I saw the Kyilkhor's fingers close on the neck of the sleeping figure and choke off his breath. Then I felt my own breath being choked off.

"How could someone who doesn't exist commit murder?" My alter ego spoke sharply from the mirror image. "Why do you keep saying he exists? You have made him a monomania. Don't you know it is your belief in him that makes him invincible? Your belief is his Elixir; if you take it from him, he'll be nothing but lifeless matter. Take it away!"

Release and new light flowed through me and an immense gratitude. I could breathe freely now and stare up at the Kyilkhor who held my defenseless body in his merciless hands.

"How could a ridiculous statue strangle me? How could a nightmare persecute me and make me run?" My thoughts swooped down upon him. "You're nothing but smoke, fog, and cloud; my imagination alone has given you meaning and form. I have done enough shadowboxing with myself. Disperse, ye elemental parasites! I hereby take back unto myself the energy and force I had loosed and dissolve the bond between us. I now take back that part of myself which I had released. You have no existence of your own. Your breath is my breath; your blood is my blood. You have no independent will; it is my will that works in you. I now withdraw these things from you. What are you now? Lifeless matter I borrowed and now return. Return to your stand and stiffen in the pose your creator commanded!"

The Kyilkhor dropped his limp hands and shuffled to his stand. When he sat down and faced me I saw rage, terror, and desperation in his face. Gradually his features froze into position, but first he gave a horrible yell of protest. The painful scream became more and more inarticulate, but it was an intolerable sound and jerked me awake. I was astounded to find that this horrible sound came from my own mouth. As soon as I recognized this, the noise ceased and my throat burned from the exertion.

The Kyilkhor sat motionless in his original pose, and his painted colors were dimly visible in the dusky light. I got up and went over to touch him; I touched cold, hard matter. The paint had peeled off one place on his face, and the yellow clay underneath it crumbled.

★

And thus the Master came to me again and gave me what I had earned — the total knowledge of things and processes. At last I had achieved what I had sought for centuries, had killed for, suffered for, fought with demons, and died to attain — I became a Magister and was accepted by the Masters. I had reached the Inner Sanctuary.

Yet the person who was initiated had nothing in common with the greedy, confused, and temperamental Hans Burgner who stumbled after eternal life. True, the mystical process had begun in his soul. He was the lead that had been thrown into the crucible, heated by the fires of centuries, and transformed by experiences and consequences into Cornelius von Grotte, the Magister. Now he had no more worldly desires, and now that he had acquired the power, he no longer wished to use it. But he had one more debt to pay and it stood in front of him.

Now the Magister stood before the last step. The next to the last step, however, involves lengthy tasks which demand great patience, and one can never ask when he will reach the end. He must first perform certain selfless duties that might take decades — or more than a century. For the difference between a Magister and Magus is that between an industrious talent and a genius.

★

I spent my days quietly with my parents, working hard. I performed exercises at dawn. In the early morning I worked in the laboratory. Then I worked with Victor Amadeus; this was more pleasure than effort. After that

I had lunch with my parents, then strolled in the park studying rocks, trees, plants, and insects. The late afternoon was spent working on the mail of the Order, and the evening belonged to reading, music, and the company of my parents.

In those days of crystal clear perfection I blocked out the past and future, for I knew this was just a passing rest to strengthen me for new events. I utilized my time thoroughly.

We hardly noticed the turmoil of the French Revolution, which was then shaking the civilized world. Of course we were aware of the various events, for we were in contact with many skillful and influential people who were doing everything they could for the victims. They could not of course interfere with individual or group Karma; they were successful only where Higher Law permitted it.

41

The Mirror Reflects the Past

In the spring of 1787, a lad of about fifteen came to the castle asking for work. At that time of year every hand was needed, and the homeless boy was hired to work the fields and chop wood. He was a large-boned fellow with pimples and wary eyes that avoided everyone else. The protruding bone over his hooded eyes suggested he might be a cunning and sharp observer, but his sloping forehead revealed little capacity for higher reasoning. He spoke awkwardly through thick lips, though his strong jaw suggested a talent for speaking. The lad positively radiated a burning restlessness. His name was Ernst Müller.

Thus the illegitimate son of the maidservant Anna Müller arrived at the Castle of Grotte to reopen old memories and bring me face to face with one of the greatest dilemmas of my life. For fate held a mirror in front of me and did not even bother to tell a new story. Only the actors changed; now a new figure took my old role, while I stood in the Magister's place.

At first I didn't even notice the boy, but gradually I became aware that curious, eager eyes were following me when I walked in the garden and when I worked by the open windows in my study. Then I noticed the boy hoeing beside the gardener. Whenever I looked up, our eyes met but then he would lower his gaze quickly and continue his work.

Once I walked over to him and asked him his name. He was so embarrassed he blushed and perspired, but it was I who was shaken when I realized who he was and observed the expression of his eyes. They were filled with brooding hunger and fanatical intensity, and they showed me a familiar hell. Those were Hans Burgner's eyes. I was moved with compassion and irresistibly drawn to the lad. He had come then to reflect the past like a mirror.

Had he come to Grotte to return an old visit and collect a debt I thought I had paid with the pain and blood of centuries? I could only consult my past, for the present was silent and the future would reply no more to me than to ordinary mortals. Yet I had presentiments, at once repulsive and attractive. There were so many clear references in Ernst Müller's life and personality; how could I misunderstand? I simply watched and waited.

A few days later I noticed that someone had been into my library; there was a book missing from one of the higher shelves. I had no doubt about the identity of the culprit; I had seen Ernst Müller's eyes and I remembered too much about Hans Burgner. I went out into the park to follow the thread that linked us.

He was beside the barn, screened by a pile of dirty wheelbarrows. Sitting on a tree stump, he bent intensely over his reading, his hands against his ears to block all sound. I recognized the book immediately; it was *The Triple Stones of the Secret Fires* by Johann Glauber, an alchemist who had been born in Karlstadt.

I touched his shoulder and he jerked up, confused and muzzy-eyed as though he had been snatched from a heavy sleep. Then he sprang to his feet terrified, and stood in front of me, making no attempt to hide the book.

"Where did you learn to read?" I asked conversationally.

It was awhile before he could comprehend the question. As he calmed, the evasive look returned to his eyes. "At the inn — from a stranger," he replied haltingly. Then he held out the book to me. "I swear I would have put it back. Are you going to dismiss me?"

I made no move to take the book. "I don't know yet," I replied.

"Please don't dismiss me," he begged. "It's just that I see these books all the time — so many of them . . ."

"Hadn't it occurred to you that you might ask?"

He shot me a glance of mistrustful calculation. "No," he admitted at last, "I didn't think you'd lend one to me."

"Why not?"

"Well, a person like me . . ."

"Don't you know you're stealing?"

"I told you I'd have put it back," he blazed.

"Why did you take this particular book?"

He refused to look at me. "I didn't mean to steal," he repeated dully.

I would not let him avoid the question. "Why did you take an alchemist's book?"

"Because I'd like — like to learn about it — Gerber, that taught me to read and write — he said alchemists have a secret . . ."

"How to make gold?"

"That, yes, but something else too . . ."

"What?"

"The Elixir of Eternal Life — the magic wand — you can make storm and hail with it, command spirits, be above everybody!" The boy seemed to regret his vehement outburst midway through. "You know," he ended lamely.

"What do I know?"

"The whole thing. Upstairs . . ."

"What is upstairs?"

"A workshop." Now he gazed at me with boundless longing.

So he had spied on the laboratory too. He must have climbed one of the trees to feast those hungry, lynxlike eyes. There were all kinds of rumors current about the Castle of Grotte. Well-meant as well as spiteful tongues had combined to weave a legend around it. Young Müller had heard these things, and they had brought him straight to me. I took the book and said I would think about his fate.

For the next few days I was conscious of his eyes following me everywhere. Should I teach him? He was crude and confused, like Hans Burgner, and he had a great deal yet to go through. But Rochard hadn't refused Hans Burgner . . .

It was an accident that decided the matter. While I was away in Rotenburg, Ernst fell out of one of the trees by the laboratory and suffered several serious breaks in his arm and thigh. By the time I got home, my father had cleaned and dressed his wounds, put him into splints, and given him a sedative, so I had little to do when I visited him in his shabby quarters in the woodshed of the gardener's hut. He was breathing heavily and looked exhausted and frightened.

"Were you spying again?" I asked quietly. The lad bit his lips and made no reply. "Answer me!"

Suddenly he broke into bitter sobs, disarming me completely. "How else could I get there — how else?" he gasped between sobs. "And you took back the book — before I had finished reading it — I have no right to complain of course. I wish I could learn too — be in a workshop, like the lords."

There was a terrifying force behind this blind ambition; I knew it was the striving of the fallen novice for the dimly remembered Light.

"Do you know what it means to study?" I asked cautiously.

"I've done it before."

"But only once in a while, between play and chores. Could you start something and stick to it for years, study subjects that are difficult, dry, and boring? This is not just irresponsible daydreaming about sorcery, spirits, and eternal life. You have to work for knowledge and submit to discipline, curb your curiosity. Unless you submit to these conditions, there is no knowledge and no power. It's a power entirely different from what you crave. You cannot have it if you want it just to control other people."

"Then what do you use it for?" He challenged in the dim light.

"To control yourself. That doesn't sound so attractive, does it?"

"Yes, it does!" the lad retorted. "I enjoyed learning all the letters and numbers and wished I could do it all the time. I don't care about anything else, and I'll work any length of time for it, asking for nothing, just a little to eat. I'll do anything you want — anything! I wouldn't ask for pay — just the chance to be among books and in the workshop." In his excitement he struggled to sit up, then sank back with a groan.

"Calm down. You mustn't try to move!" I went and wedged open the window of the woodshed so I could see his injuries. His face was distorted with pain. I leaned over and began examining his bandages. Suddenly I recoiled. There was an old, dogeared book on his blanket, smudged and stained by dirty fingers. It was the story of Nicholas Flammel.

Then I knew I had to teach him.

★

Ernst recuperated slowly; the splintered bones gave him great pain. In the meantime I brought him books I thought would help organize his inner world. He greeted me with gratitude and doglike devotion when I visited the woodshed; I could see his emotional dependence grow greater every day. To him I was the guardian of heaven, holding the key to his life and his future.

Yet every day I saw even more clearly what crude material he was and how little I could hope for his progress. What he needed to learn could be taught only by time and experience. Knowledge could not polish his passions and instincts; only living them out could do that. Every other Master would refuse him without a second thought. Obscure feelings and violent desire were not the attributes of an occult student. Only his mental and spiritual readiness and his own progress would determine his fate.

★

Meanwhile I made myself familiar with Ernst's miserable childhood, which differed from that of the animals among which he was raised only by being more neglected. Even in their filthy pens, the animals got their food on time and received sufficient care to prevent illness, but Ernst soon became aware that he could depend on no one. The world was wicked and hostile, and he was small and weak. His mother didn't care anything about him; she noticed him only to beat him when he got in her way. His grandmother would throw him some food occasionally, but she herself was a sick woman who could barely drag herself about on swollen legs. Since both were helpless, they came to depend upon each other — a dependence mixed with jealousy and suspicion, for both knew they were superfluous and feared there would not be enough for them both. One of Ernst's first memories was hearing his mother say how much easier things would have been for her if he had died at birth, while his grandmother continually lamented that God did not take her and him with her.

And then of course the inn was on the highway and attracted many strange, diverse people. The boy saw agents, wandering journeymen, swindlers, peasants, and nobility; all roused his curiosity with their alien customs and boastful tales. They implanted the lust for faraway adventure, fantastic, unusual, and wonderful. But the most important influence in his life had been a wandering barber named Gerber.

Gerber was a shiftless vagabond frequently in trouble with the authorities, but he had managed to garner some confused knowledge from randomly found books and varied experiences. Discovering that Ernst had a receptive mind, he began to teach him. Even he would go off from time to time, not caring that the boy needed him like warm sunshine after a cold and terrifying night. Yet every time the barber returned he was touched by the child's joy, love, and good memory. Ernst never forgot anything; he cherished his knowledge like a holy relic. Indeed it was his only treasure, the only meaning of his life. His knowledge increased with Gerber's every return. The barber taught him to read and write, but also a good deal of twisted information, half-truths, and fantastic theories.

Ernst had seen many fights at the tavern and knew all about knifings and spilled blood, but none of this prepared him for the experience of seeing Gerber die of gastric hemorrhage. And no one even wanted to help the dying man. The tavern folk responded to his situation by debating whether or not they should take him out to an open field, since it was going to be a messy death and might lead to complications with the police. Then the owner and the bartender hauled the helpless man out and dropped him in a ditch full of nettles. Ernst followed them, sobbing and trembling, and sat beside the dying man as the last drops of blood flowed out of him and his eyes grew glassy.

The boy was horrified by such mercilessness, and something snapped inside him. He began to remember something Gerber had told him.

"Do not work only for ordinary knowledge, my son; acquire the knowledge of magic spells that will put you above the common herd of men. If you don't, sooner or later they'll trample you. It is only by terrifying them that you can get them to respect you. I made the mistake of my life by not taking service with a Magus. I met one when I was a young man, and I knew right away who he was. Once I defended him when he was attacked by robbers — they couldn't really hurt him, of course, because the Elixir had made him immortal. He could have struck all of them down just by waving his hand, but he liked my courage and took me into his confidence. He even offered to let me become his famulus, and sooner or later he would have given me the Elixir too. If I'd just stuck with him, I could be making gold right now and not give a damn about death."

"Why didn't you stick with him?" Ernst had asked out of a pounding heart.

Gerber had just waved a hand. "You wouldn't understand yet, my small friend. There was this woman I was crazy about, a big blonde. She was a mean, cold bitch. But anyway the Magus moved on and I stayed, and she promptly betrayed me with a coffin maker. I gave up eternal life and endless gold for that woman. You see, I couldn't find the Magus again. I looked for him for years — even today."

Now Ernst sat beside the dying man and stared at the highway, hopelessly waiting for a miracle. "Surely the Magus will come now," he thought. "He'll come and bring the Elixir and heal Gerber. He couldn't let Gerber die like this. Gerber is the only person in the world who cares about me."

But the Magus didn't come, and Gerber died in the muddy ditch. After that Ernst could bear his home no longer. He ran away, taking with him only the book about Nicholas Flammel and his implanted monomania. He went to find the Magus.

★

When Ernst had recuperated, I began to teach him. First I laid a foundation of cleanliness and order. I taught him to eat at a table, keep himself clean, and behave politely and provided him with the necessary clothes, books, and writing materials. He was allotted a small room in the heated pavilion in the park.

Ernst responded by keeping his quarters immaculate. There was never even a speck of dust on his bookshelf, and he cared for each object on his desk with devout love. His hair was always well combed, his suit pressed, and his nails clean. He was humble and compliant and would do anything to please me, no matter how small or simple. As a pupil he devoured everything with surprising speed. He was exceptionally perceptive and interested in everything. In two years he had finished what most students do in eight. He threw himself into the study of languages, and his excellent memory allowed him to master French, English, and Latin.

I might have been dazzled by this beginning if I had not been aware of his quick temper, uncontrolled sensuality, and natural guile. These alarmed me. I knew he was at war with the servants. This was not altogether due to their envy of his changed status, as I had at first thought. Ernst took good care to make them feel inferior, especially the gardener for whom he had once worked and who ironically had had pity on him.

The gardener came to me and complained that Ernst was stealing the new red roses and tearing them out so roughly he injured the roots. When I began to question the lad about this, he blushed and avoided my gaze.

"I like roses," he said finally.

"If you left them on the rosebush, they'd be there longer for you to enjoy."

"I can't enjoy them with the gardener around; I can feel his poisonous hatred." Ernst spoke heatedly, all the time watching from under his eyelids for my reaction. Now I was alarmed. His eyes looked so sincere, and he was lying.

"The gardener used to be your friend," I responded. "Why should he hate you?" I wanted to see how far the lad would go.

"Because you've been so good to me. None of the servants can forgive me for rising above them. They'd love to see you get angry and dismiss me."

"So they've changed their attitude toward you?"

"Yes."

"Have you perhaps changed your attitude toward them?"

"Of course not. I leave them alone."

"If you leave them alone, then you have indeed changed your attitude toward them."

"I have nothing to say to them!"

"And that is precisely how you have hurt them. Remember you've nothing to be particularly proud of. You haven't risen above them; you've just taken another path. Your path is no better than theirs, not by any means. They are good servants who do their work well, and their path is useful and honest. You are a servant too. The fact that you've begun to study doesn't mean you're a sage. You're only standing at the threshold of knowledge, and it has not yet been decided if you are worthy of the higher knowledge. Good perception and a shrewd mind are all you need for earthly knowledge, but you need other qualities to penetrate occult truth, qualities like moral strength, love of truth, unwavering courage, humility, self-denial, and the ability to experience nonsensual ecstasy. I see little of these qualities in you. Your every ambition is directed out toward the world. You collect the treasures of knowledge only to flaunt them like medals so the ignorant will admire you. That is not a proper goal for a true student of the occult. You're still on the downward road. What did you do with the roses?"

I had caught him unawares, and he could only stammer. "I — I took them to my room."

"And then?"

"I put them in a vase on my table or the desk."

"I've been in your room every day and I haven't noticed any roses."

"I was afraid . . ."

"You hid them when I came in?"

"Yes — that's it."

"Why won't you believe you can tell me the truth?"

"The truth!"

"Do you really believe you can keep me from finding out what you're doing and thinking? If you aren't ashamed to do something, don't be ashamed to own up to it. You needn't be afraid. I'm not angry with you and I won't look down on you. I'm just your teacher. Just don't ever lie to me. That's the only condition I exact. Lying won't help you anyway because I can see through you. Elisa is very young and inexperienced. You're putting her in danger with your braggadocio — and stolen roses."

He stared at me, crushed. "You know about that?"

"Yes. That should amply prove my point. I know all about your other affairs too but they don't bother me. Until you are mature enough to channel your sexual energies into creative forces, it's better for you to discharge them this way to keep them from hindering your work. Now do we understand each other? You leave Elisa — and the roses — alone!"

He promised implicit obedience — but he broke his word before the next morning.

★

Elisa was the red-haired, sixteen-year-old daughter of the cook, a whimsical, sensuous girl. The local miller wanted to marry her and she had been inclined to favor him until Ernst appeared on the scene. By now

Ernst was eighteen, well-built, well-groomed, and unusually mature in his appearance. He could talk intelligently and colorfully, and boundless confidence gleamed in his eyes. Elisa fell blindly in love with him. She was beautiful and willing, and Ernst was totally callous in his desire. He had no intention of refusing this ripe fruit that fell into his lap. For a while the affair was secret; the girl would sneak out to the pavilion during the night and return at dawn. When Elisa became pregnant, she went to the dirty, ignorant village medicine woman for help, and Ernst somehow scrounged up the money for the old crone.

One evening the cook rushed into the study where my parents and I retired after dinner. She was frightened and crying and begged us to return with her to the servants' quarters. Elisa was in convulsions and would not let anyone touch her. We all answered the summons, but Elisa refused to see anyone but my mother. We waited while she made the examination.

My mother sent the cook away as soon as she returned and then told us what had happened. The clumsy old woman had bungled the abortion and mangled the unfortunate girl. Elisa was hemorrhaging badly; there was no time to be lost. We ignored the girl's protests and went in. Together we cleansed her and administered sedatives and certain essences to heal the infection.

The girl's horrible screams rang through the night; they drew Ernst, deadly pale and trembling, to the open window. While her bloody, naked torso writhed in our hands, I happened to glance up and meet his eyes. Despair, pity, and guilt contorted his features, and for a moment I almost hoped the incident would cure him of irresponsible sexual escapades.

When Elisa had finally calmed down, we turned her over to the care of her mother, with instructions to wake me immediately if she got worse. We returned to the castle, and I had already started undressing when I felt Ernst standing outside my door, not daring to knock. His mental turmoil was almost a palpable force burning through the wood.

"Come in, Ernst!" I called softly. "I was waiting for you."

The door opened and the boy staggered in, terribly agitated. Before I could stop him, he knelt before me. "My God, my God!" he kept repeating. "Never again. Oh, my God!"

I made him sit down, and he stared at me with his eyes full of the one question he dared not ask. "She will live," I answered, "but just fifteen minutes later would have been too late. Why did you let her go to that butcher?"

"We were ashamed . . ."

"Were you ashamed to perform the act?" I countered.

"It's just a madness — you don't even notice when you fall into it . . ."

"By all human reasoning, Elisa should be dead because of your madness. Worse, if you hadn't crossed her path and dazzled her eyes, she would have become a good wife and mother. Now she has no choice but to turn to harlotry, for the village will drive her away from here. I can't save her from that. It's not even as though you really loved her; you just wanted her to satisfy your passion. You wouldn't marry her if you had the opportunity because in your heart you look down on her. You think she's only fit for sexual pleasure. Yet you seduced her, and that at a time when you could have satisfied your desires with the baker's widow. Are you beginning to understand the nature of the power you keep burbling about? It is the power to control yourself and the weak moments you have to conquer. Otherwise you'll be buried under an avalanche of consequences.

Ernst readily admitted the truth of what I had said and accepted his guilt. Then he asked if I was going to make him leave the castle.

"Your future behavior will determine that," I replied. "I'll give you a chance to change. But if you prove you can't, you need expect nothing more from me." This statement calmed him considerably. He had confidence in himself but even more in — my lenience.

Now that his personal affairs were settled and he was absolved of all consequences, Ernst reverted to his monomania. "Was Elisa saved by the Elixir?" he asked suddenly.

"What made you think of that?" I tried to avoid his question.

"You said that by all human reasoning she should be dead. Since she is alive, it was not human knowledge that saved her; it was . . ."

"The Elixir. Yes. It would have been wiser for you to wait to learn of it until your own efforts changed the old legends into natural understanding."

"Why? Don't you believe there's an Elixir?" It was a raw challenge.

"You'll have to eat a lot of biscuits yet to learn the answer to that."

"Well, can't you just *tell* me?"

"I will tell you everything you're ready to learn."

"But the books write about it openly! Why do they do that if I'm not supposed to know about it?"

"The Elixir you're talking about is very dangerous — because it exists only in the minds of fanatics. I know of nothing but medications."

"Well, isn't that just semantics?" I felt his excitement surge around me.

"No. You're imagining an Elixir that will give your body immortal youth, sexual potency, and attraction, some kind of miracle drug that will cancel out the effects of every debauchery. You want to live forever simply because you think it will take that long to sate your desires. I'm afraid I'll have to disillusion you.

"There are certain medications that can heal the body and prolong the life span, but to be effective they must always be accompanied by a healthful lifestyle. The body can never really become immortal; it is a transitory form, an experimental workshop that is the prey of death. The body contains death within itself. It is the spirit that is eternal. Yet the spirit must struggle with its own body to gain this eternity. The two are like fire and water; they don't mix. One inevitably consumes the other, and man is the battleground of this war.

"The body's weapons are passion, desire, sensuality, and yearning after beauty. The spirit's weapons are the aftereffects of gratification of these desires — nausea, disillusionment, suffering, aging, and death. The soul is the bridge on which the two forces fight continuously.

"Sometimes the body captures the spirit, starves it, and believes it has killed it. But the spirit has a weapon that eventually wins the victory — immortality. The victory of the body is only temporary. When once the spirit defeats the body, it is annihilated forever.

"The true Elixir of the alchemists is merely a weapon in the battle, a method of extending the life span and prolonging the spirit's existence in a hostile territory so it can perform its tasks with an older, finer-tuned brain and be better prepared for the final conflict. Only a truly aware spirit can acquire the Elixir, and even then only if it will not be used for treachery."

"And this Elixir — or shall I say medicine — is it a powder or a liquid?" Ernst asked. He had not even slightly understood the meaning of my words.

It was frightening to relive the same old argument on the other side of the table. I remembered so well how I had sat across from the Magister in Hans Burgner's body, driven by a passionate monomania. Now I knew the helplessness and sorrow Rochard must have felt when he realized that he could not really pass on his knowledge; his profound truths fell on barren rocks in Hans Burgner's soul.

This ominous memory made it clear to me that it was futile to work with Ernst Müller any further; he was such raw material as to be unworkable. He wasn't interested in what I could offer, and he cherished the firm belief that I could initiate him into a secret that would make him immortal and happy. There was no way to explain why I didn't do this. I knew it would be vain to pour the clearest white magic into his grimy soul; it would immediately be churned into the thick poison of black magic. He would promptly use all his strength and knowledge for his own selfish passions and interest.

Now I realized I could stop teaching him. We had been brought together only so I could give him a start. I must remove him from the Castle of Grotte immediately. Of course I felt responsible for the boy's future; I couldn't leave him alone.

Thus I took the first step into the dark corridor of the Temple of Mysteries. I did not know whether I was going upward or about to crash into a deep well. I only knew I could not stop.

42

The Lion's Claws

I soon found an excellent way to forward my plan.

For some time I had corresponded with Jean-Marie Ragon, the outstanding Belgian mystic, and together we had established a lodge in Brussels. I had met him through Saint-Germain, who thought a great deal of his occult abilities and intelligence. When the business of the lodge called me to Brussels, I decided to take Ernst with me and get him a good clerical position there. I knew the city would attract my student like a magnet, and the sooner he submerged himself in the ocean of astral passions, the sooner he would rise from it.

At first I told Ernst only that I meant to travel and take him with me. I didn't mention my other plan because I wanted him to feel that accepting the new opportunity would be his own idea. Ernst's joy was boundless and his fevered preparations took his whole time, even distracting him from his studies. Time and again he told me he could never repay what I had done for him.

We started in March 1801, passing on the way the inn where Ernst's mother served. I wondered if he would ask to visit her so he could show off his new finery, but he drew back into the carriage and wouldn't even look out the window. He abruptly grew silent.

"What's the matter?" I prompted.

"I hate this place!" he burst out.

"I thought you might want to see your mother."

"I never want to hear of the place again!"

"I understand," I replied. Hans Burgner had felt the same way.

★

I had calculated correctly. The city of Brussels captivated Ernst, and I saw to it that he had free time and money to spend while I worked with Ragon.

When he had had his fill of sightseeing and public entertainments, I took him to meet some of the high-ranking families. The magic name of the Order opened all palace doors to me and insured a cordial, hospitable welcome.

We began to attend fine evening parties I would never have gone to on my own, and Ernst became immersed in the atmosphere of refined splendor and immense wealth and the assured bearing of the chosen caste. He had never seen anything like this at austere, monastic Grotte. Suddenly beautiful women with skin like fragrant petals and dazzling jewels buzzed around him. He began to hear delicate yet playful and enticing words directed at him, and an assortment of wines, spices, and exotic dishes tickled his palate.

The brilliant, ostentatious splendor of these gatherings would have crushed a more sensitive and sophisticated person, but it inspired Ernst and set his sensuality aflame. He was as self-confident as though he was at last on his own home ground. I was surprised at how easily he assumed a supercilious, aristocratic demeanor. He handled the ladies with a sure, easy hand, arousing them with his hungry, disrobing eyes. It was as though he and not they were experienced in the sophisticated art of love. Here was a casteless nobody, the illegitimate son of a servant bridging the social gulf like a skilled tightrope walker. He used his excellent powers of observation to store everything he heard, then use it selectively at the proper time.

People began to notice Ernst. They thought him original, unusually intelligent, and dangerously attractive, and he really was all that. He ported and played like a lion cub, but already his bloodthirsty claws and teeth flashed experimentally.

I discussed my plans for Ernst with Ragon. We agreed that his employer must be selected carefully. First we had to make sure there were no young women in the household in any capacity. Eventually we decided on Charles de Blancourt, a wealthy old bachelor who was an avid book collector. He was anxious to hire a reliable, educated young man to supervise his library and find rare books for him. The old man's love of books and generosity made him an excellent choice. De Blancourt was no real student of the occult, just an avid amateur; he did not practice in any way. Since Ragon had helped him get rare books and was an erudite companion, de Blancourt was more than ready to perform a favor for him.

De Blancourt made his offer to Ernst in the midst of a splendid party at his palatial home. He offered the boy a salary, luxurious appointments, and considerable free time if he would take on this pleasant and comfortable job. It was all a not-yet-established young man could dream of; still Ernst asked time to think it over.

When we got back to the hotel, he asked if he might come into my room to discuss an important matter. He was pale and his manner was humble. I knew what he was going to say and I knew how I had to answer him. He told me about de Blancourt's offer, and I congratulated him on such great personal success.

"I am well aware of the advantages of the position," Ernst stared at me sternly, "and I passionately love everything he offers me. But I'd give it all up without a second thought if you would continue teaching me and give me some hope that someday you would initiate me into the most important secrets of life. They are the only things that really matter."

"Well, I can at least give you a straight answer, Ernst. If I could give you a single spark of hope that I could initiate you during your present life, even in old age, I would tell you to stay with me. But I can't. I could only help you start — your goal is still far away — many lives and deaths away. I wish I could tell you something different, for I have grown fond of you and I shall miss you. But the best advice I can give you is to take de Blancourt's offer. Grotte could not give you any more."

He stood up, a picture of anger and despair. "Then what is it I need to do to be found worthy of the Opus Magnus? Am I not intelligent, persistent, and hard-working? Oh, I admit my passions defeat me, but I would subjugate them all for the Great Goal if you would but give me the word. Have you thought of the lengths to which you might drive me? I shall never stop seeking the occult, you know, regardless of what it costs me or anybody else. Why don't you lead me down the straight road?"

"Because it is better for you to go through the detours of experience that will purify you. Otherwise you would leave the straight road at a later point and use your occult knowledge for the wrong purpose. I do not doubt your intelligence and persistence, and I know you will never cease your search for occult secrets. When you arrive at the point where you can win the keys to the Three Gates of Knowledge, I know you will make outstanding use of them. But there are other things you must do first. I'm not belittling you by refusing; it's just that I cannot give you these forces to use in gratifying your passions. You see, these forces can be used properly only by Adepts who are beyond the temptations of passion. I know you're bitter and feel I've misjudged you. If I have, I'll gladly admit it. The best way for you to prove me wrong is for you to remain steadfast and keep on working without my making you a definite promise. Actually you can get closer to your goal if you don't stay with me. If you stay on the straight road all by yourself — that would be a definite indication of maturity. Let this be a trial. Prove me wrong and I will share all my knowledge unconditionally."

He rose. "All right." His response was serious. "Should I contact you or will you send for me when you realize you were mistaken?"

"I'll contact you, Ernst. You needn't doubt that."

So Ernst took de Blancourt's offer. For several months I received regular, long letters from him in which he faithfully recounted every thought and action. The youth had an original and colorful style, and he could give very droll descriptions of the people he met. He respected de Blancourt and adored his work, throwing himself into it wholeheartedly. For a while he was interested in nothing else.

Ragon also wrote me favorable reports. Ernst seldom left the house, he reported; instead he spent all his free time reading and making notes. De Blancourt liked the boy and appreciated his efforts, for he had managed to get two rare books the old man had wanted for years. He was glad we had recommended him.

Then toward the end of the year Ernst's letters became less frequent, though Ragon was still sending me good reports. Ernst was still doing well; in fact he was, if anything, overworking. De Blancourt began to worry about his health, for he had lost his appetite and had difficulty sleeping. The old man urged him to relax but Ernst would not hear of it.

The brief letters he wrote me revealed that Ernst had found something that occupied him greatly, something he didn't want me to know about. His broad script narrowed and the letters now angled backward, indicating a withdrawal from society and concentration on some subject.

Then I knew that Ernst had left the straight path.

43

Isabelle

When Ernst had been in Brussels for three years, a tragedy occurred that at last revealed the young man's secret, dangerous activity. At this time de Blancourt received a visit from his younger sister, who lived in England, and she brought her daughter Isabelle with her.

Ragon said that Isabelle was a cold-mannered beauty, tall and slender, with darkish blonde hair. The gray eyes and vivid lips of this extraordinary girl contradicted her apparent coldness, but she was wickedly witty.

There was tension between Isabelle and Ernst from the time they first met. The girl was wealthy, spoiled, and sophisticated, and she took every occasion to make Ernst feel like an upstart. It was her custom to make him the butt of her sarcastic jests during meals. According to Ragon, Ernst bore up with remarkable self-control and frequently managed to get the better of the girl with his agile responses.

Isabelle was engaged to Lord B., the eldest son of one of England's oldest houses, and upon her marriage would have a close connection with the royal house. Yet there was no doubt she was intrigued by this handsome lad of impossible background. She used her scorn to discharge this attraction and convince herself she could not possibly be interested in him. Ernst responded with polite reservation and avoided her whenever possible.

This was the state of affairs that brought about the tragedy. There began to be a change in Isabelle. She no longer threw scornful jests at Ernst and she seemed quiet, listless, and inattentive. Soon she became noticeably pale, and her lips grew dry and bloodless. Her mother, thinking she pined for her fiancé, planned a speedy return home but Isabelle would hear nothing of it. She even wanted to stay longer than they had originally planned; her mother could go home without her.

Then Isabelle's mother got a letter from Lord B. asking about his fiancé, who had not answered his letters in weeks. The girl was undoubtedly sick, but she protested desperately when her worried family sought to call in a doctor. When they sent for one anyway, she locked herself in her bedroom and could not be persuaded to come out.

Now de Blancourt and his sister were thoroughly alarmed and bewildered. They suspected some emotional involvement, perhaps a love affair, but they could find no evidence among Isabelle's acquaintances in Brussels. During the last few weeks she had withdrawn completely from Brussels society.

The truth came out in Isabelle's suicide note. The girl had taken poison and was dead when they found her. She had addressed the note to de Blancourt, and Ragon was the only person outside the family who ever knew the truth. De Blancourt gave him permission to send a copy of her statement to me.

Isabelle had begun by asking that de Blancourt stand by her mother and support her in her time of sorrow; then she asked him to cover up the affair and use his influence to find a doctor who would certify death of natural causes. Finally she told her story.

"It started two months ago, on September 2nd, a warm, overcast evening. I could have chosen between two invitations, but I had a slight headache and didn't feel like going anywhere. I felt weighed down and oppressed. At dinner I sat opposite Ernst Müller as usual. Every time I looked up from my plate he was staring at me, as had been usual of late, but that night it annoyed me greatly. For some reason, I could not think of the scathing sentences with which I usually pricked this conceited busybody. I could not but despise him because he always cunningly pretended to be a much grander person than he was. There was something strange in his face that night, and his eyes burned with hatred. Also — I can say it now since it doesn't matter any longer and I want you to know what a horrible thing this monster has done in stealing my will from me — his glance rushed through my veins like a living fire. I was desperately ashamed and worried by this sensation, but I could not defend myself against its perverse attractiveness. I was filled with a mad yearning. He was repulsive and revolting; I hated him. If I had been in full possession of my mental faculties, he could never have conquered my resistance.

"I became very drowsy after dinner so I retired early. I don't know how long I slept before I was awakened — but that's not the proper word. Only part of me awakened; my will and memory still slept. My body raged with burning desire. I heard someone call my name softly. 'Isabelle — come — come to me . . .' The voice intensified my desire; I trembled and cried out with the pain of it. Then the inner storm washed my will and memory away completely.

"I awoke fully to a situation so horrible and crushing I can't even describe it. I found myself on Ernst Müller's bed, dizzy, defiled, and bleeding. My body was scratched and my shoulders bore marks of human teeth. There he stood by the ravaged bed, illuminated by the light of a candle. In a cold, commanding voice he told me to return to my room quietly, since the servants would soon be up. Then he added that he was sure I would be sensible and not change my manner toward him publicly. I burst into tears and began to berate him savagely, using words I did not know I knew. Rushing up, I beat his chest with my fists. He shoved me back onto the bed.

" 'Shut up! After all, it's more important to you that you not be found here than it is to me. What a little wildcat! She uses her teeth and nails in love and her fists in hate.' Scornfully he bared his chest to show me the marks on his neck and shoulders. 'Now get out. I'll call you again.'

"I almost fainted with humiliation, but I managed to drag myself back to my room, moaning. My one thought was that I must quickly dress and go to the river and drown myself, but as soon as I got to my room I collapsed in exhausted sleep.

"My mother woke me at noon. I told her I was sick so she let me stay in bed, but she stayed with me. It was evening when she finally left. I felt desperately ashamed when she kissed me, and I longed to cling to her and to that bright, sunny young life I had lost in a night. After she left I prayed for a long time, then began dressing to carry out my purpose. Yet while I was dressing I felt again the sweet, debased yearning that conquered everything in me. I heard the voice again. 'Come, Isabelle.' Nothing else existed for me except the voice and my raging passion. Before dawn I awoke to find myself in Ernst Müller's bed again.

"That was what kept happening. Every day I started to go kill myself and every day I defiled myself yet again. Once I was right at the river when the monstrous puppeteer jerked me back on his thread of dark passion. But now I've got some poison and I'll take it the first chance I get. I have no other recourse, for my will is completely broken. He has infected me with desire as with the plague. Now I lust after his cold fiend's face and muscular body even in the daytime. I find myself being jealous, and I await the night with a terrible, joyous anguish. Also I know I am pregnant. That is the final blow. I cannot remain alive and bring such shame to the parents and fiancé who so trusted me or give birth to Ernst Müller's unwanted bastard.

"I, Isabelle de Blancourt Welles, by my own hand"

★

Ernst disappeared without a trace when Isabelle committed suicide. He probably left Brussels altogether.

Ragon and I both realized what had happened. Ernst had found a large collection of books on sexual magic in de Blancourt's library. This exposure had been fatal. His natural sensuality and ambition had sucked him into the womb of the dark forces. He must have practiced for months before the Isabelle incident; I could calculate his progress almost exactly from the change in his letters. Now this unfortunate suicide had proved the success of his labors.

Ernst was dangerously talented in this area; he had enormous sexual energy, great intelligence, and diligence in all he pursued. What he did not know, or wouldn't believe, was that the dark forces always turn against the one who uses them and avenge all at once the injuries he has done to others. In the meantime — well, in the meantime he could cause many tragedies, for he was loose in the world with supernatural powers. Of course he could only assault women who were morally weak and passionate — but how many women are truly strong? Ernst Müller would bring them bitter suffering with his evil pleasures, but he would stiffen their resistance in their next life.

There was no stopping him now. He was on the downward path and would have to reach bottom before he turned in the right direction, just as Hans Burgner had. Isabelle's death may have shaken him momentarily; perhaps he even understood my attitude now. But again maybe he blamed me for putting this temptation in his path. I was sure he never meant to drive the girl to suicide. He had just wanted to humiliate her.

But the forces of black magic always drive the sorcerer who conjured them farther than he meant to go. They become independent and use him to ravage and destroy. He may think they serve him, but in actuality they direct and will finally crush him.

44

The Black Magician

In 1805, the Trinosophist Freemasonic Fraternity formed a chapter in Paris "for those who investigate the three sciences." Ragon invited me to come to the opening, and I stayed in his house. It was here I encountered Ernst Müller again. I was just getting out of my coach when I saw him coming up the street. He was tattered and disheveled, obviously reduced to beggary. When he saw me, his eyes dilated with shock and he ran away.

★

Soon after this I went home to say goodbye to my parents, who were going to spend some time in the Orient. I had some things to finish at Grotte before I could join them, but I accompanied them as far as the border. By now we were so united in spirit that their bodily absence did not sadden me. I knew of a certainty I would not lose them.

★

The years that followed at Cassel were busy and peaceful. Amadeus gradually became a diligent partner in my work and climbed rapidly in the Order.

In 1818, Ragon presented a series of lectures on ancient and modern initiations at the Paris Lodge and, since I had business for the Order in Paris, I was glad to have the opportunity to hear my illustrious friend's lectures. My main reason for going though was to acquaint him with Victor Amadeus.

During this trip I got more news of Ernst Müller. The female relatives of one of my colleagues were chattering enthusiastically about a wonderful

357

man who had healed Madame X and Mademoiselle Y simply by putting his hands on them and breathing upon them.

The two women had long-standing and singular illnesses. Madame X had been a widow for twenty years, though she was still quite young. This very religious woman suffered from agonizing headaches that forced her to stay in a darkened room and scream with pain. The malady had grown steadily worse and was completely engulfing her life. She confided to my informant that these attacks were always preceded by shameful dreams she could not bear to describe.

Mademoiselle Y's case was similar. She was a woman no longer young who had vowed never to marry when her fiancé died, and she had held to her oath despite the proposals of many men captivated by her wealth and beauty. Her problem was shortness of breath, difficulty in swallowing, and vertigo. The problem had become so intense that she scarcely dared leave the house; it became even worse when she was in company. If someone stared at her or she heard a deep male voice, she would choke immediately.

Both women had been completely healed by this gentleman after only a few treatments, and now they were his devoted followers. He had gained a large number of adherents by similar phenomenal results. His name, they said, was José Maria de Chassin.

When we were alone I asked my colleague what he thought of the man with the high-sounding name.

"I don't know," he replied thoughtfully. "There's something peculiar about him. For one thing all his patients are women. As for what he's like, he is a muscular, handsome fellow of about thirty who grooms himself like a dandy. He's intelligent enough and highly educated, and he must be wealthy because he has a huge palace and a vast establishment of servants and carriages.

"His palace is peculiar too. It's all hidden lights, heavy draperies, exotic statues, and hidden music. Luxurious lounges alternate with glass cases full of snakes. The whole thing produces an astounding, hypnotic effect. Nobody seems to know where he got his money — but maybe it's obvious. He treats only women who are very rich, past their prime, and suffering from nervous disorders.

"His treatments are suspicious too. The treatment room is draped in deep red, with matching furniture. In the center is a pedestal containing a soft chaise lounge. The patients — the ones who talk — all describe the treatment the same way. They remove their clothing and put on a long red gown to cover their nakedness. Then they lie down on the sofa, facing their own image in a mirror suspended from the ceiling. The room is slowly filled with the smell of sweet incense, and the light burns down to a dull red. Soft, delicate music is heard from behind the draperies, and they are soothed to a pleasant drowsiness. Then the marvelous man appears, a red silk gown billowing about his muscular figure. He leans over them, and his warm breath touches their eyes. Then he lays his hands upon them, and they lose consciousness with a shudder that spreads the concentrated healing force.

"Mademoiselle Y says that before going to sleep she feels as if nectar and ambrosia had been poured into her veins, and Madame X confessed still more to an indiscreet friend. She said, 'You wake up with a pleasurable weariness, victorious and sated upon a bed of laurels. All tension is dissolved and every longing is satisfied. Even your skin breathes, and the blood feels youthful in the veins. You are full of hope and the joy of life. The weariness is followed by a fine appetite.' "

This description was a disturbing silhouette of my fallen student. My suspicions were verified when Ragon and I paid an unexpected visit to Madame X's salon.

There he sat like a pasha, surrounded by aging, lonely women who basked in the flame of his sensuality. The path he had traveled was written in his face. His eyes were hooded and his lower lip was divided by a faun line repeated and reaffirmed in that aggressive jaw. He had had his hair arranged artistically in a mass of shining black curls. The blind sculptor of passion had certainly done a marvelous job on him; in just a few years it had formed from his willing raw material a demon of sexual rage.

The moment he saw me, the bumptious confidence vanished. He made his excuses quickly and left, fearing I would question him. At that point I didn't have a single question to ask him.

I knew I couldn't disillusion his followers. He had bound them to himself with the cords of tremendous lust. The victims themselves could have loosed this bond by freeing their spirits, but their spirits yet slept in the glowing crucibles of their bodies. Any attempt I could make would be futile. My words would be washed away by the pulsing of their veins as the skilled sorcerer put their moral senses to sleep and freed them to act their lust.

★

Some time later Ragon wrote to me about the scandals that were ending "Chassin's" career in Paris. The police had had a series of complaints from the families of his followers, and their investigation brought several studies to light. For example, they discovered the real secret of Mademoiselle Y's early death. She had suddenly realized after several months of treatments that she was pregnant. A highborn lady had thrown away her life because Chassin had no use for her after he had taken her fortune.

It turned out that Chassin's unfortunate clients had almost without exception spent themselves into ruin because of him. Deprived of their free will, they had signed promissory notes that made them beggars. The man was an insatiable Moloch; nobody could imagine what he had wanted with all that money. It was more than he could possibly spend on the most luxurious life.

When the truth came out, several other "clients of the red room" destroyed themselves rather than face the scandal. Chassin was arrested and sentenced to death after a lurid trial. He still had some influence left, however, for the sentence was changed to life in the galleys.

★

I wished I could believe that was the end of the episode and that Ernst Müller had disappeared from my life. Certainly the few miserable years he would spend in the galleys would curb his appetites. Their horror would serve as a danger signal in his subconscious, a barricade at one of the beaten paths to hell.

But I kept thinking about him. Gradually I became aware of a certainty that the thread that bound us had not been severed. He would come back, regardless of how much it cost him — so I waited for the return of Ernst Müller.

45

The Circle Completed

He came back to Grotte in 1830. Nobody recognized him, but I knew immediately who was the horrible human wreck who begged for lodging. In truth there was little enough left of the Ernst Müller we had known. The fine voice was a rasp, and he had lost three fingers. Scars showed through his thinning hair, and his eyes were rheumy and uncertain. He was stooped and bent and showed obvious signs of syphilis.

When he saw I recognized him he began to tremble and would have fainted had I not helped him to a chair. "Forgive me," he croaked. "I've waited so long to see you — I've tried to get here for years. It's the one goal that has kept me alive. It would have been so much easier to die."

He was gasping for breath and I urged him to lie down, but he would not. The impatience of the soul on its deathbed to finish some uncompleted business drove him on.

"No — I've got to talk now — you must understand me now, or we will be too late — much too late . . . I'll be stronger in a minute — it's just the excitement . . . could you get me a drink? . . . I'm not a drunkard . . . That's one thing I never stooped to — but it doesn't really matter anymore what I haven't done . . ."

I mixed him a mildly alcoholic, fortifying drink and he drank in great gasps. Then he closed his eyes and leaned back in the chair. Abruptly he began to speak in a low, even voice, speaking of the events of his life as though they had happened to some stranger.

He began with Isabelle de Blancourt Welles and his discovery of black magic, describing his experiments that had met with such frightening, intoxicating success. The events he described were much as I had reconstructed them, but I had been wrong about his feelings toward Isabelle. Nor had I known that he had already experimented with a well-

361

known socialite before Isabelle entered the picture; that affair had ended quietly.

"I broke out in a sweat when Isabelle responded to my command," he told me. "I was jubilant, but frightened. She was wearing only a sable coat to cover her nakedness, and beneath it was pure fire and fragrance, a living flame. I learned later that any virtuous woman becomes an insatiable hetaera once she is freed of her moral scruples. I didn't induce the passion that made them crave more sophisticated sensual pleasures; it was their own passion to which they surrendered."

Isabelle's suicide had forced him into a crisis. "I didn't mean to kill her; I really and truly loved her. She was the kind of woman I could respect and admire; she captivated me completely — a perfect lady and a perfect lover. She was brilliant, a true partner in lovemaking, a beauty of inexhaustible variety. No other women can be as beautiful as gray-eyed ash blondes. The delicate nuances of her skin and lips, those daring, firm breasts, the refined yet sensual movements of that slender body — she was the jewel I coveted most of all. I knew I was the only one who could satisfy her passion, her natural master and mate, and I was sure she knew it too, for all she tried to deny it. She soon became so inflamed with passion that she would hurry to my bed, humble in her hunger, without my even commanding her. I thought that surely then she would admit she loved me.

"I knew she was pregnant and I meant to elope with her and marry her honorably, but she slipped away from me. And just a few moments before she had clung to me like an obsessed animal. I hadn't called her; she just came into my room in broad daylight and threw herself upon me. Then she took the poison.

"All of a sudden the whole world collapsed. I was deathly afraid, remembering your warning. For the first time I realized I had committed a sin — a dreadful, transcendental crime with horrible consequences. I remembered how I had promised to stay on the straight path and had even been arrogant enough to ask if you would contact me when you realized you were mistaken. I was horribly ashamed and wanted more than anything to return to the path. Isabelle's death and its attendant scandal made it impossible for me to stay in Brussels, so I went to Paris, determined to make an honest living and never use black magic again.

"But I soon used up my savings, and those dark powers I had summoned blocked every possibility of employment. I was soon homeless and starving, spending my nights in doorways or the shrubs of the Bois de Boulogne and eating garbage from the streets. No one would trust me to do the simplest of jobs. There was something about me that made them suspicious. It was apparent they didn't know how to place me. Everyone felt I belonged to a higher social stratum and had fallen to this estate through crime.

"I became embittered at living in filth and starvation. I realized it was no good struggling; I couldn't rise honestly from the depths to which I had sunk. No one cared that I was trying to go straight — yet I obstinately hung on. Finally I became dizzy with hunger.

"Then I remembered Ragon. I had known he was in Paris, but I had avoided his neighborhood. I decided to visit him, confess my error, and ask for help. I was sure he would help me . . . Then I saw you standing by his gate. I can't explain exactly how I felt. All my bitterness and sense of futility rose to the surface, and I found myself blaming you for everything. I was ashamed and afraid when I saw you, but this soon gave way to hatred. You were the one who had let me taste the fruit of the tree of knowledge and then sent me out into the world half-prepared. If I had stayed at Grotte I would never have gotten into this situation. You had known I would fall and had cynically exposed me to temptations I couldn't resist. Now I was an outcast from both heaven and hell, and I saw you turn away indifferently.

"You see, a man has to belong somewhere with his whole heart and soul. Those weak creatures who try to straddle the road without choosing a direction are always outcast. Woe to the lukewarm and hesitant! The people who really count in life ride one road or the other openly and proudly. Whether they are the deepest villains or the greatest saints, they drink the cup of their lives to the full and accept the consequences.

"Now I had one road barred to me. The other way was clear, but I was scared to go down it. Suddenly I asked myself why I should humiliate myself by a life of beggary when I could make all the secret lewdness of the city open before me. I merely had to want to . . .

"By this time I had reached the Bois de Boulogne, where I saw an aging but still beautiful lady sitting on a bench fanning herself languidly. Her carriage waited respectfully in the distance, and her jewels and clothing were clear signs of great wealth. When I first glanced at her, she met my gaze, then looked away in unutterable boredom. That glance was like a whiplash across my senses, and I swore in all the bitterness of my soul that I would change that bored look — hers and that of other women like her. Thus I burned my bridges and consciously, willingly stepped back upon the road of black magic. You know at least part of the results.

"Like a child who believes it can cheat the death that takes its elders, I thought I could escape the consequences of my deeds. I did some facile reasoning on the subject and blocked every approach by which I thought myself vulnerable. I knew of course that if one dealt in the venom of emotions he himself had to be immune from them. I never permitted myself to feel either love or pity. Though I descended into the most sophisticated sexual inferno, it was always for my own pleasure, never anybody else's. I had no scruples and no emotional attachments. I exploited every opportunity to the full and enjoyed the riches of life behind an impenetrable fortress of selfishness.

"For a few years I lulled myself into an illusion of safety. Then one day I realized that despite my efforts to conserve it, my sexual energy was diminishing. I was being consumed by the very fire I used to lure my victims. So I decided to retire with the fortune I had acquired and regenerate my energies by a period of total abstinence.

"I didn't realize that I couldn't quit. I needed rest and quiet but wherever I went, my dreadful profession followed me. Women crept into my bed at night, aflame with lust. I tried to chase them away and lock my door, but they knew well enough how to rouse the passion of my sick imagination. Time and again they drained the strength I was trying to conserve. I was bound by the spell I had conjured up; it lured a hungry swarm of women to me everywhere.

"In desperation I went back to Paris, not realizing I was putting my head into a noose. My past practice had begun to come to light while I was away, and the whole thing blew up in my face before I was even aware of it. About the same time I realized some nocturnal succubus had given me syphilis. My whole world collapsed and I didn't much care. The court sentenced me to death, but one of my patients, a kind and influential lady, got the sentence reduced to life in the galleys.

"The inhuman life on the galleys broke me physically within a few months. I crouched on the bench I was chained to, unable to lift an oar despite the cruelest lashing. The sound of my tortured breathing filled my ears, and I waited for death . . . Then I had an inexpressibly horrible experience that drove me back into the land of the living. I seemed to be looking into a chasm swarming with slimy reptiles — no human mind could understand the dreadful, transcendental monsters that were waiting for me on the other side, their eager, demoniac eyes gleaming with a promise of torments far more terrifying than any torture. I clung to my body like a drowning man; I had to save this decaying clay that kept me in the physical world. Desperately I struggled to stay alive with superhuman will. I had to stay alive; what I faced was something worse than hell itself — *the destruction of my personality, smashed into little pieces of animal existence.* If I could just stay in Ernst

Müller's body, I could work to attain a higher plane and reach a path where I can return as a penitent human being.

"And so I'm still alive, despite every law of nature. They maimed me twice for trying to escape. They beat me till I was half dead, and once they staked me out in the blazing sun. But here I sit. I've finally reached my goal. You know why I came. It was the memory of my life with you that sustained me through every hell. The very fact that I've made it here proves that I deserve the chance I'm asking; I've already won the right. Restore my health! Give me just a few decades to climb from the abyss, to regain my right to a conscious personality. I don't care to live any longer than that. I don't want eternity, just one human life span!"

Now sheer fatigue silenced him. His face was covered with perspiration. What compassion he roused in me! Yet I was helpless. How could I deny the frantic request of a dying man, even when it was based on gross error? I could not argue with a man in that condition or crush him with a blunt refusal. I decided I would examine him, treat him with any means I could, and strengthen him as much as possible. Maybe I could give him a few years at least.

But my hopes were crushed by the examination. There wasn't a sound organ in his body, and the syphilis in his bloodstream had gone beyond control. His body was just a decomposing hulk held up by willpower, a corpse containing a damned soul. Already his decaying form gave off the stench of corruption.

Ernst sensed the truth when he saw my distress. "That doesn't matter" he waved this away. "I am alive by a miracle of willpower, and you can work a yet greater miracle. Don't waste my time with your scholarly game of natural explanations; I don't *have* any time. Give me THE ELIXIR! Nothing else can save me! You can't let me be debased into an animal existence while I cling to your hand and beg with my whole soul!" He grasped my arm with one mutilated hand, revealing a ghastly, feverish strength.

"What makes you think I can give you a thing like that?" I asked helplessly.

He shoved my arm away and pointed with cold rage. "Look in the mirror!" Automatically I turned and looked into the mirror over the washbowl. "Now I know perfectly well you're nearly seventy years old. Can you think of some natural reason why you don't look older than thirty?"

What could I tell him? I couldn't tell him the method I had used to preserve my physical condition; he wasn't ready for it. And the medication itself I had adapted to only gradually and had prepared it to suit my own constitution. It would kill a weaker person, especially one as ill as he was. But I had to tell him something.

"I have stayed young looking," I admitted cautiously. "It's the result of occult exercises and a certain essence. But unless you have decades of conditioning exercises behind you and have learned other things, things that cannot be revealed to the uninitiated, the essence will corrode the life energies like a powerful poison. If I gave it to you, I'd be committing murder."

He was deaf to what I said, seizing only on my admission the fluid existed. He would take responsibility for the possible adverse side effects himself. "I know it won't destroy me. Surely you can see that I have superhuman willpower. And I've done plenty of occult exercises. Even if the direction was wrong, I gained from them."

When I denied his request, he threw himself at my feet, begging, promising, and cursing, until he exhausted his frail strength and fainted.

I put him to bed and injected some strengthening essences. When he began to come to, I left him.

★

It was an ominous and nebulous mass of problems I carried to the study that night. Despite the hour, I couldn't go to bed. I had to decipher the hieroglyph that kept confronting me. Now it was so urgent I couldn't avoid it. Three rooms from me lay a man in agony, a man who in his extremity depended on me for salvation. He wouldn't listen to the truth; all he heard was the tale of magic within him. He wanted the Elixir, but I had none for him. Now he was resting, gathering his strength to extort a few more hours from death and win from me what he wanted.

Since I could find no answer myself, I consulted the stars, mapping astrological calculations by the peaceful lamplight. I could hear the wind sighing in the moonless park outside. Then suddenly I remembered. *I had been here before.* The same feelings, the same dark silence . . . In imagination I sat upon a blue box in a dark barn making calculations in a book on my knee. I was even drawing the same aspects of the planets in the two circles of the Zodiac — my destiny, and Hans Burgner's — Ernst Müller's? Yes, I now sat in Rochard's place.

The House of Death, the Eighth House, was very crowded in my horoscope tonight, the same dark judges now and then — no, not then; it was all now. Hans Burgner's circle — Ernst Müller's — overlapped my own in terrible conjunctions, making the judges executioners. Mars with Mercury in the sign of Gemini, Saturn in close conjunction. The moon gathered their whole destructive force in her chalice and flung it upon me — and upon him who lurked silently, Hans-Ernst.

Suddenly I could see through the walls. I saw him shuffling hesitantly along the slate floor of the laboratory, his haggard figure black against the white walls. One maimed hand held a candle while the other searched the shelves, cabinets, and drawers. Impatiently he tore covers off vials and crucibles, spilling powders and liquids. It was lucky for him I had labeled them in the Latin he could read; otherwise he would have poisoned himself. Of course he couldn't find what he wanted.

Now I could feel his sick anger and erratic thoughts. His monomania was taking complete control of him. He had to get the Arcanum I hoarded and gain the life I maliciously denied him. Even if it were sealed by the most holy sacrament, he had to break the seal. And if flesh and blood should try to stop him — well, it would be just one more corpse to put beside the women who had died for him. What did it matter if he got the Great Arcanum? His body could not stand much more; he had to get it. And what else could be protecting the great secret but human flesh and blood? The moon rose blood-red over the park.

Now the problem was laid bare in crystal clarity, and I was tranquil. I left a letter for Victor Amadeus, giving him instructions about the Order and where and how to deposit my important papers. There was nothing else to do, for my father and I had long agreed the castle and estate should go to the Order.

The moonlight drew silver columns on the floor as I lay down peacefully. A slight draft told me the door had opened and closed. The transparent curtain billowed in the window.

Then I heard his irregular breathing. I did not move but listened to the painfully careful steps. I felt a deep compassion for this poor creature with his monomania, approaching to do something he had no intention of doing, something I had done once.

Now he stood motionless by the bed, staring at me intently to detect the rhythm of my breathing. Satisfied, he leaned cautiously over me, feeling under my pillow and searching the night stand. He opened the night stand drawer and searched there; then I felt his hand run over my chest. Suddenly he felt the small, flat box I wore on a gold chain, and he stopped, trembling.

Just then the moon emerged from a cloud and illuminated my face, showing him that I watched his every move. He stared back at me in terror, like a man who sees a cobra. Stumbling back, his hand encountered the bronze night lamp and he grasped it without conscious volition and struck me between the eyes . . .

The first blow crushed my brain, so I felt no pain. Ernst kept on beating the crushed shell madly, determined to crush out those two points of light and tear his own life from my body.

OPUS MAGNUM

I found myself stumbling down a steep tunnel. There was a dim pentagram of light in front of me. As I got closer I saw it was a star-shaped opening that led to a staircase. There was a soothing fragrance in the air, a light blue mist that lulled me into semiconsciousness as I moved slowly on. It was a joyous, mystic fragrance that resonated through my soul in melody and idyllic colors. I felt I had always known that melody, and the delicate kaleidoscope of pastels was dear and familiar to me.

The corridor I was now traversing led to a small rock-carved room where the astral double of my body lay unconscious on a stone bench. The mist came from a vessel on a sacramental pedestal; here it seemed to give both fragrance and light.

Then I heard the Master's voice beside me. "Cornelius! Wake up!"

My dizziness was gone, and my soul surged with weightlessness and joyous freedom. The little room widened and became a fantastically huge, columned hall. I looked back at the stone bench. My astral body lay motionless, and I saw behind it in the middle distance my physical body crushed on the soiled bed. I turned away and looked about me. The pastel curtains of many alcoves opened and I saw quiet, smiling faces, faces unknown but familiar. Rows of alcoves mounted to inconceivable heights till they became hazy in the distance. Marveling, I looked to the finials of the columns. They reached to the starry horizon, and beyond them I could see only the peaks of the snowy mountains, white arrows pointing to heaven. The beauty of the place overwhelmed me. Focusing on these heights, I gradually made out the angular lines of monastic cities sheltered among the peaks. I could hear the mournful Tibetan bone horn and the festive sistra.

Now I knew I stood in the spiritual equivalent of the Order's Hall of

Initiation, and the mountains were the spiritual Tibet — true wisdom towering invisibly over the primitive, sectarian masses.

The Master called again. Now I saw him. He wore the saffron garb of the monk, with shaven head. A form moved behind him; obviously he still lived embodied among men. Here he appeared in its refined semblance. Motioning me closer, he stretched out his right hand over my astral figure, speaking the eternal formula of the ancient mysteries.

"Burn thy body with the fire of thy thoughts!" The astral form began to glow as though in a furnace and burned with a blinding white brilliance. Now he recited the Lord's word in the Book of Ezra:

"They perish like vapor,
Like the flame and the smoke thereof,
They are kindled and extinguished."

Turning to me he continued, "But thou hast burned and been extinguished to form a fire-tempered jewel — Lapido Rubro! The initiates did not choose unworthily. One of the Just has returned."

Triumphant bells and trumpets proclaimed transcendental festivity over the hazy heights, but the voice of the Magus soared over all.

"The transitory form has turned to ashes; the shadow has become light. Living gold was born from this fire. The Opus is finished and the Great Arcanum is before Thee, my Lord. The work is perfected. Rejoice, ye sons of Light! Let the immortal gates be opened and the veil which covers the eyes of men be stricken. The Magus has been acknowledged by the elemental spirits as their master. He has arrived! May the Lord and Only Life bless the one who returns to Him!"

I stood in the white glow of completion, dissolved into the flowing melody of the Divine Masterpiece. Faces, sounds, colors, and places showed me their true form. I saw the Masters of the Order, some hidden on the Earth in hermitic abodes where they could close their lives to glittering illusion and be flooded with the light of infinity. Others were already in the spirit, besieging the frozen darkness of human existence to prepare the future Golden Age. I saw the Guardians and teachers, instruments of the Divine Forces, the ecstatic Seers and Preachers of the Word. Then there were the scattered fragments of the Divine Plan, those who blindly persevered through torment, and I saw the Lord of the Earth, Adonai, leaning with solicitous love over the flaming crucible of the Earth, with its wailing and horror, hate, and rivers of blood and tears. He tended the fire to keep it burning so it would boil away all the impurities so that after the feverish crisis of the End of Time the planet might be raised in the Cosmos.

I also saw the people who had been important in my own life's radius in order that all the uncertainty of Time would be dispelled. Amadeus Bahr was a teacher in a saffron robe bearing the signs of the Order. His disciples sat around him on a rocky plateau, the Roof of the World to which they had climbed by the sufferings of millennia.

Among those disciples was a skinny, bright-eyed boy, the Milanese Marietta who had once given me birth and had done more for me than anyone else, even after her death. Her soul mate, my father Francesco Borri, was with her; now they were companions without the bondage of sex.

Poor, sentimental Sophie Pétion still hid in the dim arcades of a convent, her life a round of candles, incense, fear, shivering penances, and the aching demands of her flesh. Though she prayed and tortured herself, her body defeated her time and again, and incubi appeared in her dreams. Her being was still riddled with superstitions and nightmares, but her naive faith remained and was leading her out of the chaos. I knew this with radiant certainty, and her present circumstances did not rouse anxiety or pity. I knew her life would soon be resolved, as mine had been. The more she suffered, the stronger she would become.

Dr. Péloc's path was already smooth, like that of all those who demand nothing for themselves. Whether in Paris, England, or Germany, he healed and learned without prejudice or inhibition. He used his powers of observation, memory, and intuition to give to others and, though he made no efforts on his own behalf, the ties of Karma fell from him. He became One of the Just.

I also saw the sin-laden figures of Lepitre and Rosalie. The human mind could never have conceived their tragic new relationship as a poor washer-woman and her neurotic, invalid son. They had had a great deal of difficulty in achieving rebirth and had simply revolved for a long time in the astral ocean. Finally Rosalie achieved birth and herself gave birth to her idolized victim — the ironic justice of Karma! For now Rosalie had given him her own blood in place of that she had spilled, and he had dim memories of nameless guilt that led him to torture his mother daily and make her life a living hell.

Lepitre's disease also was a fitting punishment of Karma. He was anemic, and his mother would have given him the last drop of her blood to cure him. The son she worshipped was the only meaning of her life. She drudged willingly for the flabby, unhappy youth whom she had borne illegitimately; yet he was slowly dying. His life was being drained quietly and steadily, just as it had the night she had opened his veins. For Rosalie had not been an ordinary murderess; the fruit of her vindictive passion was returned to her in this way.

Charlotte Bruggendorf wandered in the maze of passion as a bisexual gnome, a crippled outcast of unrestrained sexual curiosity. Her husband, the fat mayor of Straubing, was a clumsy charlatan and fairground swindler. He was ever the dilettante, a borrower of reflected light.

The Marquis of Brandenburg-Ausbach had come to hate and condemn his former actions after a few short lives. He was always careful to conform; yet somehow he always managed to bring the anger of irresponsible authority upon himself. He was executed three times, once because of a careless word, once because he happened to witness a crime, and once because he was thought to have a valuable secret. It was this final execution that moved me most. He was gradually entombed in a tower leaning over a precipice. The opening through which he was given food and water was slowly filled, and every day they shouted the question to which he had no answer. Despite his pleading, he was finally entombed. He scrabbled at the rocks till his fingers bled, then wrote his innocence in his own blood. This tower was really a sealed well in the sky, the inverted image of the well where Hans Burgner reached the lowest point of his path.

Then I saw the women who had first given me birth, the mothers of Hans Burgner and Heinz Knotek, as they developed with the experiences of various lives and circumstances.

Hans Burgner's lecherous and whimsical mother went through several lives on the stage and in the circus; then after 230 years she attracted the attention of a ruling prince. By now she was calmer and more refined, but she was also more daring and had developed her pretense into an art form. Yet her uncontrolled self-love always made her obese. Time and again she would start with an enchanting form only to become a gigantic mountain of flesh. This flesh weighed her down; yet it served as a barricade to further downward paths. Obesity served as her guardian, torturer, and teacher. She fought against it in vain, for she had never learned self-control.

Periodically she would go on a starvation diet, but this was always broken by compulsive gluttony. To forget her misery she began to drink and lost the prince's favor. He gave her a modest annuity on which she lived amid covered mirrors, drunk and crying, a prey to her servants.

Heinz Knotek's mother blossomed beautifully. The hard-working, simple, and good creature thought clear, bright thoughts and had original ideas she kept to herself for a long time. It is the quiet who truly observe others and hear more than those who love the sound of their own tongue. She had known there was a great discrepancy in the words and actions of her drunken husband, but she did not judge him. She had listened to the murderous quarrels about kindness, the venomous battles about love, and the impatient demands for patience; yet she never judged or tried to measure imperfect persons against the perfect Christ. Hers was a pure and discriminating spirit, and her new incarnations were fitting garb for it. She was reborn in England, Sweden, and in France, always in an environment where she could receive a good education and develop her talents. Wherever she was, she was a center of spiritual activity, giving and warming those about her. The attention she never sought always came to her. Though she was modest, she was always preeminent. Her French sonnets are still considered some of the finest gems of literature; they have been translated into many languages because of their beauty and immortality.

The preacher Knotek wandered through all the sects and filled each one with his personal malevolence. When his bad heart killed him in 1570, his fanaticism drove him to Russia. Here he was the son of a Greek Orthodox priest who himself became a militant priest, feared and hated. This treacherous servant of Christ scandalized his parishioners not only by his drunken debauchery but also by his extraordinary cruelty. It was his greatest pleasure to incite pogroms and take a personal part in them. In this life he died relatively young from syphilis.

Next he became a Moslem. He snatched up the prophet's banner like a spear and joyously killed Christians with it. The Koran was now his bludgeon; the holy books have ever been helpless and patient in the hands of bigoted fools. He kept the prophet's rules just as he had kept the Christian commandments, endlessly scrutinizing words and letters while his whole soul and body sinned against their spirit. Finally he died in a "holy war."

Then he was reborn in Russia in the ghetto where he had gloried in so many pogroms. Now he was a part of the suffering of this strange people with their great and terrible fate. Again he became a religious fanatic, transcribing the Talmud and the Torah. He learned to hate his persecutors but he also learned what it was to be defenseless against fanaticism, living with fear and the leaden horror of murder. He heard the futile pleas of his fellow Jews and watched the executioners turn a deaf ear to the screams of dying children. This bitter life of the perpetual fugitive filled him with the thirst for revenge. Finally he was tortured to death during a pogrom, unaware that he himself had killed a defenseless Jew by those same tortures more than a hundred years before.

Then the man's dark force was used where the logic of events demanded — in France just before the revolution. A firebrand of the revolution, he was able to consummate all his hatred and make his name infamous, but the forces he had conjured up swept him away with them. Before he could complete his killing, he himself fell to the guillotine.

Giuseppe Balsamo had been executed in the Castel Sant'Angelo in 1795, condemned as a Freemason and a heretic. All his efforts to prove he was not Cagliostro had been in vain. He had lied so consistently that no one believed the only truth he had ever uttered. When he had insisted that he was the illegitimate son of a peasant woman who had taken the name to impress people, they only laughed. There were witnesses to testify and date paintings, and even the date and place of his birth were against him. Everyone wondered why he had told such a clumsy lie.

But I also saw where Balsamo's frightful death would lead him, the direction determined as early as his meeting with Saint-Germain. The magic warning remained in his thoughts during his terrible torment and sowed the seed of something he had never known before — faith and fear. He began to believe in the supernatural powers and fear the consequences of his actions. Thus he learned his first moral inhibitions and began to have ambitions in the direction he had once scorned. His meeting with Saint-Germain had started him from his lowest point, and Cagliostro's name turned his mind to white magic.

Meanwhile Jeanne Girard/Lorenza Feliciani, whose ties with Balsamo were far deeper than those of the flesh, spent her days in ecstatic prayer in a convent. She surrendered her will completely to a forceful and bigoted Mother Superior, who formed her into a flaming prayer mill. Lorenza confessed her faults and Balsamo's endlessly, blaming herself for all, and begged salvation. She had truly loved her husband, despite her terror of him. Once in her dreams she saw him on the torture rack, reduced to a whimpering stump. Lorenza could not forget the vision, which she felt in her soul was true. From then on she forgot her fear and wept bitterly over him.

Really these two could not exist without each other. Lorenza needed Balsamo's strength and will, and he needed her receptive intuition. Balsamo had always turned her spiritual eyes and ears toward hell, but now in his misery he was turning toward higher things.

As for Ernst Müller, he was destroyed immediately by the Red Lion, which he had mixed with wine and drunk greedily on the night of the murder. The tremendous force broke his will and consumed his decomposing body. No longer could his personality be torn apart by demons; he had crashed into the innermost astral hell, an unprepared living being — just like Hans Burgner.

I saw the ebb and flow of the lives and their driving force and meaning, the justice that reconciled their miseries. In this solemn moment I saw that grotesque actions proceed from grotesque and sick minds and that these actions themselves produce the painful fruit that cures the disease. It is only transgression that can produce the healing, and there is never more suffering than is absolutely necessary.

Then a Voice rang out, the Voice of Uriel, who sends out the Word to the beings in the Cosmos. It is Uriel who directs the Divine Light into a Live Flame in the souls of the Messiahs and Seers. What a Voice it is, the sound of all holiness and revelation!

"I salute you Who Have Arrived, Magus of the three worlds. At last you have untied your bonds. You have withdrawn your personal forces from the rule of matter and now you may use them as you wish. Determination binds you no longer, for you know the secret gates, and the keys are in your hand. No'e do physical laws bind you still; you can go where your spirit wills and create what it desires. If you wish, you may create worlds and become a Titan of the galaxies. You may build your own Paradise of sublime artistry; its flowers will wither only at the end of time. You may visit the most marvelous planets and the mysterious realm of Hades. You may penetrate that which is large and that which is small and perform majestic experiments until the manifest world returns to God . . . Or you may depart alone on the Straight Path which you know and leave all transitory illusion, even the illusion of Paradise. You may leave this Cosmic crucible of suffering and experiment, for you are indeed free.

"Because of your freedom I give you one more choice, a difficult one; I offer you a mission. You do not need to accept and will suffer no penalties if you refuse. If you accept, you will return as a servant to live through a Messianic Age, a terrible and magnificent time when the old Eon will die and a new one come into being. The cataclysm of Death will be mixed with the agony of Birth and the mystery of Resurrection.

"You will have to wait many earthly years in anonymity, unknown to the world. Then will come the Time when the Star appears while Saturn is in conjunction with Jupiter in the sign of Taurus. The Cosmic Gate, which admits only Him Who Is Sent, will open. Only Hermes Trismegistus, Rama, Krishna, Buddha, Moses, Lao-tze, Zoroaster, Mohammed, and Christ have entered through this Gate; now someone will follow them. It will be your duty to announce Him, to chronicle the Truth, to preserve the traditions of the past and weave them into the present and the future. You will record your own life and how it has been imbued with the transcendental restlessness of occult force. Your life will be a window of Eternal Light to people in deepest darkness.

"Many thousands of years ago I predicted this to Ezra in Babel and told him the signs that must first appear. If you take this task, you will see it — all the Chosen Ones present at the beginning will be present at the end, that the number of the Just shall be full from Abraham to Abraham. These are those who have gathered strength and never tasted death. You will also see the deepest hell, the most terrible suffering, the greatest lie, and the most terrible crimes. The sky will be darkened, brother will betray brother, and friend will fight friend. Innocents will be massacred and all law and truth destroyed. Every value of the human spirit will be defamed, and Hell will triumph over the Earth . . . You will have to endure all this and stand firm in the midst of desolation, hatred, dangers, and threats. It is your mission to write about God and the new Messiah of the Spirit, and the new Eon to be born from the decay of Evil. You must write to the accompaniment of the trumpets of the Apocalypse, while the sky is rent asunder and the earth opens in death and flame. You must be ready for the appointed hour, for the Book of Life can be fulfilled only with the sound of the orchestra of death; the song of resurrection soars only from destruction. Choose!"

There was silence after these words, the silence of a listening infinity. Every creative possibility silently offered itself to me, with no lurking traps. The Universe was an open plain in all directions, with the vast, starry heavens round about. These were the ancient forces gathered in Lilith's womb to be commanded by the Creative Spirit. I saw the mysterious gates of Hades glimmering below, promising fulfillment of all mysteries. The macrocosmos and microcosmos drew me toward them . . . And the miserable Earth, drifting toward the crisis, awaited the Messiah . . .

Now after years of anonymity I have returned to announce Him.

Rejoice, for a star has risen!
A Liberator hath come forth from the deepest darkness!
He announceth the Reign of the Spirit, the Invisible Kingdom!
He came to defeat death with Life!
The circle soon closeth; be ye watchful!
And this is the circle, from Abraham to Abraham.
Hasten into the narrow path while it is yet open,
Hasten unto the new Eon, that ye be not locked in Outer Darkness!
Make haste; the number of the Just is about to be fulfilled!

For the signs which were spoken have appeared.
  'The chasm of agonies and the way of Resurrection,
  Behold, they are before us!'
Hasten, for few of those remain who bear the Holy Name and Number.
As for the others, they shall perish.
  'They perish like vapor;
  Like the flame and the smoke thereof,
  They are kindled and extinguished.'